A GAME OF
FALLEN
STARS

A GAME OF
FALLEN
STARS

S. E. BERKELEY

CITY OWL
PRESS

A GAME OF FALLEN STARS

CITY OWL PRESS
www.cityowlpress.com

Cover Design by MiblArt. All stock photos licensed appropriately.

Edited by Jessica Shearer.

For information on subsidiary rights, please contact the publisher at info@cityowlpress.com.

Paperback Edition ISBN: 978-1-64898-494-5

Digital Edition ISBN: 978-1-64898-493-8

Printed in the United States of America

CITY OWL PRESS
Escape Your World • Get Lost in Ours

To my beloved husband, who bent over backwards entertaining our feral kids so I could make my dreams come true.

Author's Note

Dear reader,

If you would like to review the potential triggers and content warnings found within this story, please see the list found on my website. Your comfort while reading is important.

https://seberkeleyauthor.com/#a-game-of-fallen-stars

One

The sun sinks behind the meadow's large hills, the last of day disappearing from the kitchen window. It's one of those breathtaking sunsets that reminds Ethan why he chose to spend his sabbatical out here in Parkfield, California.

But instead, Ethan is trapped inside, talking to his mother. Not that he has much of a choice. The weekly call is mandatory, the terms carefully negotiated with her after a very long session with his therapist. It would be nice to take the call on the porch and watch the stars wink into existence, but the kitchen is the only place he gets reliable cell service. So, he's stuck.

He checks the kitchen clock and his heart plummets. He is two minutes and forty-five seconds over the allotted time, and she shows no signs of stopping. Which means it's up to him to end it.

Ethan keeps his sigh silent, eyes closing briefly. Trying to end these calls is always tricky. There are two wolves warring in his mind. One snarls at him, *Be a good son, she only has you,* and the other snaps, *Maintain healthy boundaries, these are not healthy boundaries, my God, you moved out here for this exact reason.*

Well, not the *exact* reason. Sure, making it difficult for his mother to hop on a train to see him was one benefit of spending his time in Parkfield.

Because Parkfield, where there are more coyotes than people, is absolutely isolated. Nothing but deer, raccoons, and the occasional boar family. And cattle. Lots and lots of cattle.

His sister, Andrea, had painted a beautiful picture of him getting out of San Francisco and being only a short distance away from her. His therapist warned him he was running away from his problems instead of dealing with them. She was right, but the idea that Andrea had put into his head sounded like paradise.

Speaking of which, Andrea glares with a judgmental arch of her brow. She mouths, "Hang up."

He glares back at her. Like it's that easy.

She points at the phone, and he tilts it away from his ear to hear her harsh whisper. "Do it. I did not hook you up with this place for you to cave like a little bitch. Come on, Ethan. Grow a pair."

His jaw clenches, but she does have a point. His sigh is audible now. His mother has yet to take a breath, and the energy required to interrupt her and instigate hanging up still hasn't manifested. His therapist would be disappointed in him. If she was here, she would remind him that he needs to end the call before his mother—

"And how's your hair?"

—starts criticizing him.

He leans on his forearms, and his shoulder-length brown hair falls into his face. He usually ties it back in a man bun or half up, but he didn't have the care to do that today. There's a pause as he searches for the patience to answer his mother's superficial question. All he comes up with is a bland, "Manageable."

Andrea smirks at him. "Should've listened."

He nods. When she's right, she's right.

His mother's disapproving hum is straight out of his childhood when she adds, "I'm surprised you haven't been written up at work."

"Mom, I'm on sabbatical. I have no work rules, that's the whole point of this break." His patience falters and out slips a mumbled, "And, no one fucking cares." Blessedly, she doesn't hear.

He eyes the fridge. If he hangs up, he can drink his beer. That's his deal with himself. A little incentivizing. God, won't that cold one be lovely…if he can just get off the phone.

"Well, Mary Anne said at her son's tech company they..." He starts to tune her out again. If he wanders out of the kitchen, the call will drop. A simple solution to his problem. But she will call back. Repeatedly. And if she gets too worked up, she might do something horrific like visit. He shudders.

Ethan watches the clock, his mother's voice a muted echo in the back of his mind. It's one of those analog clocks, and it's stylized to match the kitchen's "rustic chic." Ethan couldn't care less about what kind of chic it is, but he does appreciate the movement of the second hand. It gives his eyes something to settle on while he waits.

It's a miracle his mother hasn't passed out yet. She can easily set the record for longest stream of consciousness without breath. It's impressive. Annoying, but impressive.

A sneered "your therapist" from his mother penetrates Ethan's wandering mind. He snaps his head down to glare at the granite counter-tops, his shoulders rounding. "What?"

"I'm telling you, baby, they want to stuff you full of useless big pharma poison. What's the point of a therapist if you're still being all mopey like this? You don't need a therapist, Ethan. You're the most put together man I know. What you need is a wife. And kids. Theresa's son was just like you but then he—"

Ethan scrubs his face, frustration bubbling in his chest. It's always the same, and nothing he says will make a difference. He tried. He really did. He dated. They were all nice, but every partner sensed the same thing: Ethan is stagnant. And they left him to flourish with others.

As for having kids, well, he'd rather die, something his mother would gladly assist with if she ever found out about his vasectomy.

Andrea cracks open one of his beers and envy sweeps over him, his throat drying. She takes an extra-slow sip. He flips her off and mouths, "Ungrateful." She gives a satisfied "ah," tilting the bottle toward him. "If you had a spine, you could have one too."

"Have you tried calling Jenny?" His mother asks.

His gaze slides to the fridge. Out of all his exes to bring up, she chooses his college girlfriend from nearly two decades ago?

"Jenny is now happily pregnant and married." To a woman, for God's sake. "Remember?"

His mother's disappointed "hm" prickles his insides. "It's too bad. She was a delight. Much better than what's-her-face. You know. That last one."

His anger spikes, his gaze on the chrome fridge door hardening. He knows she remembers Taylor's name. His mother made it very clear to everyone involved how much she hated Taylor.

A tornado of emotions swells in him—shame, sadness, anger—all building, making his stomach twist. He cracks his neck, eyes closing, trying to breathe the discomfort away, but it stays, coating his insides.

Andrea's harsh voice cracks through the roaring in his ears. "Ethan. Hang up."

His lips thin. She doesn't understand. It's not that easy.

"Ethan."

The warning in her voice makes it worse. His jaw clenches. His mother's disappointed tone sets his heart pounding faster, the beats hammering in his ears. "It's funny how you mention Jenny's little family." He feels his stomach lurch as he clutches the phone harder. "It could've been you if you hadn't messed it up."

He sucks in breath, eyes snapping open. His phone is gone, his hand smarting from where it's suddenly been ripped free. Andrea glares at him, her voice hard. "Ethan, breathe."

His breath trembles, some of the chaos in his mind ebbing. Only some. Not nearly enough. He forces in a second breath.

Andrea adds a soft, "Should I get the Ativan?"

His jaw clenches again. "No." Shame. Guilt. Fear that his mother might've heard her. It starts building again. It gives him the incentive he needs—he can't do this anymore tonight. "Give me the phone."

Andrea scans him carefully before handing it over. He holds it up to his ear. Relief hits him. His mother didn't even notice, still prattling on about God knows what. His voice is harsher than he intends, and he would curse if it wouldn't make it even worse. "Mom, I have to go."

Her tone instantly goes defensive. "Go? What do you mean go? It's only been thirty-two minutes! And you don't answer my calls or text—"

"Mom, I get shit cell service here. There's nothing that can be done about it." God, he does love that. It was the selling point, really, for moving out here. Shitty cell connection. Bad internet. Easy excuses that allow him to ignore his mother, and the rest of the world. When he had packed, he'd dedicated two suitcases to the books he had thought about reading for the last decade.

"Can't you do something about it? You work in tech! You're an engineer. Can't you just figure it out?"

"Yeah, it doesn't work like that. I'll call you next week." Maybe. Probably. But his therapist would be so proud if he didn't.

"Ethan."

That tone. It prickles the back of his neck, and he stretches again. He forces his voice to be perfectly smooth. "Please, Mom. I'm really tired. I'll try to do better. Promise." Empty words that make his insides curdle.

"Okay, baby."

He releases a silent breath. "Thank you. Goodnight, Mom. Love you."

"Love you too. Be safe out there. You know how horror mov—"

He hangs up. It was that or another ten minutes of fear mongering to try to get him to come back to the city.

Andrea eyes him, and he can detect the anger simmering in her. He wasn't lying about the exhaustion. It hits him like a wave, and he leans heavily on the countertop. She searches his face, choosing her words. "You're iced out again."

His jaw ticks. "My face?"

She nods slowly. "She makes you do that, you know that, right?"

He doesn't want to talk about this. It's a familiar argument and not just with Andrea. Unwanted memories surface, making his heart hurt. They still feel raw, and he knows without needing a mirror that it makes his face "ice out," as Andrea likes to call it. His face is perfectly smooth, not a hint of emotion, not even in his eyes. Taylor hates it…or, hated it.

He stretches his neck one more time, forcing himself to straighten. "I'm fine." He's only constantly haunted by the best relationship he's ever had, one that he ruined. With momentous effort, he stomps down all the feelings and memories. He forces a smile, a carefully practiced one he's perfected. "Now where is my promised beer?"

It doesn't fool her. Fifteen years his junior and Andrea can read him like a well-loved book. Teenage Andrea would've called him out on it, but adult Andrea lets it slide. She flashes her own dazzling smile. "Coming right up!"

She flings open the fridge. "Hello, lovelies. Come to mama." He feels his lips twitch. Pulling out his favorite IPA, she tosses him a playful smirk. "And an iced mug, because you *fancy* tonight."

That twitch turns into a genuine smile, one that washes away his fake one. It's small, but still a smile. He accepts the frothing mug. They clink their drinks together, and he takes a hearty gulp. "Oh fuck, that hits the spot."

Andrea's lip curls. "You have froth on your nasty-ass beard."

He wipes it with the back of his hand. It has gotten rather overgrown lately. Usually, it's trimmed down, but he can't bring himself to care since going on sabbatical—before that even, if he was being honest.

Andrea takes a swig of her bottle. "What happened to the grooming kit I got you? You know, with the wash and balm and—what was it? Oil?"

He scratches at his beard, and she slaps his hand. Her lip curls higher. "That's disgusting."

He shakes out his stinging hand. "First of all, ow. Rude. And yeah, I have it with me, and I'll have you know I wash this beautiful beard every day. I just need to trim it."

"And your hair too while you're at it." He rolls his eyes and she scowls. "Don't give me that! Look, just a touch. I'll even do it for you." She nails him with a harsh look. "You used to look like one of those thirst traps on social media." The judgmental sweep of her gaze rankles him. "Now you have people wondering if you're homeless, and not in that 'oh, but maybe he's secretly a millionaire' kind of way."

He runs his hand through his hair. "It's not that bad! Look." He gives his beard a tug, using his fingers to measure. "It's not even that long."

"Yeah, but you're screaming *unkempt*." She points at him. "No one wants to fuck unkempt."

"Oh, yeah." Sarcasm and anger drip from every word. "A real pressing issue out here in the middle of fucking nowhere where the only person I interact with is my sister."

"There is a whole town—"

"Population eighteen."

She raises her voice to speak over him. "A *whole* town that would be interested. But you're screaming 'is he an off-season movie star or is he homeless' and—"

"I thought it was millionaire?"

"*Trust* me, Ethan." She points her beer aggressively at him, and his mouth shuts. "You want to land on the 'not homeless' side."

Silence stretches. Ethan decides his sister has used up her welcome. The rocking chair on the front porch is calling his name like a siren, and one overbearing woman already kept him from its loving embrace for the sunset. He'll be damned if the other takes up anymore of his evening.

Andrea's hazel eyes sweep him again, and Ethan's dark gaze meets hers defiantly. Both siblings take after their father in every way except for the eyes. Andrea inherited her mother's, while Ethan's deep-set dark ones mirror their father's. The only things Ethan got from his mother are a funhouse selection of behavioral disorders.

Andrea looks away first. She runs her hand over her hair, smoothing along the buzzed sides to grip the shock of longer hair on top. She straightens, the breath she was holding rushing from her. "I just want you to be..."

"Happy?"

"Ideally. But I'll be satisfied with at peace. That's why you're out here, right? Work was burning you out. The city wasn't serving you..." Her hand wraps around her beer again. "I don't care what your mom thinks. You have some soul searching to do, and going home now and just being miserable there isn't going to work. It hasn't been working for a long time."

He nods, gaze dropping. She's right, just like all the other times they've had this conversation. He's been pretty fucking blessed all his life. Got in with a tech startup right before it took off, catapulting him through the ranks and landing him a nice VP position where he does very little programming and a lot of paper pushing. The money is great. His investments, retirement, company stock...it would make the average millennial weep. Hell, he even purchased a large condo in the city before the housing market bounced back. And yet, he still feels the suffocating oppression of ennui. He just doesn't get it. He should be happy.

He takes a fortifying swig of beer. "I know." His fake smile is back. "I'm okay."

Her eyes narrow, but she drops it. Her empty beer bottle clatters in the recycling can. "I should head out."

He nods. "You good to drive?"

"Bitch, please. It was *one* beer. I could drink you under the table."

"Yeah, don't remind me, or I'll be forced to lecture you about my concerns with your level of drinking."

Andrea's gasp of outrage drowns out the creak of the porch door swinging open. "How *dare* you. I'm fine." She starts mumbling as she stomps out. "Sexist bullshit. Just because I'm a woman, I can't win a drinking contest? My liver is an overachiever!"

He walks her out to her car. Well, his car. His old truck, from before he bought his brand new souped-up one as a present to himself for his thirty-eighth birthday. With no marriage prospects and no chance of a "whoops baby," he didn't see the point of having such a thick savings anymore.

It had made him feel better. For a second.

Andrea hauls herself into the truck. "Night, Ethaniel!"

He smiles fondly at the nickname she bequeathed him when she was six. "Night, Andy. Drive safe."

The headlights flash and he's alone. Slowly, he makes his way through the cabin until every light is clicked off. Finally, there is nothing but blissful darkness. Grabbing another beer from the fridge, Ethan steps out onto his porch and sighs as he eases down in the old rocking chair.

Andrea was right in setting him up in this place. When she heard that one of the ranchers, her friend Lisa, built a vacation rental on their acreage, she immediately used her copy of his credit card, without his permission, to lock the place for the first two months of his sabbatical. He forgave her impulsive spending of his money once he saw the place.

The small cabin sits nestled between two massive hills on a large, grassy meadow with lots of oak trees and no light pollution for miles. The first time he beheld the night sky in all its glory, it felt like he was gazing upon the quiet splendor of heaven and his mind went quiet.

And yet here he is. Far away from both the corporate life that was eating him alive and the overstimulation from the city, and he still feels like absolute shit. It's downright aggravating.

He rocks in the chair, his eyes steadily adjusting to the darkness. It's a lovely evening, the kind he dreamed of when Andrea first texted him photos. The grass of the meadow takes on a light blue hue under the full moon. His eyes slide up to the twinkling stars, abundant and beautiful with a billowing stretch of cosmos. The knot of tension within his chest finally loosens and his head rests against the weather wood. It's everything the city isn't, and it helps quiets the frustration within him.

This is why he's here. The peace. Fleeting, hard-earned peace.

The scent of sweet dry grass and rich cooling soil fills Ethan's lungs as he breathes deeply. The way they blend with the crispness of night always settles his mind. It's better than any aromatherapy he's tried. His beer is empty, but he cannot bring himself to stand. The light creaks of the chair and the chirping of crickets are all he needs in this moonlit serenity.

Moonlit serenity that is steadily growing brighter.

Ethan's brows furrow. "What the f—"

The world explodes. His eyes burn under the oppressive brightness. His chair topples sideways, and he crashes to the ground hard, arms covering his head. The Earth shivers, tectonic plates shifting angrily.

Ethan pants, not daring to move while the earthquake rumbles all around. A cacophony of crashes from inside the cabin deafens him. The dishes he left on the counter shatter on the floor. Furniture topples over and decorative knickknacks rain down. He can hardly think of the mess he'll have to clean as he covers his head and waits.

Slowly, as the Earth settles, he dares to uncurl, his arms hesitating before lowering from his head. His hand brushes against the sharp edge of his smashed beer bottle that now lies on the ground next to him, and he flinches from it.

In the middle of the field, below the massive hills, is a giant glowing crater.

A wave of sickness washes over him. Suddenly, the isolation with terrible cell service no longer feels like paradise. Instead, the cold talons of fear sink into his mind at the possible pending death sentence of it all.

Maybe he should've listened to his mother's warnings.

He racks his memory for every science class he's ever taken to figure out if asteroids usually glow a light pinkish-purple. He wants to say no, and his brain unhelpfully suggests that if this is an alien of some sort, none of what he learned in high school science class applies.

He swallows thickly, trying to calm himself and think. He needs his gun.

The door is jammed from the house shifting with the earthquake, but he forces his way inside the house. Every shadow becomes a creature lying in wait to snatch him. Every creak of the floorboards is a monster slithering up behind him. His creativity offers horrendous combinations of abduction and slaughter to agonize over, his skin crawling with the creeping horror of it all.

He shakes his head violently. He needs to focus. Plan. And not become a plotline of *The X-Files*.

His numb fingers find the light switch and flick it. Nothing. He uselessly tries a few more times before pulling out his cellphone for the flashlight. The illuminated room is a mess, his interpretation of the sounds during the earthquake proving to be accurate, with furniture overturned and debris strewn around the small place. Cleaning up would have to wait though.

With a steadying breath, he carefully steps around the mess toward his gun locker. The time he spent shooting with Andrea and her friends is about to come in handy. He loads his Mossberg pump-action and cocks it swiftly, the *crack-crack* helping to soothe his quaking nerves, and steadies his hands.

He hesitates to consider the merits of searching for a bigger flashlight, but there isn't a need for one. The ominous purple light glowing outside is plenty to see by. With one last deep breath, he slides his phone into his back pocket and exits the house.

The light from the crater has changed. Instead of a bright, steady, lavender glow, it has begun to emit flickers of luminescence. The dry grass under his boots crunches until he reaches the soft upturned earth. He blinks, squinting down into the hole. It's much shallower than he expected, with a massive orb of light taking up most of the impression in the earth.

The light flickers again, and the outline of something small and crumpled in the center burns into his retinas. In the span of Ethan's slow intake of breath, the light takes on an opalescent hue. It's like the air is coated in mother-of-pearl, but it morphs, dances. The gun in Ethan's tight hold sags, his pupils dilating. Whispers of the world hum, the soil beneath his feet erupting in fresh sprouts. Wildflowers peek up before blooming, shedding, wilting, and starting over again from the seeds. Endlessly, over and over, the cycle of life coils and unfurls before him.

His gun falls to be cradled by the lush grass.

Ethan steps into the crater.

The light is losing its blinding quality, and he can clearly see the shivering form in the center.

His knees sink into the soft earth, the whispers becoming louder. Something is not right. Fear, not of what he is seeing, but of the wrongness of the form in front of him, blooms in his chest. It is leaking. He reaches out, touching it. He expects his fingers to burn, but instead a vibrant hum echoes within him. Unable to stop himself, he rolls the form over, its soft body falling into his lap.

A pulse echoes through the valley, the grass lying flat.

Ethan's eyes flutter, the mass of opalescent air circling. His chest jerks as his heart throbs. Pleasure, unfathomable pleasure, burns through him. His voice is gone, his mind is gone. The world glows and the air shimmers. His arms tighten around the form, and it shifts beneath his hands—but he cannot see. All he knows is this wondrous light glowing within him, consuming him, and he falls into the sensation joyfully.

The world sucks inward, the aura around them shooting in, and Ethan gasps, an echo of the same sound beneath him.

Just as quickly as it began, it ends. Only a few seconds pass, but it feels like an eternity. Ethan blinks, the night sky slowly becoming visible again. He wavers, limbs suddenly weak. Confusion makes his brain feel hazy, and his stomach rolls.

He needs to lay down, maybe have some water, but he definitely needs to get out of this hole first.

He looks down at the thing in his arms and jolts. Blinking up at him is something he can't quite comprehend. It looks human, but its skin radiates light with the same opalescent lavender sheen that he saw from the crater before. Ethan hisses in a breath when he sees a head wound, a nasty one, the mysterious being's skull nearly concaved on the upper right side of its forehead. White, shimmering liquid flows from the gash to drip down to the soft earth below, the soil sucking in the liquid greedily.

He looks the creature up and down, a wave of sadness and empathy hitting him right in the chest. He can't abandon it, hurt and alone. Not in this cruel world. Ethan swallows thickly, his voice harsh. "It's going to be okay." He's not sure why he says it, only that the sense of absolute rightness hums within him when the words come out. "I'm going to help you."

Eyes blink open again, settling on his face. Humanlike, but with soft blue irises that almost seem white. So mesmerizing that Ethan finds himself lost studying the different shades within them, until he notices the pupils, his brows furrowing. The black depths reflect the cosmos above. Beautiful and mystifying at the same time. He feels himself sucked forward, his own eyes widening and his heart thudding painfully against his ribs. In a great feat of self-control, he rips his gaze away, his chest heaving with the force of his breaths.

Ethan looks around wildly to see if there is anything nearby that could offer an explanation. When he finds none, he tilts his head back to look up to the dark sky. The stars watch him silently and offer no answers. He looks back down at the creature unconscious in his arms and wonders, *What the hell do I do now?*

In the deep dark of the world, in the cold watery depths of the enraged Ocean, the pulse of life washes through the abyss. Life stirs. Starved hunger, glowing eyes, and echoing bioluminescence flesh.

Magic has finally landed.

So long have they waited. Too long. But the magic, the star, it is too far away. Much farther than what was promised by prophecy. The creatures wail, writhing in despair. Great bodies slash through the water, circling round and round, snapping great fanged jaws at each other.

The largest of them, his milky white eyes blind to all, lifts his wide head. Ancient, far older than he should be, he is the last of the secret keepers of the great sea. He remembers what his father told him, whose own father told him in the great chain of tales. Not all is lost. His webbed, clawed hand reaches into the rock and pulls out a small glowing pearl. Hope in a small, round token. So few when there used to be so many. So precious. But one must go, or all is lost.

He turns to the other that is waiting, silent, watchful. The pearl passes between them, for it is not the ancient one's place to enter the Great Game. He must stay on his rock and protect the last few pearls. The other, the

Contender, curls his webbed paw around the precious drop of magic, his thick skin blocking the glow within.

The ancient one turns his blind eyes toward the surface far, far above. So far that the light does not even twinkle in these dark depths. His throat works rhythmically, squeaks and whirls of sound coiling out to the Contender. "Go, brother. Find the fallen star. Feast and claim the prize. Do not fail for we both know...death is the only outcome." A whirl sounds in his throat, his claws sinking into the sacred volcanic rock. "Yours or his."

Two

Pain. The star has never felt such a thing before. At least, the star doesn't...has never...Where...

Newly formed eyes blink. So many colors. So much...*sensation*. Air sucks into lungs that expand and push against a hard rib cage that stretches skin. Such...*feeling*. A body. Never has the star had a body. Or at least...they don't remember having a body.

It's wondrous, glorious. Painful, yes. Such pain. But *feeling*. They suck in a breath. *Life*.

"It's going to be okay."

A fluttering sensation. What could that be? It's somewhere in their chest beneath these expanding and contracting ribs that stutter. Could it be a heart? A heart that pumps oxygenated blood through a body. *Their* body. A body that is finally their own.

"I'm going to help you."

Such beautiful sounds. Words. Meaning. The star looks up at the creature holding their newly formed body. Painful throbbing in their head pulses as memories flash. Memories of watching, cold and trapped, but always watching. The world. The humans. Yes, that's it. A human. A human is holding the star and gazing upon them with such wonder and warmth in its lovely, kind eyes.

The star smiles. How lucky they are to have found such a human.

Water pools in their new eyes. Tears. The star smiles brighter. They can make tears. What a wonderfully uncomfortable feeling, light and heavy with the fluttering of their new heart. The vision of the human blurs and they blink to see it again, casting the tears from their eyes. Hot rivers stream down their face, and their breath shivers.

The human shifts its hold, and one of the arms wrapped around the star releases them. Coldness shivers across the star's new body. Their mouth opens, breath panting, and they try to summon the sounds to beg the human to keep holding them.

The human slides a thumb down their face, collecting the tears, and the sensation within the star's chest erupts in a wave of flutters. They never want it to stop, never want this tenderness in this human's face to leave, never want to be outside its warm embrace.

The star tries to lift their arm to touch the human, but splintering agony shatters up their new bones. Air sucks harshly into new lungs, making them burn. Different types of tears, those of pain, pour down their face faster and hotter as the sensation begins to ebb.

The lovely man's face contorts, those earthy eyes shimmering with concern. The star wishes to help it, to make the worry go away. A little tremor shivers through their newly formed body, other aches and pains making themselves known.

Though it pains them to do so, they close their eyes again. It's time to rest. This new body isn't ready yet. The star needs to rest, to heal, to make the pain stop, to give their body time to settle into itself. The human will still be there in the morning. Hopefully. Their new fingers twitch, brushing the human's clothes and catching on the edge of his shirt. *Please. Stay.*

Ethan's heart seizes when the body in his arms goes limp. He quickly feels along the neck, and a pulse flutters against his fingertips. He releases a heavy sigh. Alive, with a strong pulse. That's good. He looks down at the glowing, shimmering body, trying to make sense of what he's found. It's some sort of mysterious, sexless humanoid, but not an alien. Alien no longer seems...right.

How does he even know that? It makes no sense, but there's this thing, this *voice*, that whispers to him that he's wrong about this thing.

This...entity?

No. Life.

This life he's found. It is something *other* for sure. Something wondrous. Something that requires protection. His protection?

His breath shivers out past his lips, his brain hurting from trying to process what he's seeing and feeling. It's easier to push it all down and not think about it, and the more he does, the more the discomforts eases. Soon it becomes easy, shoving it all away, out of mind. As easy as breathing. Just don't think about it.

Accept.

He takes his first truly steady breath, and it washes away all the pain and panic. In its wake, soothing sensibleness settles in like an old friend.

He looks around. It's cold. It's dark. It's...*unsafe.*

He needs to get them out of this hole and inside. And... "Christ. I'm an idiot." The life is nude. Sure, it doesn't exactly have anything to hide in its glowing, sexless form, but that doesn't mean the life doesn't deserve respect and dignity. He quickly shrugs out of his flannel and wraps it around the body. With the sun fully set a few hours ago, the temperature is dropping quickly. A chill trembles up his exposed arms, and he tightens his hold. Whatever he's found will at least be warm in the flannel. Maybe it will help stave off shock, if that's a thing that could happen to it.

Yes, this is good. Productive action and thoughts. His shoulders slump with the relief of having a plan before he gathers his strength. He hefts the surprisingly light body up, and the shimmering light radiating from it flickers wildly before settling back to a steady glow.

He hesitates. That doesn't seem like something that should happen. A surge of panic flares, uncertainty and fear taking over Ethan's mind and robbing him of rational thought. He has no idea what to do. This mysterious creature defies all logic. Cold sweat coats him, chilling him to the bone. He shivers, his breath huffing. His brain begins to ache again, pressure building, panicked sickness pressing against his throat.

Soothing calmness eases through him, whispering sweet words. Don't think. Just...*accept.*

He swallows and releases a slow breath, the tight ball of tension in his chest loosening. He concentrates, centering his panicked mind on the important steps. He needs to get the life inside. Then...then whatever happens next will happen. He'll deal with that when the time comes. He just needs to stay calm. To relax.

Focus.

Slowly, Ethan ascends the crater. He eyes his fallen gun. There is no way he can juggle both it and the body. The flickering of the light from the life's body is still lingering in the back of his mind. Whatever that was, it's probably not good for it to happen again. Best not to jostle the life too much. The gun will just have to sit tight for now. He'll come back for it later. It's not like there is anything out here that will take it.

The light glowing from the uncovered parts of the body helps Ethan navigate his way across the field, up his porch, and through his earthquake-damaged house. They make it through the living room and down the hall with Ethan stumbling only twice before getting to the spare bedroom.

Ethan pauses, ears straining against the world's haunting silence. Not even the crickets dare to offer an opinion. Hell, even the air is still. His lips press together, his white undershirt sticking to the cold sweat down his spine. One step at a time.

He kicks the door to the spare bedroom shut behind him. His boots stomp loudly in the silence, making the ominous air worse. He tries to shake off the feeling of wrongness when he steps up to the bed. Offering up a small prayer for no more unsettling flickers, Ethan moves slowly, carefully, as if the form is made out of the most delicate glass that could shatter at the slightest misstep, to lay the body out on the bed. He pauses, his hands hovering midair. The glow appears steady, no flickering or fading. It seems like a good sign, one that he readily grasps with both hands. He releases the breath he's holding, raking his fingers through his hair. So far, so good.

His flannel around their shoulders doesn't seem enough. He eases the blankets out from under the body to drape over them. He always enjoyed the cozy comfort a heavy blanket offers, even on the hottest of nights. Perhaps the life will enjoy it as well.

As Ethan pulls the blanket to cover them, his hand brushes the life's chin. Blue eyes flutter open. Ethan pauses, caught up in the unusual pupils again. Before he can figure out what to say, the eyes close, and the life's breathing evens out into one of sleep.

He straightens, cheeks puffing as he rakes his fingers through his thick hair for a second time and balling his fists into it. The pain of his scalp helps anchor him, and he exhales harshly, hands releasing and clapping against his thighs.

What the fuck now? Leaving an unknown creature that fell from the goddamn *sky* alone in his house seems like a bad idea.

He should rest. Rest. And watch.

His feet drag as he makes his way to the chair in the corner of the bedroom. Other than the decent-sized dresser, it's the only other furniture in the spartan room. He collapses into it, the sturdy leathered chair rocking slightly under his weight. He props his temple against his fist as he stares unblinking at the glowing creature.

The rise and fall of the blanket-covered chest synchronizes with his own, and his skin prickles with an unease that soon smooths out with a soft whisper of calmness in his ear. The silence slowly fills with the sound of the world returning to life, the crickets resuming their nightly song once more. The tightness in his chest eases at the return of normality. It's as if his body was waiting for that moment of peace, that hint that everything isn't absolutely fucked. Finally, exhaustion sucks him down into the abyss, and his head lolls back.

The Council of Elders circle the scrying pool, silent as all seven behold the flashing lights revealed by the water. Tension ripples through the underground room that was built when their Order first traveled over with the Spaniards. The blood of the natives that were forced to sculpt it still paint the walls to keep the secrets held within.

The Eldest speaks, his voice a whisper. "The Vessel has landed."

Another echoes. "Late and not where it was foretold."

"The Ocean seethes."

"The creatures move."

"The game has begun."

The Eldest turns to the lone man by the doors. "Come forward, priest, and receive your blessing."

The priest obeys with confident, swift steps. Young, strong. Birthed and trained for this very moment. He stands, feet apart, hands behind his back. An acolyte holds a golden chalice, bowing their head in reverence.

The Elder dips his trembling fingers into the ash. "Birthed in battle and blood, master of the ancient arts, vanquisher of all those who challenge you. Contender. Go forth and seize thy prize. For the Land. For the sovereign of humanity." He draws a circle in the air between them. "As it was foretold, in the mighty Game there is only death. Yours, or his, no other possibility. Failure is not an option."

He smears the ash onto the center of the priest's forehead. Another acolyte steps forward with a box of pure iron in their hands, the embedded diamonds sparkling to imitate the night sky. The Elder loosens his collar to withdraw a small key on a chain. It takes several tries before he manages to remove the rusted clasp. The lock screeches as the key turns. The priest's breath catches when the Elder extracts one white pearl, glinting blue in the low lights of the candles.

The Elder holds up the pearl for all to see, his hands shaking, voice unnaturally strong. "Blessed be the Contender!"

The words echo all around. The priest takes the offered pearl, holding it between his scarred fingers. All fall to their knees, the chanting becoming louder, stronger, until it fills the vast stone room.

But the priest does not kneel, he does not bow, he does not bend. He is elevated above that now. He is the Contender. He is humanity's only hope.

He looks up, beholding what only a blessed few are permitted to do, what he is now permitted to do. The carvings. The secrets of the world, so precious that they necessitated the artists' sacrifice to protect them.

He lifts the pearl, offering it to the stone. His voice, strong, rings out above the rest. "Blessed be those who look upon the Shepherd. Blessed be the Harvester who drops the fruit upon the soil." The blue-tinged pearl is lowered to his lips, and he swallows it, feeling the exact moment when it reaches his stomach. His hands shake, his voice growing as he bellows, "Praise be the Reaper! Praise be the Order! For the Land! For humanity!" He gasps. "I will not fail!"

His back bows and he screams, cerulean light flaring through his eyes and mouth. The room trembles, the chanting growing even louder, the veins in his body glowing beneath his skin.

As one, the group bellows a single word. "Contender! Contender! Contender!"

Ethan wakes to morning birds singing merrily and sunlight pouring in through the open bedroom window. He grits his teeth, shoulders pulling back. His whole body feels like a giant cramp. What he wouldn't give to be able to call his chiropractor in San Francisco. He could really use someone to crack his body back into place. He rolls his neck, his gaze landing on the bed.

Blue eyes stare back at him.

Ethan's heart jumps and he freezes. Silence stretches as the two beings study each other. At least Ethan isn't the only one who isn't sure what to do. He tries to speak but hesitates, uncertain if the being before him will understand English. After all, it is a glowing humanoid that fell from God knows where.

Ethan wets his lips, scanning the injury on the humanoid's smooth, glowing skull. The head wound has stopped leaking. That's good, even if the wound itself still looks grotesque. In the light he can see the mottled coloring is tinged with a curious pearlescence. The bluish, purplish bruise, has a closed wound in the center shaped like a flickering lightning bolt.

It's been quiet for too long. He should say something, even if he's unsure if there's a language barrier. He needs to try to...connect.

He takes a steadying breath. "Um...hi?"

God, he wishes he was less awkward. But what does one say to a glowing humanoid that fell from the sky and may or may not understand him? He tries again. "My name is Ethan."

He's out of words. Those blue eyes just stare at him with growing awe, and he shifts awkwardly. It's not like he did anything impressive. He wets his lips. "And you are?"

Fingers peek out from under the covers, feeling the hem of the bed's quilt. Those blue eyes shift to it, flaring, fingers fiddling faster. A smile stretches across the being's face. Just like last night, it is one of the most beautiful smiles Ethan has ever seen, those blue eyes turning into lovely crescent moons of pure, unadulterated joy. His lips part in amazement, his gaze rapidly scanning the being, as their light twinkles merrily.

Blue eyes turn to him. "Ethan."

He jolts. Whatever he expected, it was not his name in a breathy, deep tone, one neither overtly masculine nor feminine but holding all the beauty of ringing choir bells. The sound of his name from the being's lips draws him forward until he's resting on his elbow, his ears craving more.

He wets his lips again, his fingers rubbing together for want of something to do. "Yeah. Ethan. And your name?"

The life tilts their lovely head, blue eyes drifting. For a second, he thinks he's lost their focus again but then they speak. "Star."

"Star?"

Brows furrow as the being slowly nods. "I think...Star." Star focuses back on him. "Yes. I believe Star is correct."

"Do you not know?"

Star seems to take a moment to collect their thoughts. "Not really."

Interesting, but also not helpful. "And where did you come from, Star?"

"I'm not...sure." The being's fingers touch the blotchy discoloration on their forehead. "It's hard. To think. To..." Blue eyes focus on their hand now, turning it this way and that in the sunlight. "Remember." Star's jaw drops open, and their fingers wriggle.

Ethan nods slowly.

Blue eyes slide to him, the intensity of the stare pinning him in place. "I think I was up high, watching. Then I fell and you were there." The blue warms, Star's lips curling in a small smile, and he wonders what they are remembering. Their voice softens. "That is all. Ethan."

He shifts, uncomfortable with the awe being directed his way again. Wanting to change the subject, he points at Star's injury. "Do you know if there's anything I need to do for that?"

"I don't think so. It feels much better already. The pain." Their face scrunches unhappily. "That terrible sensation. It is finally gone. Just little... twinges. Much better."

Star sits up, making the blankets flutter down, flannel left behind on the sheets. Ethan bolts upright to his feet. "Let me get you some clothes."

Ethan practically flees to his room to dig through his dresser. What would even fit a glowing, genderless humanoid creature? His brows furrow as his mind strays. Their eyes. That blue stays with him. So real. So hauntingly beautiful.

He pulls out one of his shirts and a pair of pajama pants. It will have to do.

As Star changed, Ethan excused himself to clean up from the earthquake. Now, as Ethan continues to tidy up the house, Star follows him like a lost duckling. A lost duckling that can't stop asking questions. Ethan doesn't mind too much. He may have no idea what Star is, but at least they're a thoughtful and curious thing, helping him slide the sofa against the wall and straighten the bookshelf on the other.

The cabin isn't particularly big. Two bedrooms with one bath down the hall that separates the bedrooms. The front door sits smack dab in the middle of the wall between the living room and a modest dining area adjoined to a kitchen. There's just a small four-chair table in the dining area, and a sofa and two armchairs in the living room. An unused TV sits against the wall. Nothing special, but he's grown quite fond of the place.

Star's eyes light up with excitement when Ethan clicks on the lamp. They squeal, "Can I try, Ethan? Please, oh please?" Then they click it on and off, on and off, over and over, faster and faster. Ethan thinks to intervene before the lamp breaks, but Star's giggle of pure, unadulterated joy stops him.

Those blue eyes turn to him. "It's the strangest thing. If I think about it, I know that the light this object makes is from an incandescent bulb housing a tungsten filament that electricity enters from the base of the bulb to make a controlled fire display." Their eyes sparkle. "But to *experience* the control over the filament heating up as it clicks on and off due to fingers in a hand that I control..." Their breathing is coming faster. "It's just *amazing*." Blue eyes mist. "All of it wondrous."

Ethan isn't sure what to say, but the amount of emotion coming from Star moves him. He looks at his own hand, his fingers rippling. An idea strikes him. "Have you tried eating?"

Those blue eyes flare.

In the kitchen, Ethan enviously watches Star eat with more enjoyment than he's felt in the entire last year. Just drinking water—warm, hot, cold, iced—Star is obsessed, prattling on about water cycles in the world and how they can't wait to feel rain on their skin. Star rubs their arms, beautiful eyes sparkling as they explain how they imagine the sensation. Ethan cannot tear his gaze away, his lips twitching in an almost smile. He refills their water glass and lets himself become lost in their infectious enthusiasm for life.

This is good. He feels...good.

A thunderous call shatters their peaceful moment. "ETHAN!"

He turns toward the window, but Star jolts, the table shaking from their knees hitting the bottom. The water sloshes, and Ethan barely has enough time to catch it before Star falls into him. He catches them instinctively, drawing their small trembling body against his. "You okay?"

Those blue eyes are closer to Ethan than ever before. The pupils are blown wide, and Ethan falls deep in the darkness until the galaxy of stars within glints back at him. Such amazing, impossible eyes. He could get lost in them for hours.

Star's hands curl around his arm, their voice hushed. "What was that?"

Ethan tilts his head toward the door, unable to keep the smile off his face. "Come out and see." He rubs Star's arms to sooth their trembling before standing and leading the way. Star's shoulders curl, eyes wide. Ethan keeps a steady hand on them and his voice light. "If you liked the lamp, then you're going to love this."

Star nods, relaxing under Ethan's confidence. The smile returns to their face, smaller than before, but Star can't seem to look away from Ethan's smile. Encouraged, Ethan leads them to the front door and pulls it open. The morning sun streams in, and Ethan steps out onto the porch to greet his sister.

Andrea sits astride her ginger gelding, Monty, and stares at the crater. Except it's no longer a crater. Fresh grass and wildflowers fill the once empty hole, and life overflows and tumbles out of it in long tendrils. Golden poppies, bluebells, lupine, and so many other wildflowers that he can't begin to name paint an awe-inspiring picture in the middle of the surrounding brown summer grass. The sweet smell of flowers and grass catches Ethan's breath as the wind kisses his face. He looks back at Star in wonder. "Did you do that?"

He receives no answer, and Star shows no interest in it. Instead, they can't tear their eyes away from Andrea and the horse, mouth ajar in wonder. Ethan bites his lip in anticipation for Andrea's reaction to Star. A small bolt of excitement stirs his withered heart.

Andrea swings down from her horse, her eyes unable to look away from the burst of life in his front yard. In the light of day, he notices how much darker his sister's skin is now, the result of hours spent working in the sun as a ranch hand. Like their father, she and Ethan both have the same easily tanned skin, as if it's trying to soak up as much of the sun's rays as possible. He shifts his far paler arms. He needs to get out more.

Andrea still hasn't turned, her hand resting on Monty's reins. "Okay, seriously. I'm pretty damn sure that wasn't there yesterday."

Ethan clears his throat. "Andy."

She points at the grass. "Like, did it rain in just that one spot?"

"Andy."

"Did a pipe break? Are there even pipes there? Wait, can flowers even bloom that quickly? I swear, Ethan, that was not like that yesterday. Did you see it?"

Star and Andrea are going to get along great. Ethan snaps. "Andrea!"

She whips around, a glare behind her aviators. "What! The fuck?" Her jaw drops, shoulders straightening. A small scream like the high-pitched squeak of a balloon catches in her throat.

The world goes still, a *hum* washing over the space.

Slowly, Star descends the steps, bare feet whisper-silent on the warm earth. Andrea removes her aviators, and Ethan can see her hazel eyes dilating rapidly. Her breath hitches.

Star stops a mere foot away from Andrea, and Monty's ears swivel forward as he sniffs. Star's voice is hushed with awe. "What is it, Ethan?"

Ethan's head tilts. "The horse?"

Star's fingers lightly graze Andrea's cheek. "Horse."

He snorts in amusement. Andrea still looks too shocked to react to anything. He's not sure if she's breathing anymore. "Oh no. That one is my sister. Andrea, or Andy. Andy, this is Star. They kind of fell out of the sky last night."

Andrea's mouth moves wordlessly, and Star continues their enraptured scanning. "Sister. Does that mean..." Star beams, eyes lighting up. "Is this a *woman*?"

Ethan feels the beginning of an amused smile on his lips, and it surprises him. Usually, that is only reserved for Andrea's antics. He nods. "Yeah. Andrea is a woman."

Star shivers with excitement. "Woman. Ethan. Oh, Ethan. Woman is...*beautiful*. More beautiful than I ever could imagine." Star turns back to him. "I want to be woman. Please, Ethan. Can I be woman?"

Ethan's lips part to answer, but he's unsure where to begin. His mind spins around how gender is a construct, but there's also a chromosomal sex definition. Still, that doesn't explain what it is to be a woman and how society defines sex and gender and the sociopolitical implications—

He shrugs his shoulder. "Sure. You can be a woman too."

Star radiates joy, literally. Her glow shimmers about her, and Monty's nose bumps her gently as he sniffs.

Andrea's harsh exhale breaks the silence, and she staggers like she's deflating. Ethan had forgotten about her little freak out, too enraptured with Star's discovery of a woman. He gives her a once-over as she gives herself a little shake, her breathing rapid. Her pupils contract to normal again. "What...what...what *are* you?"

Star turns her smile on Andrea. "I am Star." Her eyes sparkle. "*Woman*."

"Yes. He said that. But..." Her hazel eyes scan Star carefully. "What are you?"

Star's head tilts, a line appearing between her brows. "I'm Star."

This is not productive. Ethan interrupts before the conversation circles too much. "They—" He shakes his head. "Sorry. *She*." Star's eyes widen, and the sparkling radiance of the galaxy within her eyes glows. Her beautiful smile appears, her eyes curling into half-moons. Ethan's neck warms, and he clears his throat, looking away before the flush reaches his face. He mumbles the rest of his explanation. "She has a head injury."

Andrea's brow arches. "A head injury."

"Yeah. I think she—" He can't look at Star again or he's going to lose his train of thought. "—hit her head when she landed, and her memory is all messed up from it. But she seems to understand English and is learning to connect the words she doesn't recognize to objects." He shrugs dismissively. "It's a little odd."

Andrea's eyes flare. "Oh yes, *that's* what's odd. Not this glowing…" Her fingers lightly touch her forehead, wincing. "Star…thing."

Star reaches out a hand to stroke Monty's muzzle, and the horse nudges her. She rubs the velvety snout. "Hello. You're very lovely."

Monty snorts, and Star's smile widens. "It's nice to meet you too."

Andrea is too pale, her throat working. She gasps and touches her chest. "Can you talk to him?"

Star blinks. "Can't you?"

Andrea's voice tips to high-pitched again. "Yeah, but he doesn't talk back!"

Ethan rolls his eyes. It's too early for this much yelling. He claps Andrea on the shoulder, giving it a firm squeeze. "Come inside. I'll make some coffee. It'll help." He catches Star's eyes and nods toward the cabin. "You too, before Andy has an aneurysm."

Andrea and Star sit at the kitchen table while Ethan prepares the coffee. Andrea drills Star for as much information as possible, but Star keeps getting distracted.

"So how did you fall?"

"I don't know." Star eyes Andrea's chipped blue nails. "Why are your nails colored differently than Ethan's?"

Andrea fans her fingers. Ethan pretends not to notice how horrendously chipped two of her fingers are in an otherwise perfect self-manicure, just like he's ignoring the poorly hidden hickey on her neck. More evidence to support his theory that Andrea has a secret new girlfriend, but he'll be damned if he thinks too hard about it. He sighs. It's like she's in high school and living with him all over again. Hopefully, Star won't ask about it. There are some details he just doesn't need to know.

"Oh. It's nail polish." Andrea wiggles her fingers. She gives her head a little shake. "But back to the way more pressing issue. What did you fall from?"

"The sky. Can my nails be color too?"

"Um, yeah. I'll bring some polish next time." Andrea shakes her head sharply again, eyes narrowing. "But what part of the sky?"

"Um." Star's face scrunches. "Up?" She points at the ceiling. "High?" Her face lights. "Will the polish be the same as yours?"

"Like a spaceship?"

Star tilts her head. "Spaceship?"

"Like..." Andrea throws Ethan a desperate look that he studiously ignores. She huffs. "Like a house or a car in the sky?"

"No, I don't think so." Star leans forward to examine Andrea's nails closely. "I like this color. Are there more colors of polish? Like Ethan's shirts? In Ethan's closet there are all sorts of colors! Do you want to see?"

Ethan's eyes crinkle and his lips tilt as he measures out the coffee beans into the grinder. Andrea is having as much luck as he did trying to rein in Star's curiosity.

Andrea slumps back in her chair, her arm draping over the back of it. "No, and his clothes are boring as shit. I have all sorts of colors."

"You do? How many?"

Ethan starts the coffee grinder, the loud noise drowning out the increasingly dull conversation about nail polish and different colored clothes. By the time he dumps the grounds into the filter and starts the coffee machine brewing, Star has shifted the conversation back toward gender.

Her blue eyes are wide, and she leans toward Andrea. "Were you always woman?"

"Um, yeah. Always."

"Since you were born? From..." Ethan swears Star's eyes turn into glowing blue suns. "*Another* woman? Oh! I wish I could see other women. There is only Ethan here, and he is a boring man. Are there many women? Do they all look like you, Andrea? Are they all beautiful?" She frowns, touching her forehead. "I wish I could remember what others are like." Sadness radiates off her, and a dull ache in Ethan's chest turns his mouth into a frown.

He shakes off the sensation and pours himself coffee. He sips while Andrea falls under the spell of Star. His sister becomes more and more relaxed, the conversation gliding away under Star's lead. Star's infectious enthusiasm catches Andrea, and she pulls out her phone. "Women come in all different shapes and sizes. Here. We can use this to look at pictures. See?"

Star vibrates. "Oh! Look, Ethan! Look! This little screen has a whole bunch of women! Oh...they are all so *beautiful*." She sighs wistfully. "Oh, how lovely."

Ethan looks over Andrea's shoulder and rolls his eyes at what he sees. "Can you not show her thirst traps?"

Andrea glares up at him. "It's my social media and I'll scroll through what I want, thank you very much." She turns her attention back to Star. "See. I like her. She produces great content."

Ethan snorts into his mug, then covers it with a slurp. Andrea elbows him, and he chokes on burning coffee. He retreats to the safety of the adjoining kitchen.

Star runs her fingers along the phone's frame, her face softening. "She is lovely. Oh!" She jumps. "It's moving!"

"Yeah. It's a video. Look, if you swipe like this, it goes through more videos. And if you push this little heart, more videos like it will show up."

"Can I try?"

Andrea hands over her phone. "Sure. Here."

"Oh, I like this. Look! They're dancing!"

Andrea laughs. "It's a thing influencers like to do. They all do the same dance trend. If you click this, you can see what everyone has made so far."

"I like this. I like the dancing."

Once Star gets the hang of the phone and has swiped through a few more dance videos, Andrea gets up and saunters over to Ethan, who's leaning against the kitchen counter. She pours herself a mug of coffee, leans on the opposite counter, and arches a brow at him.

He glares suspiciously. "What?"

She clicks her tongue, and his skin tightens, his eyes narrowing further. He could tell her she's acting like her mother, but he's not in the mood to fight right now. He holds his tongue and waits.

Andrea sips her coffee slowly, her eyes not leaving his as she glares at him from over the brim. "So, a star falls in your front yard and you just, what? Let it into your house?"

"Yeah? What else was I supposed to do? Leave her outside? She was hurt. I had to do something."

"Uh huh. Didn't you, you know, *call* someone?"

"And say what? 'Hello, police, there is a glowing humanoid that fell

eyes wide, her thick lavender hair sliding over her shoulder. Even at a distance their eyes meet, and Ethan's heart stops, his breath catching in his chest. Her surprise shifts to joy, and her eyes curve with the full radiance of her beautiful smile. The warmth floods him, and his breath releases in a trembling exhale. His knees weaken, and he nearly sinks to the ground from relief.

He gives a small wave back, trying to hide the embarrassment of his over-reaction. His feet sting from various sharp twigs and rocks that he ran over in his panic, and the morning chill nips at his shirtless chest. His lips thin, head ducking as his free hand runs through his tangled hair, his gun dangling from his limp fingers. "Idiot," he rasps to himself, his voice still heavy with sleep.

He wipes his brow with a shaking hand, as the tendrils of his horrific dream tighten around his chest. It's odd. He usually doesn't have dreams, but his nights since Star's arrival have been riddled with them. Some he can't remember, while others, like this repeating nightmare featuring scales and sharp teeth, have no ending no matter how many times he jerks awake.

The memory of the dark hunger crawls over his skin in sickening ripples.

He gives himself a shake to disperse the lingering horror, turning back to the house to pull on his boots. Once inside, he takes the time to carefully lock his gun away, then starts the coffee brewing. It's at least an hour before he would normally consider waking up, but there is no hope for sleep now. Might as well list it as a lost cause. He snatches an abandoned hoodie off the back of an armchair and pulls it on. At least he put on pants before running outside like a paranoid fool. Back in the kitchen, he smears some peanut butter on toast, grabs his cup of coffee, and goes back outside to meet up with Star.

She's holding her hands out, and he squints to see the reason behind it. There is a family of deer hiding in the trees. They sniff her and allow her to approach to rub their snouts. Large ears swivel toward him, and the buck huffs a warning, the others shifting with unease. Star strokes his long neck. "Oh, that's Ethan. It's okay. He's nice."

Ethan hopes they don't tell her about his recent participation in hunting season.

Not wanting to ruin Star's fun by spooking the deer, he keeps his distance. But not too far. He's still close enough to run to her if need be, and he watches her closely while eating his breakfast in efficient bites. The coffee in his hand steams delightfully as he sips it, eyes trained on her. She glows less, her skin looking more humanlike, yet her hair gives her away as something otherworldly. It shimmers its rosy hue so strongly in the dawn light, that it is more pink than lavender in this moment.

Then there's her cosmos eyes. He sees them every time he closes his own. Watching him with such awe.

Feeling like a creep, he forces himself to look away, wiping the crumbs from his finished toast on his jeans. His messy hair is in his eyes. Using his now crumb-free fingers, he works out the knots a touch too roughly while his gaze sweeps the terrain. It's early enough that the large hills still cast shadows on the meadow, and the chill seeps through his sweatshirt. He sips his hot coffee, hoping that it will help to heat him. He turns, pausing mid-comb.

His mug lowers.

Hovering in midair over the center of Star's crater is an oak sapling.

Cold unease washes over Ethan, reminding him that Star is not just some woman he stumbled upon. Something unnatural is happening, and the hovering sapling most certainly does not alleviate his concerns. The pressure of anxiety builds into a headache but eases when he lets go his thoughts of her otherness and focuses on the tree, while moving toward it across the grassy field.

He toes the edge of the crater. Below the floating sapling, the oak's root network stretches through the space to touch the earth. Birds sing their early songs and hop along the roots completely unperturbed. If he wasn't living with what he's pretty sure is a literal star, he'd say it is the strangest thing he's ever seen.

He calls behind him. "Hey, Star? Come here for a second."

Her merry reply echoes through the clearing. "Coming, Ethan!"

She hops over to him with her normal joyful exuberance stemming from her new ability to move and dance. She has yet to miss an opportunity to bound through the grass, even trying—and failing—to do a cartwheel. But failure to do things the "human way," or rather, with her human body, never stops her. She tries two more times before she reaches him, slightly out of breath and covered in dried leaves and stray grass. The endearing sight almost distracts him from the odd tree in the crater.

Her blue eyes look up at him expectantly, and he nods toward the hovering sapling. "What do you make of that?"

Her blue eyes scan the tree. "It's beautiful."

"Did you make it?"

She tilts her head. "Maybe."

"Can't remember?"

"No. But it's probably me."

He arches a brow at her. "Probably?"

She smiles mischievously, and her joy is infectious, setting his heart humming and chasing away the cold. "Of course. It's magic, Ethan. *Magic.*" She hops in the crater, eyes flashing. "Come on! Let's touch it."

His lip curls. "Somehow saying 'its magic' and 'let's touch it' in the same breath seems like you're asking for trouble." He follows her anyway, careful to keep his precious coffee from spilling when he stumbles. "Remind me to teach you how to play D&D later."

"What's D&D?"

"It's a game where you strategically play pretend."

Star effortlessly winds through the impossibly long roots and stands under the sapling, which emphasizes how shallow the crater really is. Star is just a few inches shorter than he is, and she clears the tree easily while he has to duck.

She pokes the trunk.

He snorts. "That's what you meant by touching it?"

She smiles. "Well, some unnamed asshole—" Andrea has clearly already been a bad influence on her. "—made me think it was a bad idea." Her long fingers run up the trunk to stroke a tiny leaf. "It's so cute. Hello, friend. I'm Star."

Ethan forces himself to blink and stare only at the tree, not at the way she strokes it. "I don't think it understands you."

Her fingers curl around the root. Ethan's hand tightens on his mug, and he mentally slaps himself. Star gives him a chastising look, and panic lances him. Her smile is playful. "Of course it can understand me."

Ethan releases a breath, his hand loosening. Out of all Star's mysteries, he'd rather not find out that she reads minds. No need to traumatize her with what his hormones are trying to conjure in his imagination. Star is beautiful, but he has to control himself. What she needs is a friend, and he's happy to be that for her. Now he just has to convince his dick the same thing.

Star's husky voice shivers up his spine. "Here. Touch it."

Ethan jolts, blinking, before realizing that she's talking about the tree. He shakes himself and keeps his tone light. "Hm, yeah, see my previous comment about how 'it's magic' and 'let's touch it' tend to be bad ideas." And yet, he extends his hand and grazes his fingers along a root. It feels like a standard tree to him. He's not sure if he's supposed to feel relief or disappointment.

Nothing should surprise him anymore.

Star circles the tree, drawing his attention. The roots partially obstruct her full female form. For a moment, all he can see are her plump lips that are pinker than what is considered normal. Then, her high cheekbones catch the sunlight as the dawn finally peeks over the hills, Star's long lashes kissing her cheeks when she closes her eyes in pleasure. She tilts her head toward the rays. Her smile is soft, her hair shifting over her face.

He forgets to look away when she opens her eyes. The sun hits the blue, and he can make out the different hues, from icy near-white to deep sapphire.

His lips part, his eyes soften. Beautiful.

Star's gaze slides down his body, her head tilting. A curiosity sparks in her eyes, and Ethan's breath falters. Something shifts between them. Something that makes his heart flutter.

He wets his lips, brows furrowing. "Star?"

She takes her time roaming up his body to meet his eyes. "Yes, Ethan?"

He swallows, forcing his mind to focus on the curiosity at hand. "Do you really not know why this," he nods at the tree, "happened?"

She looks back up at the tree, her fingers gliding along the roots thoughtfully. "I don't. Whatever the reason, I like it. I think it's wondrous, don't you?"

"But aren't you curious at all? The tree, the magic you spoke of, the crater, *you*. Your past. Any of it?"

A shadow crosses over her face. It's brief, like a flicker, so fast he's not sure if it was real. "No. I don't." Her fingers tighten on the root in her hand. "I like how I am in this moment. Here. With you." Some of her carefree spirit floods back into her face, a smile sliding in place. "That's all that matters."

Something tugs at him to let it go, so he does. If she doesn't want to talk, then it's her choice. God knows he understands the feeling. He offers her a small, gentle smile, and her gaze fixates on it, her eyes wide and bright. Her intensity took him a few days to adjust to, but he doesn't shy from it. Instead, he nods toward the house. "Come on. I'll make real breakfast."

Star loops under an oak root and bounces after him excitedly. "Can we have pancakes again? Oh please, Ethan. Please."

He holds his hand out to steady her when she ascends the rim of the crater. She takes it, her grasp strong but her skin buttery soft. His thumb runs over her hand before letting go the moment she's cleared the edge. He slides the disobedient hand into his pocket before answering her. "I was thinking omelets instead. Andrea did bring over all those eggs yesterday."

They walk back to the cabin, side by side, while Ethan ignores the way his heart is beating too fast, or how his hand can still feel hers against it.

Star's mighty shriek exploding from the living room announces Andrea's midmorning arrival. Ethan peeks his head out of the kitchen to see the front door slam open, lavender hair whipping around the corner.

He flips the pancakes—evidence of his complete and total inability to deny Star anything —one by one on the griddle. He prods them with his spatula to ensure doneness before sliding them onto a plate.

A loud, strange wailing noise echoes through the open front door, nearly making him lose control of the plate. The mountain of pancakes wobbles dangerously, and Ethan cusses loudly when one tries to fly off. He catches the escaping breakfast just in time. The plate hits the counter loudly but doesn't break, and Star's pancakes are saved.

Ethan exhales harshly and quickly turns off the stove before anything else happens. Snatching up a dishcloth, he wipes his hands clean before making his way outside to check on all the commotion.

Five ranch dogs are suffocating Star with a kind of manic love that he's never seen before. Star is laying on the ground, the dogs' bodies wriggling all over her. She hugs each one and wails along with the five animals, the noise of all of them ungodly. Star looks up at him, gesturing at the border collies while she cry-laughs, and he can't help the smile that briefly tugs at the corner of his mouth.

She hiccups. "Ethan! Dogs! *DOGS!* Canis lupus familiaris, originating from the extinct Pleistocene wolf! They're here! Look, Ethan! Look!"

He nods, his usual calm tone lilting with amusement. "Yes. I see."

She cries harder, and the pack licks her face furiously. "I l-l-love them."

Andrea speaks up from on top of Monty. "I can tell. Glad my hunch was right on that one."

The leather saddle creaks as Andrea leans up to dismount. Dust rises when her boots hit the dirt, and she secures the reins. She carefully scans Ethan and darts her gaze away when he catches her. Ethan's eyes narrow, and Andrea turns her back to him. Not sure what to make of her unusual behavior, he shifts uncomfortably and points to the two saddled mares strapped to Monty. "What's with the horses?"

Andrea strokes the snout of one. "We had a trail ride scheduled, but the tourists cancelled last minute. With the horses all ready to go and Star's head healed, I figured we could show her more than your little hovel."

"And the dogs?"

"They were excited for the ride and followed." She loops Monty's lead around the porch. "Try not to be such a dog-hating asshole about it."

His lips curl. "I don't *hate* dogs. It's just..." He eyes all five of them. "A *lot* of dogs."

"Mm-hm." Andrea skirts around the writhing chaos of dogs and Star that separates her from her brother. She halts in front of him and stares expectantly.

Frustration flares in his chest. "Jesus Christ, *what*?"

"Aren't you going to ask what I found out?"

"About what?"

Andrea's lip curls, and she kicks him. He hisses, rubbing his stinging ankle. It was her favorite move as a child, and she's perfected it to inflict the maximum amount of pain with no mark. It's one of the many reasons he misses being an only child.

She glares. "In my research, you ass. Remember? I told you that I was going to look into Star and her crash landing?"

"Oh." He'd forgotten. "I guess."

She scoffs. "You guess."

He rolls his eyes. A headache coming on again. "Oh please, Andrea. Tell me everything about your findings in great excessive detail."

"See, was that so hard to ask?"

Silence.

He and Andrea may have not been children together due to their age difference, but even as an adult he gets why siblings usually beat each other up as children. "Andrea!"

His snap startles the dogs. Star blinks at him, all wide-eyed and concerned. Immediate guilt humbles his frustration, and he clears his throat, wiping the tightness off his features.

Andrea notes the shift, her eyes darting between Star and her brother. She props her hands on her hips, takes a deep breath, and blurts out. "Nothing."

He waits and shakes his head when Andrea doesn't elaborate. "Nothing? What does that mean?"

"It means just that. I found nothing. Nada. Zip. Not a single fucking thing." She scrubs the buzzed sides of her head. "I even searched for news articles for anything about her landing. I mean, it was a giant asteroid-falling-from-the-sky-looking thing, right?" She glares at him when he fails to answer her. "That's what it *looked like*, right?"

He nods obediently. "I would say that's an accurate description, yes."

"There's nothing except some notes on the earthquake, which isn't that newsworthy for the earthquake capital of California, but still." She stares at him expectantly. He must not be showing the reaction she wants, because she bursts out in anger, "Isn't that weird, Ethan? I even found a website that shows the status of satellites to see if any got damaged, and there wasn't anything!"

He nods before she tries to kick his ankle again, saying what he hopes meets her standard of a thoughtful response. "Weird." His gaze drifts to Star and her radiant smile. "Why do you think that is?" Star hugs one of the dogs, its whole filthy, matted body curled up in her lap. The border collie furiously licks her neck and chin. Jealousy has his teeth clenching. Lucky bastard.

"Now hear me out on this one." He forces his attention back to his sister, her eyes sparkling in a way that concerns him. "Government cover-up."

"Jesus Christ, Andrea."

"I said, hear me out! I'm just saying it makes sense, right?"

He rubs his forehead, a headache now truly blooming at his right temple. He's going to run out of Tylenol at this rate. "I need more coffee."

"Hey, at least I'm doing something. What are you doing? Do you even have a plan here?"

He turns away from her toward the house. "She's hurt."

His sister stomps loudly as she follows him. "*Was* hurt. She healed remarkably fast, right?"

He drains his mug, ascending the porch steps. "But her memories aren't back, so something is still wrong. It's called giving it time and having patience. You should learn it sometime."

"Fine. Whatever. I'm still going to try to figure it out." Andrea's boots echo loudly on the wooden steps behind him. "Did you make breakfast?"

He nods toward where the kitchen would be through the wall. "On the table." He pauses at the screen door, and Andrea shoves by him in her quest for coffee. He looks back at Star having a grand time with her fluffy new best friends. "Star, you want some breakfast?"

Her full attention snaps from the dogs, and she beams her response. He feels his expression soften. "Come on, but leave the dogs out."

Star's face falls. "But, Ethan—"

"Star." He'd idly wondered where the line was when it came to her whims, and now he'd found it. "They're filthy and live in a barn or kennels on the ranch. They are not housedogs. They stay outside."

Her sadness is unbearable. He feels himself wobble, and Andrea's called-out "dog hater" from inside doesn't help the situation. He grinds his teeth and cracks his neck. One calming breath later, he offers a compromise. "Maybe we could eat outside with them? It's a nice day."

Star's excited "yes, please" has his shoulders slumping in relief. He really didn't want to clean up dog mess from his rental. It would've wrecked his mood for the day.

The picnic on the deck ends up being a very pleasant idea, and Ethan rocks in his chair with his fresh mug of coffee, the tight tension in his chest gently easing with each sway. Star sits cross-legged on the ground, sharing bites of her short stack with each of the very attentive border collies. Andrea reprimands her from her seat in one of the wooden chairs she'd dragged out from the kitchen table. "I've *seen* what those dogs eat. I would just not. Trust me on this."

But Star ignores her, smiling brightly when one licks syrup off her cheek.

Dressed and ready for the day, Ethan steps out of the house with his sunglasses dangling from his teeth, still working on tying his hair back. His nails rake against his scalp to make sure he's not missing any strands. Once satisfied, he twists the mass of hair into a tight bun and secures it with the tie around his wrist. Just then, he notices Andrea scanning him carefully. Again. Suspicion rising, he rips his sunglasses from his mouth and snaps, "What?"

Shrugging, she tests the horses' saddles. "Nothing. Just noticed you've started maintaining your beard again."

Subconsciously, he runs his hand over his beard. Not only did he trim it today, but he oiled and waxed it as well. Several ex-girlfriends would be proud. Not that he'd give Andrea the smug satisfaction of admitting that she was right. He had been looking "unkempt."

He smacks the dust off his hat grumpily before sliding it on with his sunglasses.

His mare for the day greets him when he steps up. He strokes her long neck and gives it a friendly pat. There is a bustle of dog excitement behind him, and he can't help himself. He looks back at Star.

Her hair flows behind her as she runs to her horse. He's sure she's at a normal speed, but to his eyes she's in slow motion. Jeans have never looked better on a woman. They hug her hips and ass smoothly, the bootcut balancing the look perfectly in a way that some women would pay large quantities of money for.

The horse waiting for Star doesn't flinch at her exuberant approach and steps forward to nuzzle her chest. Star's hands smooth over the long neck as she murmurs sweet words of praise.

Ethan forces himself to look away and nudges his mare into a walk.

Andrea frowns at Star's loose hair. "Are you sure you don't want to tie your hair back? It's going to get hot."

Ethan darts a peek and sees Star gracefully mount her mare. His throat bobs as she shifts in the saddle. One of his old Giants hats is on her head, and her long wavy mane overwhelms her narrow shoulders. Star runs her fingers through the length. "I like it down."

Andrea has worn her hair cut short for years, and in the summer heat she nearly buzzes it to her scalp. When she first did it herself at sixteen, their father called it off-puttingly masculine. But Ethan always thought it suited his sister. Something about it brings out a different kind of beauty. Besides, when he first discovered her in his bathroom with his trimmer in her hand, she'd said cutting it felt like shedding a bad fur coat. Good enough for him. He'd helped her even out the back.

Pulled back into the present, Ethan watches Andrea's lip curl. "I don't know. The way it *sticks* to sweat is just, ugh."

Star beams. "I love it. Sensation. Feeling. Sweat." Her face tilts up to the sunlight. "The pleasures of a body."

And that's enough eavesdropping for him. His hormones are way too interested in knowing more about these "pleasures." Ethan quickly nudges his horse farther away until he can no longer hear their conversation.

Andrea takes the time to teach Star how to ride, but she soon learns that the horse does what Star wants without her even touching the reins. Ethan adds that to the ever-growing list of unusual things. Rather pointless, really. Everything with Star is unusual.

They ride into the hills, their pack of ranch dogs romping about merrily. Star takes on the activity with her same joyful exuberance as always. She smiles brightly, her hair flowing behind her when her mare races the dogs. Her laugh echoes through the California wilds, her arms outstretched and her head falling back.

Her hat blows off when a mighty wind hits. Her blue eyes shine bright, her hand combing her hair back to witness the cap cascade down the cliff-side they've climbed. She looks guiltily back at Ethan. "Sorry, Ethan. I can try to get it."

The hint of a smile that comes to him is soft, and he lifts one shoulder in response. "Don't worry about it. We'll get a new one."

Her whole face lights up. "In town? Can I go?"

He can say nothing else but, "Sure, why not?"

Andrea arches a brow, nudging Monty forward until he's in line with Ethan's horse. "Oh, yeah. She'll really blend in."

She has a point. Some of Star's happiness begins to dim, and Ethan cannot bear it. "We'll put a long-sleeved shirt on her. Tie her hair back. Sunglasses. It'll be fine."

"She *glows*, Ethan."

"Not that much anymore. Besides, I doubt anyone will guess she's not human."

"Is this what it's like to be Dad when you side with me all the time? Because you're making me sympathize with him and I hate it."

Star turns her charm on his sister. "Please, Andy. I promise not to do anything magical and be the perfect average human."

"It's not the doing something magical I'm worried about. It's all of..." She gestures vaguely up and down Star's body. "That."

Star looks down at herself thoughtfully. "Maybe the hair?"

She runs her hands through the thick tresses, and the lavender bleeds away to inky black. Ethan's jaw hinges open, like someone has struck him dumb with an anvil. Her eyes are impossibly bright now, and the black, rather than a true black, shimmers wildly with sapphire-blue highlights.

"Somehow that's even worse!" Andrea's voice is a touch too high-pitched, and Ethan can relate. "It's like looking at Star in her Villain Era." Andrea glances at him. "Am I wrong?"

Ethan shakes his head and is surprised to hear his own voice even and calm. "That you are not." This new Star is making things even more confusing. His mind wanders unhelpfully to all the wicked things Villain Star could do to him, and he closes his eyes. He takes a steadying breath. A leather-clad Star with ropes is not what he needs straddling his subconscious. The visual of her hips moving on the horse now is adding a particular vivid reality to the moment, and he finds himself struggling to cast the fantasy from his mind.

Andrea's voice grates against his eardrums. "What is that called again? The evil version of something? Omega Star?"

He swallows. "Nega-Star."

Andrea points. "Yes, that. Sorry, girl. It's rough being so hot. My condolences."

Star sags in her saddle and shakes her hair, the black dispelling in a fine powder that the wind sweeps away. Her head lowers, eyes drooping. Even her horse walks slower.

Ethan cracks his neck to try to shake the discomfort. To his great relief, Andrea sighs loudly. "Lord help us, *fine*. We'll do what Ethan says and cover you up so we all can go to town. I need to hit the store anyway."

Star brightens instantly, eyes sparkling. "I promise, Andy. I'll be the most human you've ever seen."

Star's mood is infectious, and soon all three are racing through the oaks, Andrea and Monty wildly outpacing the others. She whoops her victory, flipping them both off. Star races by her, her laughter like chiming bells, her mare weaving expertly, dogs giving chase.

Ethan nudges his horse into a run to close the gap between him and the women. His posting abilities are not on par with Andrea's, and soreness sets in. Luckily, the racing seems to run its course, and the horses take a break to slowly trot through the grass.

They make their way back to the cabin, and Ethan is glad for it. It's a beautiful day, but it's getting steadily hotter by the second. He's sweating by the time he dismounts, leading his horse over to the water bucket that Andrea has filled up. The horses happily drink down the cool liquid, and Andrea takes the opportunity to shed her outer layer. She stretches in just her tank top, and Star's eyes light up when she spots the black ink etched on her skin. "What's on your arm?"

Andrea looks down at her forearm. "This? It's called a tattoo. It's like permanent art on the skin. Ethan and I have matching ones." She smiles at the memory. "Got them on my eighteenth birthday."

Star whips toward him. "Can I see yours, Ethan? Oh please?"

He sighs, rolling up his left sleeve and holding out his arm. Twin compasses, both with long, stylized arrows. Andrea's arrow shoots from south to north with a wilderness-themed compass face showcasing trees growing past the rim. Written in scrolling cursive around the compass is "Not all who wander are lost." She thought it was the deepest shit she'd ever heard while camping with her friends, and nothing Ethan said could convince her otherwise.

Ethan's, luckily, is different. His arrow shoots from north to south, and his compass face is split down the middle with a clock. He hides his grimace.

Every date has asked him the deep hidden meaning behind the tattoo, but he has nothing. Andrea wanted the design and was too scared to go by herself, so Ethan let the tattoo artist do whatever she wanted. The clock seemed cool, and the geometric accents around the design aesthetically pleasing enough for him. He refused to have any writing with it. No "Carpe diem" shit for him.

Star looks down at her bare forearms. "I want one."

Andrea smirks. "Sorry, Star. Montenegro sibling exclusive. You'll have to think up something else."

"Like what?"

"I dunno, something that *speaks* to you." Andrea ignores Ethan's snort. "Or something that will remind you of a good memory. Look." She lifts up her shirt and shows a stylized dahlia on her rib cage. "My friends and I got this during spring break in Cabo. We were drunk off our asses, and every time I look at it I think about how fun that trip was."

Star continues to stare at her forearms pensively. It's the most subdued Ethan has ever seen her. Her mood lingers even after Andrea leaves to take care of the horses, returning hours later to join them on their afternoon trip to town.

Star was so lost in her thoughts that she only stuck her head out of the truck window once on the drive.

As they enter town and pull into the local gas station, Ethan notices that Star is still staring at her arm. He tries to pull her attention away by buying her a soda at the gas station, the first one she's ever had. He feels a little stupid doing it, but his instinct was spot on. Her whole face lights up when she sips the carbonation, and his lips twitch, his gaze warming. Catching it, she smiles at him, her eyes searching his face. Her shoulder nudges him, the softness of Star's low voice humming inside him. "Careful, Ethan. I almost saw a smile."

His hand flexes, the desire to put his arm around her overwhelming. Luckily, Andrea the Mood Killer is with them.

She gasps in mock horror. "A *smile*? Oh God, but what if your face cracks open from the pressure! Or worse..." The back of her hand smacks against her forehead. "Your face gets stuck that way."

He rolls his eyes, her cackling laugh grating on him.

Tank filled and drinks procured, Ethan parks along the street before

Andrea can start bitching about where to park. She grumbles something from the backseat of his truck about him clearly missing a shady spot farther down, and he rolls his eyes as he climbs out. He hasn't even shut his door before Andrea grabs Star's hand and drags her off, leaving him with only a flash of purple hair disappearing into Leather and Goods for directions. He sighs and shuts Andrea's car door before following the two women.

He should've walked slower to the shop. The two women try on every hat in the store until Andrea declares that the light cowboy hat suits Star perfectly. Which means for some reason Andrea needs one too. And new sunglasses to go with the new hat. The two women try on frame after frame until they get matching oversized aviators.

Star glows, and not from her normal light. The hat, the sunglasses, her long, thick hair that falls over her shoulder to curl along her tight shirt that fights to contain her chest...all of it suits her perfectly. Star twirls in the small mirror, her smile wide and eyes bright, and Ethan gets the full pleasure of seeing her ass in those jeans. She bends to grab a silver belt buckle, the waistband pulling low to tease the edging of lace beneath. Ethan's teeth sink into his lower lip, his eyes darkening.

Andrea slams her hip against the counter besides Ethan, and he startles, blinking rapidly. She slides her new sunglasses down her nose, nailing him with a knowing look. "You're drooling there, Ethaniel."

His glowers at her, but it's diminished by the heat crawling up his neck. He wrenches his body back toward the cashier and shoves his credit card into the machine harder than necessary.

But no matter how much he tries, he can't ignore Star's low voice from behind him. "Maybe I should get a tattoo of these sunglasses."

He signs the receipt as Andrea replies, "Why?"

"Because this has been the best day of my life."

"Girl, if that's true then you have a whole lot more living to do."

"I guess you're right. I'm just so happy."

Ethan nods a thanks to the cashier and turns to see Andrea melting under Star's smile. Before Star can reply, Andrea cuts her off. "What would really make this the best day of your life is by getting ice cream. Follow me."

The pharmacy at the end of the block has a little ice cream parlor. Ethan is pretty sure watching Star try mocha almond fudge ice cream for the first time is in his top ten most enjoyable moments.

That night, Ethan emerges from the shower to find Star on the living room couch, staring down at her forearms again in that quiet, pensive way. Heart aching, he slowly approaches her, glad he threw on his ratty old sweatshirt and sweats before exiting the bathroom. "You know, you can do the compass if you want."

He's sure that somewhere in Andrea's home, she's having the sudden urge to be an only child by violent means.

Star sighs, arms falling. "It's not that. I just..."

The silence stretches, and Ethan eases onto the couch next to her. She swallows, hugging herself. "I don't know. I feel..."

When she doesn't continue, he takes a leap. "Is this about your memories?"

Her lower lip trembles.

He nods. "I think time will be needed for that. Try to give yourself the grace to heal. You went through what I'm assuming was a pretty damn traumatic ordeal."

Her voice is so quiet he almost misses it. "What if I don't want to remember?"

He tilts his head, waiting for her to continue.

She swallows. "What if I remember, and I don't like what I do? Or I'm a different person?" A tear slides down. "What if I don't like who I was? I like this me. I like how I am now. I like the joy of discovering all the things. I like all *this*. And..." Her arms tighten around her body, a slight tremble shivering through her. "I like this body. It's *my* body. All mine." She hiccups a breath, tears falling faster. "Mine, Ethan. Mine."

His hand lifts, but he clenches it into a fist and forces it back down on his thigh. He shrugs. "Maybe the opposite is true. Maybe this is just an extension of who you've always been?"

She shakes her head. "I don't think it is. It's hard to explain, but it's like my body and subconscious know more than I do." Her voice drops, emotion making it crack. "I've been having these dreams. They don't make sense, but they always make me feel dread, Ethan. I don't think I want to know my past."

His heart clenches, his voice dropping to a low whisper. "It's going to be okay, Star. One day at a time." His fingers twitch, and this time he takes her hand in his. "We'll figure it out. And I understand about dreams. I've been having them too."

She looks at him with her large, tear-filled eyes. "You have?"

"Yeah. Weird nightmares of creepy monsters. They're hard to wake up from."

She uses her other hand to wipe her tear trails. "Mine are variations of the same dream. A bleeding woman who never looks up."

His brows lift. "Well, that does sound disturbing."

She nods. "They are. I don't like them. I wish they would stop."

Star sniffles, looking down at their joined hands. She shifts their hold to twine their fingers, and his thumb strokes her soothingly. It seems to help, and she leans against his shoulder. They stay like this, Ethan's heart beating in his ears, until he rests his head against hers.

After a stretch of comfortable silence, Star straightens with a quiet whisper. "I think I know what I want my tattoo to be."

Shifting his left hand more in her lap, she slides his sweatshirt up to his elbow to inspect his compass. His skin shivers when she runs her fingers over the ink. He tries to stay perfectly still. With a delicate touch, she traces the north, west, and south points of the North Star and the little markers in between. It feels nice, her touch and attention. Something pleasantly snug unfurls in his chest to take space, his gaze trailing her profile. He swallows, unable to look away.

Suddenly, she shifts, swinging his arm over her shoulders. Panic lances through him as his lap, once empty, is filled by Star's body, her hair in his face. All Ethan can breathe and see and fucking *feel* is Star. He sucks in a breath, but by doing so, he takes a gulp of her sweet scent, making him want to curse violently or roar in pent-up frustration. It's all too much, and he considers bolting. But to get up and run would mean throwing her off his lap.

He has no choice. He grits his teeth and bears it, locking down as much of his reaction as humanly possible. It takes almost everything he has, but he manages to smooth out his facial expression into a placid one, perfectly hiding his inner turmoil. But fuck, does he *burn* inside.

Oblivious, Star presses their left forearms together. Ethan's skin tingles as if his arm has fallen asleep. It's the distraction he desperately needs. Before he can so much as gasp at the sensation, she hops off and presents her forearm.

He blinks, the sudden whiplash a bit much for his still spinning brain. But then he sees it. Brows furrowing, he slowly reaches out and holds her arm gently to look down at what she's done. It's the other half of his compass face, but instead of the clock, there is a colorful star in lavender, pink, and blue within a night sky. Around the circle are golden poppies, oak leaves, antlers, horseshoes, paw prints, and—Ethan sucks in a breath, a smile softening his face—a pair of aviator sunglasses.

She points to the North Star of the compass. "See, this is you." Then, she traces the colorful star. "And this is me."

He looks up at her.

She smiles, a touch of uncertainty in it. "And these are all our memories. This way, no matter what happens, I will always remember that every moment with you is the best moment of this new life of mine." Her blue eyes dim, and he can see something ancient within them that makes his heart clench. "I like what I am now. I like learning and feeling and *being* here. With you. With everything. And if I change, hopefully I can look down and remember what it was like to feel such..." She takes a pain-filled breath. "Happiness."

Ethan's eyes burn, and he swallows thickly.

She wets her lips nervously. "Do you like it?"

It is the most special thing anyone has ever done for him. He looks up at her, studying her face, and everything he's pushed down when it comes to his feelings for her comes rushing up. All the intense longing, the hot painful desire, and the growing desperation to touch her. The intensity steals his breath away. This woman, this whatever-she-is, has wrapped his heart up so tightly, he feels like he will burst if he doesn't kiss her.

His eyes flick to her lips, and he lets out a shaking breath. "I love it. It's beautiful, Star." He lets go of her arm. *Coward.* "I'm glad you figured out something you like."

She smiles happily. "Me too." The cushions bob when she flops down next to him. She leans against his shoulder again, body softening. "I want to learn everything, Ethan. I want to live. I want to be. Please, Ethan. Promise me. You'll teach me how to be human." Her voice is a whisper. "I just want to be human."

He settles back into the couch, head resting against hers. "Of course, Star. Whatever you need."

A hum of rightness resounds in the space. They stay like this, staring at nothing, listening to the crickets sing. Existing together.

It's the peacefulness he's been craving all this time.

White, glowing eyes flash in Ethan's dreams. Bright lights. A mouth forming words he cannot hear or comprehend. A dream that wakes him in the dead of night, the tendrils of which slip from his mind like sand through his fingers. He struggles for consciousness, but sleep drags him back down to forget.

He dreams of a monster sliding through dry, brown grass. Sniffing. Hunting. Hungry.

Four

Black shimmering dust dances playfully upon the wind until it encounters flat nostrils. The creature snorts a sneeze before excitedly snuffling the wind again.

For days it slithered through the countryside, its hunting fruitless. Frustration growing, it risked the town, its dark body melding perfectly with the shadows. The risk was well worth the reward. The storefront metal bars peeled away beneath its claws, and it licked and sniffed small things of plastic and the larger firm fabrics. Delight within its cold heart grew, eyes glinting in the moonlight.

And the humans that came to investigate were delicious as well.

Now the scent grows, the excitement of the hunt pushing its slithering body to cover the terrain quickly. There are large rocks again, a cliffside just like the one it crawled up when leaving its watery home. There at the base is another small fabric item. A forked tongue slithers out to taste, eyelids fluttering and body shivering. Still fresh. It's getting close.

Star made breakfast all by herself while Ethan slept in and now presents the results to him with an artistic flair. The plate is decorated pleasantly with little edible wildflowers, longer cuttings of which are added to a coffee cup in the middle of the kitchen table. It's sweet, and kind, and yet Ethan stares down at the white ceramic in cold fear. The consequences of Star's first attempt at cooking stare back at him. They could very well have been pancakes once in their lives, but now they squat on the plate like sad, black hockey pucks begging for death.

He glances back up to see Star's bottom lip tremble, her hands twisting in his old t-shirt, the one she likes to sleep in. He can tell their conversation from the last night still weighs heavily upon her. She touches her tattoo with unsteady fingers and shifts her weight on her feet, her pajama shorts rustling with the movement.

He picks up his fork and takes a crunchy bite. Without gagging, he forces a smile and a jaunty thumbs-up.

Star is about to burst into tears. "I tried so hard so many times and it won't work!"

Chewing any more might crack a tooth. He chokes his bite down until he swallows. "It's," he hacks, "great. So impressed."

She tries to snatch his plate away, but he grabs it, holding it out of reach. She stomps her foot. There's flour on her face and clothes, and batter stuck to her elbow. She's a mess, but an adorable one. "I'm throwing it away!"

The force of Ethan's dodge skitters his chair across the tile. "No! It's great. I've never had anything better."

She swipes again. "Ethan! It's terrible."

"It's not terrible." He tries to stab another with his fork, but the tongs bend. *Fuck.* He switches tactics. "Practice makes perfect! Don't give up."

She succeeds in yanking the plate out of his grip. Before he can stop her, she stomps over to the kitchen trash and dumps the whole thing in. Ethan slides to his feet, retrieves the fork and plate, and sets them in the sink. "Really, it's not that bad."

Her back is to him, her arms hugging herself tightly. Tentatively, his hands rest upon her narrow shoulders, her hair sliding between his fingers. "Seriously. Star. I really appreciate you trying." He strokes down to her biceps and gives a gentle squeeze. "Thank you."

It happens so fast, he doesn't have time to properly prepare himself. She collides with him, her arms wrapping around his chest tightly. His brain processes too quickly the feeling of her against him, the smell of her hair, the sad, wailing words. "Don't be nice to me! I'm a failure."

"Oh, Star." He returns her hug tightly. "It's okay. These things happen."

She melts into it, sniffling and turning her head to listen to his heart. "I just wanted to do something nice for you, Ethan. You make it look so easy." She hiccups a breath, her voice lowering. "Sometimes it feels so futile. It doesn't matter what I do or how hard I try..." Her arms tighten with her shoulders. "I'll never be human."

Words escape him, her despair robbing him of thought. His hand slides up and down her back, searching for some solution to her pain. "Does it make you feel better if I tell you Andrea can't cook for the life of her?"

Star looks up with a sniffle, watery eyes wide. "She can't?"

"Nope. The woman can fuck up toast. She sometimes risks a microwave and that's about it. Why do you think she eats here every day?"

Star gives a wobbly smile. "Yes, that does make me feel a little better." Her shoulders sag. "I did want to do something nice for you though."

"Look, let's do it..." Bad choice of words. "Let's *make* breakfast together." He forces her away before he does something very stupid. "What you really need is a teacher, and luckily for you, I'm a pancake expert."

She wipes her face. "Really? You'll help me?"

"Of course. What kind of teacher of humanity am I if I can't teach you the most essential human female food group. Brunch." He gives her a soft smile and she returns it, some of her light sparking in her eyes again. "Come on. It'll be fun." His thumb wipes the flour off her cheek, lingering longer than it should, his fingers resting on her jaw.

He cuffs her chin, forcing himself to take a step back. "Maybe you'll even get another tattoo out of it."

She beams, giggling softly. "Okay. Yeah! Maybe it'll be fun." Her shoulders set in firm determination. "It will be fun."

The rest of the hockey pucks clunk into the trash. He feels the seed of an amused smile try to bloom, but he hides it away so that Star doesn't think he's laughing at her. "That's the spirit."

They clean up the kitchen, and Ethan starts pulling out pancake ingredients. He shows her how to crack the eggs and keep the shells out of the batter. Then, the proper way of measuring the dry ingredients. Once everything is mixed, he slides the bowl to the side. "The secret is to let the batter rest for a couple of minutes before putting it on the heat. That's how you get them fluffy."

She nods studiously. "Okay. Yes. Waiting. I can do that."

He highly doubts that. Amusement bubbles within him when her patience runs out a minute and half into the process. She leans forward, her long hair skimming across the newly cleaned counter, and she peers into the bowl. Her fingers tap, her bottom lip sucking into her mouth to chew, and it's the most delicious thing he's seen all morning. He swallows, unable to tear his gaze away.

She shifts, her elbows resting on the granite counter, and her hair sways dangerously close to the batter. Ethan darts forward, catching her hair before the sticky mix can ruin it. Star jumps, eyes wide, his hand inadvertently brushing her neck. His fingers flex, the backs stroking down to her collarbone. Goosebumps bloom along her skin, begging to be kissed. Her hair in his hand is heavy. He could twist the length around his wrist like a rope and pull her against him. But he can't. His fingers curl. He *can't*.

With every fiber of self-control he has, he forces his hand away and disguises the movement as sliding her hair over her shoulder. His insides mutiny, enraged at the missed opportunity, but friends don't kiss. Friends don't lick and suck each other's necks. Friends don't rip off each other's shirts, even if this friend is wearing *his* shirt. Technically, he would be reclaiming it. Her chest expands with a breath, and he knows with absolute certainty that she is wearing nothing underneath when her hard nipples press against the cotton, begging to be licked—

Oh fuck, he needs to *stop*. If he could slap himself without alarming Star, he would. Instead, he takes the world's most subtle deep breath and shoves it all down, deep into his psyche, stomping on these treacherous feelings until they're back where they belong. Once he's in control again, he speaks in a miraculously calm tone, "Sorry, I didn't want your hair to fall into the pancakes. It would've been a mess to clean up. Do you want to tie it back?"

Star blinks and touches her hair. He can't get a read on her expression, probably because he can't stop watching her mouth as she releases her swollen, chewed-on lower lip. Every fiber of his being begs to suck on it. To bite. To soothe the sting with a lick. His lips tingle with awareness, parting, and he presses them firmly in a tight line. No. None of that.

Star shakes her head no, a few shorter strands of hair brushing her pink cheeks. Goddamn it, someone needs to stroke them, softly, with the back of a finger, before catching the loose hair and tucking it back behind her ear, but that someone cannot be him. Not right now. He doesn't have the restraint to do it as a friendly gesture. He wouldn't be able to resist leaning in to kiss her full lips softly like she deserves.

He grinds his teeth and shifts his stance, slyly moving away to give her some much-needed space. He folds his arms across his chest so that she can't see his balled fists and leans against the counter.

She's watching him, her blue eyes darting between his. His stomach jolts, fearing what might be leaking through his carefully controlled face. But instead of calling him a sick pervert, she asks softly, "How do you know all this stuff, Ethan? Is this normal human knowledge?"

Relief hits him, but he feels none of the peace that comes with it. The morning light is streaming in through the kitchen windows to dance play-fully on her face. The picture of her glowing captivates him, robbing him of a reply. Something deep in his chest stirs, something he thought was dead. His traitorous heart skips, and his stomach clenches.

He needs to get away. Now, before he does something incredibly stupid. He grasps desperately for the first distraction that comes to mind. Cleaning. He grabs the cracked eggshells and turns away to toss them in the trash. "My mom taught me. Then, Andy came to live with me when she was fifteen, so I became very good at it. Didn't want her living off junk food."

Star watches him snatch the kitchen towel up and start wiping down the spotless counters, her hip leaning against it. Her large eyes glitter with barely contained curiosity. "Is that what humans do?"

He tosses the kitchen towel in the corner for the laundry and pulls out a fresh one. "No. Definitely not." He wipes his hands on it. "I happened to live in the best public high school district in the Bay so she could get in with my address, but really that was an excuse. Our dad is old and was tired of raising kids, and they weren't getting along well at that point. Her mom is nice, but the fighting was getting to be too much for her. So, Andy came to live with me. Her grades went up. Not the best, but you know, she gradu-ated. Started college, but hated it. All she wanted to do was ride horses and be in the wild." He gestures. "That's how she ended up in Parkfield. Found the job online. She hasn't looked back since."

He turns and startles. Star's close, too close. She looks up at him with those blue cosmos eyes. It feels different. It *is* different, but he's not quite sure how or why. Maybe his growing desperation is messing with his mind, making him see things that aren't there.

Her gaze flashes to his lips and back.

His heart jumps, body swaying forward before he takes an unsteady step back. "The batter is ready."

It most definitely is not, but he's going to get in trouble if she keeps looking at him like that. Innocent, joyful Star. Curious and new-to-a-human-body Star. If she is feeling even a fraction of what he is, it's probably just her body responding to his proximity. It would be wrong for him to take advantage when she's still learning.

He wants to do right by her. Kissing her in the kitchen without ever discussing such things is not doing right by her. He's better than that, and Star deserves better too.

"Okay, so we plop some butter in our hot skillet and once that bubbles, we add a scoop of batter." He demonstrates, Star's body warming his arm. Silence stretches, his arm hyper-aware of her, and Ethan is grateful when the batter starts cooking. "See these bubbles? Time to flip. You can use a spatula or do this."

He tosses the pancake, catching it perfectly in the pan.

Star gasps, eyes sparkling. "Do it again!"

He pulls out a second skillet to restart the process. "Want to learn?"

She does an excited little hop. "Oh yes. Please."

He demonstrates on the done pancake. "It's all in the jerk. Forward and back. See?" He flips it a couple of times. "Then you can get really fancy." The pancake goes high in the air. Now he's just showing off, but Star's rapture is like a drug.

He holds out the skillet. "Want to try?"

She takes the pan hesitantly. He can tell by the way her eyes slide to the trash that the hockey pucks are still heavy on her mind. He wraps his hand around hers, bringing their bodies close. Too close for his barely there self-control. He takes a steadying breath. "Like this."

The pancake flips perfectly.

Star sets her shoulders and tries. The pancake smacks against the wall. She blushes.

Ethan shrugs. "Eh, that's why the ranch dogs are lingering." Not that he could get them to leave even if he tried. Andrea couldn't get them to leave with her yesterday. The collies are obsessed with Star, following her around like she's their new pack leader. Andrea gave up and assured Star that there were at least a dozen other dogs at the ranch. No one would mind if a couple hung around the cabin for a few days. Ethan, on the other hand, did mind. They whined and scratched at the front door all night. But Star loves them, so he can learn to live with the beasts. At least they're about to come in handy.

Ethan nods at the pancake batter. "Try again."

Fifteen minutes later and there are pancakes all over the kitchen, some plastered on the ceiling, others oozing down the walls. But Star is determined, and Ethan is happy to keep making her batter.

Star's eyes narrow in absolute focus, her body rigid. She takes a deep breath and flicks the pan.

The pancake flips perfectly in the air and lands back in the skillet.

She screams, jumping up and down, and Ethan's smile blooms. The pancake flies out of the pan with her hopping, but neither of them care. Star celebrates by jumping around the kitchen, Ethan briefly interrupting her to carefully confiscate the hot skillet before releasing her to jump away. He huffs a small laugh as he sets down the pan and turns to her to join in the celebration. Laughing in a cloud of lavender hair, she jumps into his arms. It's his instinct to catch her, her arms wrapping around his neck and her thighs gripping his hips. She feels good in his hands, and the way his fingers sink into her thighs sends a little jolt of want through him.

She beams, her whole body sparkling. "I did it!"

He nods, his smile warming with affection. Her excitement is intoxicating, and he happily drowns in the moment. "Congratulations, Star. You'll be a five-star chef in no time."

Her eyes search his face, her features softening. Her fingers trail down the hair that escaped his bun, sliding it back behind his ear and lingering. He wonders if she is experiencing the same temptation he did, and he huffs with the delusional hope that she might be feeling anything other than a basic physical reaction to his body. Still, he can't stop thinking about how easy it would be to plop her on the counter, grip the back of her neck, and kiss her. He could make it so good for her. Whatever she wanted. Whatever she was curious about. He could sink down on his knees and show her what mouths could do. His fingers tighten ever so slightly on her.

She grazes the edge of his jaw, and his breath hitches. Sheer force of will has him gently setting her down on the ground. He nods toward the kitchen table. "Should we eat one or keep practicing?"

Star's cheeks are bright red, and she gathers her hair back in a twist as if she's trying to cool down. Sympathy stings him. He let it go too far. He could've kept this morning tame, but he failed. Guilt has him averting his gaze. This is his fault.

Her voice is breathier than usual, and he clenches his teeth. "Eating sounds nice. I'm sure if we look hard enough, there could be one edible one." Her eyes sparkle, and his heart flutters in response. "Andrea said something called *jam* also tastes good on them. Do we have that, Ethan? Do we?"

Grasping the excuse to move farther away to give her space, he turns toward the fridge and yanks it open, scanning the contents. "I think there might be—ah! Here we go." He pulls out a slightly sticky glass jar. "Strawberry."

They eat the non-floor-or-ceiling pancakes cheerfully, Star spreading generous globs of strawberry jam on hers. As he promised earlier, and to witness Star's eyes light with joy, Ethan permits the ranch dogs brief entry into the house to feast upon the practice pancakes around the cabin.

Midmorning, Andrea stops by on an ATV for coffee and a quick bite. Star beholds the vehicle with sparkly-eyed anticipation. Andrea waves her off. "Listen, I'm all for a little joyriding, but coffee and food first." She tucks her sunglasses in her tank. "Don't give me that face. I'm not Ethan. I don't just melt to your whims."

Ethan is about to argue, but even he knows she's right. He's weak and happily twisted around Star's fingers.

Star sighs, dragging her hand longingly down the vehicle. "Okay."

Andrea gives her a little smirk, nudging her. "Don't be so sad. I have work, but later I'll take you out on it."

Star brightens a little at this. "Promise?"

"Promise. Now coffee, for the love of God."

The three of them file back into the house, with Ethan careful to lock the whining dogs outside. Andrea slides into her seat at the kitchen table, hazel eyes tracking him while he fetches her a cup of freshly brewed coffee. He sets down the mug before her, and she picks it up without breaking eye contact. Her slurping sip makes his skin crawl.

His eyes narrow, arms crossing. "What?"

She bats her eyes innocently. "Breakfast?"

"I've got it!" Star flips the pancake expertly. "Did you see Andrea? Did you see?"

Andrea nods. "Yes! Great job."

Her gaze slides back to Ethan, and he snaps, "God, *stop* that. Just tell me!"

Andrea's mouth opens and closes wordlessly like a fish out of water before she scoffs loudly, "Can a sister not just look at her brother without it being a thing?"

"No sister in the history of siblings has ever made eye contact without planning something nefarious. Spill."

It takes another loud slurp and an equally slow gulp before Andrea's gaze drops. The mug clicks against the table, and she spins the porcelain between her fingers. "Have you been on any socials today?"

"No. Why? Did you send me something?"

"No." Her short, freshly painted hot-pink nails clack rhythmically against her drink. "Just wondering."

His lips purse. Social media really isn't his thing. He only has active accounts because it seems like a generational requirement. That and the odd meme Andrea likes to share. "Is there something I should see?"

He pulls out his phone from his back pocket.

The cup almost splatters out of Andrea's hands. "No! Seriously, good for you. Stay off that shit." Her eyes sparkle. "Look at that! Star!" Star beams happily, setting down the plate of perfectly cooked pancakes. No more burnt hockey pucks for her. "You made these? Beautiful!" Andrea takes a huge bite and moans. "Oh fuck, girl. Yes. Queen." She points enthusiastically with her fork. "Ethaniel! Get on these before I eat them all."

He sits down and takes a bite. They are good. He gives Star a proud smile, and she glows. Andrea gushes lavish praise, while Star's bliss adequately distracts him from whatever it is that Andrea doesn't want him to see.

Fed and caffeinated, his sister slides on her sunglasses, preparing to head out to work. The dry grass crunches under her boots. "A bunch of us are stopping by the Saddle Up for some beers and pool after work today. You two should come."

Ethan's lip curls, but Star lights up. "What's that?"

"It's a local bar. It'll be fun."

Star turns a hopeful look at him. "Can we, Ethan? Please?"

Maybe it's how much she loved going into town last time, or maybe it's because she looks exceptionally lovely, her eyes bright with anticipation, because he doesn't even try to put up a fight. Perhaps Andrea is right and it will be a fun experience. "Sure. If that's what you want. We'll come."

Andrea startles, whipping around to face him. "Really?"

Ethan snorts. "Don't act so surprised."

Andrea's face changes. A smile spreads wide, her eyes shining. Just then, Ethan realizes what a burden he's been on his sister. A burden she volunteered to take on when she brought him to the country, but still. It's such a little thing to go out with her, and it makes her so happy.

The moment lasts too long, and both siblings break eye contact before anything happens to spoil it. Andrea presses her lips together and ducks down, the longer hair on the top of her head falling forward. She slides on her hat and lifts a shoulder. "Okay, great. See you after dinner? Nine-ish?"

Ethan nods and scuffs his shoe against the dirt. Andrea mounts her ATV, and with a merry wave to Star, she speeds off. The dogs halfheartedly chase but soon turn back to mill around Star.

Except for one.

The female stares out to the thicker tree line at the far end of the clearing, ears perked and twitching. Ethan follows her line of sight. There's nothing there, or at least nothing he can see. But she stays there, the intensity of her stare setting him on edge. He whistles, and one ear flicks toward him before snapping back.

Slowly, the dog turns away and trots back to the house. She passes Ethan to join the others in a game of romp with Star with not a care in the world.

Ethan gives the tree line one last look before retreating into the house to clean up.

The Saddle Up is one of those old, much-loved small-town bars. During rodeo season it's packed to the gills. Decorated with an overabundance of cattle paraphernalia, the arched ceiling holds an array of bull horns, all with their own cowboy hats that the occasional drunk frisbees up there.

The bar wall is practically painted with photos. Rows and rows of winners of gladiatorial-style drinking matches sit along it, some photos badly aged to the point of being nearly indistinguishable from the wood paneling. Everyone in town shows up for those nights. Sitting in a place of honor in the very center of the bar is a makeshift trophy someone in the '70s welded together. A photo is taped to the top featuring the latest winner, who happens to be Andrea.

She steps through the front doors to an earsplitting cheer, bottles and fists slamming on the bar and tables. Ethan grimaces, lightly touching his ringing ears, while Star jumps, gripping his arm lightly in surprise. Andrea saunters through with arms raised like a Roman emperor, similar to the moment when she beat her competitor two weeks ago. Drunkenly climbing onto the chair, she'd planted her boot on the table with the two empty beer pitchers lifted to the heavens. The crowd joined her in a thunderous roar followed by a wave of bowing and chanting. Two of her friends lifted her on their shoulders and carried her in an unsteady lap around the room. Ethan barely managed to catch her before they all came crashing down.

The morning after remains the only one that Andrea did not show up at his place for breakfast.

The fun and horrendous hangovers aside, Ethan prefers the more subdued evenings at the Saddle Up. His personal favorites are the ones that feature live music. Rarely predicted, they begin when someone sits at the old piano in the far corner. Then a guitar will strum. Then another. Soon the bar will fill with a song that reaches every corner. It's the kind of melody that is felt rather than heard. Old friends, new friends, and tourists all join in to create a beautiful blend of emotional sound so joyous that it never fails to spark a flicker of happiness, even within Ethan's darkest moods. He could spend the whole evening at the bar with his eyes closed, feeling every second of it.

Tonight happens to be one of those nights. Two people are playing guitar, with a third ready on the piano. It's not an especially crowded evening, mainly Andrea's ranch crew shooting the shit and playing pool, which suits Ethan just fine. He can easily hear the melodies while he leans against the bar, observing how Star melds with the crowd. Ethan catches more than one gawker, but Star becomes instant friends with everyone she meets. She laughs and chats with all of Andrea's friends, her enthusiasm and authentically keen interest addicting to all. One of the cowboys, Danny, who Ethan swears has never said more than eight words to him in the entire time they've known each other, tells Star his life story. She nods throughout, eyes wide, question after question pouring out of her like a river.

Ethan eyes the number of drinks people buy her. There seems to be an unending stream of them that Star guzzles down, though she doesn't seem even a little drunk. He starts to relax at that, letting his attention wander.

He drinks his beer, trying and failing to follow the rambling conversations around him. He stretches his neck, thumb scratching at the sweat-dampened label. The noise burrows into his brain like the buzzing of a fly that he can't shake. He closes his eyes in hopes of filtering through the sounds to find the music, but it fails. There is a feeling of tension growing in his chest, a discomfort that sends his jaw clenching. Unbidden, his eyes open, and his gaze slides over to settle on Star.

She's standing at the end of the bar, and he slowly follows the enticing trail of her long legs to the jagged edge of her cut-off shorts. His attention snags for a heartbeat of a moment. Her shirt is loose, tucked partially in to show where her hips dip toward her waist. The way she leans, the way her hair tumbles over one shoulder to display her neck, makes him swallow, his thumb pausing in its incessant picking. Her neck curves to her shoulder in a perfect slope that begs to be kissed.

He sucks in a breath before taking a hearty swig of his beer. His vision zooms out to see who she's with. Andrea is perched on a barstool on the other side of Star and talking with Christina, the barkeeper and quite possibly Andrea's secret new girlfriend. Christina leans forward to talk excitedly to Star in a tone that is too low for Ethan to catch what they're saying. The woman's smile is wide, and her brown eyes are sparkling, her bottle-red hair tied high in a messy bun. Star sits with rapt attention, nodding studiously at whatever the woman is saying. Andrea glances at him, and he startles, gaze snapping away.

He forces himself to watch the man playing the piano. They've definitely met before, but Ethan can't quite recall his name. Then again, he's met almost everyone in town and the ones neighboring it, but he can recall only a handful. The fog he was in when first moving here didn't allow for much retention.

"Ethan?"

He turns to Star. Her smile is soft, eyes wide. "Will you teach me how to play pool?"

That sounds infinitely more enjoyable than what he's doing. He nods, finishing off his beer. The bottle clicks down on the bar, and he slides it back so Christina can grab it easily. He catches Star looking back at both women before following him to the vacant table.

He racks up the balls, going over the rules. Christina sets down a fresh beer next to him and a pink cocktail for Star. He didn't know they made specialty cocktails here, and his brows raise in surprise. Christina rests a hand on Star's shoulder briefly, giving it a small squeeze as she saunters away.

Star does a little wiggle to prepare herself for the activity ahead, and Ethan's gaze softens, some of the tension leaving him. The intensity with which she tackles a task is endearing as all hell. He takes a hearty swig to ease his parched throat when Stars bends over the table, cue stick all wrong in her hold. "Like this?"

He tilts his head, forcing his gaze to be professional. "Lift your elbow more."

She overcorrects. "This?"

Instinct screams at him to make this moment a cliché, lean around her, feel that perfect body against his. He takes another calming swig. "Lower." Damn, he felt that word all the way down to his toes. Her ass is a thing of beauty. Not that he's looking or anything. Because that would make it creepy. His throat works.

She straightens, looking distressed and frustrated. "Help me!"

He pushes off the wall and sets his beer down. "Here." Careful to keep his body away from hers, and using the smallest of touches, he readjusts her. "Now try."

She hits the cue ball perfectly.

He snatches up his beer before he does something truly stupid like hold her generous hips. "See? You did it."

Star stares at the table, her brows furrowed. Blue eyes flick up to him, and he hesitates, unsure if she's angry at him or just deep in thought. Regardless, he racks his brain trying to figure out what the hell he did. Was it that he didn't ask for permission before touching her? They only started to touch here and there, usually in comfort, never so casually. That must be it. There is no other explanation.

Star looks back at the bar where Andrea is sitting with Christina. His sister takes a swig of her beer, her brow arching. She does the smallest of nods, so subtle that he questions if it was real or simply a movement to end the long drink. The exchange sets his anxiety on edge, guilt creeping up his insides.

An apology is on the verge of pouring out when Star turns back with a wicked smile. It is so different from her other smiles that he finds himself caught in it, his body stilling as something within him stirs warmly. She cocks her hip, a small shift that takes his breath away. "You better get ready, Ethan Montenegro. Because I'm going to kick your ass."

He startles. A smile stretches across his face, and he takes another swig. A little thrill vibrates in his chest. "Alright then. Go ahead." He nods toward the table. "Show me how it's done."

They play round after round, Ethan solidly beating her. But every time, the score gap gets narrower and narrower, until they are neck and neck.

Christina goes to put down another unordered beer, but Ethan stops her. He's not sure what number this is, and he's supposed to drive them home. "No more beers, Chris."

She sets it back on her tray. "Can I get you something else? Bourbon?"

He shakes his head. "Nah. I'm tapped. Can I get water instead? Thanks." He measures his shot, focusing on the targeted ball.

The cue slides along his fingers, and movement before him captures his attention. Star's body slides down her stick, her loose tank straining against her full breasts.

His shot goes wide, the balls cracking chaotically around.

He guiltily looks up at her to see that wicked grin on her lips again. His jaw drops, and she bites her lip. The sway in her hips has a level of confidence he's never seen before, and his whole body tightens like a coil.

Her fingers graze along the table. "My, my, Ethan. You seemed awfully distracted that time."

She's flirting with him. She's flirting with him and his mind is short-circuiting, alarms blaring in his ears. She grazes by him, his body on fire. She hinges at the waist, the curve in her back deeper than he's ever seen it. She makes a perfect shot, the solid red ball *thunking* into the pocket soundly.

He feels himself smirk, the slow curl of his lips happening without his permission. He leans back against the wall, and he lets himself take her in, that simple luxury humming through him. She pauses, her breath hitching just a touch when she takes her shot. He's not completely stupid. He knows he's attractive. He also knows how to use that to his advantage. He may suck at keeping girlfriends, but he sure as hell knows how to catch them.

He runs his tongue along his bottom lip while he considers his next move.

She scratches.

He says nothing, letting the silence build tension. He swoops up the cue ball and brushes past her, letting his fingers linger on her hip in a way that makes her shiver.

They enter a new kind of game, a dangerous one. A game that his brain, if it had any blood left in it, would tell him not to play. But she started this game, wants this game, and by God, he's not strong enough to deny her, especially not this. Like in all things, he is a slave to Star's whims, and he wants nothing more than to see what that looks like in every aspect.

As he lines up his shot, his head low to the table, she steps up to stand too close to him, bringing her breasts right to his face. She leans slightly, like she's trying to see his shot too, and he knows his face will graze her chest if he straightens. God, he wants to grab her mouth first, plop her on the table, and feast.

Okay, maybe he has had one too many beers. He feels absolutely cut free in every single impure thought he's had since the moment she formed her body, as if she'd peered into his mind to watch his deepest, darkest fantasies. He cracks his neck, exhaling harshly and hitting the cue ball harder than necessary, almost sending it arcing off the table. Star giggles, blue eyes flashing mischievously, like she's reveling in his suffering. He almost groans with want. What he wouldn't give to have her be as cruel as she wants to him. Preferably with him tied to—

He snatches up his water and chugs it down. No way is he letting his mind go there.

Soon, they're both vying for the eight ball. He leans against the table next to her as she takes her shot. He's lost. Even before she pulls back the stick, he knows this. His aim is completely gone. Hell, if she breathes even a touch harder than necessarily, he misses. Meanwhile, she's only getting better and better. "You're a quick learner."

Her smile has a triumphant edge to it. "You're a good teacher. Eight ball, corner pocket." The stick strikes the cue ball, the eight cracks and sinks solidly into its new declared home, winning the game for Star.

His lips curl around the rim of his glass. "I strive to please."

She wets her lips, moving closer. "Ethan?"

His pulse quickens. "Yes, Star?"

She looks up at him, her blue eyes all he can see. He can practically taste the growing tension, the charge nearly a physical thing. He's sure if he touches her, he'll see crackling magic. He waits, because he wants her to say it, he wants her to choose what they have. Wants to ease her into this aspect of humanity not because of curiosity, but with a wholehearted enthusiastic excitement and readiness.

Because he wants her, oh *fuck* does he want her. But he wants her to want him too, not as an easily accessed body, but as a genuine interest in who he is.

"I believe…" Her breathless voice sends a little shiver down him. "There are all sorts of things you can teach me."

"Is there?" His head tilts. "I've taught you pancakes. Pool." His smile is wicked. "All the essentials."

She wets her lips again, her breaths coming shorter. Her gaze flicks to his lips and back. "There are other things."

"Oh?" She's so beautiful. The desire to see her in even shorter breath is overwhelming. "Andrea taught you how to ride a horse."

A flicker of nervousness shows, like she's unsure how her words will land. "Yes, and I was rather good at riding, wasn't I?"

Her eyes flare with victory, confidence soaring when her words essentially take him to his knees, every neuron of his brain onboard with teaching her whatever the hell she wants. Let her ride whatever she wants. Show her all the things she could straddle, the first of which is his face, in his truck, which is plenty spacious with enough determination.

He swallows and takes a deep, steadying breath. And another. And a third, because the first two didn't work. By the sixth, he regains some semblance of his mind. He wants to do this right, and pouncing at the first opportunity isn't the right choice. Not for her, and definitely not for him. He wants her to stay with him after, not just take him for a test ride. He stretches his neck to ease the tension and to give himself a moment to center his thoughts for his next move.

"That you were." He pushes off the wall, walking up to her. Her eyes are all glittering hope, and he almost gives in. "However tempting what you're suggesting is, I think we should take that one step at a time."

The perceived rejection hits her hard, and it hurts him deeply to see all that newfound confidence waver. "Hey." His hand slides to stroke her hair behind her ear and tip her head up to look at him. "It's not a no, just a slow down."

Her smile is soft. "Yeah?"

"Yeah." He steps closer to her, head tilting, and her eyes flutter. "I rather enjoyed our game, didn't you?"

Her voice is breathless, eyes flicking to his lips. "Oh yes."

"So, let's keep playing. Trust me, Star, it only gets better from here." His voice drops low. "We have nothing but time. There's no rush."

Her smile lights up her face. She nods. "Yeah. Yeah, we do." Her hand closes around his wrist, and her touch sends tingling pleasure down his arm. "I think I'd like that."

"Good." He hands his stick over to her. "Why don't you put these away and I'll close our tab? I think I'm ready to head home."

Her usual chipper self emerges. "Okay."

He makes his way over to Christina, whose smile is a little too wide to be innocent. He pulls out his wallet. "I'd like to close out, Chris."

She bats her long, fake lashes at him. "Oh? Leaving so soon?"

He barely hears her and hands over his card impatiently, his attention wandering to what Danny is telling Andrea and their crew. "—dead. All three cops. Gutted and dragged across the street. Looked like something tore them apart."

"Was it an animal?"

"Maybe. Looked like teeth took whole chunks out."

Ethan goes still. His nightmares of cold, dark, teeth, and claws come to him unbidden. He turns to Danny, stepping up. "What happened?"

Danny repeats his story. "Two stores were broken into. Morrison's Deli and Grocery and Leather and Goods over on Main. The storefronts ripped clean open."

Andrea is pale. "That's insane. We were just there yesterday. Did anyone see anything?"

"Security footage caught some sort of large animal, but the attack was out of view."

One of the cowboys, Ethan can't remember his name, snorts. "Bullshit."

"Oh, it's true. You can go down and see the damage. And Lisa's brother's sister-in-law works down at the precinct and said the dashcams caught nothing but some audio. Gruesome shit too."

He feels warmth to his side and catches Star staring wide-eyed at the group. Her hands clasp together over her heart.

Christina taps down a tray holding Ethan's card and receipt. "Here you go."

Ethan startles, blinking down at them, and hesitates.

"Hey, Chris?"

The woman leans on the bar. "Yeah?"

He pauses again, unsure if what he wants is a good idea or not. He glances at Star's hands and notes a slight tremor. His jaw flexes, fist clenching. "Do you have coffee I can get to go?"

"Yeah. No problem." She efficiently grabs a cup and fills it up at the little station behind the bar for the breakfast crew. She slides it over to him. "On the house." She smirks knowingly. "Have a *fun* night."

He replies automatically, his mind elsewhere. "Yeah. Thanks. You too." He slips the card back in his wallet, eyeing the coffee.

Something tells him to take it and sit on the porch with his loaded gun all night. But that seems incredibly unhealthy. Obsessive even.

He sees flashes of needle teeth, sparks of light, feels the cold, dark, damp *hatred*.

Unsafe.

He grabs the cup and takes a sip, turning to Star. "Ready to go?"

She nods, her voice weak. "Yeah."

He walks her out of the bar, one arm around her to keep her close to him. The cool night air sobers him, and Star leans into his warmth. Gravel crunches under their shoes, and the cosmos glows above, thousands of stars twinkling at them. The ranch dogs are still in the bed of his truck and wag excitedly when they approach.

He opens Star's door for her and scans the darkness around the bar. It's going to be a long night.

Five

They ride home silently, Star rubbing her forearm the entire time. Ethan notes her tattoo now has a little stack of pancakes sitting next to the sunglasses. The corner of his mouth lifts.

It's not enough to ease the tension though.

He sips his coffee, hard eyes staring into the pitch black of the road. The light from the truck brightens the space as much as possible. Perhaps too much for his current on-edge state. Every reflective set of eyes has his heart jolting, his hands tightening around the leather-clad wheel. But it's never more than the average animal he would expect to see. A family of racoons. A coyote. No creepy man-eating monster.

Yet.

He feels a tickle of relief when the glow of the cabin appears in the distance, but it's quickly swallowed up by fear. The porch light is warm, but the world beyond is a menacing black void. He now regrets not having his gun in the car.

The dogs jump out, milling about and sniffing. He watches them carefully, noting every twitch of an ear, every flick of a tail, waiting for any sign of alert. If one so much as lifts its head too quickly, he'll drive them right the fuck out of here, straight to San Francisco.

"Ethan?"

He swallows and forces all the tension out of his body so he can look upon Star in his normal relaxed way. Her eyes are wide, the lights from the dash making them shine. "That creature they were talking about? At the bar?"

He tenses. "What about it?"

"Do...do you think..." Her lip trembles, voice quiet. "It scares me, Ethan."

He exhales harshly, reaching out and taking her hand. "Hey." He squeezes. "It's going to be okay. Let's just get inside and try not to think about it." He'll think about it for the both of them.

Her eyes glisten. "What about the dogs?"

He doesn't hesitate. "They can sleep inside tonight." If they destroy the rental, he'll just have to beg Lisa for forgiveness.

A small smile teases her lips. "Okay. Thank you."

"Of course." He swiftly scans their surroundings once more, noting the relaxed dogs, and quickly opens the car door. He does his best not to grab Star and sprint to the house.

The dogs are ecstatic to sleep inside. They bolt around, getting into everything and jumping on the couch. Ethan tosses his car keys on the little table by the front door like always and makes his way around the house. He locks all the doors and windows for his own mental well-being while Star heads over to the kitchen. The dogs jump around excitedly as she sets out a water bowl and feeds the beasts some of the food Andrea brought over.

Maybe tomorrow he'll remind her that they actually live somewhere else and should go home with Andrea at some point. But not now. Tonight, he appreciates their presence and heightened senses.

Star gives him one last smile at her bedroom door. "Good night, Ethan."

He returns it. "Night, Star."

The dogs go in with her, and the door shuts.

Silently, he opens his gun locker. He loads up his Mossberg with all seven shells. He even gets his pistol and holster. He doublechecks the magazine and clicks it in place. A trickle of doubt wheedles in, and he almost puts the pistol away, but then the cold, dark nightmare comes back to him and he slams the locker shut.

He sips his coffee, pacing the house. He turns off all the lights but the porch. Round and round he goes. Watching. Waiting. Ready.

The dogs barking to be let out wakes Ethan. He finally went to bed fully dressed when the coffee wore off. Now he has a terrible headache. He peeks open an eye, sees the dim gray light of dawn, and groans.

Fucking dogs. Should've left them outside.

He feels sick, heavy.

The dogs won't shut up, and it sounds like they have started scratching. "Stop that!"

But they don't listen, only getting louder.

Where is Star? Shouldn't she let them out? It was her idea to let them sleep in the house in the first place.

He blinks, forcing himself to sit. He stretches his back and neck. The stupid coffee is making his heart hammer. It was a bad idea. He let paranoia get the better of him.

Whining, scratching, and high-pitched barking drill into his eardrums.

He's very uncomfortable from sleeping in his clothes and shoes. It seemed like such a good idea at the time. He picks up his Mossberg from where he propped it against the nightstand. The clock states 3 a.m.

He looks outside. The grayish light of dawn shouldn't be there so early. Maybe the clock is wrong.

He rubs his chest. The racing of his heart is getting worse. He swallows, gasps for breath, and calls out, "Star?"

Only the dogs answer him. He takes his gun with him as he walks through his bedroom and opens the door. "Star?"

Her bedroom door is open. A chill shivers through him, and he turns toward the front door. His boots thud against the wood floor, and he finds the dogs clawing at it, barking and jumping on each other in their desperation to get outside.

Ice-cold dread has Ethan moving faster, his gun gripped firmly in his hands. His tattoo starts tingling, and now he's running, tripping over the dogs as he forces his way to the front door, finding it unlocked. His stomach plummets. No hesitation. He rips open the door.

His whole body freezes, the scene before him so horrific that it takes his mind a moment to comprehend it.

A massive, oily creature with shiny, black scales, the face of an anglerfish, and the body of a salamander on steroids sits on its hindquarters. A tendril extends from its forehead to dangle a large, glowing orb before Star, leading her forward. Her bare feet drag along the ground with each trembling step.

The dogs burst out of the house, nearly knocking Ethan from his stunned position in the doorway to the ground. It is enough to unstick him. His panicked bellow echoes through the wilderness. "STAR!"

She falters, jerking.

The dogs charge forward. They snarl and bark, distracting the creature. Its head lifts, its massive mouth with horrible teeth opening in a hiss. Star falls to her knees, and Ethan doesn't hesitate. He shoulders his gun and fires.

The bullet hits the creature in the face, and it rears back, stumbling. The dogs take advantage, biting and snapping, throwing the creature further off-kilter and giving Star a few extra moments to wake from her trance. For that alone, Ethan will never speak ill of a dog again.

He cocks the gun, shell flying. "STAR, RUN!" He shoots again, hitting the creature in the chest. It's still up, and he makes some quick calculations. He has only five shells left. And it's still standing. "STAR!"

Star falls back, hands fisting in the grass before she pulls herself up. She staggers but rights herself and runs as fast as she can to him, her blue eyes glowing in the dark and her body a muted gray. He already knows her terrified face will never leave his memory.

He grabs her arm, not taking his eyes off the creature. "Get the car keys! Go! Now!"

The creature rights itself, oozing, but standing. Ethan fires, cocks, fires, cocks. The creature staggers and shakes itself, then notices Star getting away. It shrieks, front limbs pounding to the ground to give chase.

The dogs refuse to allow such a thing. They charge at the beast, barking and snapping, keeping it at bay. Swift, agile animals, they dodge swipes of deadly claws, working like the unit they were bred to be. It gives Ethan time to turn and run toward the house.

He finds Star hesitating at the doorway with the car keys in her hands, her terrified eyes on the dogs. He jumps up the steps and grabs her. "Go!"

Her eyes fill with tears. "I can't leave them!"

"They'll be fine. Get in the car!"

He shoves her toward the car, and she stumbles but listens. She runs to the car, unlocking it. He's close behind her, but he stops when a horrible shriek raises the hair on his neck. He turns to see the creature surging forward, ignoring the attacking dogs. They snap and bite, but its armor is thick. It moves swiftly, long claws glinting as it races after Star.

Ethan steps in its way, aiming and firing. Two shells left. He shoots again. One. His eyes flick up to the glowing orb dangling from its head. Like an anglerfish. Instincts alters his aim, and he shoots the orb. It bursts apart with a sickening *pop*, causing the creature to stop and thrash in agony. A little flicker of relief sparks in Ethan's chest. At least now it can't hypnotize Star again.

The creature shrieks and rears back, clutching its head while it thrashes back and forth. Ethan draws his pistol. He doesn't count shots this time. It doesn't matter. Either it dies or he does. He keeps shooting, his mind empty, his ears ringing, the creature faltering. His heart races. Star is screaming. And he fires and fires and fires until the gun clicks, empty.

He takes a small trembling breath in the humming silence.

Out of the darkness, claws slice down him. He roars, his arm and chest mangled. The pain is mind-numbing, and he goes down in a crumbled, broken heap at the creature's feet. There is no more fear, only a pang of regret that he never took the time to teach Star how to drive. Hopefully, she runs or tries to drive the truck anyway. Whatever she needs to do to escape.

The creature hovers over him, an unnerving gurgling-clicking sound in the back of its throat, the last thing Ethan will hear. He looks up into its soulless black eyes, reflecting the car's headlights.

A hum pulses through the air.

A scream echoes through the night, building to an excruciating pitch. Ethan sucks in air, a silent cry leaving him when his eardrums pop, blood trickling down to soak his hair. Blinding white light flashes, turning the night to day in a single impossible second. The creature looks up as something hits it, ripping through its body. Limbs splay, chunks splattering everywhere. A fine mist rains down.

Ethan blinks, unable to clear the shadows from his vision, and he wonders vaguely if he's blind. Doesn't really matter. His blood is pooling all around him, his arm barely attached. His breath rattles in his lungs. Cold shivers through his body. Pain. So much pain. But now numbness. Slowly building...numbness...

Awareness begins to flicker like an old movie. He's being dragged. Not well, but he's moving. He blinks and his body rolls down a hill. No. Not a hill. His vision hazes in and out, but he sees the oak sapling hovering over him. The crater.

Then there is Star, her tear-streaked face still beautiful even when swollen and splotchy. He wants to touch it, to tell her it's okay, but he can't move. She holds him to her chest, rocking, sobbing. He thinks she's speaking, but the only thing he hears is ringing. His blood is filling the crater, and he closes his eyes for just a moment to experience her hold.

He should've kissed her this morning. That would've been nice.

Andrea better take care of her or he's haunting her ass.

Warmth fills him, a hum vibrating through his body like he's full of bees. He blinks open, confused, and sucks in a painful breath, body arching, hot, fizzling *pain* searing through his entire being from a hand that's been placed on his chest. He looks into glowing neon-blue eyes, full of rage. No, determination. No, some sort of anger-fueled will power as she screams, her lavender hair whipping around them in a maelstrom.

An odd suctioning in his ears builds and stings like bees swarming into his skull until finally it stops. He gasps, blinking. With no more silent ringing, he's able to hear the word she's screaming. Just one word spoken repeatedly. A word cried to the heavens with such raw feeling that he hears it echo in his very soul.

"Live."

The first thing Ethan becomes aware of, when his mind surfaces from the darkness, is that he's wet. Not just wet—soaked. Which makes sense, since he's neck-deep in water.

His eyes flutter, refusing to work for a moment. True dawn greets him through the roots of the oak tree. No longer a sapling, it's a full-grown monstrosity, the biggest oak he's ever seen. Through the arching branches and rustling leaves, birds chirp merrily with not a care in the world.

The water sloshes when he turns his head, trying to comprehend the pinkish liquid he's in. Pink water. He blinks. Water tinged with blood. His blood. Fuck.

Five pairs of dog eyes catch his attention. They stare at him from the wildflower-covered rim of the crater, whimpering softly.

A ragged breath has him whipping around. Star watches him blearily through heavily hooded eyes. She looks haggard, her lavender hair dull and limp, her skin ashen and matte. Her arms shake around him from the effort of keeping his head afloat.

Tears well and pour down her face.

Water splatters when he flails, trying to get upright. Everything aches with a deep-bone exhaustion, but he gets his body to obey, his feet hitting the soft ground of the pool. He tries to stand but groans, the ebbing buoyancy too much. He sinks back down until just his head is above water.

He cups her neck, his other hand touching her face, thumb wiping away the tears. "Are you okay?"

A little sob escapes, and she leans into his hand. She shakes her head, and her body gives out as if she's used every last molecule of energy to hold them both out of the water. Water sprays in his face when he surges forward to catch her. He draws her limp body tight to him and swoops her into his arms. He tries to stand, but his legs buckle. The two of them almost go beneath the pink water before he gets his feet back underneath him.

Short of breath, he leans against a knot of roots. They're more expansive now, thicker, and they form a little shelter around the two of them. He's able to find one root to half sit on, his head *thunking* against the wood. "Maybe...maybe we'll just sit here for a little bit. Just a bit."

The sun peers over the hills, and light streams through the roots. Ethan lifts his head to watch. It almost seems magical, peaceful, if not for the horrors of the night before.

Star shifts in his hold, her head against his shoulder turning to look as well. Her hand moves through the water to touch the light. They silently watch the grayness of her skin bleed away. Slowly, but surely. He shifts them, moving her more into the light but still within their root cocoon. It feels safe here, and he's loath to leave that feeling.

Her voice is a soft whisper in the silence. "I'm sorry."

He waits, his hand sliding into hers.

She shudders a breath. "I didn't...I didn't know I could do that, with my magic." Her hand turns in his, palm facing up, and he gently holds her wrist. Her voice wobbles. "If I'd done that sooner then—"

"Hey." He tightens his hold around her. "It doesn't matter how or why, the important thing is the outcome. We're alive. The dogs are alive. *It* is not. How we got here is inconsequential."

She turns in his hold to face him. Tears stream down her face, a tremble in her fingers when she lifts them. They touch his brow, her eyes darting between his with a desperate edge, like she's uncertain he's real. "I was so scared, Ethan." Her other hand joins in her gentle reassurance. "Then I was so angry. It changed the power inside me. This...anger." Her fingers softly trail down his face to linger on his cheekbones, her thumb stroking. "I didn't know I had such a thing in me." Her eyes flash, the blue darkening, the morning light dimming for a moment, and a darkness swirls over her skin. "It tried to take you from me." Her hand slides down to his tattered shirt. Scars show through, thick white lines from where the monster's claws nearly severed his arms and split open his sternum and ribs. "I will *never* allow that to happen."

Her hands slide into his hair, the band holding it back finally giving up the fight and falling away. She fists it, their foreheads touching. "You are *mine*." Her breath ghosts over his lips, and his eyes flutter. "*Mine*."

He looks over her, her darkened blue eyes glowing bright. Even her hair is darker, matching the shadows swirling over her skin. A small tremor goes through her body, and his hands slide up her back to rest delicately on her neck.

His voice is soft, barely above a whisper. "I'm not going anywhere, Star."

A shiver wracks through her, the force of it shaking her breath.

Everything that he's felt since the moment she landed before him, everything he's pushed down for the various reasons, he now pours into his face, his eyes, his smile, and her skin flickers with light. He tightens his hold so that their bodies are flush. "I'm not going anywhere." He nuzzles her, and a tear escapes her lightening eyes. "I'm alive because of you. That's all that matters."

She collapses into his hold, face buried into his neck as she sobs, her whole body wracking. The light brightens again, warming the space. He rests his head against her, rocking the both of them. His eyes close, breathing in her scent. Her lavender hair shimmers pink in the dawn, and he smiles.

His phone is ruined from the water, so he sits on the deck's steps waiting for Andrea. He lets his mind wander, circling around and around a memory from decades before that he can't seem to shake. A photo. A vase. The image is so hazy in his mind that every time he blinks, it flickers out of his grasp. His jaw tightens. He has to see it again.

Star is prone in the long grass, sunbathing with the five dogs curled around her. She's looking better, her skin less matte and back to her usual glowing self.

Except her solemn mood. She can't seem to shake it.

Ethan's truck is destroyed, the front blown out like a bomb went off in the passenger seat. But that is what happened in a way. Star blasted her magic forward and killed the thing. What he thought were the car's head-lights was actually her magic building.

The creature's long-clawed limbs are scattered around the yard with vari-ous-sized chunks of flesh. Ethan thought of collecting them but couldn't quite bring himself to get near it yet. He'll allow himself a few hours of reprieve before facing that daunting task.

The dogs lift their heads. A horse whinnies in panic and a string of curse words that would make a sailor blush breaks the silence. Ethan heaves himself up to standing, dusting off his jeans. Star doesn't stir, and concern flutters through him. He rounds the house to encounter Andrea, her hazel eyes wide.

He tucks his hands in his pockets, not sure what to say. He waits for Andrea to collect herself. It doesn't take long.

"Wh-wh-what the *fuck*?!"

He looks around at the gore.

She throws her hand out. "And your fucking truck! I LOVED THAT TRUCK!"

The stress might be getting to him, because he laughs and it isn't exactly a sane sound. He combs his hand through his loose hair. "Yeah, I don't think insurance is going to cover a creepy fish-monster attack."

Andrea wobbles in her saddle, and Ethan quickly crosses the yard, Monty skittering away from him nervously. He holds the lead steady and helps his sister down. "Come on. I'll tell you all about it inside."

Andrea says nothing during the whole story. Her coffee goes untouched, her mouth gaping. Ethan takes a contemplative sip, gaze drifting to the window where he can still easily see Star outside. She refused to come in. Whatever is going on in her head, the sun seems to be giving her comfort, or perhaps even recharging her. The dogs are pressing against her side, relaxed but alert, and she idly strokes their matted fur.

His hands are tight on his mug. He doesn't like her out there alone. He kept the front door open so he could sprint out if needed. His gun is propped against the table just in case. But he needs to talk to Andrea in private. What they're going to talk about could upset Star, and she's had enough of that.

"Ethan."

He turns his attention back to his too-pale sister. She swallows, body tense. "What if there are more of those creatures?"

His lips thin. "I know."

She looks around the small cabin. "This place. It's too rural. If I didn't come by every day, you would've been stranded." She gestures to his chest and the scarring his fresh shirt hides. The words are lodged in her throat, but he knows what she's trying to say. What if Star couldn't heal him?

He nods. "Yeah." The shaky breath he takes evens out, and his shoulders straighten. "I need my old truck back."

"Yeah, no shit. I'll use the ATV or figure something else out until you get a new one. But, Ethan, what's your plan here?"

"We can't stay out here. I'm going back to my place in the Bay."

"Yeah, okay. Makes sense." She glances out the window, her voice quiet. "What about Star?"

His brows furrow. "What about Star?"

"What are you going to do with her?"

Anger roils in him, but he pushes it down. He's had enough therapy to know that he's trying to outlet his stress on his sister. "She's coming with."

Andrea's eyes flash. "Ethan!"

"Andrea."

She glares. "Ethan. A fish monster, who destroyed metal bars and *ate* three people, hunted her down—"

"We don't know that."

"Don't be an idiot!" She throws her hand toward the window. "*Of course* it was after her. A fucking star fell from the sky, and a fish monster appeared to lure it out with its special fucking angler orb that didn't work on you. It was coming for her, and if there was one, there has to be others."

She has a point, except... He keeps his voice calm. "Andrea. And if I abandon Star, what do you think will happen to her?"

Andrea swallows but refuses to back down. Ethan holds her stare, keeping the silence, and waits.

She lets out a harsh breath, wiping furiously at her eyes. She takes a big swig of cold coffee and gasps before speaking. "So, a giant fish monster is hunting Star and your plan is to go *closer* to the water? Seems, I don't know...suicidal. Head inland. Montana could be lovely this time of year."

He nods. "I thought of that, but there's something I need to do in the city."

"What thing?"

"Something." He shrugs. "It shouldn't take long."

"Ugh, can you just not?"

His brows raise. "Excuse me?'

She points an accusatory finger at him. "You're doing that fucking annoying *thing* where you get vague and shut people out with that icy face of yours. Just tell me. I know I was upset earlier, but I promise to be supportive. Don't shut me out." Her glare cuts right through him. "Tell me your plan, Ethan. I can handle it."

He sighs. "Okay. Fine. Jenny."

This time Andrea's brows raise. "Jenny? Which Jenny?"

"Jenny Henderson-Galt."

She stares at him blankly, head tilting, before jolting with realization. "Jenny *Henderson-Galt*? As in your very gay, very pregnant ex-fiancée Jenny Henderson-Galt?"

"Ex-girlfriend and current friend, thank you very much." She'd confessed her love for another grad student, who is now her wife, during his proposal, so technically never his fiancée. Their once-a-year lunch to catch up is still a highlight of his Octobers. A very odd anniversary of their breakup that his therapist isn't quite convinced is healthy. But Jenny finds it funny, and he enjoys her company. "I think she might know some things about Star."

Andrea's interest is piqued. She sits up in her chair, leaning forward.

Ethan smooths his hand over the table, gathering his thoughts. "It came back to me while I was waiting for you to arrive. Jenny's dissertation was on this vase she was obsessed with." The image of it flashes in his mind, sharper this time. "There was a woman who held a star, and the back depicted some sort of battle between man and fish creatures. One was a mermaid thing, I think." The needle teeth in its gaping jaw stand out sharply in his memory. "And there was just something about it that reminded me of the thing I saw last night." He will never forget those teeth. Or claws. Or creepy orb that lured Star to its maw. "I don't know. Could be nothing, but could also be something. And worse comes to worse, her wife Katie is a marine biologist doing deep sea research at UC Berkeley so she might know something." He exhales heavily, his shoulders sagging, as he looks back at Andrea. "It's better than nothing."

Andrea nods, her eyes glistening. Her voice cracks. "Yeah. It's definitely a plan. More than I've found." Ethan watches his sister's throat bob, her eyes flicking to the window. He waits for her, his heart clenching. She fiddles with her fingers, averting her gaze again. "You could die, Ethan."

He takes a sharp breath. "Yeah. Maybe."

Her fists clench, her angry gaze meeting his. "I don't want you to die."

"I know. I don't either." A playful smirk spreads across his face. "But if I did, think of all the money you'd inherit. You could go get a much nicer truck. Jack it up even higher so everyone knows you have the biggest dick out here."

She snorts, smiling despite herself. The chair rattles with the force of her flop back against it. "Please." She snatches up her coffee cup. "Everyone already knows that."

Victorious, he reaches for her hand, and she allows it. "It'll be okay,

Andy. It will be better in the city. Harder for a creature like that to hunt discreetly. But you. I'm worried about leaving you here. Come with us."

Andrea fiddles with her mug, contemplating his words. "Maybe. It's not that easy to leave work. I'll think about it. There are some things I'd need to tie up first."

It tears his heart asunder to leave her alone, but he forces the words out. "Okay. Whatever you want."

Andrea helps him dig a shallow grave and plop all the monster parts in it. It's the best they can do for the time being.

She leaves them to ride back for his old truck. Ethan waves her off, solemnly watching her disappear into the distance. His gaze slides to the wreckage beside him, eyeing the twisted metal and melted insides. He rests his hand on the still intact side and heaves a heavy sigh, permitting himself to feel a moment of grief. He did like this truck. His hand slips away as he steps back and turns to go find Star.

She hasn't moved from her prone position in the grass. Not wanting to startle her, he lowers himself beside her—well, as beside her as he can get with all the obsessed dogs. She doesn't flinch, her eyes not moving from where they stare blankly at the cloudless sky.

His lips thin, and he brushes her hair back in hopes to wake her from her trance. "Star?" Her chest expands with a deep breath, and he delicately traces her cheek with the back of one finger. "What's wrong?"

Her throat works, blinking as her eyes focus back on the present. "There's something I need to do, but I don't think I have the strength to do it."

"Oh?" He scoots a dog away to shift closer until his legs touch her. "What's that?"

"I should leave you. Here. Everything." Her eyes close, the wind blowing her hair over her face. The grass rustles loudly. "I'm a danger to you."

A small, tender smile softens his face, one that appears only when with her. Unable to resist the opportunity, he moves the hair out of her face. "I'm not so sure about that." His thumb skims the curve of her ear, and he's mesmerized by the resulting shiver. The deep hunger to see it again nearly steals his train of thought. He swallows, his voice rougher. "Pretty sure you saved my ass back there."

"If it wasn't for me you wouldn't need saving!" She sits up, and his hand falls away. Her eyes flash as her shoulders tighten. "It wanted me and I'm too damaged to even know why. I'm a burden. A danger. I should..." Her voice grows small. "I should go."

"Hey." He reaches for her hand, their fingers twining together. "I thought I was yours."

Her lip trembles.

He leans forward, smiling softly. His voice lowers. "How can I be yours if you're not here?"

She ducks her face, and he has to strain to hear her mumble, "You can be mine at a distance."

A lightness builds in his chest, and his smile brightens. "Nah. I get into way too much trouble for that. Someone else might try to come along and claim me."

Her eyes flash with violence, and he huffs a low laugh. She fights a smile, her hand tightening on his. She uses her other hand to pick at dead strands of grass and toss them away. "Stop. You're baiting me."

"No, I'm seducing you. There's a difference."

She blushes, her hand stilling. She turns back to him, blue eyes meeting his again. A strong gust tunnels through the hills, blowing the grass flat. It pulls the shorter strands of hair from his bun and his shirt tight against his chest. Star's so close, her long hair tickles his face. He breaths in deeply, memorizing the sweet scent of her hair mixing with the dry, heated grass of the meadow.

Sorrow shadows her face, dimming her glow and darkening the blue of her eyes. Her whisper is barely a sound. "I'm not strong enough."

He squeezes her hand, wishing he had the right words to make her feel better. No matter how hard he searches, he can't find them. He wants to pull her into his lap and wrap his arms around her. He wants the warmth of his body to warm her, to comfort her, but he's not sure she'd welcome it. So instead, he holds her gaze and strokes the back of her hand with his thumb until the tightness in her shoulders dissipates.

His eyes soften. "Want to hear my plan?"

She nods and leans toward him, her shoulder brushing his.

"I think we should leave this place and go to my home in the city." He props his knee up to lean his arm against it. "I think you'd like it, the city. So many things to do with lots of people to mask your scent, or however that fish thing tracked you."

He remembers Andrea calling him out earlier about keeping his cards too close to his chest. He doesn't want Star to feel like he's keeping things from her. Andrea is never afraid to speak her mind, but he's not sure about Star. The thought forces the words from him. "I have a friend there. She's a researcher at a university and might have some answers. I'd like to take you there, if you're open to it." He swallows and shifts, his eyes trained on Star's face. He speaks carefully, calmly, to make the words land softly. "Maybe it'll help you remember some things."

The wind gusts, her hair whipping around them. The sadness is there again, and he cannot bear it. Her eyes drift to the dogs, then to the cabin.

Ethan wets his lips, and his resolve crumbles like sand. "Or we can stay here and figure something else out." Andrea would be ashamed if she heard him. When Star doesn't answer, he squeezes her hand to get her attention. "Whatever you want, Star." He'll just never sleep again. That's fine.

Star takes a trembling breath, her eyes closing. "I don't want to leave here." Tears shimmer on her lashes. "I love it here. I love our life here. It's been beautiful, everything I think I could ever want."

She falls silent and he waits, sensing the "but" before it slips free.

Finally, with a small, cracked voice, she whispers, "I hate that we can't stay." A tear slips down her face. "I don't like this change. I want to be still. Why can't it just be still?"

His lips tighten, his throat burning. He leans into her, his forehead brushing against hers. "I'm sorry, Star."

She chokes on tears. "Ethan."

"Yes?"

Her eyes open. They're full of such anguish, he almost breaks and pulls her into his arms. "My dreams."

His heart clenches. "What about them?"

"I think, I think they're trying to tell me something. There is a woman. She cuts herself and—" Her voice cracks. "She doesn't bleed red." She turns their hands so that her inner wrist is exposed. "Her blood is like mine, her eyes are like mine. And she never looks up, because if she does there's... there's—"

He doesn't look away as Star's hand tightens so hard his bones ache.

"Screaming. Such terrible, terrifying screaming. It makes me wake up all sweaty and shaky, parts of me hurting, but there are no wounds to see. But last night I didn't wake up. I saw her crumble to shimmering ash and then..."

The look in Star's eyes fills him with such deep foreboding fear that sweat breaks out down his spine. Her voice is barely a whisper, her hand shaking in his. "There is death. Death like I never thought possible. The world trembled, life changed forever. And a whisper. A woman with glowing eyes. She whispered..." Star's eyes go far. "There is no running. There is only death."

Cold washes over Ethan, his body stilling. A dream so similar returns to him that he can see the white, glowing eyes and a mouth moving with no sound. But this time, he hears the voice, a hissing from afar. *Death is the only outcome. Yours or his.*

Ethan can't breathe, he can barely think. He breaks eye contact with Star, staring at their joined hands. Their fingers are white, sensation long gone.

Star is so quiet, he almost doesn't hear her. "I don't want to remember. Nothing since the moment I woke in your arms has led me to believe that remembering will bring me joy." Her voice trembles, and it forces him to look back up to see her haunted eyes staring into the distance at the massive oak tree above her crater. "But I don't believe I have a choice. I have to try to remember."

She looks at him, older and tired, and it pains him to see her so. She nods. "Okay. Let's go to the city and meet your friend."

He gives her hand a squeeze, his voice hardening. "Together."

Her eyes soften, and she squeezes back. "Together."

Far out on Highway 99, at a nothing truck stop near Tulare, the priest rests on his motorcycle. He keeps his heavily tinted helmet on so that no one can see his face, a map of the state stretched out on the handlebars. He hovers his hand over it, tendons straining, his eyes white. The magic burns his veins, constricts his throat. He chokes, air cutting off, but he does not stop. He must find the Vessel. It's been days of weak traces. He cannot fail.

A surge, his heart leaping. There.

His hand snaps into a fist, and he sucks in breath. He shakes his head, his eyes unrolling from the back of his head. So, the Lophian is dead. He'll take that as a gift from the ancient one. Now the Vessel is moving north, but toward the coast.

He sighs, head tilting back and offering a prayer of mercy upon his haggard soul. Going closer to the ocean is never a good idea. He needs to haul ass before the Lophians rally and send another Contender for the prize.

He packs away his map carefully and kicks his bike alive. He peels out, speeding up the highway toward San Francisco.

Six

In the dark depths of the ocean, the Lophian waits on the very edge of the white coral. Hidden within, his mate curls protectively around their clutch of eggs. Her fins rhythmically flutter over their young to maintain a constant, life-giving current. She can never stop, never rest. Their growth is dependent on it.

She stopped speaking to him days ago, going deep inside herself to reach a primal state. His side burns from her long, sharp claws. He cannot blame her. He got too close, paused for too long, but it was worth it for the brief view of their eggs. Little wriggles of life within the flexible clear shell had his heart leaping, his fins pausing. Their young. Their future. Their hope.

The nine eggs are the largest laid brood seen in the last century, and he swelled with pride when she finished laying, his gill fins unfurling to flutter for her. But four eggs have begun to yellow, the life within moving slower than the others. A bad sign, one that has him resting forlorn on the soft sand instead of circling the coral.

A screeching yowl vibrates the water, and he tears his gaze away from his mate, turning his broad head toward the noise. His mate hisses, unknowing to the meaning of the sound. But he knows. His gills ripple, fin spines spreading.

Malnki is dead. Failed in retrieving the magic in the Game.

What a waste of a magic pearl.

He turns back to his mate and the five healthy eggs, fear ripping his scales. No magic means no Life. No Life means...no. His fins flare. He will not allow it. He chose to breed with his mate instead of participating in the Contender selection, a choice that seemed clear when she went into season, but now here they are. Four yellowing eggs. And the wrong Contender chosen.

He chose poorly that day, he will not do so again.

With one final look at his mate, he whispers an apology she will not understand but will hopefully feel. He shoves off the sand and swims toward the sacred volcanic rocks where the ancient one sits and protects the pearls.

Star is quiet on the drive. Every once in a while Ethan sees her stroke her tattoo, her eyes distant in that cold, ancient way she gets when she thinks about her memory loss. He contemplates taking her hand but decides against it, a sudden shyness overtaking him. He lets her be, hoping space is what she needs to process everything.

The scenery begins to change. Suburbs. Cities. All the endless brown grasslands giving way to civilization. Star sits straighter, eyes brightening. Then, the Bay Area consumes them.

Star glows, face plastered to the window. Words pour endlessly from her. "Ethan, did you see how tall that building is? Or that building? Or *that* building? Oh, ETHAN, THAT BUILDING!" There's a meaty smack when her hand collides with the window. "I know human engineering advances allowed for greater structurally sound buildings but to *see* it from ground level is-is-is..." Her eyes sparkle. "*Amazing.*"

He smiles. "If you think this is great, then I should take you to New York. You'd have a field day." Maybe the Atlantic Ocean is less fish-monster-filled than the Pacific.

Or maybe the fish monster just traveled very far.

Flashes of teeth and claws absorb his vision, his hands tightening on the steering wheel. Phantom pains in his arms and chest ache, and he recalls the odd feeling of his partially severed arm flopping along the ground as Star dragged him. It's a memory he can't wait to bury deep in his psyche.

Star's breathless, excited voice draws him back to the present. "Really, Ethan? What's it like? What would we see?"

So, he tells her a story. A lovely one of hopes and plans for the future that chase away the haunting memories. He details what the cross-country drive would be like, though he's never personally done the trip. The different cities they would stop at. What they would do, what they would see, what it would be like. Star lounges in her seat, smiling brightly, her hand propping her head up. She's so beautiful like that, body curved, one leg tucked up on the seat so she can see him better. Her lavender hair is caught up in her hand and tumbles over her shoulders.

He stares at her for longer than is safe while driving. He forces his eyes back on the road, continuing his story. Yet, no matter how hard he tries, his gaze keeps straying in time with his wandering mind between beats of his story. He chooses to not linger on the horrors of the night before, but thinks back to earlier that evening. When they played pool together and what could've happened.

What should've happened.

What he dearly hopes will still happen.

At long last, Ethan pulls into his building's parking garage. The relief of getting home is remarkable, making his shoulders slump. Putting the truck in park is almost a religious experience.

Star, on the other hand, is practically vibrating next to him. Her words are an open stream of consciousness filling the space, her voice echoing as she marvels at the types of cars, the sensation of being underground, the firm decision that she doesn't like it, and her excitement to get upstairs.

She follows him, bouncing on her toes, distracted by the various artworks in the building's hallways.

Then, they reach the elevator.

She jolts, eyes flashing in alarmed excitement when the doors ping closed. The lift rises. It's a tall building, a new one too, so the elevator is fast, and the sensation undoubtedly odd for any person's first time. But Star seems to struggle with the concept of gravity while moving upward. She slides down the wall to squat oddly as she grips the railings for dear life.

It's a small blessing that they're alone on this ride.

She tries to stand, but her leg slips out. Her blue eyes are pale and bright, her smile wide. For once, she has no words, just a jittery sense of overwhelmed pleasure.

A grin tugs his lips, his eyes warming. "You need some help?"

She nods vigorously, her smile growing. The way her eyes glitter warms his heart. "Yes please. It's fun, but I feel so unsteady." Her eyes flare. "Do you think we could ride it again?"

He huffs a small laugh, shifting the bags around to free an arm. "If you like this, then you'll love a rollercoaster."

Her other leg slips when she tries to stand. It's like watching Bambi on ice. "Help, Ethan."

"Here." He holds out his hand. She snatches it in a viselike grip. Her clawed hands sink into his clothes as she grapples her way up his body. He widens his stance, dropping their bags to get a hold of her when her leg slips again. She's flushed to him, arms around his neck, head whipping all around as if the metal box they're in will provide any sort of information.

A vibration of exhilaration trembles through her. Her breathing picks up speed, marking the beginning of the longest elevator ride of Ethan's life. God, she feels amazing, and he's such a creep for thinking that. He keeps his eyes trained ahead on his own reflection in the metal doors. He glares himself down. Self-control. Self-goddamn-control.

He curses violently to himself. If he can't last in this elevator, then how the hell is he going to get through living in an apartment with her? The cabin was small, but at least it had outdoor space. There is no outdoor space here. Not even a balcony. And it will be just them. Alone. No dogs. No Andrea. Just Star, and him, and whatever they get into trouble with.

If she wants him still.

He tilts his head back in a prayer. Please, lord, let her still want him.

She shifts in his hold. He looks down and away a moment after she looks up and away, then suddenly their eyes collide. The world goes still, the vast cosmos hidden in her eyes sucking him down into the wonder that is Star.

Her fingers slide up his shoulder to tangle in his hair. His breath hitches.

The elevator dings. Ethan is severely tempted to hit the stop button, push her up against the wall, and sink his hands into her lush hair. Their kiss would be everything, he'd make sure it was everything, so that she'd get a taste of what a different kind of high feels like. Just a taste, one that would leave her breathless and achy in the way only good chemistry and painful desire can.

Except this is a new building, and the alarm will go off if he does that.

His hand slaps out when the doors start to close. He looks at her with regained composure. "You okay?"

She slides her hair behind her ear and nods. If he didn't know any better, he'd say she looked a little breathless. But that was the ride, not him.

Carefully, he helps her stand. Once assured that she is indeed stable, he collects all their bags and leads the way to his unit.

A door opens and slams down the hall behind them. Ethan looks over his shoulder to see which neighbor it is, but there's no one there. Shaking off the odd feeling, he slides his key into the lock and swings the door open. "Welcome home."

God, he loves the way she lights up with every new experience. He likes his place, but not to the degree that Star loves it, and it makes him appreciate the apartment more seeing it through her eyes. It's a two-bedroom, two-bath place. The long hall from the front door houses one of the bathrooms and Andrea's bedroom, then it turns right to the decently sized open kitchen and large living room with floor-to-ceiling windows. That was a huge selling point for him. All that natural light. Then his bedroom is right off of the living room with a private bathroom.

He places the bags down by his kitchen island and hears a *smack* as Star collides with the huge windows. Terror stutters his breath, and he shuts his eyes tightly. God, that aged him ten years. "Please don't do that. It's glass, and glass can break." He pulls his hair into a sloppy half-up bun, securing it with a tie from his pocket. "I know you fell from the sky and everything, but that was before this body, and I'm not sure how you'd fare in a twelve-story drop."

Her breath fogs the glass, her hands sliding down it in a screech. He looks to see what she sees. The sun is setting, and the city sparks to life. It is lovely, but in the way all sunsets are. He cannot detect anything unusual or exceptional about the view. Perhaps it's the way the sun shines on the windows, or how the lights flicker on in a strange limbo of half-day, half-night existence.

He glances at her, then back at the view. The silence stretches, and concern begins to bleed into him. "You okay?" Silence is her only reply. His chest tightens, his brows furrowing. It takes him only a few short steps around his large couch to reach her. His fingers lightly brush her elbow. "Star?"

Still sucked into whatever mind space she slipped into, her head slowly tilts, her hair falling to the side. "Ethan...it's so beautiful...so many little lights that..." Her voice goes far. "Seemed...like one large cosmos..."

He pauses, the strap of his duffel bag slipping from his fingers. "Star?"

She blinks, lips parting as her brows furrow.

His fingers graze down her back. "Do you remember?"

"Sort of..." She touches her forehead where that terrible bruising used to reside. "It was...beautiful looking down. Some places were so dark, cold, while others were like..." Her eyes trail from building to building. "Looking at the electrical connectivity of neurons. How amazing that humans could make such things while having limited magic." Little sparks crackle between her fingers, and she becomes lost again.

He looks at the view and then back at her, the tightness of concern still gripping his chest. He nods toward the outside world. "Care to join me in a walk? Do a little exploring, maybe grab some dinner?"

Her eyes instantly shed the haunted coldness. "We can do that?"

He nods, relief that she's back to her old self easing the tight knot that formed in his chest. "Of course. Come on." He steps back, smiling softly when she follows. Step by step, he pulls her from the windows deeper into the apartment, and she follows, those blue eyes trained on his lips. He scoops up her bag when he passes and dumps it into Andrea's room.

He snatches up his keys from the side table, and his insides hum when she doesn't release his hand. "I'd like to show you around my neighborhood, if you're willing to indulge me." His voice is low, enticing, and a thrill speeds his heart when she smiles in response.

"Yes, Ethan." Her eyes glow lightly in the dimness of the hall to the front door. "I'd like that."

Walking through the city with Star brings the streets to life in a whole new way. How many times has he walked these same streets and never noticed the wonders of the city around him? Too many. His eyes wander up the tall buildings that Star points to before sliding back to focus on her, the tension he didn't know he was holding easing.

Star pauses before a chic new bar, her hands lightly clasped together while she looks all around it in wonder. He stands next to her, examining the place as well. He nods toward it, his hand resting on her lower back. "Come on. Let's eat here."

She hesitates for a moment but leans into him when he steps forward, his hand on her back guiding her. Oh, he does like that. It's almost too easy to slip his hand over a little more to grip her side, tucking her in close. Star inhales sharply, her thick lashes fluttering before peering up at him. "Have you been here before?"

"No." He holds the door open for her, the sound of softly playing jazz greeting them from the dark space within. "It must've opened while I was away. But it feels like a new place sort of night." The corner of his lip quirks up, his eyes softening. "A little adventure for the evening."

She smiles. "I like that. Adventure." She nudges him on her way in, playfulness dancing across her face. "Careful, Ethan. You're being generous with your smiles this evening. I'll get spoiled at this rate."

He huffs a laugh, and she beams, her beauty shining. He steps close to her, bringing his lips to her ear. "Maybe I like spoiling you."

She brushes her hair back, her side warm against his. "I like it. All your smiles."

He leads her to the sleek, modern bar, pulling out the barstool for her. She sits gracefully, her eyes searching him again. "To be honest, sometimes I find you hard to read. You're so solemn and serious. It's nice seeing this more…" She tilts her head side to side, her brows furrowing slightly while she searches for the right word. "I guess you could call it your more expressive side." She nudges him with her foot. "I like it when you emote." Her eyes search his face, her voice soft. "It makes it easier to understand what you're thinking."

He grimaces, taking his own seat. "Yeah, sorry about that." It takes him a moment to phrase his explanation in a way he knows she'll understand. "It's…a very bad habit that I picked up while growing up. Andrea calls it 'icing' or 'iced out' because I kind of freeze my face." He lifts a shoulder, hoping to convey nonchalance. "It's from my parents. They're very..." He feels his lip curl before he soothes out his expression. "Over-reactive."

Star leans on the bar, staring at him in that enraptured way that makes him feel so much more alive. "But Andrea doesn't have that. She's very expressive. I never have an issue understanding what she's thinking or feeling."

"Yes, well. She has a different mother."

Star brightens, her curiosity straightening her spine with a little hop. "She does? What's her mother like—wait, no." Her eyes bore into his, and his stomach drops. "What's *your* mother like? Will I ever get to meet her?"

Over his dead body. He lifts a hand, signaling the bartender, needing to move away from the topic of his mother. "What do you want?"

She looks around. "I'm not sure. What does one do at a place like this? It's very different from the Saddle Up."

That's right. This is all new to her. The Saddle Up's casual ambiance is very different from this place's modern chic, all dark and jazzy. He accepts the menus the bartender offers with a nod. Ethan leads her through all the basics, describing what each item means. They order a selection of appetizers and drinks, the bartender happy to assist Star in finding her preferred cocktail.

Unsurprisingly, she immediately dazzles the bartender, clapping and smiling brightly when he flips the bottles for her. Ethan contents himself with watching how Star's easy charm flows off of her, earning them a free appetizer. The gourmet jalapeño poppers are divine, the perfect balance of spice, cheese, and crunch, and the dipping sauce to die for.

With her words from earlier still haunting him, Ethan allows an easy smile on his face. The effect is immediate, and he's an idiot for not connecting it sooner. Star glows under his smile, and her body turns toward him, their knees touching. He nudges the plate toward her and lets her take the majority. He hands her the menu. "Order whatever you want."

Her eyes flare, taking the menu carefully with her fingertips as if it was some sort of holy object. He huffs a small laugh at her softly whispered words of wonder. "Are you sure, Ethan? Anything?"

This happiness is addicting. His chest aches, his smile growing. "Anything. As much as you want."

He swears there are sparkles in her eyes. "Okay, Ethan."

She orders half the menu, causing Ethan to decides to not look at the check at the end of the evening. It's worth it to see her this happy. They take over most of the bar with their orders, Star trying everything and chatting away about what she does and doesn't like with growing excitement. He picks off whatever she rejects, taking the bites she offers him of the ones she loves. He does insist on a bite of the baked artichoke heart before she inhales it.

Finished, Star leans back in her chair, arching over the backrest to stretch, her fingers twining. The bartender fumbles a bottle, and Ethan cannot blame him, because he, too, is caught in Star's spell. Ethan's gaze slides down her like a caress, from her neck to her breasts fighting to break free of her restrictive shirt to her soft stomach. The hem of her shirt rides up to reveal an enticing sliver of midriff that calls to him like a siren. He swallows, skin humming with the deep desire to kiss that strip of skin while on his knees with his hands firmly gripping her hips.

He eyes her thick thighs covered in tight jeans and imagines them in a skirt with her feet propped up on the bar edge, legs spread wide. He sucks in breath harshly through his nose, but he can't get his imagination to stop. He can practically feel her hand fisting in his hair, his scalp burning, while she holds him tight to her sex. Her back would be arched just like it is now, and she'd be grinding against his mouth while moaning soft noises of starved desperation. He'd take his time, feasting upon her slowly, his licks long and flicking to feel her hips twitch—

What the fuck is wrong with him? Ethan snatches up his cold beer and takes several long gulps before gasping for air. He still needs to be able to stand and walk home without a raging hard-on announcing his impure thoughts about his friend—companion? No. Friend. Special friend. He snorts. What is he, sixty? Complicated friend. Yes, that's it. Very, *very* complicated friend.

Maybe the combination of their sexually charged pancake making, their pool game at the Saddle Up, their moment after almost dying, and now this flirtatious datelike evening is too much for Ethan. He is but a mortal man, a mortal man who hasn't gotten a chance to properly jack off in a week. Yes, that has to be it. Ethan is a tinderbox of sexual desire, and that's why he's so filthily hedonistic at the smallest self-permission to eye-fuck the shit out of Star. But damn it, he needed that eye-fucking.

Star's smile is soft, her hands sliding through her long hair and fanning it out, the shimmer of pink catching the low light. Ethan nearly groans and adjusts himself. This time he does look away for his own sanity, but he tenses when he notices that Star has caught the attention of more than one patron's eye.

A woman in heavy eyeliner and a blue and black hair walks up, her eyes trained on Star. Ethan goes rigid, his hand tight on his glass as he tracks her with deep distrust. But she simply asks where Star got her wig, and his shoulders slump with his exhale.

There's a playful mischievousness to Star's smile, and she parrots the words Andrea gave her back in Parkfield. "It was a gift from my sister. Lovely, isn't it?"

Her eyes slide to his, and his own lips curl in the same smile. Time slows as they share in the secret. A flicker of heat ignites in her gaze, head tilting. But he blinks and the spell breaks so quickly, he's not sure it was real. Star turns away toward the approaching bartender. Maybe he imagined it after all.

Back at his apartment, Ethan moves methodically through his evening routine while Star hangs off the back of the couch, staring out at the glittering city. He turns off all the lights for her, and her large eyes reflect the metropolis.

He pauses at his bedroom door, watching her stare at the city with such peaceful wonder. This evening has been pleasant, their adventure together a small little reprieve from their current dilemma. Too small a reprieve. His chest is still tight even after their lovely time in the city, his hand running along the white scarring his shirt hides. Fear, trauma, the unknown weigh heavily on him. Maybe it's selfish, but he wants her to look blissful and happy for a little longer. He's not ready to see the tightness in her features again.

Logically, the first thing he should do tomorrow is get a new phone. It makes sense as a next move in their journey to get answers about Star's past. Then Andrea can reach him in case she needs him. And he can reach out to Jenny. It's the right thing. The responsible thing.

But if he has a phone in the city with its excellent reception, then his mother can easily reach him again too. And work. And the world in general, really. And Jenny. She might respond and want to meet immediately. His chest tightens, jaw clenching. Too soon. It's just too soon. It's only been a day since near death. What is one day more in the larger scheme of things?

"Star?"

She glances back at him.

He leans against the doorjamb. "Would you like to see more of the city tomorrow?" Just one day. That's all he needs. One. Then responsibilities can come back. "We could go get you some clothes." Yes, that is essential. She has only a handful of items that Andrea brought. Going shopping will be practical.

And if he keeps telling himself that, then maybe it will be true, and not because he's avoiding everything for his own selfish desire to spoil Star.

He smiles, making the effort to open his features. "It could be fun."

The effect is instantaneous again. Star brightens, her eyes dancing as they take in his face. She nods, her voice soft. "I'd love to, Ethan."

He nods, forcing himself to turn away from her. "Great." He stops himself from saying something like "it's a date." Hand on his door, he pauses. "Good night, Star."

"Good night, Ethan."

Ethan allows Star to drag him all over Union Square the next day. They go into every store that catches her eye, lingering for however long she wants. He buys clothes and waits patiently while she plays with gadgets in the tourist trap shops that mystify her. Her obsession with fidget spinners makes him smile. She ends up with five, because choosing one was just too distressing.

His favorite moment is their ride on the cable car. The wind catches Star's hair, the sun radiating off her skin as she turns to him, laughing in simple joy, her eyes bright. In that moment, he doesn't have to try to emote, because he can't help but to smile back. This game of playing tourist with her is more fun than anything his previous life could give him. Living in blissful ignorance of their troubles is everything he wanted from the day. His only regret is not having a hand free from all her bags. It keeps him from properly putting his arm around her. The lost opportunity pangs his chest.

The trolley dings to a stop, and Ethan leads her over to the docks and the vista of the bridge. It's a beautiful view, one that he's always enjoyed when he's explored the city on his own.

The seagulls caw loudly as they look out at the vast ocean together. Star stares, her body completely still, her eyes darkening and aging. She swallows, her head slowly turning. It's not what he expected her response to be, and he tries to see what she sees. He's always liked the ocean. He and Andrea went on the ferries a few times, even took a ride on the Jeremiah O'Brien.

He's never seen anyone look out at the water with such deep dismay before. Confusion and fear bubble up, threatening to ruin Ethan's mood. "Star?"

She turns to him, the breeze off the ocean catching her hair and blowing it in front of her face. For one eternal moment, she is this ancient being housed inside a human body, and the next, she is her joyful self again, her smile radiating from her. She slides her arm through his, even with all the bags, giving a gentle tug. "Let's go somewhere else. I like the buildings."

"Alright." He gives the ocean one last look before pointing at the Ferry Building. "Let's go in here."

Like he suspected, Star loves the market with a passion. All the vendors and shops and restaurants. The noise, the people, the chaos. Star throws herself into it, her arm through his, pointing at various things, shouting to be heard over the din. They try cheeses and candies and coffees until Ethan can feel his blood and teeth buzz.

At some point, her hand slides from his elbow into his hand, and he shifts her bags to accommodate. His right hand screams from holding too many things at once, but he bears it for the simple pleasure of her wanting to hold his hand. He feels lighter, his fingers tightening around hers, her eyes meeting his with a smile. The lingering unease from the odd moment on the docks washes away. His smile widens, and Star's chest expands with a quick inhale, her eyes large and bright. She pulls his captured hand deeper into her side, her other hand joining to hold his bicep. His heart thuds painfully when she rests her head against his shoulder while they wait in line for salt-water taffy. There is nothing he would change in this moment. Nothing, except to be able to kiss her.

It will never cease to amaze Ethan how many times this woman can take his breath away. The shimmering pink dress she saw in the storefront clings to her body, and she wears it with such loving confidence that no other woman can even begin to compete. The tone of the color reminds him of her hair in the sunset, and Star excitedly spins in his living room to show it off.

He didn't think he had a favorite item she purchased, but he finds his psyche firmly settling on this one. It takes a herculean effort to keep his gaze respectful when her body's best features are presented to him like this. The way her hips roll when walking in heels sends a little shiver of want down his spine. What he wouldn't give to fall to his knees and slide his hands up those bare thighs and under that short skirt, feel every inch of delicious skin.

He sucks in a breath, his smile tight. "You look amazing." He holds out his hand, the one small acquiescence he gives his body. "Ready?"

Her hand slides in his, and Ethan cannot look at her when she says, "Yes, Ethan," or they'll never make it to dinner.

He takes Star to his favorite restaurant in the neighborhood. It's a little bistro hidden in a brick building that he stumbled upon with an ex-girlfriend.

They sit in a small booth, cozied up, Star's arm through his as she leans into him to be heard over the noise. He turns his head toward her, smiling and appreciating the way her eyes light by the intimate gesture.

He strokes her hair behind her ear to speak into it, the back of his fingers gliding down her neck. Goosebumps ripple along her skin, and his teeth close on his own lip. *Patience*, he reminds himself. With great effort, he forces his gaze away and greets the approaching server.

They order wine and decadent appetizers. Dinner arrives, and they steal bites off each other's plates, moaning how good everything is. Star talks with her mouth full, holding up her fork for him to take a bite. He does, flopping back with an "Oh fuck, that's good." His arm drapes along the back of the booth, and Star leans into him, her shoulder against his chest feeling like heaven.

They linger longer than is necessary. It feels too good, too fun. They conspiratorially whisper to each other, their people-watching a new shared favorite hobby. Star marvels at the clothes, hair, partner selection. Ethan sips his wine, enjoying the sound of her low voice in his ear, words that are just for him. His arm over her shoulders, her fingers lacing through his.

They walk home like this, Star tucked in tight under his arm, her new brown leather jacket doing little to keep her warm.

Back home in comfy, warm pajamas, they cuddle up under an oversized blanket for movies.

He peeks down to see her stroke her forearm. Ink blooms along it, the cable car and candies and the dessert they shared gleaming with the rest of her memories. Her fingers linger along a black eight ball, a token from their flirtatious game of pool at the Saddle Up. Her voice is low, soft with a whimsical smile on her lips. "Today was a good day."

He smiles, tracing over the pieces of her ever-growing tattoo before drawing her closer to him. "Yeah, it was."

Star falls asleep like this, and Ethan rests his head against hers. He stays for longer than he should, until he, too, drifts off.

The star waits.

Her form's eyes open the moment the human's head lulls against the back of the couch. She turns to take in his softened features. It's her favorite moment, the sleep. It opens him in a way that the day never does. Usually, the star has to sneak into his room to watch, but this is far more preferable. She revels in the feel of her form against his, the warmth of his body heating hers, the soft fibers of the blanket capturing and amplifying it. Pure bliss.

She knows it is wrong to watch. It feels wrong, clearly an invasion of his inner sanctum. But the star cannot help it. The compulsion to watch is strong, like it is in her very existence to watch. And the human... Ethan. He is lovely.

The star does not move, her fear of disturbing him strong, overriding the compulsion to stroke her fingers along his face. Her gaze slides to the windows. The brightness of the city keeps the night blessedly hidden. It's a small reprieve and an easy excuse to not look up.

For looking up...she shivers and does not know why.

Her dreams. That bleeding woman from them did not look up either, and a part of the star understands. Better to look down, to look upon Ethan, to look upon this world. This magicless world, and yet it still sparks with something. Her gaze slides to study the rise and fall of Ethan's chest. A flicker of magic. Life. This world with its rules and restrictions, but still so full of wonderment.

She makes sure Ethan is truly asleep before lifting her hand. Magic crackles effortlessly between her splayed fingers, though the sharp stinging makes them twitch. It's much easier than days ago, but the pain is far worse. Trying to call a spark that exists outside her form makes this body sweat, like it is not made to express magic so. The feeling is unnatural, yet her inner soul calls upon it.

Part of her mind rejects the magic vehemently. She does not want it. Being here, being human, *that* is what the star wants. To shed this other otherworldly part so she can meld with *this* world. And then, perhaps, Ethan will consider her as something...more.

She brightens at the thought. Today was filled with so many smiles, so much emotion from him when there is usually cold restraint. Perhaps there is hope for this not so unrealistic dream of being a human and living here... with Ethan. Her heart swells.

But no. She must practice her magic. The creature got too close. It hurt Ethan. Almost robbed her of him. Almost took this form from her. Almost devoured everything.

She was helpless, and she hated that.

Her fingers curl into a fist, her eyes hardening as she looks upon the world. Never again. Whatever it takes, in any way. She will master this pain, master this power. She will be free. Her gaze slides to Ethan. Magic crackles along her fist, her eyes burning into the darkness. They will be free. Nothing and no one else matters.

Seven

The Lophian makes his way through the black waters. Flares of light here and there catch his attention. Some communicating. Some luring prey. Some giving deadly warnings. He ignores them all and focuses on the dangerous trials ahead.

The sacred rock looms before him. He flattens down, skimming the sand until he curls along the dark basalt, his bioluminescent pouches a dull black to hide his presence. The six elders swish in enraged circles around the sacred rock, wailing and screeching their displeasure. Such useless, unnecessary noise for a failure that is their own fault. Malnki should never have been chosen for the Game. He was too rigid in the ancient ways.

The Lophian turns his attention to his quarry. The ancient one, so old that his name is lost to the great Kraken himself. He is a terror to behold, his massive size dwarfing the circling, wailing ones. The ancient one stares up, his long fins wrapped firmly around the seamount. Below him are the very last pearls.

The Lophian listens to the wailing complaints until he learns what he needs. The magic is still unclaimed. There's hope.

He slips from his hiding spot, and his pouches flicker to announce his presence. The reaction is instantaneous. The massive forms of the elders flare to life, deep hums of threat tightening his insides. He does not balk. He lengthens, spines splaying, his light flaring to rival theirs. He may not be of their size and age, but he is strong and more than capable.

Their dark hisses fill the watery depths. "You dare approach?"

He does not bend. He does not writhe. "I dare."

The hisses are deafening. Lesser Lophians would flee, but not him. His eggs are on his mind. He will not fail them. "Your Contender is dead." His claws flex, ready to take by force if he must. "Malnki wasted his pearl. He chose brutal strength over strategy." Dark shapes glide in the water, his own senses flaring to track their movements. "I have a plan."

"A plan?" One gets too close, but the Lophian shows no fear. A tail softly grazes his side. "What plan could you have that would rival the Great Unnamed's choice?"

"One that will succeed. One that will bring magic back to our kind." His gills flare. "One that will bring Life magic."

Hisses of rage echo, clicks of skepticism, but silence from below. The dark shape curled over the ancient volcanic rock does not stir, but the Lophian can sense it watching.

If he fails to persuade the elders, he will need to lure the Great Unnamed off his perch to take the pearls. It will be his greatest battle yet. "I require two pearls for this."

The outrage is thunderous. One snaps at his head, but the Lophian is swift. He shoves up, sending the elder off course. It swims away alive, a gift he shall give it. For now.

He directs his words below, for that is the way forward. "I fear if we fail to obtain Life magic now, we may never achieve the chance again. Every season, fewer and fewer eggs hatch. More and more females perish from the effort. Devouring the star is not enough. We must prime it and seize the Life magic." His teeth flash, his lights flaring. "Death magic will not save us. We must find a way to obtain the Life, and that way is my plan. Two pearls and I will claim victory. Just two." His lights flicker. "Trust in me, for I am more than capable."

The Great Unnamed considers him, his large head tilting for a moment. The Lophian wonders if he can hear the Ocean itself, perceive the whispers of the Kraken. He sincerely hopes they side with him. The battle for the rock would be costly, and he is uncertain how that cost will hinder his plan.

The massive body shifts, and the Lophian tenses for battle.

Reaching into his rock, the Great Unnamed pulls out the pearls to a chorus of dissent. He offers the two white spheres to the Lophian. "Go, my pup. But go knowing you take the last of our magic." He reverently tips the pearls into the Lophian's waiting webbed hands. "Failure is the death of us all. Those born...and yet to be born."

The Lophian's hand curls around his treasure. "I will not fail this. I swear, sire."

Someone is incessantly ringing the doorbell.

Ethan groans, rolling over to eye the clock on his bedside table. 8 a.m. Not *completely* ungodly, but it *is* a Saturday. So more like incredibly rude.

He already woke up once this morning on the couch with a fucked-up neck. After he tucked Star into Andrea's bed, it took him way too long to fall back asleep. Now, groggy and in desperate need of at least two more hours of rest, his mood plummets.

With an incensed growl, Ethan whips off his warm comforter. It's too cold, and it prickles at his exposed arms. Whoever it is better have a damn good reason or he's punting them down the hall. He shuffles to the front door, scratching at his knotted hair, and peeks through the peephole. Star's sleepily yawned "Who is it?" echoes from behind him.

He groans loudly, *thunking* his head against the door. "Sweet baby Jesus, spare me."

He wrenches the door open to glare at Lilliana, Andrea's best friend from high school. Lilliana slurps her coffee loudly, phone pressed against her excessively pierced ear. "Yeah, he's right here." She holds out the phone with a bright smile. "Here you go, asshole."

Ethan rolls his eyes, taking the phone. Lilliana bursts past him into the apartment, her overly processed platinum blonde hair smacking him in the face. Her loud gasp as she sees Star almost drowns out the receiver. "My GOD, you're hot. I'd leave my boyfriend for you, just say the word."

Ethan gingerly puts the phone to his ear.

"Where the fuck have you been?" His sister's enraged tone is too much this early in the morning.

He shuts the door. "Good morning, Andy. I'm fine, thank you for asking."

"Hey, asshole, I'd ask if you'd gotten your shit together and bought a replacement phone, instead of making me track you down like an animal, but obviously the fish creature isn't enough motivation."

He powers on his espresso machine while Andrea continues to rip him a new one. "And what about me! I could be monster fish flakes right now and you wouldn't even know!"

"I don't think I'd know regardless." He pops an espresso pod in.

"It wounds me that you wouldn't even call."

"Okay, *Mom*. I'll call more." He pokes the start button harder than necessary. The machine groans to life.

"Wait, which mom? Yours or mine? And keep in mind that my rage will be dependent on your answer."

"Mine."

Andrea gasps violently. "How dare you! Rude! Fucking rude! Here I was worried about you, no word in days. Don't even know if you're alive or d— okay, you know, now that I'm hearing it out loud, I might be sounding a touch like her."

"Just a touch." He hands the first espresso to Star, and she gives him a dazzling smile. She doesn't look the least bit perturbed that a stranger is in his apartment, who somehow got past the doorman and the key-required elevator.

His eyes narrow suspiciously at Lilliana. "Did you give Lilliana a key fob to my place?"

"Of course I did. Bitch is my sexless wife, and I need her for exact moments like these."

He points at Lilliana. "Hey. You. Key back now."

Andrea's wail is a near-perfect imitation of his mother. "Why do you continue to wound me, Ethaniel? After everything I do for you!"

"I swear, you speak to Lilliana for ten minutes and you transform into your high school self again." He glares at his sister's friend. "I'm not joking. I want the fob and any keys back now."

Both women speak at the same time. "That's not going to happen."

Ethan sighs loudly and burns his tongue on his coffee. "Is there a point to this call, or was it just to annoy me before I have my coffee?"

"You mean other than to confirm you're alive? Yes. It's called get a fucking phone or I'm sending Lilliana over every single day."

"Fine. I'll do it tomorrow." He pops some bagels in the toaster. "But I'm rather enjoying being off the grid. Should've done it years ago."

"Yeah, bet it makes it harder for your mom to stalk you."

"She doesn't do that." Anymore. "And be proud of me. I missed my weekly call with her." His therapist is going to be so proud.

"Yeah, I don't think 'couldn't call because I drowned my phone after nearly dying from a fish monster' counts. Seems like one of those exception cases."

The toaster pops, and Ethan tosses the bagels onto plates. "Now look who's being rude. Please support my healing journey in whatever form it takes." He spreads the smear on each. "What did you...share with..." He's at a loss. There is no way he can think to covertly ask Andrea what she told Lilliana.

"Are you asking about Lils? Don't worry. I told her that Star is a friend from Parkfield who was born in a cult so she's missing an ID. That's why she's with you. You're helping her get established. Oh, and that she's cult traumatized so don't ask about it."

Ethan blinks. "Elaborate." And effective.

"Well, I couldn't quite tell her the truth, could I? Besides, if we don't become monster fish flakes, she'll need a story to get citizenship."

His heart warms, gaze sliding to Star. "Clever. I like it." He hands Star her bagel, and she gives him a quick glance before going back to charming the socks off Lilliana. "Thank you, Andy."

"You're welcome. Now get a phone and call me the moment you do. Stay safe. Love you."

"Okay, bye."

"I SAID I LOVE YOU!"

He sighs. "Love you too. Don't be fish flakes."

"Samesies. Bye."

He hands the phone back to Lilliana, who is so deep in the Star haze that she doesn't even notice. Being ignored by Lilliana while she's sitting on his couch takes him back nine years, minus a sixteen-year-old Andrea, and a little wave of nostalgia hits him.

Lilliana clasps Star's hand. "You should come out with us tonight!"

Ethan sputters his coffee.

Star's eyes light up. "I'd love to!" She turns toward him. "Can we, Ethan?"

He nearly pulls something from the effort to hold in his groan. Going out with Lilliana tonight is not his first choice. He had plans to take Star out to dinner again. Maybe walk around, go to another high-end bar. Alone. See if things continue to escalate. Maybe he'd see if she'd like him to kiss her afterward.

It would be her first kiss, and he's feeling oddly nervous about it. She deserves for it to be wonderful, and damn it, he's going to make sure it is. Now, he'll have to figure out how to make the evening romantic with Lilliana's friends around, or else postpone it. His teeth grind. Damn Lilliana.

It's not that he doesn't *like* Lilliana. They have a sort of love-hate relationship that comes from having to parent her as a teen. Besides, it's not completely unheard of for him to join her and her eclectic group of friends, who happen to have some of his friends wheedled in. He just hoped to continue to take Star on unofficial dates.

His skeptical gaze meets Star's hopeful one, and he immediately caves. "If that's what you want."

Lilliana claps excitedly. "Yay! We're starting at White Rabbit's at nine. Get some drinks. Then maybe go dancing later at like eleven."

Ethan's old ass tries not to groan. Sounds like pure hell. However, dancing with Star could be fun. She'll probably love it. He tries to hide his grimace as Star smiles excitedly at him.

They spend the daylight hours at Golden Gate Park, Star marveling at the beauty of the place. To get through all of it with her level of curiosity would take days, so instead they linger within Strawberry Hill. Star particularly enjoys the Pavilion's brand of peaceful serenity. She leans against the railing overlooking the pond, her lavender hair nearly glowing in the midday sun. She smiles, the reflection of the water playing across her skin as she points to the ducks and various birds in the area while Ethan stands solemnly beside her. A few sparrows land on her shoulder, singing merrily and nibbling on strands of hair.

Murmurs hum in the air, phones getting drawn out and pointed toward Star. Pictures and video are taken to be posted on God only knows where. Ethan's anxiety spikes. Maybe he should take them somewhere else, where Star's unusualness will be less obvious. He waves a fluttering bird away from his face. Perhaps a place without birds.

Ethan eyes the sparrows perched on several of Star's fingers. She perfectly imitates their songs in a lovely harmonization, the kind of sound that seeps into one's soul to haunt listeners for the rest of their days. A sound that the mind likes to latch onto to bring back in lovely remembrance.

Star turns her smile on him, and his heart throbs, all thoughts of leaving evaporating in her light. She beams, teeth sinking into her full lip, the birds taking flight. Her laugh fills his ears, and he eases his hip against the railing, his eyes not straying from her. A smile comes to him, his hand lifting to encourage the birds out of her hair. He strokes back a strand, his fingers lingering. Their eyes meet, hers the color of pure cerulean in the sunlight as she searches his face.

She shifts closer, leaning into his chest. It's only natural for his arm to wrap around her middle, his fingers settling on her hip. They stay like this, Ethan resting his head against hers as they watch the ducks swim in silence. A warm pressure grows in his chest, his arm tightening, until his fingers lace together to encase her in his hold. Star's hands rest on his arm as her weight sinks into him.

In that moment, the world melts away to nothing but the two of them and their shared space. Ethan feels his soul ease, his mind letting go of all the stress and worry over the looming threat of fish monsters and unsolved mysteries.

For one beautiful moment with Star, Ethan just exists.

The evening is pleasantly brisk as the ocean air wafts through the streets, cooling the city. Ethan chose a place for dinner not too far from the White Rabbit so they could walk together afterward. The night is just starting to wake, clusters of people laughing as they pass by on their way to their various revelry-filled destinations.

The bar's lights are in sight, and Ethan's steps falter, a thought occurring to him. "Star..."

She pauses, turning toward him. He loses his train of thought as his eyes hungrily take in her form once again.

Star used magic to pull her mass of hair up into a chic ponytail. Her glittering dress and choker necklace do something to him, something he's trying to not think too hard about. At dinner she saw some other women stroll by looking glam, and in a blink her features changed to imitate their makeup. A smile of satisfaction curled her lips as Ethan's gaze darkened with a different kind of hunger. A pair of earrings he doesn't remember buying glint in the streetlights while she waits patiently for him to finish his statement.

He gives himself a little shake. "Star, I don't think we can get in."

Her face falls, eyes growing large. "What do you mean?"

"Well, you don't have an ID."

"What's that?"

"It's a way for places like this to verify you're old enough to go in."

She bites her glossy lip, brows furrowing. What he wouldn't give to be that lip. Maybe this will work out for the best. Now they can go to a place where no one will card her. Just the two of them.

"And this is a thing I need? This ID? It's important?"

He nods. "Yeah. Kind of essential if we're going to do this regularly. We've been lucky so far that no one questioned your age."

"Okay." Mischievousness flashes over her face. "Don't worry, Ethan." Fire blazes in her eyes. "I've got this."

He'd be more concerned if he wasn't thoroughly obsessed with this new confident side of her. She takes his hand, and his mind goes blank. "Okay."

She tugs him, and he follows a step behind, his gaze devouring her from head to toe before he steps up beside her. The bouncer does his own covert once-over before clearing his throat, professionalism back in place. "IDs, please."

Star places a hand on the bouncer's forearm, and a hum pulses. Ethan blinks rapidly, as does the bouncer. The man's pupils dilate, and Star's smile widens, her blue eyes practically glowing in the night.

The door opens. "Enjoy your evening."

Star's shoulders roll back, head tilting. A hint of smugness bleeds into her tone. "I plan to. Thank you."

Ethan is dragged behind her. The small hallway darkens when the door shuts loudly. He stops abruptly, the force of which pulls Star to face him. He inspects her, eyes darting all over like he's not sure where to land. "What did you—how did you—" He gives himself a rough shake, mind clearing. "What happened?"

She gives him an impish smile, her blue eyes a shade darker and slightly glowing. "I used some magic." She holds her free hand between them to hide the crackle of energy from the room beyond, white tendrils winding over her trembling fingers in a playful dance. "I've been practicing."

His jaw drops. "When?" They've been together nonstop.

She lifts a shoulder. "When you go to sleep. I don't sleep like you do. It's more like bursts or a short rest than an entire night." Her fist clenches, the tendrils crackling harshly before disbursing. "I want to be ready. I want us to live undisturbed." Her hand squeezes in his own. "Together, like you said."

His eyes lock with hers. "You are...*incredible*." A sense of ineptness washes through him when he tries and fails to find the words to eloquently express his feelings. Instead, he lets it bleed into his face. Just a hint, but enough for her to notice.

Star's smile grows, and the radiance of it shines upon him in the dimly lit hallway. It's like she reached in and stole his breath, replacing it with a growing, aching warmth. This woman, soft, sweet, and kind, but so fierce. Everything he's ever dared to hope for, and the universe dropped her in his front yard.

He steps up to her, hand leaving hers to slide around her middle. His lips graze her ear, and he feels a little tremor ripple through her. "You never cease to amaze me."

Her breath tickles his neck, and he pulls back just enough to see her expression to assure himself he hasn't overstepped. A thrill vibrates through him when he finds her willing and excited, a blush tinting her cheeks. She licks her bottom lip, capturing it between her teeth to bite lightly, her irises back to light blue. Her gaze sweeps over him, and he senses a hunger growing within her. It takes everything he has to not press her against the hallway wall and suck that lip between his teeth.

She copies his move and wraps her arms around him, her lips brushing against his ear. It's hardly fair. His knees almost give out. "I'm thirsty, Ethan."

He could live a happy life with his name on her lips. Always. Constantly. He wants to hear it said in every way. He gives her his most coy smile, and her eyes flare, hand on his shoulder tightening. "I can assist with that."

The entrance doors behind them open, and Ethan gives her hand a small squeeze, stepping away to lead them into the main bar before the newcomers run over them. The bar is beautiful and styled like a classic speakeasy with modern touches. Copper and black are the predominant color scheme, with a massive, gilded mirror behind the main bar reflecting the space. The bar itself is sizable, with a good amount of space on all three sides. They take a seat at the corner of the bar, a flash of Star's thigh visible when she crosses them. It doesn't take the bartender long to notice the beautiful woman waiting for a drink. After all, it's nearly impossible to not notice Star.

He comes over, leaning on the bar. "What can I get you two?"

Star leans forward as well, lips pursed in thought. The man can't help himself, eyes darting to them, dipping down, then guiltily flicking toward Ethan. Ethan's lip quirks in response.

"I want..." She gives a little sway. "Something pink. The pinkest, girliest drink you have."

The bartender smiles. "You want cherries with that?"

Her eyes flare. "Oh, *yes*. Please. Thank you!"

He looks at Ethan. "And you, man?"

Ethan's hand rests on Star's lower back. Her dress is sinfully low to expose her spine, and his thumb grazes her skin there. "Boulevardier. Thanks."

Alone, Ethan leans forward, his body closer to hers than mere friends' would be. "You look beautiful tonight."

"Thank you." Star gives him a heated look, leaning into his warmth. "You do too."

He smiles, a small laugh huffing out. "I look beautiful?" He did try tonight. Beard trimmed tight, hair pulled back. He dusted off his favorite blazer and a nice button-up for the occasion. Hell, he even found cologne an ex gave him.

She purrs, "Oh yes."

His smile takes an edge. God, the things he wants to do to her. Maybe this will finally be the night they tip over from friends to more. The way Star is leaning into him is giving him all the hope. She pulls her long ponytail forward over her shoulder, and he contemplates trailing his lips across her bare skin.

Their drinks arrive, the light clank drawing Ethan's attention. It's like a switch flips within Star as she goes from lethal temptress to her usual boisterous self, buzzing with excitement. The bartender taps the pink drink with an excessive amount of cherries in a decorative glass. "Love potion. Vodka, peach schnapps, grapefruit juice, and some grenadine."

Star takes a sip, fingers touching her lips with a little jolt. "Oh! I love it!" God, she's adorable. One minute she's got crackling destructive energy in the palm of her hand, ready to mulch a fish monster, the next she's excited about an excessively pink drink. "What's your name?"

The bartender leans on his forearms. "Anthony."

"Anthony." She whispers it like she's trying out his name on her tongue. Ethan momentarily pities the man. She gives her patented Star smile, leaving Anthony looking a little dazed. "Thank you, Anthony. This is amazing."

Anthony nods. "Um, yeah. Course. Let me know if you two need anything else."

Star takes a large sip. "Ethan, you should get one too."

He taps his nail on his glass. "I have a drink."

"Yes, but then you can have two drinks. It'll be even better."

"Two? No. That would be excessive. Unlike you, I would get very drunk drinking that fast." He gives her a playful smirk. "Unless you're trying to take advantage of me?"

Star's smile curls. "I don't know what that means." She leans forward, and Ethan's gaze drops to take in her curves. Her low, soft voice shivers through him. "But I like the way you say it. Should I be?"

The alcohol burns from his too large of a sip, and he catches the way she watches his throat move. The smirk comes to him unbidden, his voice velvety. "Well, we went to dinner. We got drinks. Seems logical. If that's what you want."

She bites her lip again, heat curling between them. Her eyes flick away, her shoulders playfully nudging his chest. He watches mesmerized as she brings that fancy glass to her lips, taking a slow drink and catching a cherry in her teeth. She sucks on it, and his hands clench, his eyes tearing away to look at his own drink. He takes a careful breath to steady himself. Patience.

The bar has filled up by now, people pressing to order drinks. They've just finished theirs when Lilliana and her crew show up with a burst of chaotic excitement. Hasty introductions are made, Lilliana taking control of the space and drawing Star forward to meet all her friends. Ethan claps the shoulder of Mike, a fellow programmer at Ethan's company. The gang jostles away to find a table, but Ethan lingers to order another round. Anthony shows excellent customer service and appears practically the moment he lifts his finger.

Then, the crowd shifts and reveals the last person he expects to see across the bar.

Taylor Coleman. His last girlfriend. The one who left him a depressed, heartbroken wreck.

She watches him with her dark eyes, slowly assessing. Her smile is warm, welcoming, and she wiggles her fingers at him. An engagement ring flashes, the silver band practically glowing against her dark skin.

Ah. His mind clicks. This is why Andrea asked if he'd been on socials. Taylor and Andrea were thick as thieves once. Andrea would've seen the engagement announcement and worried about Ethan's reaction.

Taylor. She's exactly how he remembers her. Stunning, strikingly so. And radiating the kind of confidence that makes the whole room pause when she enters. Her eyes slide to Star, who is beside him chatting animatedly with one of Lilliana's friends. A perfect eyebrow arches. Taylor nods her approval, lips pursed, and he can practically hear her purr *Nice.*

His smile widens. That's why he always liked Taylor. Easy. Fun. Direct. One of the best relationships he's ever had and built on a foundation of amazing sex. Shit, the entire relationship was sex. Easy. But not brief, *never* brief. Not with Taylor. Even when they meant it to be, they'd get lost in it. Pure body chemistry and barely anything in common other than that she wanted to do what she wanted, and he didn't care what she did.

Then, it all came crashing down. His mother's constant hatred, Taylor's growing open disdain for the toxicity. And then, the final nail in the coffin, one that Taylor couldn't look away from. What did it was his fateful "If I have to" combined with "If that's what you want" to the statement "Then I guess I could get it reversed" regarding his vasectomy. He can still see the way her face changed, her eyes searching his.

He swallows down the discomfort at the memory, the sense of failure hitting him hard. Taylor Coleman wanted children with a man who also wanted children. Not one who would settle for them after sterilizing himself. Especially not one with a mother like his. A "mother-in-law bullet dodged," as a mutual friend put it.

So yes, it was him who fucked it up, and he offered Taylor an easy out to walk away. So, she did.

A man next to Taylor slides a drink over, pulling Ethan back to the present. He's handsome and they're quite the pair. Ethan nods toward the man with a question on his face. Taylor's teeth sink into her lip, and she nods, her brows wiggling. Ethan does his own appreciative nod, and her shoulders shake with a suppressed giggle.

It would be nice to be friends with Taylor again. His heart aches a little at the thought. The absence of their easy companionship is a pulsing open wound that hurts a little less than it used to. Hell, a lot less, now that he permits himself to drop fully into the sensation. His face softens, knowing what's finally initiated this healing.

Maybe now that he has Star and she has Mr. Taylor Coleman on her arm, friendship could work out. Alas, she made it clear that it would be too weird to stay in touch.

To this day she's the only ex he ever occasionally wondered "what if." What if he had set boundaries with his mom? What if he firmly sided with Taylor during one of their fights? What if he stood up to his mom instead of leaving it to Taylor? What if he had shown excitement for having children? What if, what if, what if.

Taylor's fiancé slips his hand along her back, and her perfectly manicured nails tap against her glass as she cheers Ethan. A goodbye, her smile blinding. He can tell she's happy for him, and he smiles back so that she knows he's happy for her too. He really is.

"Who's that, Ethan?"

Ethan turns to Star. Uncertainty floods him. He doesn't want to get into it. Rehashing it will just stir too much within him. But he can see Star waiting, watching him expectantly. He wets his lips, choosing his words carefully. "She is an ex-girlfriend of mine."

Star's eyes flare, flicking to where Taylor once stood. "Ex?"

"Yeah. We broke up." He searches for the words, feeling prickly discomfort. "My mom...didn't like her." He shrugs a shoulder, hoping the nonchalance ends the conversation. "It happens."

Star nods. Her eyes flicker with uncertainty, and he wonders if he should explain. But no. Taylor is his past, Star is his future. That fact settles in the moment, and a sense of closure he didn't know he needed washes over him. Besides, Star's curiosity is a powerful thing. If she has questions, she'll ask. Simple as that.

His gaze drifts back to look at the spot where Taylor stood, and he releases a long sigh. End of an era, really.

His face softens, a small smile sliding in place. *So long, Taylor.*

Eight

F resh boulevardier and love potion glasses click down before Ethan, snapping him out of his Taylor Coleman daze. Anthony the bartender taps the counter twice before slipping away to tend to the writhing mass of thirsty customers.

Ethan delicately holds the artful glass of pink alcohol and turns to hand it to Star, but she isn't there. He blinks, trying to clear his head. It takes him only a moment to locate her vibrant hair in a sea of humans. Perched on a couch at the far corner of the bar, she's chatting animatedly with Lilliana and her group of friends. They laugh, Star twisting her hair around her wrist and Lilliana playfully slapping her arm.

She's so far away, gone without him even noticing. His brows furrow. Was he really that distracted? Or did she move that quickly?

Shaking off the vaguely disturbed feeling, he grabs his wide tumbler and makes his way over. There are so many people now, too many. He is forced to move slowly, inching his way without spilling the drinks. A miracle, really, with Star's overly full drink in his hand.

Her blue eyes flick up to him when he stands at her side. There is no room for him, and none of Lilliana's fully captivated friends look willing to give up their coveted places by Star.

Star plucks her glass from his hand and flashes a smile. "Thank you, Ethan."

Her attention immediately slides back to Lilliana, her crossing legs causing her body to shift away toward her new friend.

Ethan hesitates in a moment of confused silence, the feeling of being dismissed mingling with the "disturbed" sensation from earlier. Needing something to do, he lifts his drink to his lips. The alcohol burns his throat and distracts him from his own prickly reaction. His features smooth out as he dismisses the uncomfortable feelings, settling on it all being an overreaction on his part. Star's simply enjoying her time with this group of friends, just like when they were at the Saddle Up. Nothing more.

With a nod, he steps back and falls into conversation with Mike, easing into an open chair beside the man.

Just an overreaction, he reminds himself. Nothing more.

The Lophian swims as fast as he can, not wasting a moment more. Up and up. Higher and higher. The darkness is still so oppressive, no hint of this surface that tales have whispered of—a brightness that burns the eyes, a ceiling of the world.

The only hint he receives that he is nearing it is the massive school of fish that he startles. It distracts him, his spines flaring and lights flashing. The school scatters, darting away from his massive teeth and clawed hands. Never has he seen so many fish. The deep, dark depths, beautiful with its variety, are sparse. He'd only seen the ragged carcasses of these ones when they fell from above.

They're the sign he's been waiting for, and he swallows the first of his two pearls.

The burn inside is agonizing. He writhes, twists, and flails. His bones crack, re-forming, densifying. His gills tremble and give way to his amphibian form's freshly carved lungs. His tail thrashes as it lengthens, the ends splaying open.

He looks at his long arms, watching fingers form and webbing shed away. Yes. This is what he needs. He touches his head to feel the flattened front and spherical shape. A skull with a tapered neck. Tales from the ancient ones spoke of their siren brethren trapped in a mighty, distant sea. Powerful cousins who warred with humans for centuries.

His new form has done the tales justice.

Victorious, he powers on, his changed tail propelling him even faster, the speed making his heart soar. Such speed. Such power. On and on, his maw stretching in a grin until he bursts through the firmament. He arcs, eyes wide as his lungs gasp, his body suspended in this strange dry existence.

He crashes back to the depths, stunned.

Slowly, he rights himself. His new fingers stretch, the oddly glinting ceiling of his world warping with the roaring waves.

He surfaces, blinking, sucking in a full breath. Night. That is what it is called. Sparkling, glittering balls of magic wink at him from above, a glowing heavy orb among them. He bobs with the strength of the waves. So odd, this new world. So odd...and *wrong*.

He breathes in another gulp of this stinging, arid hell. The common ancestors long ago should never have allowed the land to break the wall dividing the heavens from the waters. Foolish, arrogant. The ocean will swallow it whole once again, correct the wrongs, then finally his mighty people will be reunited once more in one glorious ocean.

The way the great gods meant for it to be.

He closes his eyes, stretching his newly acquired magic until it touches something. Something not above in the sparkling web, but down on that cursed land.

Not far. And calling to him.

He does not delay.

Boredom swirls within Ethan. He's run out of work topics to discuss with Mike and, if he's honest, he really doesn't give a fuck. He's on sabbatical. He doesn't want to talk about work. He wants to talk to Star.

His gaze slides back to her. She's absolutely riveted by something Lilliana's friend is saying. His brows draw together. He's not familiar with this one. Knowing Lilliana and Andrea, this woman is probably around twenty-five. Probably a senior when they were sophomores in high school.

That is, if this is a high school friend who didn't clog up his apartment for years.

He interrupts whatever the exiled menfolk are talking about, nodding toward the mystery woman. "Who's that?"

Mike leans back to see better. "Oh, that's Rachel. I don't think you've met her. She's Devin's ex-girlfriend."

"And Devin is...?" He's really out of the loop. The last time he went out like this was during Andrea's last visit, back when he was still with Taylor... So maybe a year ago?

He blinks. That's right. He and Taylor broke up only a year ago and she's already engaged? No wonder Andrea was concerned. Seems awfully fast. Well, maybe they had that spark. She does want kids, and she was acutely aware of the ticking clock.

Mike sets his empty glass on the table. "You remember Devin. She was an engineer with Courtney's crew before she switched to a bigger company and moved to LA. So now we have Rachel."

Rachel. Stylish Rachel in her skintight leatheresque pants and loose button-up shirt tucked into the waist, chic, effortless. Her short hair curls in ringlets around her sharp but not-unpleasant-to-look-at face. Her long, elegant fingers with artful, minimalist tattoos tuck a few ringlets behind her extensively pierced ear. She leans closer to Star to be heard over the noisy bar.

Ethan's eyes narrow. Too close.

Blonde hair whips in front of him, efficiently cutting off his unhealthy staring. Lilliana cocks her hip, thumbs flying over her phone's screen. "We're going dancing."

He'd rather be skinned and set on fire. His lips part, but Lilliana cuts him off. "Star wants to go with us."

He gets the distinct feeling that he's being played. Lilliana and Andrea excelled at such things. His eyes narrow further, and he leans back to glance at Star. Rachel is inclining against the back of the sofa, her arm propping her head up, listening as Star animatedly talks about something.

What Ethan wants is for it to be last night again. Curled up in a private booth together, splitting a nice bottle of wine while in their own little world. A wave of shame hits him. He's being selfish. It's good for Star to make friends and experience life. And if she wants to go dancing, then he'll take her dancing, because he'd rather be eaten by the fish monster than leave Star on her own with Lilliana and her friends.

And Rachel. Whoever the fuck Rachel is.

The ice in his glass clinks when he tilts it to look at the empty contents. Maybe he should switch to water.

"Ethan."

He looks up at Lilliana. She arches a brow at him. "Dancing? Going? Close your tab, friend."

He nods, getting to his feet. He sends one last look at Star before heading over to close out.

God, Ethan hates clubs. The darkness with the blinding, multicolored lights. The deafening music that does *not* need to be this loud. The gross heat that has him regretting his jacket.

The only thing he doesn't mind is the dancing. Taylor loved to dance, and there were nights where it was just another form of foreplay. Now *that* he could get behind with Star. Feeling her body against his and moving rhythmically sounds like pure heaven.

But Lilliana's clubs are the three S's: sleazy, sweaty, and sticky.

And Star is dancing with her new friends. Without him.

Which is fine. He's happy for her.

He takes an overly long swig of his drink.

On the walk over, he had trailed behind with Mike as Star walked arm in arm with Lilliana and Rachel. She did give him one look to make sure he was following, one smile, but it flickered away. Very different from their walk to the White Rabbit, when it was him that she held.

Mike nudges him and yells over the music, "Go dance with her!"

Ethan swallows the mouthful of alcohol. "Who?"

"Don't play dumb, man. The hot one. Star."

He shakes his head. "We're just friends." It's like a punch in the gut.

Mike raises a brow. "Uh huh. But you know...it could be more if you stop being a coward and go dance with her."

Mike is drunk off his ass. It's the only explanation. Ethan shrugs a shoulder and takes another drink, Mike scoffing in overexaggerated disappointment.

Star being Star, with the help of Lilliana, charms her way into a booth. Lilliana might not know what Star is, but she very quickly caught onto Star's effect on people and expertly weaponized it. Ethan would feel bad for the club owner if he didn't hate this place so much. There is bottle service at a discount and a waitress who comes by steadily with sparkly eyes on Star. Ethan is happy to have a place to plant himself where he's away from the writhing bodies but can still watch everything.

Maybe if he thinks "happy" enough times, he'll start to feel it.

Needing a break, he downs his drink and heads to the bathroom. He catches a glimpse of himself in the mirror. He looks normal, closed and blank-faced. Then again, he is an expert at hiding all outward indicators of his suffering.

Star is having fun. He just needs to chill.

He sighs, does what he came in to do, and washes his hands without looking at the mirror again.

Opening the bathroom door is like walking into a wall of noise. He cringes, head tilting as he tries to adjust to the sound. God, he hates it here. He sullenly makes his way back, trying to avoid touching too many sweaty bodies. A few girls try to catch his eye, but he averts his gaze, in no mood for their interest. He steps up toward the booth and pauses, feeling ice drip down his insides as his heart plummets.

Star is sitting on the couch with Rachel, who leans forward to kiss her.

He'd lunge forward to stop it if he didn't see the way Star smiled and leaned into it as well, her beautiful blue eyes closing as she melts into the kiss.

Her first kiss. And it's not with him.

He swallows, taking a painful breath, his eyes burning. The kiss becomes heated, Star's leg draping over Rachel's lap, the woman's hand touching the thigh he wants to be touching, kissing the lips he wishes to kiss, pressing against the body he could've pressed against if he hadn't fucked it all up. As Rachel's hand slides upward, Ethan forces himself to turn away.

He doesn't need to see this.

Ethan is drunk. He is self-aware enough to admit that.

Is he stopping? No. Because if he stops, then he will see Star kissing Rachel over and over and over and—

He throws back his drink, the whisky not burning anymore, and the glass clinks on the bar. God, he's a mess. Eventually, he will be happy for her. Star has merely seen what all the other women eventually saw. He's stagnant. It's the truth. Nothing can grow in infertile land.

He runs his hand through his hair, but belatedly realizes he's tied it back. His hand taps the bar again, looking longingly for the bartender. He needs water. And then another drink. Also maybe food. Oh yeah, something greasy from a truck would be perfect. And then he'll go home, pass out, and wake up as a better person who is happy for his friend for finding someone to show her the joys of a body.

Oh fuck, he's going to cry in this shitty ass fucking club. It's going to be the lowest he's ever been in his life, and then he'll have to call his therapist first thing in the morning to reestablish care, and then he's going to have to *talk* about it, and then call his fucking *mother* because he's a shit son and—

"Ethan!"

His eyes squeeze shut for a moment. God, help him get through this.

The stool swivels around, and he almost topples out of it. He smiles lazily as Star beams at him. He reaches out to tuck a loose strand of her hair behind her ear and remembers as he does how her hair got loose from her tie in the first place.

His eyes flick behind her. Using every drop of self-control, he reins in his glare. He sways from the sheer effort, and it takes a moment for him to control his too-large tongue. "Rachel."

Rachel offers a half-hearted wave. Her lipstick is smudged. He reminds himself not to cry. The shame would be unbearable.

Star is glittery with excitement. "I've been looking for you! Oh, Ethan. Rachel invited me to her place!"

He's going to throw up and cry at the same time. He beams, but he fears it's more of a grimace. Focusing on Star helps. Her lovely, pure happiness helps remind him that he's a good person who will *not* ruin this moment. His cheeks hurt from the effort to not scowl. "Wonderful."

"Come with us!"

The bar hits his back. He's not the only one. Rachel staggers back a step as well. He blinks rapidly, scanning the woman, before focusing on Star again. "What?"

"Well," Star twists the ends of her ponytail around her finger, "I don't want to leave you here, and Rachel's place sounds like fun. She has a cat!"

He scans Rachel, who looks as confused as him. Oh, his sweet, innocent Star. The false expression melts off his face and leaves behind a soft smile that he only has for Star. He huffs a laugh, shaking his head. He leans forward and holds up a finger to Rachel. "A minute, please. Trust me." His bleary focus zeros in on Star. "I'm not invited."

Her whole face falls, her blue eyes glistening in the flashing lights. "What? Why not?"

He drapes an arm around her middle, drawing her closer so she can hear better. "Star..." He drops his voice, whispering in her ear. "Rachel is inviting you to her place to have sex." His eyes dart to Rachel, who silently confirms it.

"Oh." Star's eyes sparkle. "Ooohh." She scans Rachel and slithers closer to Ethan to whisper conspiratorially back at him. "That does sound fun. She's so pretty and soft and kisses so nicely..."

This is nice, being playful with her, even if his heart is shredding into a million pieces. "If you want to have sex with her, then you should go."

She bites her full lip, and Rachel gives her a heated smile. Star's lip slowly escapes, and she leans into Ethan's side. "I think...I'd enjoy that."

A selfish part of him wishes she'd hate the idea. Wishes that she confessed that it's him that she wants to have sex with. That she kissed Rachel but thought of him. Fuck, he's so desperate that he'd take anything that says he hasn't been imagining this whole romance from the start.

But maybe the Saddle Up was simply her being curious about sex and Ethan being her only option.

He's going to throw up, but he gulps it down. With every fiber of his drunk being, he forces down all his emotions deeper and deeper into his psyche until his face smooths out into the perfect iced-out expression Andrea hates. It's necessary to do what he has to, which is be her friend. And friends support each other.

With a heavy heart, he nudges her. "Then have at it."

Star and Rachel share a heated look, the intensity of which forces Ethan's gaze to drop. He breathes through his nose and waits for Star to proclaim that she'll see him in the morning. Then, he'll throw up in the bathroom and drag his ass home. Alone. And drink in his room until passing out. Maybe even dig in Andrea's room to see if she left any weed behind.

Star's hand on his bicep isn't enough to bring his eyes back up to hers. He can't let her see his raw feelings. She needs to make this decision on her own.

Star mumbles, "I don't want to leave you alone." That small morsel is enough to lift Ethan's head. She worries her lip, brows tight. His heart hammers, hope rising.

She smiles brightly, her whole body lighting up with an idea. "Oh yes, Ethan. You should join us! The three of us will have so much fun!"

Ethan must truly be in a dark place to consider the idea. The thought of guiding Star through the experience does sound intriguing. He chances a glance at Rachel. She locks eyes with him, and they both come to the same conclusion: they are not two people who can share a woman. A small part of Ethan is relieved. Yes, he is enough of a loser to take Star any way he can get, but the chances of him being utterly ruined after the act are high.

Besides, deep in his withered, broken heart, he's a romantic. He'd want it to be just the two of them the first time he makes love to Star.

He swallows around the lump in his throat and whispers to Star, "I don't think it's a good idea."

Star turns her back on Rachel to look at him, her face full of sadness. His brows furrow, his guilt for being a shitty friend getting him back on the "be supportive" track. "Hey, don't worry about me. Do what you want to do." The lie slips out fluidly. "I'll be fine."

Star hesitates, and Ethan can see Rachel drawing her own conclusions. Her eyes narrow ever so slightly on him before she reaches out and touches Star's arm. "Look, don't worry about it. I'm going to head out."

Ethan could slap himself. He ruined this for Star. What a fucking asshole he is. He swallows and fights the alcohol to find a way to save it, even though his heart is celebrating that Star will go home with him. His tongue is too thick and sluggish, but Star wants this and he swore he would help her. Even if it includes a romantic liaison that doesn't involve him. He just wants her to be happy.

He reaches out to Rachel and does his best not to slur. "Listen, I don't know if Lilliana told you, but this is all very new to her. Here. Give me your number—" Fuck, he doesn't have a phone. "Write down your number. I'm getting her a phone tomorrow." Well, guess he's adding Star to his family plan now. "Maybe you two can hang out and get to know each other, if you're down."

Rachel hesitates, her eyes sweeping Star hungrily but wavering uncertainly on him. He gives the most dismissive, casual shrug he can muster, and against his better selfish judgment he says, "We're just friends. Don't worry about it. Trust me. It's nothing."

Rachel sweeps him suspiciously one last time before sighing. "Look, Lils has my number." She lingers on Star. "Shoot me a text in the morning if you're still interested." She smiles lustily, drawing Star toward her and out of Ethan's hold. "It was an absolute pleasure meeting you."

Ethan looks away so that he doesn't have to see the way Star shivers into the kiss. When he looks back, Rachel is gone, and Star is dragging Lilliana back on the dance floor. A chill washes down his arms in the heat of the club. Loneliness sinks its talons deep into him, and he orders another drink so that he has something to do while he waits for Star.

It's here. He can sense it.

The priest pulls off his helmet, securing it to his bike. His heart hammers as he tugs his gloves off one finger at a time, eyes wide and searching. The music of the club thumps, and the bouncer stands up from the stool he's perched on as the priest approaches. The priest waves his hand, and the magic shimmers in the air before the bouncer sits back down, looking a little dazed.

The line outside the club yells angrily at him, but he ignores it.

He pulls open the doors, and the aura hits him so strongly he stumbles back.

The Vessel is definitely here. He can practically taste the humming magic. The people around him have no idea the effects of it. They writhe together, high off the proximity of pure Life. It's too potent for them to react to his magic commanding them to part to make a path for him. He sighs and dives in.

He pushes and squeezes through, shoving off the occasional wandering hands that are starved for any sort of physical sensation. He gets stuck at one point, being drawn into an undulating ball of pleasure seekers that are high off the magic from the star, the same they sense within him from the pearl. It takes a moment for him to wrench his body away.

Then, he sees it.

Or her. The Vessel has mortal form. No, not completely mortal. Almost. Yes. It's getting closer. He's made it in time.

He reaches her and stands there for a moment, taking her in while she dances, lost in the heady moment of her own magic and the undulating humans reveling around her. By God, she's...*beautiful*.

Finally, he reaches out and touches her, his bare fingers wrapping around her bicep. The echoing hum of the pearl vibrates through his whole form. His thumb smooths over her skin before pulling her to him, turning her. His hands slide up to cup her face, slipping to feel her hair, drawing the long ponytail forward. His breath shivers with his body, with her body, their magic twining. Her blue eyes flare, light growing in them, and he feels his own heat in response.

His voice is a desperate whisper, his blood hammering in him. "Come, Vessel. Let the priming begin."

Her pupils expand, full lips parting. A moan hums in his chest, and he leans down to kiss her. He should wait, but the call of the magic, of the *Life*, is too much for him to resist. He must taste her. Just one taste. No more, or this club will rapidly spiral out of control.

The first touch of their lips sends a pulse so strong that the crowd ripples with the strength of it. He draws her tight against him, his fingers touching the band securing her hair. It bursts apart, the heavy length cascading down. He runs his fingers through it until his hand fists in her hair. Oh fuck, the call is strong. Too strong. He deepens the kiss, his mind shuttering away with his whole-body shiver. She's tense, body twitching but lips soft.

Her hand lifts, fisting in his leather jacket. Magic crackles, stinging him. His brows furrow, pulling back to look at her glowing eyes. There's something within them, something that twists his stomach. It's almost like an... aversion? Reluctance? His head tilts. Hatred?

A voice breaks through the fog of magic. "Hey!"

Someone grabs his shoulder, ripping him back. He only has time to briefly take in a bearded man before a fist collides with his face, breaking his nose.

Ethan doesn't understand the unbridled rage that fills him. There is a painful stinging in his tattoo and a strange panic that echoes in the back of his mind. It's oddly sobering, and he can feel the alcohol burning out of his blood. When the sensation hit him at the bar, he'd thrown up suddenly and violently, like something out of *The Exorcist*. But it wasn't bile that he threw up—it was the alcohol he'd drank. He'd only had a moment to realize it before his tattoo began to burn like crazy, and he whipped around to see that man touching Star.

Rage surges in him again, his teeth baring. He's not a violent man, but he feels like he could kill the fucker before him. It's ruined by a second round of puking, less intense this time, and blessed sobriety returns to him. He spits to clear his mouth, ready to punch the idiot a again.

Star is breathing rapidly, her hand trembling when she wipes her mouth. She swallows, and the fear and anger in her face tell Ethan all he needs to know.

He refocuses on the man in front of him. Young, with dark hair buzzed short, and a strong body with wide, muscular shoulders. The stranger shakes his head, hands lowering from his face. His nose is somehow intact, and the blood staining the lower half of his face and down his neck sizzles away in a shimmering mist. Ethan's eyes flare when the man's green eyes meet his to reveal glowing white pupils, the same glow that the fish monster's orb had.

The stranger flicks his wrist toward Ethan. "Away." Then, he reaches toward Star, his pupils like two flashlights. "Come, Vessel."

Star goes rigid, her jaw tightening. She yanks her body back violently, shaking her head, eyes squeezed shut. "No!"

The stranger freezes. He gives his head a little confused shake. "Excuse me?"

Why is the crowd not doing anything? They all seem oblivious, still dancing like nothing unusual is occurring.

Ethan shoves the man away, his finger pointing right up in his face. "Get the fuck away from her."

They can kill a fish monster and get away with it, but murdering a human in a crowded room is going to lead to too many complications, no matter how much the hammering in his head is telling him to do it. Ethan's body goes rigid, fighting the urge to lunge again. His voice deepens with the repressed violence. "You need to go. Now."

The stranger looks between the two of them, confusion written all over his face. He gives his head another shake before his features harden. "I don't have time for this. Fuck off." And he shoves Ethan's chest.

It's like a battering ram hit him as Ethan flies several feet across the room. All the air knocks out of him, and the ground is merciless when his body smacks into it. He sucks in air, hand fisting his shirt in shock. Fuck, it *hurts*. He wheezes, coughing, but no matter how painful it is, he needs to get back up. He needs to get to Star before—

Star has the stranger's wrist in one hand, her other hand wrapped around his throat. Her skin darkens, not like how it was when the fish monster attacked, but a flash of something deeper, like a void of deep, cold space, not in color but in feeling. Her blue eyes turn to sapphires, the man's stunned face illuminated by their deep neon hue.

Her hand slides up in what could be interpreted as an affectionate way if not for the crackling magic that sizzles against the man's skin. Her deep voice ripples the air. "If you ever hurt Ethan again, I will peel the flesh from your bones, strip by strip, until you're trapped in a living nightmare that no god can wake you from. Do you understand, human?"

The stranger doesn't speak, doesn't move.

Star pats his cheek tenderly. "Good." She shoves, the man stumbling back, the oblivious crowd rippling away from him. "Do not follow us."

Star struts over to Ethan, her hair rippling like she's underwater. She hauls him back up to standing, her hand resting on his aching chest. He puts his hand over hers, panting, their eyes meeting.

She swallows thickly before her jaw tenses. Anger washes over her face, and she takes his hand in hers, leading them through the club. He follows her, giving one last glance at the stranger, who is staring after them in slack-jawed disbelief.

The door blasts open. Star keeps her gaze trained ahead, not looking at anyone or anything. The cold night air hits Ethan, and he blinks blearily as if surfacing from a deep daze. Car horns blare and brakes slam when Star steps right off the curb and into the street. Ethan gives a cry of alarm, heels trying to dig in to stop her.

She ignores him, her staggering strength dragging him along. She saunters up to the first car and raps on the window. It rolls down for her. She reaches in to run a hand affectionately over the driver's cheek, her thumb catching his lip. The driver's eyes dilate, and Ethan feels a thrum resound in his chest as Star speaks, "Take us home."

The doors unlock.

Star opens the backseat, drags Ethan toward her, and folds him into it. She slides him over like he's made of nothing. The door slams behind her, and the hypnotized driver speeds them straight to Ethan's apartment without needing a single direction.

Pain. So much pain. The needling, sharp, electrical agony of the star's flesh nearly sends her to tears. Too much magic escaped this form, and the mortal flesh recoils against it. Her hands tremble, spasm. Ethan does not see it. His back is to her as he unlocks the front door. She swallows, her breath shivering, the sounds drowned out by the door creaking open.

Ethan steps to the side, holding the door open for her. She slips by, curling her shoulders in to keep from touching him. Her skin stings, and the feel of her dress is too much. Ethan pauses at the door, but Star doesn't look back. She hurries to her room.

Ethan gasps, his voice a low, broken whisper. "Star..."

She pauses, hand on Andrea's door. It *hurts* and it's more than the flesh now. Her insides shatter, the beating heart within her cracking open. Her vision blurs. *Friends*, he'd said. A sob nearly escapes, but she twists the knob and the bedroom door swings open. Of course he doesn't want the star. The star is not one of his kind.

Her voice is ragged, the unshed tears nearly robbing her of sound. "Good night, Ethan."

And she slips inside, the door shutting behind her. She rips off her dress, throwing it in the corner harshly. It's like insects are burrowing under her skin, their tiny needle feet and sharp pincers driving the star to the edge of madness. She rubs her arms, chokes on air. She just wants it to stop.

She's spinning, panicking as she collides with the floor-to-ceiling window in the room. She slides down it, her forehead thudding against the glass. The coldness helps focus her, helps ease the horrible crawling sensation. She sucks in a breath, arms wrapped tight around her chest, as she tries to center herself. Her eyes slide shut, and the spiraling slows.

But then, the whispers. Her eyes snap open. She forgot to close the curtains. The night sky glares down at her through the unobstructed glass, the hissing, crawling sounds burrowing into her mind. She squeezes this form's eyes close and tries to retreat from its senses, covering her ears, but it's no use. The whispers follow her, anchoring her in the form. Her teeth grind, her body curling in on itself, trying not to hear. Trying not to comprehend. Trying not to internalize the terrifying displeasure in the cruel words. But they're not words, they're *feelings*, a language of sensation that none of this world knows but her.

She tries to get away to hide in a dark corner of the room, but the bones within her ache too much. Trapped nausea rolling in her belly, her hands still covering her ears and pressing as hard as they can against them. She rocks, crying softly, trying to make it stop. *Displeasure. Disappointment. Rage.* Why does it make her glow within this flesh tremble so? She doesn't understand. She doesn't remember.

Her dreams try to rise in her mind, but she shoves them away. No. She doesn't want to think of the bleeding woman or the glowing wraith with its horrible words. She wants it to stop. She wants the pain to stop.

Her heart longs for the sweet grass and rustling of oak leaves, as her skin quivers with the ache of overstimulation. Oh, how she yearns for the warm embrace of the pool beneath the oak. But she can't, her crater is too far away. She's trapped, forced to feel, forced to hear. Forced to exist beneath this oppressive flood of sensation. She sobs harder.

Suffering. Alone.

Nine

E than drums his fingers rhythmically on the desk at the AT&T store. The whole task is taking twice as long as it should, giving him too much time to introspect about the disaster that was the night before. He sighs harshly through his nose. At least he's not hungover, even if the memory of him projectile vomiting across the bar will haunt him for the rest of his life.

And yet, he *wishes* that was the only haunting memory. He sighs again. What a fucking mess.

The rhythmic, incessant *ching ching* of Star's fidget spinner beside him is not helping his mood at all. She's been obsessed with the stupid thing all morning, and it is slowly driving him insane.

He takes another calming breath, one of many today, to keep himself from chucking the toy across the store. No matter how satisfying it would be to watch it shatter against the wall, she'd be sad and he'd be an asshole. And her being sad would be far worse than the noise. Well, sadder than she already is. They've barely said more than a few words to each other all morning. Just a "We should go get new phones this morning" and a silent nod of agreement.

He pinches the bridge of his nose, eyes closing. Maybe it is all his fault. He got drunk because he couldn't deal. And because of his drunkenness, he wasn't with her to stop that psycho from kissing her. No wonder Star was so cold to him when they got home last night. He needs to come up with a way to fix it.

Maybe Mike was right. Ethan should've gotten over his hesitancy and danced with Star like he wanted to. Hell, he would've *loved* to dance with her.

Then again, she didn't want to dance with him. She wanted to dance with *Rachel*.

Jealousy roars, and he tries to shove it down but can't. His lips thin, and he mentally slaps himself for being such an unsupportive asshole. This is exactly what got him in trouble last night. He couldn't handle the rejection, and that creep got an opening while Ethan was distracted.

That psycho magical fucker touched her. Hurt her. Assaulted her.

Rage pulses in Ethan's veins, drowning out the sounds of the store as he fixates on what could have happened. Punching that man once wasn't enough. He should've kept hitting him until his knuckles bled and his arm fatigued. He should've protected Star. He *needs* to protect Star.

Ethan groans, his hand uncurling to rub his face. Andrea was right. He should've driven them to Montana.

"Here you go, man."

Ethan startles, blinking blearily at the salesperson. He eases off his elbows, hands resting on the table. Two brand new smartphones sit on the counter with the sturdiest, most waterproof, lifeproof, monsterproof cases they sell. His gaze slides over to Star, waiting for her to say something about the more heavily designed but less solid cases along the walls.

Her continued silence unnerves him.

He half listens to the breakdown of the phones while his mind wanders to his previous obsessive thoughts. His jaw clenches, teeth lightly grinding. He should've stayed sober, should've stayed present, should've been there to protect her. He was a fool to get lulled into a false sense of safety while they enjoyed being tourists.

Never again. Focus. Productive action. Safety. Those are what is important.

Their phones up and running, he and Star leave together to walk back to his place. Ethan looks around, taking in the lovely San Francisco summer day. The sun is out, and a cool ocean breeze ruffles his hair. He pulls out a spare hair tie and combs his hair out of his face, securing it into a tight bun. A "business bun," as Andrea likes to call it.

Hair now under control, he gets to work. Pulling out his phone, Ethan drafts and sends a series of texts. The first to Andrea, informing her of his new phone so that she doesn't send Lilliana after him again. The next to Lilliana herself, apologizing for disappearing suddenly the night before. Seeing as the crowd was under some sort of hypnosis, he doubts she was aware of anything that went on. Hell, he's not even sure how he was aware of what went down.

His tattoo catches his eye from under his rolled-up sleeve. That's twice now his tattoo has alerted him of Star's impending abduction, or devouring, or whatever the fish monster wanted. It's clear that whatever magic she did to make her own tattoo must've connected them in some way.

His lips part to ask, but he hesitates. If she knew or remembered the details of how her magic worked, she would tell him. What he *should* ask her is everything else that happened with that strange man, but Ethan is loath to bring up anything from last night. If *he's* feeling traumatized by it, he can only guess how she's feeling. Best to leave it be for now. Give her space to process, space that he desperately needs too.

He peeks at Star from the corner of his eye. She's looking down, arms lightly around her middle. Even her hair is muted. It's painful to see, even more painful than his personal discomfort.

He presses his lips in a tight line before looking back at his phone. He needs to focus. He taps away a quick text to Andrea. *What the hell do I say to Jenny?*

He doesn't have to wait long for her reply. *Hey gurrrl, I've got a fish monster trying to slice me up like sashimi and wanna know if you've heard of it. Congrats on your successful procreation! Hope the sperm is biologically sound.*

He snorts. *Be serious.*

Just send something. Like she's pretty cool, right? And you're friends.

She has a point. He's about to respond when another text from Andrea pops in. *If she was comfortable enough to ask you for sperm, then you have the right to ask her about creepy fish.*

There are many reasons he's grateful for his vasectomy, but the most unexpected one by far was the easy bow out for when Jenny and Katie asked for his genetic donation almost a year ago.

Flattered though he may be, there will be no little Ethans. Ever.

Emboldened, he drafts a text. Redrafts it. Almost walks into traffic. Redrafts it again.

Lilliana texts him back. He saves his drafted text to Jenny and opens Lilliana's message. His heart pangs, and his eyes tighten. The urge to delete the text is strong, but he resists. It's time to work on fixing the wrongs he made with Star. With a wave of grief, he forwards the message. A little *ding* sounds next to him, and Star pulls out her phone from where she slid it into her back pocket. Her brows furrow.

He tries on a smile, but it's not quite natural. Hopefully, Star doesn't notice. At least he manages to keep his tone light. "It's Rachel's contact." This is the right thing. It hurts, but this is what she wants. "So, you can message her if you decide you want to meet up."

"Oh." She tucks her phone away again with a soft "thank you."

Now it's his turn for his brows to furrow. Okay, maybe he misread her needs and he should really talk to her. Something is wrong, and giving her space is not helping. He nods toward a café. "Lunch?" He's not hungry, but she should eat. He'll sit with her and try to coax her into talking. He can do that for her. Listen and hold her hand.

She gives it the briefest of glimpses. "No." Her eyes go back to the ground. "I'd like to go back home."

Now his heart hurts for a different reason. "Like...home-home? As in," he points to the sky, "up?" How the fuck is he going to accomplish that? But more importantly, would he survive sending her back? It's a punch to the gut, and his pain reflects on his face before he can mask it. He really did ruin it.

Star catches his flash of pained grief before he manages to smooth out his expression. Her face softens, and she tilts her head back to look up. She smiles when the sun bathes her face in warm light and marvels at the towering buildings' reflective windows. "No. I mean *our* home, Ethan."

The relief is staggering, the reason behind it much more than her planning to stay on the ground. It's the flicker of the old Star shining through the dark clouds over her soul. In that moment, she smiles, admiring the world in that awed way she loves to do. And even deeper than that, the idea of his apartment being their home warms his cold heart and softens his tone. "Alright." She glances at him, searching his gaze for something. He nods toward his building. "Let's go home."

Her eyes shine, shoulders rolling back with an extended breath. She nods, a smile flickering over her lips again. "Okay, Ethan."

A gaggle of tourists comes bustling their way. He places a hand on the small of her back, gently guiding her closer. Her small, delicate smile remains, and he keeps his palm there, the warmth of her body pleasant against it. They walk down the street until they reach his building. He holds the door open for her, guiding her in.

The elevator ride up brings back memories. He glances at her at the same moment she does him, and they both share the remembrance. He sees his reflection behind her and realizes he's smiling. His gaze goes back to her, and her smile takes a secretive hint. His heart jumps.

She scuffs her shoe and nudges him with her shoulder.

He can almost feel the heat of Parkfield and smell the fizzy sweetness of her first soda at the gas station when she did the same thing while teasing him about his smiles. But this time, there's no Andrea to interrupt the moment. It's just the two of them. Alone. And Ethan's heart soars.

His hand slides from her lower back to her hip, and she shifts her weight subtly from one leg to the other to bring her body closer to his, their sides brushing. His pulse quickens as their gazes meet in their reflections. Star wraps her arm around her middle, and his breath catches when her fingers lace with his on her hip. Her other hand lifts to stroke the neckline of her sundress, her lips parting.

All that from just one genuine smile from him. He's a fucking idiot. She told him she finds him hard to read, and in a single day he's completely forgotten about that. No more. He's going to fully commit to showing his true emotions from now on.

His iced-out face and instinct to bury his feelings were always a point of contention in all his other relationships, but he could never bother with breaking the habit. It always felt like too much work to be worth it. Maybe this time it won't feel the same. Already, slips have easily happened. Maybe if he works on it, uses some of the tools his therapist gave him, he could break the instinct.

He squeezes her fingers and leans against her. He can do this for Star.

Her head rests against his shoulder, her eyes closing, like this small affection is taking a great burden from her. His heart aches, and he rests his head on hers. The sweet scent of her hair fills his nose, and he breathes it in deep to the bottom of his lungs, the tightness in his neck and shoulders easing as he exhales.

The elevator pings at their floor. Begrudgingly, he lifts his head. He keeps his arm around her and uses his other to ensure the door stays open as he leads her through it. They walk side by side, still wrapped together.

Star rests her head against him, a sleepiness slowing her speech. "Thank you for the phone. Maybe Andrea can teach me how to get those app things I liked so much on hers."

"I'm sure she'd love that. I put her contact on your phone so you can message or call her."

Her eyes regain some of their previous sparkle. "I think...that would be fun. I do miss her." She looks up at him excitedly while he pulls out his keys. "Do you think she'll come here?"

He shrugs, opening the door for her. "Maybe." He locks the door firmly behind them while Star waits expectantly for him. The hall is too narrow to walk comfortably side by side. He misses her warmth acutely as he leads the way down the hall and takes the right turn by Andrea's bedroom to the living room and kitchen. "She can be hard to predict like that. If I keep fucking up, then for sure she w—JESUS FUCKING CHRIST!" He slams his arm out protectively against Star's chest. "Mom!"

His mother smiles brightly from her position on his living room sofa. It's not a normal smile though. There's a hint of pent-up rage behind her dark eyes that sends a cold shiver down his spine. The rest of her is deceptively relaxed in her immaculate smart black pantsuit, her Birkin sitting in a place of honor beside her. She still retains an elegant ageless quality, the artfully streaked grays in her black hair the only hint that she's a touch over sixty.

Her calculating eyes sweep Star before locking on him. He instantly feels nine years old before he remembers he's almost forty. Her musical voice fills the room, even though it's softly spoken. Always softly. "Baby, I was worried."

If he dies at fifty from a heart attack, it will be because of this woman and not the burger a day he consumed in college. Catching his breath, he tosses his keys on his kitchen island with a jarring clatter. "The key was for emergencies *only* and how the fuck—"

"Language."

Christ, spare him. He resists rolling his eyes. It will only make things worse. Her breaking into his place again tells him all he needs to know about her current mental state. There's a manic edge in her gaze that sharpens further, her shoulders tensing. In response, his voice smooths out with his facial features, and she eases slightly. Maybe they'll get through this conversation without her throwing something. "How did you know I was back?"

Her smile widens. "Well, you know my good friend Kathleen lives down the hall. *She* let me know, even though my own son couldn't be bothered."

Ethan has a decision to make. He can either get into a fight with his mother about spying on him or ignore it in hopes of getting her out of here before—

"And who is this lovely woman?"

—she gets too interested in Star.

God fucking damn it! His eyes dart to where Star hasn't moved from the hallway's shadow. His hands turn clammy, and he clears his throat. "This is Star. Star, this is my mother, Josette. Mom, Star is—" His mind stutters before he remembers Andrea's backstory. "Andrea's friend from Parkfield. She's staying with me while she gets established in the city."

His mother's shrewd eyes widen, placid smile firmly in place. "Andrea's friend? How nice. Does this mean you're twenty-three as well?" Her eyes flash in that hungry way that makes Ethan sweat. "Or are you older? Thirty? Twenty-nine?"

He doesn't have much time. He quickly shoves Star toward Andrea's bedroom before his mother can stand and drag her over to the couch to interview as potential marriage material. "Star, do you mind giving my mother and me a moment? Okay. Thanks. Bye." He slams the door in Star's bewildered face.

His mother's musical voice drills into his ears. "I'll take twenty-eight, but anything younger and it might look like *grooming*, Ethan."

His real emotions nearly crack through, but he reins them in hard. "Mom. What are you doing here?"

Her lips purse. "I'm hurt, baby. You don't text, you missed our weekly call, you don't tell me you're in town. You're my only baby, my sweet boy. It breaks my heart when you do this."

"Mom…" He paces slowly to lean against the kitchen island, arms crossing. "We talked about this. Remember? It makes me uncomfortable when you do these things."

Her eyes flash, and he feels dread drip down his insides. "Ethan. Do you know how it makes me feel when you say such hurtful things?"

He pinches the bridge of his nose. "*Mom*. Please. It's been a week."

"Oh, has it? A week of being shacked up with a young girl?"

This time he does roll his eyes, head tilting back. Here it comes.

"And here I thought you were more like me than your father. I guess I was wrong. What a shame. A waste." She shifts in her seat, rage clouding her face. She hisses, "I gave that man my best years, Ethan. *Best*. I was a good wife. Raised his son. Ran his business. Without me, there would be no money. None, not at all! And now my son, my *baby*, turns against me. What did I do to deserve such a fate?"

He could recite this whole speech by heart, but he knows if he interrupts, she's going to lose her ever-loving mind. All that crazy needs to go somewhere, and right now it's best to let it spew out to fizzle into nothing instead of focusing too much on him. Or worse, on Star.

"That hateful man, shacked up with the OR nurse he told me not to worry about. The nerve of him! Knocked her up when he told me he wanted only one child. Just one, Ethan! One! You! And you ignore me and hurt me so deeply." She sniffles, hand going to her chest. "I can't even see you without you yelling at me for *boundaries*."

Ethan's lips thin, breathing through the discomfort of her manipulation. He carefully steers the conversation. "Dad's a selfish dick for doing that to you. But you're so much smarter than he is, Mom." He eases against the kitchen island smoothly. "Especially during the divorce. What an idiot."

It works instantly, like he knew it would. She grows a cruel little smile, head tilting back. "Well, I did take him to the cleaners, didn't I, baby? Took half his clinic, and I still run that thing like the well-oiled money-pumping machine it is."

He snatches up the mood-changing opening. "It'd be in ruins without you."

She preens. "That it would. Does he thank me? No!" A sneer attempts to distort her face, but the Botox fights against it. "At least your half-sister isn't so terrible. I do love her energy during our holidays."

He nods. "She does prefer you to him." A sad fact, but as long as Ethan gets sucked back into visiting his mother's side for the holidays, Andrea will come to watch the show.

His mom's lip twitches. "Excellent taste. And lovely." She clicks her tongue, head tilting. "Too bad she insists on looking so manly."

And it's time for her to go. "Did you come into the city just to see me, or do you have a lunch to get to?"

She shakes her head, brushing imaginary dust from the sofa. "I was thinking of stopping by Kathleen's for a refreshment, since my son has no manners."

All he wants is to snap, *"If I give you water, then you'll never fucking leave,"* but he holds his tongue. It's like giving a mouse a cookie, the narcissistic parent edition. Somehow, Barnes and Noble never stocked that issue. He forces a smile before she tells him what he really wants to say. "Well, don't want to keep Kathleen waiting."

His mother smoothly unfolds. She was a dancer with the San Francisco ballet in her former life, and that gracefulness still follows every movement. Her stylish flats tap softly on his hardwood as she approaches him.

Her hand cups his cheek. "I do miss you, baby. I love you so much." Her smile softens. "My sweet boy. So handsome." She rests her hand on his chest mournfully. "It's a shame you have such issues with finding a wife. I do still hope for grandbabies."

The shame and guilt of his secret surgery eat him alive. "I'll walk you out."

She pauses in front of Star's door, and his pulse spikes. His mother gives him a thoughtful once over. "Are you sure nothing is going on between the two of you?"

He swallows, nodding. "We're just acquaintances. Fresh friends, if you will."

"Hm."

"I'm serious. There's nothing going on. I'm just helping her out." *Please don't hurt her with your bullshit.*

She purses her lips again, eyeing the door. "Pity. She is quite lovely. Would make excellent babies if she fixes her hair."

He might throw up from stress, and that would make three more times than he ever wanted in twenty-four hours. He thinks quickly, trying to throw his mother off Star's scent. "And she's twenty-five."

Her reaction is immediate. She cringes away from the door, her lip curling. "Oh *no*. Too young for you. Seriously, Ethan. *Grooming*." She brightens and struts through his apartment. "Isn't that a fun little term? I learned it from Linda. It's all the hot new rage in scandals. So funny. In my day, it was nothing to blink at. Just look at that filthy father of yours."

"Yes, and the divorce rates were never better."

His mother's hand is on the door handle. So close. She turns back to him, her finger on her chin. "You know, I took a look in your fridge, and you should really get some produce for salads. Not fruits, too much sugar. *Diabetes*, Ethan. Especially for that new...friend of yours."

His heart plummets. He was so close, so fucking close, to getting her out of his place before she tipped over to this shit. He contemplates punting her out the window. Star, who is lovely and perfect in every way, and has never had passive aggressiveness of any form directed at her, does not need this toxic shit anywhere near her or on this planet.

His mother's dark eyes flick over him. "For you too."

He goes cold and hot at the same time. "Bye, Mom." He reaches around her and wrenches the door open.

She smiles obliviously at him. "Have a good Sunday, baby. I love y—"

"Yeah, love you too." The door slams in her face.

He locks the deadbolt for good measure.

His whole body is winding tight, tension suffocating him. With a *mmf* he cracks his neck, rolling his shoulders, trying to shake it. It's a short distance to Star's door. He raps on it. "Star?"

Silence.

The door cracks open. She's unreadable, blue eyes dull. "Yes, Ethan?"

Where does he even begin? "I just..." *Wanted to make sure you're okay. That you didn't hear my toxic mother. That you don't think less of me because of her.* He closes his eyes, pain in his heart tightening his chest. *I wish I knew what was wrong, why there's this distance between us, and what I did wrong to cause it. I miss how it was before last night.* He clears his throat, stretching his neck again before opening his eyes and saying, "I'm going downstairs to the gym. I'll be back in about an hour." The thought of leaving her alone makes him sick, but it's not stronger than the pressure slowly building within him. "Do you think you'll be okay here by yourself?"

She hesitates, and he thinks he knows why. She's never been alone before. His lips thin. He can't bring her with him though. He can't stand the thought of her witnessing him like this. He needs a moment alone to collect himself, to get all this tension out before he bursts.

She nods, voice small. "Yeah."

"It'll just be for an hour. Tops." He'll set a timer on his phone. "Promise." He's already backing up. "I'll be back."

He doesn't wait for her response, his heart rate spiking already. He changes quickly, pulling on his gym shoes, and leaves the house, meticulously locking it behind him.

The treadmill is brutal, his burning body slick with sweat. His feet rhythmically pound against it to form a drowning white noise below the blaring death metal playing in his ears. He reaches forward and ups the speed. It's still not fast enough. He ups it again. Faster. His music and pulse and the thudding of his feet are all he can hear. Faster. The sound blares out all thoughts, all memories, everything. Past, present, everything gone. Faster. Run. Just run. Just keep running. Don't stop. *Run.*

The anglerfish face flashes.

He chokes, legs giving out. He goes down hard, the track shooting him backward and crashing to the linoleum. He gasps in pain, hand clutching his sternum. It still hurts from last night. Star didn't heal him, probably isn't aware of it aching. But it does, a little reminder of how helpless he was. Is.

He rolls over, his arms stretching out, and he freezes. Across his shoulder are jagged, bubbled scars that arc across his chest, the loose tank top he's wearing hiding none of it.

His chest pumps, his throat ragged. He's hyperventilating, but he tries to lie to himself that he's just out of breath. He's not though. He's spiraling. The room is spinning, and his hands splay on the floor to keep from collapsing in a broken heap. Sparks appear in his vision as he fights to control his breathing, to slow his lungs down.

Slowly, the sparks disappear and he exhales, head bowing.

Thank God, no one else is here. Most people on Sunday afternoon are doing their own thing. The humiliation of falling would be too much, let alone his panic attack.

He hauls himself up into a sitting position. He catches his reflection in the corner of his eye and sharply looks away. *Weak. Disgusting. Soft.*

His chest starts pumping again, and he hides his face in his hands. The tingling in his face begins, threatening to overtake him. He needs to breathe. He needs to calm. He needs to focus.

Slowly, he takes a deep breath, eyes burning. He stays like that, sucking in air, lightheadedness threatening to take him to the ground, until finally, slowly, he evens out. Another steadying breath and the tingling in his face recedes. By the third, he's able to return to his body, stretching out his stiff neck. Wrecking his body will not solve his problems. He needs to stop avoiding the looming threat coming for Star. She trusts him to keep her safe, and he's failed at every turn. No more.

It takes him a few seconds to find his phone and then even longer to pull up the correct contact. His shaking fingers are practically useless on a touch screen. Finally, he has the correct draft pulled up. With a harsh exhale, he hits send on his message to Jenny.

It doesn't take long before his phone vibrates. *I'd love to meet up! I'm on campus tomorrow morning. Does 11:30 sound good?*

His thumb taps rapidly. *Perfect. See you then.*

When he returns to the apartment, Star doesn't come back out to greet him. He lingers at her door, a sense of inadequacy keeping his hands at his side. At a loss, he turns away and orders pizza, which he eats alone. The only hint he has that she's still in her room is her quiet reply to his offer of dinner that she's not hungry.

The apartment is cold. Dark. Ethan goes to bed early to stare at his white ceiling, his mind spinning with all his failures.

That night, the star cries alone in the borrowed room, in a body that she made, in sheets that do not smell like her, in a house that is not hers. She does not watch Ethan sleep. She does not leave the room. The curtains are drawn tight, so there is nothing but darkness around. The pain in the heart she made is overwhelming, making the stomach this body uses feel sick.

The woman in her dreams haunts her. Cold and terrifying words plague her. The star does not wish for her body to sleep. She does not wish to dream of this woman again and feel so cripplingly inadequate for not remembering.

Let go of the dream...

The star cries harder, the pillow muffling the noise. She does not want to. She just wants Ethan, who clearly does not want her the same way.

Whispers come to her, and she whimpers, drawing the covers over her head. She covers her ears, begging for it all to stop. To just please leave her be.

Ten

A little light flickers on the beach like a beacon in the night. The Lophian glides silently through the water, the top half of his new head barely visible. A human is sitting alone on the sand, staring at the dancing fire before him. The Lophian observes the human, watching how he moves, the things he wears on his body.

The sand crunches under the Lophian's webbed hand.

Like a flash, he surges out of the water, tail whipping behind him, his needle teeth bared. The human looks up, and pure horror contorting his pale face. The Lophian falls upon him, the flesh tearing easily.

The human never had a chance.

The Lophian feasts, his stomach engorging, cleaning the bones until there is nothing but a white pile next to him. His long tongue wraps around each of his bloody fingers to savor every drop, even sucking little scraps out from under his claws.

He's ready now.

The final pearl disappears down his throat. The change is easier after having consumed what he wants. The magic burns in his gut, and he morphs, tail twisting under his belly until he stands on two legs.

His claws disappear to hide in his nail beds, and he runs his blunt fingers through his smooth black hair. His pure white skin glows in the moonlight, mirroring the bones beside him.

He picks up the human remains and throws them into the ocean, letting the hungry waves swallow them whole.

An offering, and a promise, of more.

His thin lips curl, his sharp teeth glinting. Soon.

The sand crunches under his feet as he walks toward the glittering lights of the metropolis where his destiny awaits.

UC Berkeley is a beautiful campus. The large trees tower over the bustling students as they shuffle between classes, the buildings glistening in the sunlight. It's been so long since Ethan has been on campus. A sense of nostalgia washes over him as he looks about.

Star is overcome with the novelty of it all. She lights up with starry-eyed excitement. She turns in a slow circle, mouth ajar, taking it all in. It's the happiest Ethan has seen her all day, and he is glad for it.

"And people...*learn* here?"

A warm flush blooms across his chest, and it's not from the hot summer day or from Star's jean cutoff shorts and pink crop top, though Star does look exceptionally stunning in both. Ethan has caught himself heatedly staring at her long legs and thick thighs multiple times on the BART ride here, and that strip of exposed midriff has stolen his train of thought until he sounded like a blithering idiot. No, the flush is from how much he missed Star's sparkly-eyed delight. It makes the hollowness of the last forty-eight hours stand out in painful starkness. "Yeah. You can take classes, and professors lecture on topics."

"And your friend we're meeting, she's a professor here?"

He nods. "Yep. Jenny. She teaches..." God, what does she teach? All he can remember is her thesis in grad school that she obsessed with and revised over and over. The one with the vase, and the woman. "I'm not actually sure. I think it's some sort of art history, with an emphasis on Mediterranean studies." Why can't he remember what she teaches? Is he as bad a friend to Jenny as he is to Star? Guilt tightens his shoulders and he checks his phone, making sure he didn't miss a message from Jenny "You'll like her. Probably. She's very...unfiltered." A common theme among the women in his life.

Star's attention on the conversation begins to wane as a group of theater kids walk by with their arms full of costumes. Her fingers graze her neck, and she bites her lip. He can practically feel her vibrating desire to follow them. "Is art that interesting?"

A warm, familiar voice laughs behind them. "Oh no. It's the absolute worst."

Ethan whips around. Jenny beams a too-wide smile at him, her bright reddish-orange hair glowing in a wild, untamed mane around her. Her brown eyes fill with fond warmth as she beholds him. "Bores the socks off most people. Hi, you." She yanks him into a tight hug, her massive pregnant stomach nearly knocking the wind out of him. He's forced into an awkward ass-out position and staggers to keep from falling. He pats her back until she releases him and turns on Star. She throws a boisterous hand out. "Hi! I'm Jenny. Nice to meet you."

Star hesitates, her eyes darting between Ethan and Jenny, her fingers curling into a fist. Ethan's brows furrow, but before he can puzzle out Star's odd reaction, she shakes off her uncertainty and returns Jenny's friendly smile. She clasps the other woman's outstretched hand. "I'm Star. Ethan's..." Her throat works. "Friend."

Jenny shakes her hand firmly, then shoves Ethan. He glares at her, rubbing his arm. "Ow. Should you be so violent even while pregnant?"

Jenny plants her fists on her hips, accentuating her large stomach in the loose, flowing dress. "When you said you were bringing someone, I thought it was Andrea. You should've warned me you were bringing a hot eligible piece of woman flesh!"

Ethan scoffs. "You're married. And pregnant."

"And the pregnancy is not helping. Give me an orgy, please God in heaven, I am *begging you*." She pauses, attention darting back to Star. "Oh. Wow. Are you, um, okay?"

Star hadn't breathed in the several moments since Ethan brought attention to Jenny's bump, her blue eyes even larger than usual. Her hands shake as they clasp together. She wets her lips, her eyes glistening. "There's...*life*." She swallows thickly, gasping. "Such...*magic*. Beautiful, pure magic. Oh." Her hands spasm, twitching to reach out to Jenny's stomach. "May I?"

Jenny is struck silent for the first time in the decades Ethan has known her. She nods dumbly.

Star smooths her hands over Jenny's bump, a little shiver going through her. "Oh. Oh, hello." She falls to her knees, and several students strolling by give them odd looks. Jenny seems frozen in place as Star leans forward, placing an ear to her stomach. Her deep, soft voice a mere reverent whisper. "Hello, sweet one."

Ethan's eyes flare as Jenny's stomach contorts with the strength of the baby's kick. Jenny jumps, hands resting on the top, but she doesn't pull away.

That hum Ethan associates with Star's magic vibrates through the air. Her whispers echo oddly. "May you grow and flourish in brightness and love, not a shadow cast upon your soul. Let darkness not linger, your life untouched by such wickedness." Star turns to rest her forehead on Jenny's stomach. "May all your wishes come true, little one. Blessings upon your journey through this world."

More and more students pause, a few of them recognizing Jenny, and Ethan feels unease creep up on him. He doesn't want to stop Star from whatever she's doing, but if a phone comes out, they're going to be fucked. He doesn't know what technology the magic creep has, but having their location broadcast on social media seems like a bad idea. He brushes his hand along Star's shoulder. "Star?"

Her trance breaks. Star smoothly stands, Ethan's hand slipping from her shoulder, and Ethan swears the baby reaches out toward her as she steps back. Tear stains glisten on Star's cheeks, and she smiles. "Thank you, Jenny, for the wonderful gift you've given me."

Ethan clears his throat, anxious to get them out of the public eye as fast as humanly possible. "Jenny?"

She turns to him, her eyes still wide with shock. He nods toward the crowd. "Maybe we can talk somewhere private?"

"A star..."

Jenny's voice is breathless, her eyes glistening. The mug of now-cold tea she's holding trembles slightly in her grasp, and Ethan plucks it from her before it spills. Her office hasn't changed much over the years. Small, just enough for her desk and two comfortable chairs. The rest of the space is taken over by wall-to-wall overstuffed bookcases, some with actual bound books, and others housing notebooks with loose papers wedged between cracks.

All the time he's known Jenny, she never got used to using a computer. She preferred writing all her ideas, always keeping a notebook on hand to jot something down, drafting on her laptop only when the situation required.

His lip twitches when he spots a familiar little bobble. From when they toured Alcatraz together, back when they first moved here after college. Back when they were together. He bought it for her when she joked about marriage having the same vibe as the famous prison. She had met his mother for the first time the day before.

Jenny wets her lips, her gaze obsessively raking Star up and down. "I'd say you're fucking with me if you hadn't, well..." Her hand smooths lovingly over her stomach, resting on the lower swell. She takes a shivering little breath. "What did you do earlier? Will it be safe for the baby?"

Star tilts her head, lavender hair flowing over her shoulder. "I spoke to the baby."

Ethan stretches his neck. He's still tender from his fall yesterday. Not to mention the ache in his sternum from his confrontation with the magic creep the day before. Damn, he needs to get his shit together. "She means the magic."

"Oh." Star offers a little smile. "I guess it was some kind of blessing. I'm not really sure myself. It just felt natural." Her fingers fiddle with the cut edging of her shorts. "I wanted to make sure the baby will have a good life. A happy one." Her fists clench before she looks up, beaming. "Full of light. And love."

Jenny's lip trembles. "Thank you."

She grasps Star's hand in a tight hold. Star squeezes it back, a softness washing over her face. "You're welcome."

They stay like that, the two women looking deep into each other's eyes. The silence stretches until it tips to being uncomfortable for Ethan. He needs to get them on track or they'll never leave. "Jenny, back when you were writing your dissertation there was a vase you were obsessing over. Do you remember it?"

"Oh, you mean..." She slaps her desk, throwing papers off until she unearths her laptop. She lets go of Star's hand so that she can wrench the screen open and turns it to face them. "*This* beauty?"

There it is. Bronze with a dark etching of a beautiful naked woman kneeling in a pool of water, her hair flowing down like a stream feeding it, her hand reaching up and holding a glowing star.

Jenny turns the laptop back around, logging in quickly. "She has been my whole life work. You see all this shit?" She gestures wildly about. "All about her."

Ethan's eyes flare, cracking his neck. "All of it?"

"Oh yeah. You have no idea. She pops up in every civilization through every great era. But subtle. One or two pieces. And always with this."

She turns the laptop around to face Ethan again. It's a shot of the other side of the vase, with two competitors facing off, both holding spears with large, curved blades at the ends. One of them is a man, standing strong and proud. Creatures of land, animals and humans alike, swarm behind him upon twisting vines. It's his opponent that makes Ethan go cold. Some sort of siren or merman challenges the human, its long tail coiled to create a base. Creatures of the deep ride a mighty wave to swarm behind it. The two creatures mirror each other. Land. Ocean. The armies of the world poised for battle.

Ethan's gaze lingers on the sharp needle teeth carefully painted on the vase, the memory swarming him of their likeness hovering over his broken body with a guttural wet clicking, his blood soaking the cold, hard ground. White noise hums in his ears until it pops, Jenny snapping the screen closed breaking the spell.

She tosses her laptop at him, and he fumbles it with a growled, "Christ, Jenny. Tech is fragile."

Firmly ignoring him, she stands and nearly smacks him in the face with her large stomach. She talks very quickly. "She's some sort of fertility goddess that's depicted as either a human woman or a siren." She throws books on the desk, sending loose paper fluttering. "Usually seen as a great gift to this world, a piece of life and magic. A blessing, if you will." She sits down heavily with several notebooks. "But not always."

She flips through the pages before slapping her hand down. "Here. Okay. So. During *my* sabbatical—which was wonderful by the way, thanks for asking—I went to Italy. A researcher over there reached out to me because he knew I had this multidepartmental catalogue. I'm not only talking about art of her, I'm talking about legends, myths. Marine biologists who find things that can't be explained. Hell. Fuck. Wait. Okay, yes. So, I went to Italy to meet him. Do you know what he was doing in Italy?" Her eyes flash. "He was part of the research team excavating Pompeii.

"He oversaw the collecting of any recounting of the volcanic eruption and found one that depicted something unusual. A fisherman witnessed a terrifying creature burst forth from the waters to capture a glowing goddess resting on the beach. A fearsome warrior intervened but ultimately failed to save her from being dragged into the water. The next day Vesuvius erupted."

Jenny takes a deep breath, her freckled face bright red with excitement. "I'm telling you, I might have the most well-known archive of this goddess, but she is one of many of her kind. There are researchers all over the world trying to figure them out. Hell, I got contacted by a researcher in Japan who was looking into the tale of the sun goddess Amaterasu as mother to the imperial line. There is a legend that she left a string of magic pearls in the imperial treasury. Well, during the Mongolian siege in the 1200s, the emperor ate one of these pearls and summoned the divine wind, or typhoons, that destroyed the Mongol fleet, saving Japan."

Ethan's brain hurts. "Okay but—"

"There are other tales of magic pearls, like the kitsune and their pearls. Eat a kitsune's pearl and you have control of the spirit."

"Jenny."

"And that's not just in Japan. Korea has the same."

"Jenny."

"And Kappas."

"Jenny!"

"And Ikuchi!"

"Jenny." He places his hand on hers, and she settles. Trying to get Jenny to focus is a full-time job. "You've lost me."

Jenny huffs a breath and presses a hand to her chest. She starts again, slower. "There are legends of falling stars all over the world. Goddesses of great magic and power. With these tales are stories of pearls, gifts from the goddesses. Each one links to great changes in history, a golden age, or a war. But there's more. Water creatures, like the one you described. Let's just choose one…" She snaps her fingers, pointing at Ethan. "Ikuchi! The ikuchi was a massive sea serpent in Japan, so large that it would take three days to sail around it. In fact, there are even tales in Korea and China of similar creatures. Sometimes they're described as dragons. Hell, up until the world wars, these sea serpents were still noted in literature. Think about it. Mermaids, sirens, giant squids, Moby fucking Dick. Monstrous sea creatures are not abnormal. Just ask Katie. Her department is currently applying for funding for another deep-sea dive."

Jenny's eyes glint with madness, her chest heaving. "It all links to the great game." She snatches her laptop off Ethan's lap, showing the back of the vase. "The Game of Fallen Stars. Two Contenders." She points to the man. "The Land." She points to the siren. "The Ocean." She flips the image to the woman. "And the Star. Whoever consumes the Star will be granted the raw, untamed magic to hold dominion over the Earth, whether for the greater good or mass destruction."

Ethan swallows, cold seeping down his limbs. The snap of Jenny's laptop shutting makes him jump, refocusing. Jenny beams. "Cool, huh?" She turns toward Star. "So, what do—oh." Her face falls. "Oh. Oh geez."

Ethan whips around, and his heart stutters. Tears fall steadily from Star's closed eyes. He reaches out, taking her hand. "Star?"

She sucks in a shuddering breath, blinking her eyes open to behold Jenny. Her voice is whisper quiet. "May I see the vase again?"

Jenny fumbles her laptop. "Oh yes. Of course. Here." She pulls up the full photo.

Star squeezes Ethan's hand until it goes numb, and he just grips back. Her fingers quiver when she reaches out and gently strokes the image. "Astra."

Jenny's eyes widen. "What did you say?"

Star's voice strains. "Astra. It's Astra." She crumbles, sobs overtaking her. Ethan doesn't think about what he should or shouldn't do. He just moves and falls to his knees in front of her, reaching for her. The first touch of his fingers and she cascades into his arms, sobbing into his neck. She mumbles words he can't hear, her body heaving with each breath. He strokes her hair, and she tightens around him. He hears his name a few times and tightens his hold.

"It's okay, Star. I've got you. It's okay." He swallows over the lump in his throat, all of Jenny's words echoing in his mind. "It's going to be okay."

Jenny hands Star a mug of fresh tea, and it shakes so violently in Star's hold that Ethan has to assist her in stabilizing it. They're in a pile on the ground, Star curled up in his lap, his arms still firmly around her.

She carefully sips at it. Her lowered voice rasps. "I don't know who she is, only a name. Astra. Like a haunting in my mind. Maybe...maybe I knew her? I don't know." She rubs her chest, voice straining again. "It hurts. Thinking of her."

Ethan rests his head against hers. His phone keeps buzzing, but he lets it go to voicemail. "It's okay, Star. You don't have to. Just push it away."

She nods numbly, sipping. Her body tightens, curling up tighter in his arms. "There's more."

He waits silently, letting his slow, calm breathing guide her until her whispers fill the room. "I dream of her. She's the one I told you about, the one with the glowing eyes. Sometimes I can't hear her, and other times..." Her hands start shaking harder, the tea sloshing. "I wish I couldn't."

Star has sunk into a deep reverie, not even reacting to the spilling tea burning her hands. Ethan pulls the cup from her grip, startling Star out of whatever deep place she had been lost in. The ceramic clicks against the ground as he sets it down beside them.

Jenny's features are tight. "I'm sorry. I should've been more thoughtful. I let my excitement get the better of me."

Star offers a strained smile. "No. Thank you. I do appreciate your help."

Ethan's phone buzzes again. He ignores it, focusing solely on Star.

Jenny holds out her trash bin for Star to deposit her tissues. "If you don't mind me asking," she wets her lips, head tilting, "what does Astra say to you?"

With trembling fingers, Star plucks another tissue. Her voice is barely above a hushed breath. "Death." She swallows, tissue crushing in her fist. "She says the same thing. Always about inevitable death."

When Ethan's phone buzzes a third time, Jenny gives him an exasperated look. "Ethan. Answer the damn thing or turn it off. My God, man. We're kind of in the middle of an intense emotional conversation!"

Star curls tightly in his hold. "It's okay. I don't want to talk about it anymore."

Another buzz and Jenny looks like she's about to introduce Ethan's phone to his colon. He sighs, finally pulling it out. It's his mother. Three missed calls and several texts. This is exactly why he didn't want to get a replacement.

Baby, I'd appreciate having lunch with you today. Armaldo's at 1.

Baby, it's rude to not confirm.

Ethan Joseph Montenegro, respond to your mother!

Her inability to take no for an answer is not new, nor are the increasingly threatening texts when she believes he's ignoring her. He sighs harshly, catching Star's attention. He grimaces. "Sorry. My mom is texting." He types quickly. *I can't. Busy. Sorry.*

He goes to tuck away the phone quickly, turning back to the waiting women. "Maybe we sh—"

His phone goes off again, and he looks. His stomach drops. *Either you come to lunch or I go to your place.*

Damn her. She figured out he wants her away from Star. He hoped he had time before that happened, but there's nothing to be done now. "Star, I'm going to drop you off at my place."

"No."

He blinks, looking down at her. She's rigid, face still streaked with tear stains and flushed, her blue eyes glinting. He grasps for words. "What?"

"No!" She wipes her face furiously. "You're not leaving me again."

Okay, they are clearly long overdue for a chat. This is all his fault. He was defaulting to his old ways of giving too much space and waiting to see if the problem goes away on its own. Things were so much easier in Parkfield. Maybe they shouldn't have left.

Ethan says gently, "Star—"

"I want to go, Ethan." The look she gives him is so shocking, words flee. Stubborn and furious, her eyes are darkening. "I want to actually meet your mother, not get shoved out of sight again."

His mouth moves soundlessly but he has nothing. No excuse why Star can't go that could make sense to her. Hell, no real reason other than the deep gut feeling that his mother is going to make everything between Star and him worse. He glances hopelessly at Jenny, but she's pretending not to be listening. Finally, he sighs. "Okay. If that's what you want."

Jenny's grimace does nothing to ease his anxiety. His mother, whose main motivation in life is to get him married and procreating, excels at chasing away girlfriends she finds unworthy. Jenny, who is still his mother's standing favorite, would argue it's almost worse when she approves.

He texts his mother quickly. *Fine. We'll have lunch.* No need to elaborate and give her time to scheme.

Star nods, pushing herself to standing. Raw determination sets her narrow shoulders, her hair wild and messy from being curled up against his shirt. Her eyes glow. "Let's go." She marches out of Jenny's office.

Ethan scrambles to his feet. "Um—I—sorry, Jen. We'll chat later." He dashes after Star before Jenny can say anything. "Thank you!" he shouts over his shoulder.

A distant "No worries" echoes back to him. He catches up to Star and begins to prepare himself mentally for this trainwreck of a lunch.

On the way there, Ethan tries his best to describe what a narcissistic parent is, and even tries to prepare Star for some of the toxicity that his mother might spew like she did with Taylor. And Lauren. And a bit with Claire too. Many girlfriends, including Jenny.

He grimaces, raking his fingers through his hair. "It's like...she doesn't *mean* to say hurtful things. She just...does."

Needless to say, it does not go well. Star is determined. Her face and posture saying all he needs to know about the situation.

Jenny's text during their BART ride does nothing to ease his anxiety. *Are you sure about this? No offense, but your mother is one of the most passive aggressive woman I've ever met, and that bar is quite high. I'm in academia. Rethink this. Please. For the sweet lamb's sake.*

He tries to feign illness, but then Star tosses him a vicious glare, the likes of which he's never seen from her before. He swallows, hands clammy. There's no helping it. This is happening.

With resignation, he calls ahead to let the restaurant know that the reservation will be for three, not two.

Armaldo's is his mother's favorite Italian café to meet for lunch. Small, always crowded, but with large windows that help dispel any sense of claustrophobia. She is known by name after becoming friends with the owner a decade ago to guarantee a spot at her favorite table by the window.

Star and Ethan arrive exactly on time, and Ethan can't tell if that is a token of his good or bad luck. Still, he gratefully accepts the blessing of arriving before his mother. At least he has that going for him. He pulls out Star's chair for her before taking his own.

Ethan orders a glass of wine, but immediately cancels it in favor of water. His mother doesn't need the ammunition. He can hear her as if she's already there. *Wine? At lunch? Really, Ethan"* Or that look she gets when she's counting calories.

God, he misses Parkfield.

Star shimmies in her seat in apparent glee, picking up the menu. A small, satisfied smile plays on her lips, and he can't help the twitch in his. He has no regrets about having stopped back at his place so they could change into something his mother might approve of—though the chances were high that nothing they changed into will meet her constantly shifting standards. All the same, he's enjoying Star's appearance.

She practically glows in the sunlight. She's pulled her hair half up, little whisps hanging in her face. She does look beautiful today, the yellow sundress an excellent choice for her body. The bodice is tight on her chest and the skirt loose in flowing waves, her hips and thighs making it flare perfectly. Her delicate shoulders hold the thin spaghetti straps nicely. He wants nothing more than to slide one down and kiss his way along the curve of her neck, his teeth closing on her earlobe.

He takes a sip of water to cool the heat building inside him. If his mother ruins this, there will be hell to pay.

"Ethan?" says a soft voice from behind.

Ethan turns, brows furrowed. A woman he's never met before stands behind him, a pleasant smile on her face. A flicker of uncertainty tightens her brows when she notices Star, her hands gripping her purse tightly. The waiter pulls out the unoccupied chair for the woman.

Oh no.

The woman slides her brown hair behind an ear. "I'm Gabby."

Oh no, no, no.

"Um, you know, Janet's daughter?" She wets her lips, shifting. "Our moms go to Pilates together?"

He's going to cut off his mother. This is it. The last straw. He always wondered what would make him do it. He never thought it would be this, but here he is. Done.

Gabby's gaze flicks between Ethan and Star. Back and forth. She hasn't taken her seat yet, as if she's still deciding what she'd like to do. He doesn't blame her.

Her gaze finally lands on Star. "Hi?"

He hears Star shift, but he can't quite take his eyes off Gabby. It's like watching a car crash in slow motion. Star's low voice is filled with confusion. "Ethan, what's happening?"

He swallows. He should've ordered that glass of wine. "I think...this is a date?"

Gabby laughs nervously, and he would too, if he had any control over his body. She presses a hand to her chest and says, "Oh, this is so awkward. I should go."

"No." Ethan isn't sure he heard Star correctly. He wrenches his eyes from Gabby in time to see the skirt of Star's dress whip around as she stands abruptly. Her voice is strained. "I will go."

Ethan sits rod straight and reaches for her, but his hand closes on air. She's already gone, winding her way through the restaurant at an inhuman speed. "Star!" Panic laces through him. He stands, his chair knocking out from behind him. He flounders, straightening it, then tries to decide what to do with the check. Idiot. They just had water. He dashes away before stumbling over his own feet back to Gabby. "I am *so* sorry."

Gabby waves him off, shoulders tight. "No, no, please. I'm sorry."

"No. Really. *Trust* me on this. I doubt your mom had any idea either." He grinds his teeth. "It's my mother who did this. I'm so sorry your time was wasted. I'd offer to pay for lunch but I kind of have to go."

She nods. "Yeah. No. Go, please. Good luck. And...nice to meet you? I guess?"

"Yeah. Thanks. You too. Bye."

He swiftly goes to leave but keeps running into waiters or other customers until he practically falls through the front doors. He looks around wildly, heart pounding. There is no sign of Star. He grabs his phone and quickly calls. No answer. "Fuck!" He calls again. Nothing. "FUCK!" Enraged, scared, confused, he does the only thing he can think of. He calls his mother.

"Ethan."

His voice explodes out of him, several pedestrians hopping away. "You had no right!"

"Calm down. You're being awfully emotional. I'm telling you, it's the carbs. Your poor pancreas can't keep up. Might as well just eat straight sugar."

"Fuck you."

An outraged gasp. "Excuse me? Ethan J—"

"No. Fuck you. I am *done.*"

He crashes into another person, holding his hands up in apology. He can't seem to get his coordination correct. If he's not tripping over his own feet every time he tries to run, he's bumping into someone or hitting a red hand at crosswalks. His apartment is not far off, but at this rate it's going to take three times as long to get there.

"Ethan. You're being dramatic. Besides, you brought this upon yourself. Lying about your live-in girlfriend to my face. Please. I am your mother."

He splutters. "So, you what? Set a trap for me?"

"Not a trap. A test. And I was right. Besides, Gabby is an excellent choice. Smart, quiet—"

"Star was at lunch! You *hurt her*, Mom. Really hurt her. She wanted to meet you." He remembers Star's little triumphant shimmy in the chair, looking so lovely to make a good impression on his vicious mother. His heart aches, his eyes burn. "She was excited to have lunch with you. How could you be so cruel to her?" To his sweet, lovely Star who deserves none of it. His throat tightens, and he starts to gasp for air.

"Please, Ethan. I did nothing. You did this."

He stops moving, his building tears drying up with the white-hot rage that simmers inside him. His vision tunnels, the crowd shifting around him disappearing. She'll never feel regret, she'll never apologize, and if she did, it would only be for pageantry. And Star deserves a true, heartfelt apology. Hell, *he* deserves an apology. Something dawns on him, something that his therapist and Andrea didn't have to convince him of for once.

This is not his fault. It's *hers.*

"Mom." His words come out low and dangerous. "You had no right to do that. You have no right to try to run my life. You have no right to hurt the people I love because of your own selfishness. You have no right to hurt me because I am not doing what you want."

"Ethan!" For once her enraged snap doesn't make him flinch. "When have I ever done any of that? I don't understand why you are constantly trying to make me the villain in your life. It hurts my heart. My own son. My baby. The things you think of me are cruel."

His teeth grind. "Really? What about your little fucking comments about everything? And your blatant disrespect of my boundaries?" Hurt lances through him. "And your constant manipulations? Right now, you're doing it again. Do you even hear yourself?" He shakes his head. "No, you don't. I know this. This is how you are and you're never changing. I am done." He releases a breath at another crosswalk. He feels freer, lighter. "I should've done this a long time ago."

"What are you saying?"

"I need a break." He starts his chaotic run again. He has to get to Star. He needs to fix this.

Another exasperated sigh. "You've said that before!"

"Yeah, well, for real this time."

A sniffle. "Baby."

"No, Mom." His chest is tight, but the fear of Star alone in the city, ignoring him, when there are fish monsters and creepy magic men out there, overwhelms him. "I mean it. Until you learn to respect my boundaries, I can't keep talking with you. It hurts me."

Twenty-four hours since seeing his mom, and he's already fallen back into those destructive cycles he's worked so hard to break. "A month. Give me a whole month. Don't call me. Don't show up at my place. Don't have your friends spy on me." He forces the words out, the ones that previously caused such horrible fights and a dinner plate smashed against the wall. His heart pounds, his hands slick with sweat. "After that, I'll call you to schedule a joint meeting with a therapist." Margaret will be so proud. She's been trying to get both of them in a room together for years. "If you want me to stay in your life, those are my conditions. Otherwise, this is goodbye."

He almost slams into a light pole. What the hell is wrong with him? Is he drunk? No. This feels weird, like its intentional. Like Star doesn't want to see him. If he's right, then the worse it gets the closer he is to her.

Which means, based on the neighborhood and the direction he's going, Star is probably at his place. Hopefully. Panic spikes.

"I have to go." He can hear her crying, and though it pulls at his heart and guilt, his single-minded determination forces the words out. "Bye."

"Ethan! Don't do this to me. I love you!"

He hangs up. She calls back immediately, but he hits ignore. At the next ridiculously long red light, he blocks her contact.

Guilt and shame rear up, but he shoves it down. He has more important things to deal with right now. No more distractions. No more avoiding it because it'll be a difficult conversation. He's going to talk to Star, and they're going to fucking fix this rift between them.

The elevator isn't working, so he has to run up all twelve flights of stairs. He's drenched in sweat, his bruised sternum screaming with each heavy pant. It takes him three tries to get his key in the door. He swallows, gasps, and turns the handle.

It's jammed.

He scowls. "MotherFUCKER!" And he kicks the door in.

It slams into the wall and punches through the drywall. He huffs a half exhale and groans, his head in his hands. He tries to not be mad at Star, but this is getting a bit much, even for him. There's a hole in his wall now. And in Jenny's office, it was Star who was adamant about not being left alone.

Ethan stomps in and wrenches the door out of the wall. He slams it shut, twisting the deadbolt. Finally, he's in his apartment, a feat he wasn't sure he was going to accomplish. He leans hard against the intact wall and wheezes in breaths.

Just then, the sounds of sobbing from Andrea's bedroom reaches him.

Heart in his throat, he limps down the hall and hammers on the door louder than he means, but the adrenaline has taken on a mind of its own. "Star?"

The sobs turn to wails.

He pounds again. "Star? Can we talk?"

A wobbly "no thank you" is muffled by the door.

His stinging eyes squeeze shut. "Please. Star. *Talk* to me." His fists tighten. "I fucked up. Somehow. Some way. I know I did. Please. Star. Just open the door." His head *thunks* against it. "Please."

The door opens like he willed it, and a sodden-faced Star stands before him, eyes swollen and the blue extra bright from the bloodshot white of her eyes. Her lower lip trembles. "No, Ethan. I fucked up."

He startles at the profanity coming from Star's mouth. "What?"

She sniffles loudly, brushing past him to pad to the kitchen. She gets a glass of water, chugging it down. The glass slams on the counter, her hand trembling.

The silence stretches, Ethan keeping the island between them. "Star?"

Her shoulders tense, drawing up to her ears. "I misunderstood. Now I hurt all inside."

Panic flares. "What happened? Did someone hurt you?"

"*I* hurt me." Her shoulders tremble. "I thought...oh, Ethan. I'm so stupid. So incredibly stupid."

He slowly makes his way around, but the moment he touches her arm she turns away. "Is this about Rachel? Did she turn you down?" He can relate to that agony.

She shakes her head wildly, hair swishing. Her arms wrap tightly around her middle, her body rounding in. Her voice is so full of pain that he feels it echo in his soul. "I thought we were friends."

He takes a surprised step back. "Are we not?" News to him.

"I thought we were becoming something...more. Wonderfully more. Amazingly more. I-I-I was so excited. But I was a naïve fool. How could you want something more with me? I am..." She spits out the next word violently. "Otherworldly."

Confusion hits him hard, his head spinning. "What are you talking about?"

"I heard you. Yesterday."

Oh shit.

"Fresh friends is a new term. I didn't know what that was until then. And you told Rachel we were nothing and then there was that-that—." Her exhale is full of deep longing. "*Beautiful* woman at the bar. The ex."

His shoulders sag. He's an idiot. A fucking idiot. "Star—"

She chokes on a sob. "I won't ever be human. Not really. I can't even look fully human, and there are all these lovely human women who are here. I'm just an idiot. I want so much from you and-and it *hurts*. My whole heart *hurts*. I feel sick." Her hands slide up her arms. "I hate this feeling. I want to curl up and drown in my own tears to make it stop."

He huffs a laugh, combing his fingers through his loose hair. He moves around the island so that they're on the same side. "Star. Jesus Christ. Star." He searches desperately for the words. "Star, I *want* you."

She pauses, snuffling, her back to him. "What?"

"Fuck. Star. You are everything I've ever dreamed of. Hoped of. I wake up every morning excited to spend time with you. I just want to be with you, help you, talk to you. To me, you are... *Perfection*."

She turns slowly, eyes wide. "Really?"

He smiles wide, bright, tears burning his own eyes. "Really. Star, I was trying to give you space to figure things out on your own. I didn't want you to be with me because you had no other option. I told Rachel that we were just friends because I thought it would smooth things out for you. I told my mom the same because she can be so obsessive. I didn't want her attention to stifle you. I know..." he swallows, "I have a history of being hard to read. Emotions-wise. And my ex? At the bar? *I* didn't want to talk to her, that's why I didn't introduce you. I wanted to be with you, not her. If you want me, I'd like to be everything for you. Whatever you need. However you want me." He takes a trembling breath. "If you'll have me."

Her hands fall limp to her sides, her eyes renewing with tears. "Ethan. But...your mom." Pain shimmers over her face, and rage burns hot in Ethan's chest. "She doesn't like me."

His anger causes his voice to snap. "Fuck her." Star's eyes flare, and he forces himself to take a calming breath before he speaks again. "I don't care what my mom thinks. It's like I told you in Parkfield. I'm yours, Star. All of me."

A little puffed exhale whispers past her lips, and Star rocks forward. And then, she's on him, her body tight against his, her arms around his neck, her fingers snarling in his hair, and her mouth covering his. Ethan's world ends and a new wave of existence blooms, one where all he thinks and breathes and *feels* is Star. His arms wrap around her, and he meets her kiss with every drop of unrestrained passion he has. There is no gentle easing in for them. Too much has happened for that, and they kiss with the raw, unleashed desire of two people starved for one another.

Excitement, passion, and scorching heat burn between them. Ethan gasps against her lips before diving in again, her mouth opening to his with a needy whimper that he feels deep inside him. They kiss and kiss, sloppy, desperate. His scalp burns from her strength, and Ethan's hands slide hungrily over her hips. She wraps a leg around his and he bends, grabbing her thigh, tightening his other arm around her middle as he lifts her.

Star squeaks an adorable gasp, and her glowing eyes flare open. Her ass lands on the kitchen island, and the gasp turns into a purr as she hooks her legs around his hips and draws him tight to her. He smiles into her kiss and she moans, shivering when he licks her bottom lip before lightly biting it.

His hand glides possessively from her thigh up over her hips to her soft stomach, smoothing over her breast, to grip her jaw firmly. He guides her head back to slide his mouth to her neck, sucking and biting, shivering from the gasps and whimpers pouring from Star's lips.

"Yes, Ethan. More."

He latches on the curve of her shoulder he eyed so hungrily earlier, sucking, and she arches into him. "Mm, more."

"Oh fuck." His teeth graze against her skin, desire nearly burning him to ash. His hand slides down to cup her breast, reveling in the fullness of it overwhelming his large hand.

Her hand twists in his long hair. "*More*, Ethan."

He shivers, his thumb glides over the center.

She gasps, arching into it. "Yes! More, more."

"God, Star." Madness is overwhelming him, lust drowning his senses. He starts drawing tightening circles, eyes fluttering from her squealed "more, more." He could die happy hearing those words, more than willing to oblige. He starts to trail open-mouthed kisses down her chest, making his way to where his thumb is, Star's viselike grip in his hair encouraging him. His fingers tug at her dress's neckline, drawing the strap lower until the dress rolls down her breast, his mouth watering as the yellow fabric catches on her nipple before releasing it, her back arching to present it to him.

"Oh fuck, *yes*," Ethan groans, cupping her bare breast, lifting it and lowering his mouth tongue first.

The front door unlocks and they freeze, Ethan's mouth still open and hovering over her.

A familiar voice calls down the hall. "Hello! Oh fuck, what happened to your wall?"

It's odd, feeling like one is going to throw up from both relief and unyielding rage. His lips curl up in a snarl, but Star breaks out of his hold, tugs up her dress, and sprints through the apartment. "Andy!"

He hears Star collide into his sister, both women laughing. There are words exchanged, but he can't hear. He picks up Star's abandoned water glass and fills it back up, the rim hovering in front of his lips. He cracks his neck, eyes shutting. A low groan escapes him as he struggles to regain control. But it's no use. Every pounding of his heart is a *want want want*, and echoing in his ears is Star's moaned *more more more*.

He lets out a shivering exhale and downs the water. Andrea the Mood Killer has arrived.

Eleven

E than barely has his shit together by the time Andrea and Star enter
the living room. He refills his glass of water, not turning around to
speak to his sister. "How did you get up here?"

Andrea scoffs loudly as he chugs the water. "Like a peasant, thank you
very much. Christina drove me to Paso, and I managed to grab an Amtrak
up here and then Caltrain took me the rest of the way. Speaking of which, I
will be needing that truck back posthaste, if you will. Amtrak wasn't too
bad, but that was a six-hour trip that could've been three. I have tasted
luxury and I am not going back."

He nods mindlessly, staring out the window above his sink. Star and
Andrea start chatting, and he can't seem to focus. The frustration building
inside him won't ease. All he can hear, all he can think, is the *want want
want* growing louder and louder. Tinnitus rings in his ears and he wants and
wants and she's right there and she wants more. Gasps more. Moans *more.
More. More!*

"Ethan?"

The ringing pops, and he blinks.

The two women stare at him from the couch. He shakes his head, trying
to clear it. "Sorry—what?"

Andrea's scrunched face clearly says how many brain cells she believes he has. "I asked if you'd like to do an order of wings with our pizza, but you're clearly having too much fun staring out the window."

He blinks again. "Pizza?"

"Yeah." She arches a brow. "Food? Sustenance? *Dinner*?"

He swallows, bowing his head and squeezing his eyes shut. "Yeah. Sure. Whatever you want."

Andrea whips out her phone and types as she turns back to Star. "That guy at the club sounds creepy as fuck, girl. Glad you got out of there."

Ethan blinks. "You..." He turns his attention toward Star. "You talked about that night?"

Guilt hits him hard when she nods. She finally opened up, and Ethan missed it. He needs to get his shit together. Whatever is happening in his mind, this obsessive ringing, he needs to conquer it. For Star. She deserves so much better than what he currently is.

Andrea blathers on before either of them can say anything. "Yeah, while you were obsessed with the window. And I'm just saying, so please hear me out on this one, it's too bad Ethan didn't unalive him. Then you wouldn't have to worry about him showing up again."

Ethan fills up his glass again, hoping more water will cool the fire burning within him. "That would be called murder."

"I mean, would it?"

"Yes. It would."

"Eh, maybe."

He has a headache brewing. "Sorry, I was...I was distracted. What were you guys talking about?"

"Oh, you know. Star catching me up on all the fun city things you've been doing. Creepy magic guy. Jenny, who sounds as delightful as I remember. Speaking of which, who do you think Astra is?"

Star's shoulders tighten, her eyes dimming. "I don't know. I wish I did and yet..." Her fists clench. "I feel in my stomach that I don't want to know."

Ethan now feels stable enough to cross the room to join them. They're curled up on the couch together, so he chooses the armchair. Close, but not too close. His eyes lock with Star's, and the heated shift in her gaze is enough to make him feel weak all over again. The temptation to call Lilliana to pick up Andrea is strong.

Oh fuck, Star needs to stop looking at him like that before he loses his mind.

Andrea blessedly breaks the tension. "Have you considered that's why you can't remember?"

Star looks away, and Ethan almost sags back. Relief and frustration wash over him, the odd combination winding him tight. His leg starts jiggling.

Her low voice sets his skin prickling. "How so?"

Andrea sits up straighter and props her elbow on the back of the couch. "Well, you've got all this magic, right? I think we've been thinking of you as human." Ethan sees the deep hurt in Star's eyes, and he nearly flips the table. "But you're so much more than that. Your human body, or head, wasn't injured. Your other form was."

The pause stretches before Star's head cocks. "I see. Maybe you're right. I'm not sure what I was before, but the form that I landed in, I don't think that was even me, not originally. It's hard to explain because I don't really understand."

"Okay." Andrea sits up, excitement brewing. "Hear me out. So, there are these stars, these magical things with pearls, right? We got that from Jenny. If you are some sort of pure magic, I mean fuck. That oak tree is evidence enough. Then, maybe you can control your own healing. How good are you at using your magic?"

Star grimaces. "Not great." She flexes her fingers, making energy crackle. "The more I try to will it, the less it obeys. It seems to work best as instinct. The most powerful shows of it, where my will seemed to command it, was when Ethan was injured. Even when that..." Rage flares in her eyes. "*Man* touched me. I tried so hard to fight it, but it wasn't until Ethan was threatened that it just..." Her head tilts, her gaze growing distant. "Flowed. Synced." A little spark flashes on her fingertips. "Became one."

Ethan's heart swells. His voice rasps. "I'm glad you were there for me, Star. You really saved us, both times."

Star gives him a truly lovely smile, her most lovely yet, her blue eyes lightening and glowing with open affection. He wants to ease to his knees before her and kiss her so softly. Really pour everything into it. He's not the best at showing his emotions on his face, but he can sure as fuck express them with his body.

Andrea shatters the moment. "Maybe it's muscle memory. Forcing it will just make things more and more awkward. Or like, I dunno, breathing. If you think too hard about it, suddenly it's laborious and annoying. If you don't think about it, you just, you know, breathe."

An idea strikes Ethan, one that isn't just about sex. "Maybe it's your fear of what you were that is causing your magic and your mind to get out of sync."

Andrea glares at him. "Thanks for mansplaining my point, asshole."

Ethan ignores her and soldiers on. "Star." Her eyes lock with his, and he can see her displeasure, but he forces the words out. "You've accepted your human form with open arms, but what you were before..." He digs deep into his years of therapy. "She is deserving of love as well. It doesn't have to be an either-or situation. You can love what you are now, while appreciating what you were."

Her body is rigid, her hands clenched. Slowly, she nods. "Maybe. I'll think about it."

Ethan senses her not wishing to discuss things further. He successfully steers them into lighter conversation, but every once in a while, Andrea brings up the magic man to speculate his motive and current location. She tries to bring up the fish monster, but Ethan asks her to drop it when his stomach clenches painfully. He's already too strung out, too exhausted. What he would like more than anything is to take things one step at a time. Or at least, take the rest of the day to just be.

So, they order pizza, break out the beer and wine, and just exist. Andrea brings a different kind of joy to the apartment, and they all laugh a touch too loud, the two siblings bickering about the truth of past arguments. Star laughs merrily, smile bright, watching them like they're her favorite TV show.

It's a wonderful night. Ethan smiles when he catches Star smoothing her hand over her forearm. The lingering sadness in her eyes melting away when she gazes at her tattoo, her smile growing when she beholds the pizza slice along the other charms she's collected on her skin. She takes the moment to touch each one, lingering on a few, like the eight ball and the cable car.

Before Ethan knows it, it's way past the time when he usually likes to go to bed. Andrea stretches, groaning loudly when her back pops. "Okay. I'm going to go sleep in my very own bed that my brother lovingly bought for me with his own money in his house that is very much also mine. Sorry, Star. I hog the blankets, and Chris would kill me if she heard we shared a bed. Consider this your eviction notice."

Star meets Ethan's gaze, and Andrea gives him a pointed glare. His brain short-circuits. His mouth opens and closes like a fish out of water, trying to figure out the correct answer to their stares. His dick angrily shouts at him to offer to share his bed with Star, but that seems like the wrong answer. So instead, he says, "I'll...take the couch?"

He has no idea if this is the right answer. They both give him expressions so complex that not even growing up with narcissistic, short-tempered parents can help him decipher them. He clears his throat and tries again. "Star, please. Take my bed. I insist."

It seems like the right answer, and chivalrous enough. And yet, both women are unimpressed. Star drops her gaze to twist her fingers, and Andrea rolls her eyes. He can practically hear his sister's unsaid *Idiot*.

He sighs and scrubs his face. Lord help him, it's going to be a long night.

Andrea shakes off her disappointment and claps her hands loudly. "Well, good luck with that. Night, you two." She marches decisively to her bedroom.

Her door slams shut, and ringing silence fills the room. Ethan doesn't dare meet Star's eyes. He knows the moment he does, he's done. The best thing he can do is keep his gaze down and get ready for bed as quickly as possible. "Let me grab some stuff real quick."

He forces his legs to move before he breaks and begs Star to share a bed with him. But he's not sure how much self-control he has, not after he was barely able to keep it together when Andrea interrupted them in the kitchen. He can still feel the warmth of Star's body against his, his lips tingling with the memory of her kiss.

His teeth grind as he leaves her on the couch and steps into his room. Despite how disappointing it feels, he knows it's better this way. He won't have to worry about making her uncomfortable and taking advantage of her now.

Clad in a white cotton shirt and flannel pants, Ethan makes himself a makeshift bed on the couch. He became a couch-bed-making pro when he used to do this for Andrea's friends on weekends whenever they were too drunk or high to go back home and face their parents. Andrea had no qualms whatsoever about lying to all her friends' parents that he was their dad. That part irked him, but he'd much prefer them getting high in his apartment, where he could keep an eye on them, rather than having a herd of teenage girls wandering the streets of the city intoxicated.

Bed ready, he quickly turns off all the lights, the city's light glowing through the large windows and casting shadows in his apartment. Too tired to draw the blinds, he collapses face first on the couch, hoping the pillow will suffocate him. No luck. He's trapped existing within this insane sexual frustration, his brain practically throbbing with it. He sighs harshly, flopping on his back, arms thrown over his forehead. He stares at the white ceiling, trying to will his mind to calm down and his hands to stay above his head and safely away from wandering down to ease some of this pent-up frustration.

It's going to be a long, lonely night.

The door of his bedroom silently opens. Star stands there, wearing a simple cotton nightgown that might as well be the sheerest lace for how his body reacts to it. The thin fabric clings to her luscious curves, her wild, unbound hair framing her shoulders. Her eyes lightly glow in the darkness, the city lights reflecting in them. Ethan's skin hums, his breath catching, as she leans against the doorframe, her hip sliding out and her hand stroking down her body. His lips part with heady want, the desire to be her hand overwhelming.

She crooks a finger at Ethan, and only an act of God could stop him from obeying. He stands, his bare feet soundless against the hardwood while he makes his way to her. Her eyes sweep him slowly, and she bites her lip as her gaze darkens. It feels insanely good that Star might want him as much as he wants her.

Her fingers resting on her thigh curl in her nightgown, sliding the hem higher. The urge to fall to his knees before her to start at those beautiful thick thighs—to sink his teeth into them and soothe the sting with his

tongue, before hooking her leg over his shoulder and licking her to comple-
tion—weakens his knees. An odd wave of uncertainty locks his legs and
stops him one step away from her. The weight of what they're about to do
has him hesitating. Star has never done this before, and he wants to make
this experience like nothing she's ever dreamed of. But what she wants and
how far are the questions he needs to ask. Talking about what sex entails and
what she would like is the right and sensible thing. Earlier, they were like
burning wildfires. Now, they should take their time and ease into this. It's
the right thing to do, and he wants to do right by her.

His lips part, but nothing comes out. His hands clench to keep from
touching her. How the fuck does he even start this conversation?

Star's head tilts, and her smile widens, a flash of deviousness glinting in
her eyes. Ethan's heart jumps, heat curling low inside him. She twists her fist
in his shirt and yanks him forward. Ethan's breath rushes out, and her lips
seal with his. He groans into the kiss and opens his mouth when she
licks him.

All his fears and concerns wash away as his arms wrap tightly around
her, pulling her tighter against him. He falls into the heady sensation of her
body against his. His fingers snag in the cotton of her dress and inch it
higher until he grips her perfect ass. Her hips tilt into his hold, and she
moans into his mouth, stretching higher on her toes to kiss him deeper. She
rips out his hair tie and sinks her fingers into his hair. Her nails scrape his
scalp, and he shivers, gasping against her smile.

He doesn't protest when she drags him with her into his room and kicks
the door shut behind them. He likes this, her taking the lead. It makes it
easier, allows him to spiral with her. He can be her toy to play with. The
thought sends a jolt of pleasure straight down his body. She walks him backward, shivering when his teeth graze her lip. Oh yes, this he can fully get
behind.

The edge of the bed hits his legs and he topples backward onto it, his
arms around her taking her beautiful body with him. The thin nightgown
does little to hide her warmth, and he smooths his hands over her, heat
flaring when he feels the absence of anything underneath.

Her kiss is living magic, and he moans, tongue sliding with hers as his
arms tighten around her. Ethan always liked kissing, but kissing Star is a
whole new experience. His mind is foggy with this intense, all-consuming

need for her. "Star..." His voice is a breathy, desperate whisper as he drags one hand up her body to brush her hair back, his fingers lingering behind her ear so he can look at her. She's so beautiful, a blush brightening her eyes and her lips all swollen.

She smiles, making his heart flutter. Her hand covers his, their fingers twining. "Ethan." Her nose brushes his, and he trails his lips along hers, his eyes closing with the tingling pleasure, before drawing her down to sink into another deep kiss.

His chest expands, a pressure building until he feels it behind his eyes. This sensation, new and exhilarating, trembles his breath, and he kisses her deeper, harder, hotter, so desperate for more and more of her, his thigh sliding up between her perfect thighs. Her hips tilt with a heated moan.

A frenzied passion consumes them. Kissing, touching, it doesn't seem to be enough. There's a fire in Ethan, one that is mirrored in Star, and she gasps and trembles against him. Her thighs spread until her legs frame his hips. Then, her hips tilt to press and mindlessly rub her sex against his hard cock. His eyes squeeze and he bucks, the ache from base to tip desperate from the heated pressure. A breathy little sound squeaks from her lips, and she begins to rock faster against the hard line of his erection.

Ethan's hands tighten on her thighs, his teeth clench as he struggles to stay passive, to let her explore this new sensation. It's difficult though, pleasure pulsing and his body shivering. He tries to breathe through it, but his hands betray him. They slide up and under that thin nightdress to grip her bare hips. God, she's not wearing anything underneath. His thumbs sink around her hip bones, and a deep, rumbling moan vibrates his chest. Star gasps, and he makes the mistake of opening his eyes. She's flushed, full lips parted, her glowing eyes heavy-lidded with desire. He can feel her unspoken *more* deep in his bones, and his restraint snaps.

He plants his feet on the bed and rolls his hips up to meet her, his hands guiding her into a sensual rotation. He's well rewarded when Star widens her knees, sinking more of her weight onto him, and purrs out a heated "Oh, *yes.*"

She sits up, her hands pressing against his chest and fisting in his shirt, her head throwing back as she grinds with abandon. What he wouldn't give to be inside her, and he bites his lip, the sharp pain helping him focus instead of flipping her on her back.

Star lowers her head, her blue eyes glowing brighter. She pants and it gives a breathlessness to her voice that elicits a shiver down his spine. "Ethan...I feel...there's..."

His chest heaves, and he licks his lips, excitement sparking inside him. "What do you feel?"

Her fingers draw up his shirt, and she watches with riveted fascination as more and more of his stomach is revealed. Her lips part with desire as she rolls his shirt until it's gathered under his arms. "There's this pulsing inside of me."

Ethan swallows thickly, his teeth clenching with the spark of pleasure that twitches his hips. It takes him a second to speak, his voice deeper than usual. "Have you had an orgasm before?"

She shakes her head, her hair rustling.

He grins devilishly. "Would you like to?"

Her breath speeds up, and she nods.

He reaches for her. "Come here." His voice rasps, "Let me take care of you, beautiful."

She shivers and lowers herself into his arms. He kisses her, slow, deep, sliding his teeth along her bottom lip to feel her tremble before tilting her head back to kiss and suck down her neck.

Star whimpers, hips vibrating, and yanks at his shirt until he lifts enough for her rip it off. Her hands roam him in greedy, hungry strokes, and he smiles against her neck. He whispers against her throat, "Use me." He grips her hips, encouraging her to rock. "That's it. However you need. I'm yours."

She gasps, trembling. "Ethan."

He slips his fingers under her nightgown straps and slides them down her shoulders, fascinated by the goosebumps that ripple down her arms. He draws the neckline under her breasts, gravity and the tight cloth bringing them toward him. He salivates and groans when he cups them, shivers of heated want rippling down him. Finally, he draws one into his mouth and gives her a slow, licking kiss, pleasure tightening his thighs from the feel of her nipple against his tongue.

Her reaction is everything he could want. Star cries out and grabs him by the hair to pull him harder to her. He nearly suffocates, but he'd die happily like this. She feels so good desperately rubbing on him, pulling on his hair, and his only regret is that she's not sitting on his face. *Later*, he promises himself.

His breath trembles, goosebumps blooming over her skin when his breath cools his saliva against her breast. She's soaking through his pants, and his hands shake when they stroke down her sides.

Star moans, her fist twisting in his hair, sending a tingling shiver down his scalp. "More, Ethan. I need...I need..."

He trails his lips along the side of her breasts until he kisses her sternum. "What do you need?"

"More, Ethan. Give me more."

He smiles and tugs at her nightgown. "Can I take this off?"

She nods excitedly. He helps her peel it off and takes a moment to appreciate her naked body. He believes Jenny. Star must be a goddess. Soft curves, hooded, lust-filled eyes, lightly glowing skin. His teeth skim over his lip as he memorizes everything, until his starved gaze meets hers. Fuck, she's so desperate for him, her hips undulating in small, greedy grinds against his cock.

He swallows, taking a slow breath to steady his vibrating body. "If you'd like, I can use my fingers."

Her eyes flash before darkening. "Yes, Ethan. Everything. Show me everything." Her hands slide over her body, and suddenly it's like he's seventeen again and his cock throbs. If she keeps this up, he's going to come way too fast and humiliate the shit out of himself. He shivers when she huskily whispers, "Teach me everything."

He bites his lip and sits up, his arms wrapping around her. "Gladly."

And he flips them. Star giggles when she bounces on the bed. Fuck, she's even more beautiful like this, her hands limp by her head and her smile bright. She spreads her legs wide, and it takes every inch of self-control for Ethan not to rip off his pants and sink deep inside her. Fuck, he'd make her come so hard on his cock. Make her scream his name while he pounded her, her nails ruining his back while she sobbed in pleasure. He'd fold her in half so she'd feel every inch of him, her perfect legs over his shoulders.

He heaves in a breath, forcing himself to stretch out beside her. *Later.* He licks his fingers. "Have you touched yourself yet?"

Star blushes deeper and nods. "I was curious."

Oh fuck, what he'd give to be a fly on the wall. "And? Did you like it?"

She nods. "It felt good."

He strokes up and down her parted thighs. "But you didn't come?"

She shakes her head. "I wasn't sure how."

He smiles, nosing her gently. "Let's see if we can change that, shall we?"

The first slide of his fingers parting her is like pure, silken heaven. His cock twitches with unadulterated want. She feels so good. And she's sensitive. Her thighs shiver, her back arching, sinful noises pouring from her lips. He kisses her, nuzzles her, breathes her in. Pure sensuality takes over, their bodies rolling together, his fingers teasing her, testing her, his eyes watching her like a starved man.

He circles her entrance until her hips lift, the tip of his finger teasing in and out of her. A breathy, high-pitched moan from her lips has him sliding in deeper and deeper, soft, gentle, easing her into being penetrated with each stroke. His finger goes in so smoothly, his brows furrows in confusion. There's not a hint of resistance, which he expected from his memory of being intimate with virgins. But then again, it has been years. And Star is soaking wet. His mouth waters, and his tongue aches to be included.

Star's eyes pop open wide, her back arching, and he clocks exactly where his finger is inside her. He strokes and circles, rubbing that hot spot he knows is going to get her where she wants. She whispers his name, head tilting back, and he presses his forehead against the side of her neck. He can't watch her come. He's too on edge, his cock throbbing with the begging chant that pours from her. She's hungry for his fingers, so he slips a second one in, circling that spot inside her while his thumb slides up to press against her clit.

Star screams his name as she climaxes, her back coming off the bed in an arch and her nails scraping along his scalp. She tosses her head, her hips snapping, fucking herself on his hand, and Ethan groans, his hips flexing against her trembling thighs. When she's too overcome to keep moving, he thrust his fingers harder and deeper in her, kicking her orgasm up a notch. The wet sounds make him grind his teeth, and his desperation heightens. He hasn't come in weeks, and he feels it acutely in this moment. There is no way in hell he can have sex with her tonight. He'd come too fast. Hell, he's nearly on the edge from rubbing against her.

Star's thighs snap together, catching his hand within her pulsing sex. She pants, eyes closed. "Wait, I need...I need..."

He nods soundlessly, understanding how overwhelmed she must feel. He keeps his two fingers buried all the way inside her, his palm firmly against her so that the heel of his hand presses against her clit to ease some of the throbbing pleasure. His lips trail along her neck as he breathes her scent deeply into his lungs. He's wound up tighter than a spring, but his soul is quiet and rested. He kisses her damp skin, tongue lightly tasting the salt. Her pulse flutters against his lips, and he sucks lightly, unable to resist hearing her sharp intake of breath and feel her hips shift to rub against his trapped hand.

He soothes the small, red mark with a slow lick, and she shivers so violently she nearly vibrates. She swallows and gasps out his name, "Ethan?"

He kisses his way up her throat to murmur against her jaw. "What is it, Star?"

"Can...can you..."

When she doesn't continue, he lifts up his head to look down at her. This might be his new favorite look for her, sweat-soaked, pink-cheeked, and eyelids sleepily lowered. He smiles, his tongue catching on his teeth in a stroke. He can't wait to make this her new normal.

Her gaze is clouded over, her full lips parting as heated desire darkens her face. "Can you do that again?"

His smiles wickedly. "Do what?" He leans down to brush his lips against hers before kissing her sweetly, his teeth capturing her lower lip to run his tongue along.

She gasps, her gorgeous hips shifting, and her sex clenches around his fingers. She spasms when he licks her again. "That." She moans, tilting her head when he kisses her deeper, his tongue sweeping in deep. "But lower."

"How low?" Delicious, mischievous pleasure coils in him as he shifts down her body, his hand wiggling its way free of her thighs to assist. "Here?"

He slowly swipes over her nipple, and she convulses, gasping. "Lower."

"Lower..." He gently bites the underside of her breast. "This low?"

She whines, and it's music to his ears. "Ethan, *please.*"

"Hmm..." He trails his lips down her quivering body to her stomach. "Where could you want me to lick..."

He leans back, grabbing her thighs and wrenching them open wide. He holds them there and purposefully, so that she knows what he's doing, trails his gaze down her beautiful body to stare with a starved hunger at her revealed, post-one-orgasm pussy. He pins her legs down, holding her splayed as he runs his tongue along his bottom lip before sucking it in to bite.

Her whimpering moan draws his gaze back up to her dark, desperate one. His voice is deep, rasped, and she shivers when he says, "Do you want me to lick your pretty clit, Star?"

She might be strong, but he is too. He keeps her splayed there, hungry and untouched, until whimpered little pleas mumble out. "Yes. Please, Ethan. Lick me like that. Please."

"I guess I could try." His eyes glint, smirk in place as he slides down her body, sliding his shoulders between her thighs. He considers teasing her more, but her body is going deliciously lax in submissive anticipation, and he finds himself unable to wait. He slides her thighs wider and licks her slowly, her voice keening with pleasure and her back bowing. His swipe from her entrance to flick her aching clit sends a jolt of mirroring pleasure within him.

Ethan has yet to find a woman he didn't viscerally enjoy eating out, but sliding his tongue along Star takes the experience to a whole new level. He groans against her, licking over and over, reveling in the feel of her hips undulating with want. She reaches down, fisting his hair. He bucks, moaning into her, as his scalp burns. He eats her slowly, savoring her as he eases her into the sensation. He could do this for hours, happy to tease and edge her for as long as she wants, but a greedy side of him wants her to come. He wants to see it, feel it on his tongue, and then do it all over again.

They have all night, and he plans to use every minute of it.

He sits up, and Star almost scalps him with a strangled cry of frustration. Their eyes lock and he smiles, licking his fingers, her eyes hungrily watching him as he does. He lowers them back to her sex and slides them inside her, her back arching with it. He pumps gently, fingers curling around the spot he found earlier, before pulling back up to circle her clit, tapping it and smiling at the little gasp she makes. Her hips roll against his hand, growing slowly in desperation.

Then he lowers back down, lapping at her clit while he rubs that hot spot inside her demandingly.

Her orgasm crashes into her hard, sweeping her away with the force of it. Her hands claw at the bed for a desperate anchor, her hips shivering and snapping. He watches her hungrily, licking her through her second peak.

His gasped-out name is his reward, and he feels it all the way down his center, his lips closing around her clit to lightly suck with a languished moan.

When she shifts away, trying to gain a reprieve, he pulls back and sinks on top of her in a warm embrace. She surprises him by turning to capture his mouth with hers, kissing him, licking deep into his mouth like she can't get enough of her taste on him. He shivers, tilting to kiss her harder and deeper, his arms sliding under her back to hold her. They kiss until he feels her body settle into a lax, melted state, her chest heaving to catch her breath.

He pulls back with one last lick, smiling down at her. She's flushed, breathless, and soft. It's so endearing that he kisses the tip of her nose affectionately before sliding over to lay on his side. She blinks up at him, her eyes a swirling glow of sapphire and cerulean. It's beautiful, this kaleidoscope of blues.

She rolls on her side too, facing him, her fingers delicately tracing his brow, following the curve to his cheekbones, then trailing down to circle his lips. He kisses her fingertips one by one with a smile. She drags down his bottom lip before releasing it.

She whispers in the darkness. "I've always loved watching you."

His smile softens. "I like watching you too."

Her gaze is distant, her hands trailing down to his throat, catching on the dip at the base. "It's why he struggled to drop me. I held on...so I'd land where I wanted..." She pauses, her gaze going far again. "I don't like the ocean..."

His breath catches. "Star?"

She blinks, her eyes focusing. She continues her soft stroking down his chest, feeling the hair there.

He touches her wrist gently. "Do you remember something?"

She shakes her head, and his stomach tightens when her fingers tickle it on their journey down. "Nothing worth talking about." Her finger snags on the waistband of his flannel pants. She slides a finger under, wiggling until it hooks around his boxers. She pulls them back, and Ethan shivers, his hand trembling when he reaches up to stroke down her shoulder. Star's eyes darken, her husky voice like a stroke down his neck. "I want to taste you, Ethan."

His breath puffs as she slides his clothes lower, the cold air kissing his heated skin. His throat works, and he struggles to speak. "Do you understand what will happen?"

Star rolls him on his back, sliding his pants and boxers off his body. She kneels before him, gloriously naked and her eyes glowing. His heart speeds, and he lifts himself onto his elbows. "Star, do you understand what will happen when a man comes?"

Her smile is slow and wicked. "Lay down, Ethan."

It's a command he cannot disobey. Like a sacrifice to a goddess, he lowers himself back down, his heartbeat pulsing in his cock.

Her whisper washes over him in a shivering wave. "Grab the headboard."

His fingers tremble when he obeys, his biceps bulging when he grips it. Star crawls up him, and the sweet anticipation has his hips twitching, a bead of precum glistening in the reflection of the city's lights from the uncovered windows.

Her hand circling the base of his cock sets his teeth on edge. If he comes all over her face, he might never recover from the embarrassment. Then, her tongue licks the tip, and his shaky, whispered "oh fuck" brings a delightfully cruel smile to her face.

A thrill tightens his insides, heightens the spark of pleasure, and then she swallows him right down to the root. Breath lodges in Ethan's throat, his mouth stretched wide in a silent cry as pleasure pulses through his cock. Ethan is proud that he's larger than average and definitely thicker. Some girlfriends have opted out of giving head for long due to jaw ache, but not Star. She must not have a gag reflex. She sucks him off with a hunger that stretches his control to breaking. His heels dig into the covers, scraping them while he fights not to come.

Star hums, drawing back with a slow slurp that he saves in his psyche to replay for later. She smiles, hands stroking his shaft. "I love this side of you, Ethan. You're always so in control." She trails her lips down him to suck on his tight balls. "I love that I can make you like this."

He pants, eyes squeezing shut. "Star—"

"Come apart for me, Ethan." She licks her way back up to swirl her tongue around the head. "I want to see your control crumble."

Her words are his undoing, and when she sucks him back down into her hot mouth, his orgasm claims him. All he wants is to bury his hands into

Star's thick hair and fuck her mouth, but he bites his bottom lip viciously, muffling the deep shout that tries to rip free when pleasure floods his system. His bed creaks as he pulls on the headboard, his hips trembling with the intense restraint required to hold them still. Star takes him deep and doesn't stop sucking as she gulps greedily. He spasms, and her moan of pleasure has his eyes rolling back. He arches, his mouth stretching wide with a groaned growl.

He heaves in breath, his body coated in a layer of sweat. Top ten orgasm and all she did was blow him.

Star stretches out on top of him, their naked bodies pressed tight together. He moans into her kiss and peals his fingers from the headboard to stroke down her back and grip her perfect ass. He huffs a laugh. "Fuck, Star. Just...fuck."

She grins. "Did I do good?"

"More than good. You were mind-blowing."

She hums and strokes down his chest. "Do you think I can do it again?"

He grimaces. "Tonight? Honestly, maybe not." His balls feel like they've been wrung dry. That orgasm was too good. "But I'm willing to give it a shot."

"In that case..." She takes one of his hands and guides it down between their bodies. His gaze darkens, heat licking up him when he finds her hot and wet again. She mumbles against his lips. "Can I have more?"

He smiles, finding her clit and stroking. "As much as you want, beautiful."

And he delivers. Using his fingers and tongue and all the combinations thereof, he draws out more and more and even more pleasure from Star. She lays on her back and holds her legs wide open for him, crying out loudly as he plays her like the beautiful instrument she is, making sure she will never want anyone else. And when his hands start to cramp and his tongue give out, he heaves her up into his arms, showing off his hours of lifting to carry her into the bathroom, where he pins her against the shower wall, hikes up a leg, and uses the shower head to finish the job.

Her cries echo off the tile like an angel's song, his lips grazing hers to breathe them in. She sings his name, and he shivers each and every time.

The sun is starting to rise by the time they collapse back into bed. Relief hits him hard when he hears Star's sleepily muttered "more" that trails off into her passing out. He lets out an exhausted breath, telling himself *well done* and giving himself a mental high five before pulling the blankets over them. He drags her body tight against his and joins her in blissful slumber.

It's midday by the time Star and Ethan wake. She stretches in his arms, and he smiles softly, pressing a soft kiss to her bare shoulder. She turns in his hold, and her kiss is like sunlight pouring into the darkest parts of him. He smiles into it, drawing her tighter against him, their legs tangling.

He could live a thousand lives and never tire of kissing her. He understands why Amaterasu was the goddess of the sun. This light, this warmth. She is the only star in the sky to him. Perhaps whoever found Amaterasu loved her like he loves Star. Maybe that's why she gifted her line with magic pearls?

It's a lovely thought, and he holds onto it in both hands. He hopes whoever Astra is, she had a moment of happiness and love under whatever trauma Star does not wish to remember.

He strokes Star's hair back, basking in a moment of pure disbelief that this is real. That she chose him, not because he is the only choice, but because she wants him like he wants her. Now, she's naked against him, the feel of their bodies flushed better than he ever imagined. It's the best morning he's had in a long time.

The lavender strands tangle with his fingers until he grips and guides her back to him for another lingering kiss, Star glowing in bliss.

She sleepily mumbles, "You're smiling."

He chuckles, lips grazing hers. His voice rasps, "I smile. At times."

"Hm." She accepts his kiss. "Not like this. This is a real smile. A full smile."

His teeth close gently on her bottom lip, drawing it through to feel her shiver. "What can I say? You bring it out in me."

She giggles, melting into his hold. "I like that. I like that I make you real."

"Me real?"

She nods. "You're so stoic, even with Andy. Even when you're having fun. It's just flickers." Her hands slide up to twist in his hair. "I want to bring you out. Make you all mine."

He laughs softly, and she beams in pleasure. "I am all yours, Star. As long as you want me."

"Good. Because I want to eat you up and keep you all to myself."

His smile takes an edge. "Good. Do it. Devour me."

She snaps playfully, and he laughs again. She joins, eyes sparkling. She rolls him on his back, straddling his hips. "When do we get to do the other kind of sex?"

His hands smooth over her thighs, his gaze bouncing hungrily all over her naked body. Oh. He does like this. His teeth sink into his lip, his gaze heating as his hand slides up her thigh to grip her full hips, watching the way his thumb sinks in. There is nothing more he'd like than to have her ride him with her special brand of joyful abandon. Perhaps she could tie him up and make him try to hold out while that perfect body takes pleasure from him, her tits bouncing just out of reach of his mouth like a tease. Her cries of pleasure from the night before echo in his ears, adding to this fantasy. His other hand joins, and he rocks her hips experimentally. Oh, this will do. He'd love to make this fantasy a reality.

His smile grows as a realization dawns on him. This is much more than a passionate obsession. Ethan is so deeply, helplessly in love with Star.

He doesn't want to scare her, so he'll keep it to himself for now. When it's time, he'll take them somewhere nice to tell her the full extent of his feelings. Maybe they'll go to Baker's Beach to see the Golden Gate Bridge. No. She doesn't like the ocean. They'll go at night instead when the city is all lit up. She won't see the ocean then, and she seems to love all the lights.

Star's hands smooth over his chest. "What are you thinking about?"

He abandons a hip to capture her hand in his. He kisses her palm. "I was lost in thought about what this 'other sex' could be."

Star beams, fingers trailing over to his lips, and he kisses each one as she presses them against him. "The one that is penetrative in many..." Her gaze darkens, hips shifting. "Different ways."

His tongue slides over his teeth, his body stirring with heady desire to discover exactly what she means. "Hm. And how do you know of these other sexes? Is this what you've been using your phone for?"

"Please, Ethan. I know *some* things." Her grin turns mischievous. "Though the phone was useful."

He laughs, surging up and taking her to the bed. She squeals, wiggling under him and giggling into his kiss.

There is a pounding on the door. Andrea angrily yells through the wood. "Okay, I am fucking bored, and this place's walls are paper thin. Stop it."

Ethan is tempted to throw Andrea through the window. He hollers back, "Then go to Lilliana's!"

"She's fucking working! Get dressed and hang out with me. I'm hungry and want to order food."

He sighs, and Star laughs joyfully. She strokes his face. "I am kind of hungry."

Good enough for him, his frustration instantly dousing. "Alright." He gives her one last lingering kiss. "For you, and only you, will I leave this bed."

He hears Andrea's muffled scoff. "Rude."

Maybe the walls are too thin after all.

They dress and leave the bedroom. Star bounds out, and Ethan and Andrea purposefully do not make eye contact. This was by far the worst part of living together. He was always very careful to go to his then-girlfriends' houses, but never to stay the night. The guilt and sense of abandoning Andrea never sat well with him. That is, until he learned Andrea appreciated the nights of him away. It was one hell of a way to find out that his sister was not only sexually active but also a lesbian.

He snorts, cackling as he combs his hair back. Andrea gives him a strange look. He tries to explain, but he's too lost in his own merriment. Eventually, he chokes out, "Remember when I came home to you and Emily?"

Andrea huffs a laugh. "Oh God, I thought I was going to die of embarrassment. You have the worst timing."

"That I do." He can't stop smiling, his face slightly aching from the strain. Such joy fills his heart. He wishes this will never end. "Let's order lunch. What do you want?"

Andrea immediately starts tapping away. "Let's do Thai! I have such a craving for it."

"Alright. Order what you want. Just get a lot of it."

He brews coffee, Andrea and Star watching some movie together on the couch. Andrea patiently explains the plot and answers all of Star's questions. It's a perfect way to spend the afternoon.

The doorbell rings, and his brows lift. That was fast. Good thing too, because he's starving. Up all night and no breakfast, he could eat the whole order himself. He sets down his mug and pads through the apartment, combing his hair back to tie in a sloppy bun.

He swings open the front door and comes face to face with the magic man.

Twelve

Ethan's whole body turns ice cold. The man, who is just as Ethan remembers with buzz-cut black hair and startling green eyes, raises a hand.

Ethan slams the door, but the man wedges his booted foot inside, stopping the door from closing. Ethan's mind switches into overdrive. He throws his body into the door, hollering down the hall, "ANDREA! GUN!"

The magic man yells through the door gap, "Wait!"

There are sprinting footsteps in the apartment, but Ethan does not take his focus off the door, pouring all his strength into keeping it as closed as possible.

The man curses violently. "Fuck! Wait! Don't shoot me."

Ethan hisses through his teeth, "ANDREA!"

"Listen to me! I just want to talk. Nothing more."

Glowing light catches Ethan's attention, his head whipping around to see Star advancing. The hall darkens as her skin marbles with blooming shadows, her eyes bleeding into neon blue. She practically throws Ethan off the door, tossing him behind her.

The door slams open, deepening the hole made in the wall yesterday, and the man stands there, wide-eyed.

Star's voice hums with restrained power. "I warned you, did I not?"

The man seems at a loss for words. He swallows slowly, skin going clammy. "You did, Vessel. Your warning was heard and heeded. I swear to you on the mighty Harvester above." His hands splay in a placating gesture. "I am just here to talk. I beg of you. Grant me an audience."

Star's eyes narrow. "I have no reason to believe you, and all the evidence to distrust you."

He nods slowly. "That...is something I wish to discuss. I admit, I am surprised. You, Vessel, are not at all what I was trained to expect. I have caused great offense, and for that I beg your forgiveness. I was misled. I wish you no harm, only to understand and help." He takes a breath, his green eyes intense. His voice drops so low that Ethan strains to hear. "The priming is upon you, Vessel, and the Lophian nears."

Star's fists clench. Something brushes by Ethan's arm, and he startles, whipping around to see Andrea with Ethan's pistol trained on the man. Her eyes narrow. "You're not making sense. Vessel? Priming? Loafynan?"

The man's eyes dart to the gun, and he swallows. "It's not for you to understand. Only the Vessel. Please. An audience."

Andrea's hold on the gun is unwavering as she stares down the intruder. "That's the thing. She doesn't know."

Ethan glares at his sister. "Andrea!"

"Ethan!" she mocks, before rolling her eyes and dropping some of her attitude. "Look. Why the fuck are we here? To try to find out Star's past, and whatever that fish monster was." She throws her free hand out toward the magic man violently. "And look who shows up! Someone who not only recognizes her but also seems to know shit. You." She nods Ethan's gun at the stranger. "Do you know shit?"

His green eyes dart from Andrea, to the gun, to Star and back a couple times before he slowly nods.

Andrea's face hardens with violence. "And you're going to be well-behaved? Not do anything stupid? Because I will put holes in you like Swiss cheese. Then, my lovely magical friend here will get rid of the body. *No one will find you.* Understand?"

Magic crackles angrily around Star to make Andrea's words land firmly.

Again, the man nods. "Yes. I swear. I will be on my best behavior. I just want to help before it's too late."

Andrea nods, lowering the gun ever so slightly. "Okay. Let him in."

"No!" Ethan stops himself right before he grabs his sister, who is wielding a loaded gun with the safety already *off* like some murdering psychopath. "Absolutely fucking not."

Andrea snarls. "Ethan!"

"No, Andrea! This is not your call."

She scoffs, her mouth opening to yell, but Ethan turns away from her. His tone softens. "Star."

Star turns her glowing, darkened eyes on him. Her lips are thin, her body tight. "Yes, Ethan?"

He swallows. "You don't have to let him in. You don't have to hear him out." He speaks over Andrea's angrily spat words of dissent. "Do whatever you need to, Star. Listen to him, kick him out. It's your call."

Star takes a trembling breath, her eyes lightening ever so slightly. Her voice lowers to a soft whisper. "I don't think I have a choice."

"Respectfully, I think you're wrong there." He slides his hand in hers. "This is your life. Your past. Your call." He gives her hand a little reassuring squeeze. "Do whatever you need to, Star."

Her chest heaves with her breath, shoulders drooping. A shadow of grief whispers over her features. She swallows, eyes glistening. "It's like you said. Maybe I do need to appreciate what I was, to fully become what I am now, and I can only do that by remembering." She cups his cheek, thumb skimming it affectionately. "I want to keep you safe, Ethan, and I fear only knowledge will permit me to do that." Her hand drops, eyes dulling with something akin to grief. "Let him in. I want to hear what he knows."

Even though a part of him hates this plan, Ethan nods. "Okay."

He gives the man one last glare before sliding his arm around Star. "Andy, if he even blinks strangely, shoot him."

Andrea smiles viciously. "Happy to. After you, magic man."

The man's brow furrows in confusion before Star wraps her arm around Ethan. She tugs, leading Ethan away and down the hall. Once they reach the living room couch, she pulls him down on the cushions with her. He keeps his arm firmly around her, and she leans into his warmth, her eyes following the magic man as Andrea leads him at gunpoint into Ethan's apartment.

The armchair that Andrea drags screeches jarringly through the living room to rest in the center of the open space. She gestures with the gun for the man to sit. With no other option, he obeys, and Andrea joins Ethan and Star on the couch to sit on Ethan's other side, legs crossing and gun resting casually on her knee. She seems way more comfortable with this situation than Ethan likes. They're going to need to talk about these violent tendencies later.

Andrea happily takes the lead. "Here's the too long, didn't read. Star got hurt, and she has no memories. A fish monster already tried to eat her, but she blew him up. Now we're in a pickle."

The man startles, wide eyes locking on Star. "You *wielded* magic? Against a Contender?"

"Hey!" Andrea taps her finger against Ethan's gun. "Focus. We want to know everything you know. And I mean everything. Let's start with who you are and work from there."

The man eyes the gun before nodding slowly. "I am Alec Volkov, and I am the chosen Contender for the Order of the Seven." He pauses, eyes locking on Star again. "We wait and foretell when the next Vessel is gifted to this world by the Harvester." When they continue to stare at him blankly, he continues, "To lay claim to the rights of magic?"

Ethan chances a glance at Star before interjecting, "You mean the Game of Fallen Stars?"

Alec's eyes light. "So, you do know."

"Just the name, and that it's a battle for magic between the Land and the Ocean."

Alec nods. "What about the Harvester?" Nothing. "Shepherd?" Still nothing. "The...Reaper?" Alec's jaw drops, green eyes sliding back to Star. "Wow. You really have forgotten everything."

She tightens slightly, and Ethan pulls her a little further into his hold. At her silence, Alec groans, head falling into his hands. He runs his lightly scarred fingers over his short hair. "Lord help me. Where to begin?"

He gives Star a weary look, and she draws back ever so slightly, just enough for Ethan to feel it. Andrea interrupts, "I believe I said tell us everything? Start at the beginning."

Alec sighs. "Alright. I guess...we'll start with the origins." He points to the sky. "The Harvester is a god. He gifts this world a drop of magic. The Vessel. A star, if you will, for that is what it looks like when the magic falls. It is magic in its most raw and pure form. Once in this world, it takes on a mortal shell." He takes a breath, wetting his lips. "Then the Contenders search.

"The Land and Ocean have been warring over the magic drops for millennia. In the beginning, the Ocean consumed the magic, making great monstrous creatures within its watery depths. Then, the Land broke free. Life magic created the first land animal. The Ocean is a jealous god and did not wish to share this world with another. This is when Death magic started."

He goes to stand, but Andrea taps Ethan's gun, and Star crackles with power. He settles back in his chair and leans on his elbows. "If the Contender finds the magic and devours the Vessel's flesh, then great and powerful Death magic is gifted to that god. Wars. Famines. Disease. But not just that. Great conquerors. Lost civilizations. Think back to great and terrible destructions, and you will find Death magic linked to it."

He takes a breath, and his eyes land on Star. Ethan doesn't like the light of hope in them. "But Life magic...it is...it is the most wondrous and pure magic there is. Powerful too. Golden ages. Evolution. Fuck, dominion over the world. Life magic is near endless. And it has been so long since Life magic has been gifted to us."

Star's face is unreadable, her hand on Ethan's knee constricting. He rests his own hand over it when Andrea speaks. "So, you *eat* the star, and you get Death magic. What do you do to get Life magic?"

Alec doesn't take his eyes off Star. "Life...Life is birthed, in a way. That is why I speak of the priming. The magic is in the mortal shell for only so long before the magic becomes volatile. It seeks a purpose. The Vessel has taken a human form this time, which means Life is for the taking for the Land. My task is to prime it, care for it, until the Life magic is birthed into this world in a new golden age for mankind." His expression darkens. "The Lophians seek the Death magic. They hunger to devour this form and land a devastating blow to our kind to take back dominion of this world." His fists clench. "With a Vessel as powerful as this one, the Lophians could do something truly terrible."

The monstrous teeth and the glowing orb leading Star away flash in Ethan's vision. That horrific night sinks its claws deep into his psyche, and his breath shivers. He draws Star closer, his hold a touch too tight, but she doesn't seem to notice or care.

Alec starting to speak again brings Ethan back to the present. "Another thing. We foretold that this Vessel would land in the ocean, giving the Lophians the upper hand." He nods. "I'm not sure why you're here, or why you're human, but I thank the great Harvester for such an unforeseen gift."

Andrea gives Star an unreadable look before speaking again. "What the fuck is a Lophian?"

"They're monstrous creatures from the ocean. Not many of them left, but they rule the deep on this side of the world. When I was tracking you down, I sensed that the first Contender was going to reach you before me. Now another has emerged, one that has more mastery of the magic pearl." He touches his brow. "It's blocking my ability to scry it. Whatever it's doing, I fear it's only a matter of time before it finds the Vessel and claims the Death magic for its own." He gives Star a sharp look. "We must leave,quickly, and go somewhere safe to begin the priming." He scans her carefully. "It looks like it has already initiated."

Ethan feels hot rage wash over him. He's about to snatch the gun out of Andrea's hands when a firm voice snaps through the room. "No."

All three humans turn to Star. Whispers of dark marbling flicker over her skin.

Alec's brows raise. "Yes, there's also that. The texts do not...how do I describe it? You're awfully..." He rolls his hand while he searches for the word. "Aware? The Vessel is a vessel. It has a form, but it's not aware. It's magic encased in flesh for the Harvester's Great Game to be played. But here you are, talking, making decisions, resisting my lure of command. It's really..." He grimaces. "Not what I expected."

Star stoically stares at Alec. Her voice is low, soft, yet it fills the room. "Yes. Here I am. A *Vessel*. A disobedient one. Tell me, priest." Ethan's heart jolts as her eyes harden. "What will you do with this disobedient one? Rob me of my control over this form? Force your 'priming' against my unwilling mind?"

Alec's eyes flare. "Wha—no—"

"Do you know what it feels like when you exert your...what did you call it? Lure of command? Let me tell you, ignorant one." Star's hand trembles under Ethan's, the only tell of her fear. "It's like I am trapped. I scream at my body *no*, but it does not listen. I try to make my voice speak, but it does not sound. A puppet to your whims, with all the horror of trapped awareness. So, tell me, priest." Her blue eyes are so dark they almost bleed black. "When your Order and the Lophians 'primed' the vessels, what do you think that was like for my brothers and sisters?" A hum of power echoes in the room. "Or when they were devoured alive. Which do you think was more violating?"

The silence that follows rings.

Alec is pale, his eyes too wide. It takes him a moment to collect himself. "I...that..." He swallows, his voice taking a hint of sheepishness. "That is not written about."

Star snaps. "No. It wouldn't be, would it? Who cares when ultimate magical power can be theirs? And this contest you speak of? Just call it the rape and slaughter of my kind. Might as well be honest about this little game that is played by your so-called god."

A wave of sickness hits Ethan, and he swallows rhythmically. Star's rigid in his hold, but her hand on his knee is like a vise. She keeps her eyes trained on Alec, waiting for him to respond. Alec doesn't look like he's going to speak for a long time as he stares at his hands.

Andrea clears her throat, leaning forward. She catches the vicious glare from Ethan and gives him an apologetic grimace, her voice gentle. "I know, but we're already this far." She turns back to Alec. "How do you have magic?"

Alec wiggles his fingers weakly, his voice mumbled. "Both Contenders eat a magic pearl, which gives them the magic to play the game."

"What are the magic pearls?"

"Exactly as described. They look like pearls that are made of magic." He clears his throat, his face tight with stress. "Created after the magic is birthed unto this world."

Andrea's eyes are wide. "And what do you mean birthed? Like actual birth? Or metaphorical—"

Star starts visibly shaking, and Ethan snaps. "Andrea."

"What! Look, like that part is a little important, don't you think?"

Alec's mumbled words interrupt them. "It's mostly metaphorical. The important part is the priming and then protecting."

Ethan and Andrea jump when Alec stands abruptly, ignoring Andrea's gun. "If you'll excuse me. You, um." He swallows, skin ashen. "You've given me a lot to think about."

Alec rushes from the room. The front door slams and the silence stretches. They don't move for a long time. Eventually, Ethan chances a glance at Star. She's muted, matte, eyes dull. Even her hair is less full. He squeezes her hand, and she shifts slightly.

Her voice trembles. "I really was looking forward to eating Thai food with you. Just for one moment longer. Just..." A tear escapes. "Just one more."

His chest tightens. "It's going to be okay, Star."

She shakes her head. "No, it's not. Everything..." She takes a trembling breath, gaze drifting to the window. "Everything he's said, it's what Astra has been trying to warn me about. There is no running." Her eyes close, her voice dropping to a whisper. "There is only death."

He wants to argue, wants to scream and rage, but can't. Star looks so small in that moment. He had hoped so fervently that the others of her kind had happiness, but now doubt creeps up. Nothing that Alec has revealed points to anything other than the horrific genocide of Star's kind.

As Ethan goes to pull her into his embrace, the door slams back open. Before he can jump to his feet, Alec storms in. His eyes are wild, skin still ashen. He paces back and forth in his leather ensemble, hands raised and gripping the back of his neck.

He stops abruptly, whirling on them. "Look! I'm not—I'm not a rapist! This is! FUCK!" He roars, kicking over Ethan's coffee table, the three on the couch flinching back. "It isn't supposed to be like this! I battled Kristof. I won the match. It was supposed to be all epic fight for the greater good and hot fucking sex with a hot magical creature and being a-a-a goddamn hero!" A look of devastation washes over his face. "Fuck. Just. Fuck."

He collapses back into Ethan's chair, his hands sliding over his scalp. "I'm not a bad guy. I'm not."

When Ethan first saw Alec in the club, he had the impression that he was young. At the time, he was uncertain how young. But now, Ethan realizes that he can't be much older than Andrea. Maybe even younger. There's a softness in his face that he hasn't yet managed to shed.

Ethan's gaze lingers at the scarring on his hands.

Alec's words are so mumbled, Ethan can barely hear what he says. "Supposed to be the hero."

The two siblings exchange a look. Andrea grimaces. "There, there? No need for a room-destroying tantrum."

She glances at Ethan again, like he can help her console this man. Ethan's lip curls in response. Young or not, that night at the club will never be forgiven, not to mention Alec and his Orders' willingness to have sex with something they don't perceive as having agency. The guy is fucked up, and Ethan wants him gone.

Andrea stumbles on alone. "Look, like, you didn't know. Right?"

Alec pauses before nodding.

"See?" Andrea gestures with the gun, and Ethan quickly takes it from her, putting the safety back on. "But now you do. So, what you do from here is important, right? So. Now informed, what are you going to be? The hero or the villain? Because I'm going to be honest, we're way out of our depth with this Loth-a-whata-thing. A hero would be real nice."

The silence stretches, and Alec slowly lifts his head. He meets Star's gaze unwaveringly, and the gun twitches in Ethan's hand. Alec's voice is low and full of misery. "I don't want to hurt you. I don't want to force you. I'm not that kind of guy, I swear. And I'm really sorry, for everything. We didn't...we didn't know. It was what we were told that needed to be done and—" He clears his throat and sets his shoulders, eyes shining. "I'd like to help you, if you'd let me."

Star studies the man before them, her dull eyes taking on a mere hint of their usual glory. She glances back up at Ethan, her face showing him all the conflict within her mind. He gives her a small, reassuring smile. "Whatever you need, Star. I'll back it a hundred percent."

She swallows thickly, eyes closing tightly. She blinks back tears and looks upon the young priest. "I need time. I don't know you, but I know of your kind." She takes a shuddering breath. "Nothing tells me that you are to be trusted. But..." She searches him. "You seem sincere in your offer. And I do believe we have a common enemy. I just don't know if that is enough to take the risk."

Alec nods slowly. "Fair enough."

"I need time to think about it. But know this, priest." Her voice hardens, head tilting down in threat. "At the first sign of betrayal, yours will be a slow and agonized fate."

"I swear, Vessel, I will do everything in my power to fell the Lophian." His lips thin, a shadow of something crossing over his face. "I do sincerely appreciate the opportunity to redeem myself in this. I'm not...I'm not a bad person. I don't want to be the bad guy."

Star nods, her voice whisper soft. "I know, Alec."

Emotion wells in his green eyes. Alec bows his head, hiding his face. "Thank you."

Andrea leans forward. "Here, give me your number. You do have a phone, don't you?"

He nods, shoulders setting. "I do."

"Excellent. Let's swap contact info and I'll text you."

Suddenly, the doorbell rings and all of them jump, Ethan and Alec both on their feet. Alec pulls a small rod from his jacket pocket. It rapidly expands into a long staff with a wickedly curved blade. Alec carefully arcs it down. Ethan eyes the weapon, recognizing it from Jenny's vase.

Andrea stands slowly. "I know Alec rang the door, but I doubt the fish monster would. Let me get our food before the poor underpaid delivery guy gets hurt."

Neither man relaxes until Andrea returns with the bags of Thai. She sets them down on the kitchen island, and Alec's staff returns to its shrunken state, sliding into his pocket. Andrea turns to him, nodding toward the front door. "I'll walk you out and get that number of yours. Come on."

Alec turns his attention to Star, his gaze intense. "A word of advice. You need to get out of the city." Ethan stiffens. "The Lophian is too clever. It's somehow blending in and moving swiftly. I already caught its trail once at the club you were at, and I'm not sure how it's masking itself with so many people. I recommend somewhere isolated to lure it out into the open. If you let me know where, I can take the opportunity to fight it. By killing it, you'll buy some time before they can rally a third Contender." He offers a small smile. "If you decide to trust me, I can prove a valuable resource. I'm strong, trained. I can kill the monster. Besides, I think our motives align in far more than that."

Ethan's eyes narrow, but Alec turns away, pulling out his phone. He quickly exchanges information with Andrea before heading to the front door. He looks down at Star. She stares straight ahead, barely breathing.

Unsure what to say, Ethan sinks back down on the couch next to her. He presses a soft kiss into her hair. She sucks in a breath, blinking away tears. Her weight sags into his side, and he wraps both arms around her. The only sounds are Andrea speaking softly with Alec at the door. He lets his strength hold Star up, hoping it provides her with the comfort she seeks. He breathes in her scent, the flowery shampoo Andrea bought her seeping deep into his soul until his heart aches.

Andrea's voice penetrates the moment. "Lunch?"

Ethan's eyes open. He hadn't realized he closed them. He looks over at his sister standing next to the kitchen island. It's the last thing he wants to do, but it's a necessary task. He nods, standing and taking Star with him. "Yeah."

If he forces down food, maybe it will help encourage her.

Andrea passes out plates, serving herself. Ethan piles food on Star's plate when she shows no move to take any. She picks at it as he forces down pad thai that he doesn't taste.

The silence is oppressive.

Andrea's hazel eyes dart back and forth between the two of them. "So...plan?"

Ethan sighs harshly, chewing and choking the bite down before answering. "I don't know. I'm open to suggestions."

She nods solemnly. "I think we should listen to Alec. Get out of the city. At the very least, we'll be able to get back to your gun locker, and mine. Much easier to shoot a fish monster in the country than the city. Don't want to accidentally hurt someone or cause chaos or get arrested."

The memory of Ethan uselessly gunning down the creature as it advanced chills him to the bone. His arm aches, and he jolts, standing straighter. He forces himself to take another bite. "Yeah. Maybe."

"I want to go to Parkfield."

Both siblings turn their attention to Star. Her gaze is unfocused, her body slumped onto the island they stand at. She swallows thickly. "I want to go back. I miss it." Her hand tightens on her fork. "I think I need it."

Andrea asks the question that is caught in his throat. "What do you mean?"

She swallows, lip trembling. The silence stretches before she whispers. "I don't know. I just...hurt. Like after I killed the creature before, I hurt. Going into the water beneath the oak eased me then, and I think it'll help me now." She looks up at Ethan. "I want to go back. Please, Ethan."

His throat aching, he nods. "Okay. Let's go back."

And just like that, their time in the city comes to a close. Ethan's heart aches at the loss. Star holds his gaze, the mournful look on his face echoing on hers. Her hand slides into his, gripping it tight. "Together, remember?"

He squeezes back. "Together."

Ethan tosses their luggage into the back of his truck. Andrea is still upstairs finishing packing, and Star stands next to him, leaning against the truck's side.

Ethan sighs, pausing, giving her a once over. "When did you get your memories back?"

Star startles, her wide eyes snapping to him. "How did you know?"

"Little things." He starts tying things down. "For one, you knew what Alec was. You called him priest and he didn't refute the term, though he looks nothing like a priest."

Star lets out a slow breath, her body sagging. She whispers, even though there is barely anyone in the parking garage but them. A few neighbors walk by with arms full of groceries, and one dark-haired man stands by his car. "Not all of it, but little things have returned. Like pieces of a puzzle that I don't quite know how they fit together." She shifts. "Alec's story helped. He added details that were missing, and then my puzzle of memories kind of... smoothed out in places."

Her sadness is unbearable. His heart aches, and he's at a loss for what to do. All he can think of is to take her hand and say, "We'll figure it out together. It'll be okay."

How could it not? He's never been with anyone who felt so right before.

Star squeezes his hand.

Just then, Andrea bursts through the door. "Okay! Got all my shit. Door locked. Let's get this shitshow on the road."

She throws her bags haphazardly into the truck, ruining Ethan's careful system. He sighs, reaching in and reorganizing them as Andrea swings the passenger door open. Her voice echoes oddly in the near-empty garage. "Hope Star doesn't mind riding bitch or in that shoebox you call a backseat."

He rolls his eyes, glancing at Star. But Star isn't there.

He startles, whirling around. She's walking through the garage, her feet completely silent. Ethan's brow furrows. "Star? Where are you going?"

Ethan left the keys on the dash, so Andrea rolls down the window, hanging out. "Star! Shitshow on the road is over here! Come on!"

Star doesn't turn.

Ethan steps away. "Star?"

Walking away from the truck gives him a new perspective. The guy that was lingering by his own car is staring at Star in an oddly intense way. Then again, if a beautiful woman like Star randomly walked up to Ethan, he too would be intense.

Ethan's eyes narrow. Not that intense though. It's kind of creepy. Ethan's hackles rise. "Star? What are you doing?"

She doesn't stop.

Her hands tremble.

Ethan is moving before he realizes it. He's running, his instincts screaming at him. Something is wrong. She wouldn't wander off like this. "Star?" He's almost to her, but she has a head start, and each second stretches as panic tingles through his senses.

He's mere feet from her when he looks past her shoulder to the dark-haired man. Ethan stumbles. The man's pupils are glowing white. Ethan's arm begins to sting. "STAR!"

Ethan lunges and grabs Star's arm. She gasps as if surfacing for air, her feet catching on themselves, her body sagging. Her knees hit the pavement, and she hisses in pain as the hard asphalt skins them. The stranger smiles, too close, Star nearly in snatching distance. Long needle teeth glint in the lights, and Ethan's breath stutters in terror. The Lophian.

Ethan pulls Star's arm, and she flops backward, awkwardly dragging herself back to her feet, then stops, her body rigid. She gives Ethan a look of pure fear, and he feels it acutely, his hand tightening painfully on her wrist, sweat slicking his hold.

The creature steps toward them, arrogance written over its angular face.

Ethan's mind blanks out as adrenaline sizzles through his veins. He throws a punch, but the creature catches it. His bones creak in its tightening hand, and Ethan gasps in pain. He hears Andrea screaming as a humming tang fills the air. Electricity crackles, Star grabbing the Lophian's arm. The monster screeches, releasing Ethan before it can crush his hand. It wrenches out of Star's hold, and she goes to strike, but the magic dies in her hand.

She gasps, trying again. The Lophian slaps her hand out of the way and grabs her neck. She chokes and grips its wrist. Her fingers turn white from her hold, but no magic comes to her aid. Ethan hears her whispered words, "It's not fair. It's not fair!"

Ethan lunges toward the monster.

Magic vibrates in the air again, and Ethan has a weightless moment, Star's wrist ripping from his grasp, before he crashes into the asphalt. Star screams, body flashing in deep marbling, her eyes such a deep blue they're almost black. Magic explodes around her, forcing the Lophian's hand off her neck, and the creature stumbles back, arms raising to cover its face from the blast.

But it's still standing. The clawed hand drips blood, but it's still standing. Its arms lower as it hisses words that Ethan can't understand, but Star seems to have no issue. She snarls at the creature. "I'll never prime for you." She slashes her hand toward it, her magic sputtering. "I am not yours to use! I am no one's!"

The creature laughs, a deep, dark noise that sends Ethan's skin crawling. Ethan regrets turning Alec away. Having a fighter trained with magic would be very useful right now. He's out of his depth, helpless and desperate. Willing to do anything to save her.

This time, the Lophian speaks English. "Your body will save my kind. A new era of Ocean will be birthed from your magic. It is your fate. The Great One has spoken. Now, we can do this the easy and pleasant way, or I can slaughter your pets and take you by force." Its dark eyes glint unnaturally. "Choose, Vessel. It will be your last chance to do so."

Star's fists clench. "No. I am not for the darkness. I am for the light."

It shakes its human-appearing head. "Lying to yourself will not help you or your pets."

Magic crackles around her. "Do not touch them."

Cruelty drips from each of its words. "Oh, I'll do more than touch them. I'll rip them apart piece by piece." Its face darkens, sharp teeth bared. "Humans are the plague upon the Earth. The world was birthed in water, and she will return to its loving embrace. Now come. I grow tired of this."

Ethan drags himself to his feet, arm wrapped around what could be a cracked rib, readying to lunge forward. Star had said magic comes easier to her when she's saving Ethan and, damn it, if saving him is what helps her, then so be it. He'll keep coming forward, keep risking himself, even dying if it means she gets away. If it means she is able to save herself, he will do this. To save Andrea. For both of them. He'll die to make sure they live.

A voice echoing in the garage sends Ethan sagging to one knee, his hand snapping out and palm stinging against the hard ground to stop the rest of him falling. "But I haven't had my fun."

The Lophian whips around, hand raising in time to catch Alec's spear as it arcs down. Alec's face glows in excitement, his voice echoing powerfully in the enclosed space. "This world is for the Land and the Ocean will slumber. Now, foul creature. Die."

Ethan drags himself to his feet once again, seizing the opportunity. His truck roar to life and Andrea pulls up beside him. Her ashen face glows in the interior, the windows down. "Get in!"

Ethan's hand snaps out. "Star!"

She turns, sprinting toward him, hair flowing, her neck bleeding from where the creature's claws ripped the flesh. The Lophian roars, magic flaring. Ethan's hand closes around Star's. He doesn't see the battle, but he hears it, Alec screaming in pain. Ethan throws open the passenger door, tossing Star in. He barely climbs in too before Andrea floors it, tires screeching. Star is practically in his lap, his arms tight around her while he holds the car handle. Andrea is screaming out the window for Alec, and Ethan barely sees the other man flash by the front of the car, blood dripping down his face. Alec grabs the truck's side, wet hand slipping along it in a terrifying moment, before he launches himself into the back.

The man reaches into one of his many jacket pockets, pulling out a rapidly expanding crossbow and fires it. Ethan cranes his neck to see bolt after bolt ricochet off the Lophian, magic crackling all around. The creature gives chase, its black eyes full of rage. Andrea almost flips the car with how fast she takes the turns out of the garage. Around and around, up and up, until light nearly blinds Ethan.

A delivery truck is making its way into the garage, leaving the door open like a gift from God, and Ethan's truck clears the gate, hitting air for a moment before crashing down. Ethan and Star bounce painfully in their seats. Andrea scrapes an oncoming vehicle, sending it careening, but she doesn't slow down. They swerve, and loud *thunks* echo, what Ethan assumes is Alec being tossed about in the back.

All Ethan can do is hold onto Star and the car, and try not to close his eyes. Andrea swerves into the other lane to avoid a line of traffic and comes face to face with another car. There is no room to dodge out of the way.

Star shifts, throwing her hand out.

A sonic boom pops Ethan's ears. The oncoming car arcs in the air in slow motion, clearing the top of them and preventing a head-on collision. Ethan tries to see what happens to it, but suddenly they're on the freeway.

Andrea does not slow down, knuckles white on the steering wheel. Their collective heavy breathing is all that sounds over the engine. Ethan touches her arm gently, and she eases off down to the speed limit. The cops are the last thing they need right now.

Ethan sags in his seat, eyes closing for a moment—just one, to collect his spinning mind. Star is warm and soft in his hold, her short, quick breaths worrisome. He reaches back, grabbing the seatbelt and stretching it around both of them. It's tight, but they fit.

They speed south and away from the city. Away from the Lophian, Alec quiet and hidden in the truck bed.

The Lophian rages. With a snarl, he unleashes his magic, cars blasting back from him. Humans scream. Alarms blare. He does not care. His prey is escaping, and not even his magic can get these legs to move fast enough to catch up to the car.

The creature turns in a circle, black eyes searching and thinking quickly. Like a tick in the back of his mind, he can feel the Vessel flicker away quickly to the south. He runs his tongue over his sharp teeth once before his mind is made. He begins walking, picking up speed until he is running. Humans scream again, trying to get away, but he ignores them. Faster and faster. He cannot fail.

He will be sucking the priest's and his companions' bones clean in a glorious meal of victory before the end of this game. He can almost guarantee it.

Wood thumps under his feet, loud in his mostly human ears, until there is no longer wood beneath him and he dives. The water hits his body like a cold shock. The magic flares within him, agonizing pain burning in his flesh. His long siren tail slashes through the murky water, moving him faster than any of those metal human-made monstrosities could ever dream.

Soon, priest. That star is his.

Thirteen

Ethan doesn't take a full breath until the city gives way to the brown, grassy, open terrain of Highway 101. His eyes drift shut for a moment, his chest heaving in great gulps of air, but his cracked ribs make themselves known. Each breath is like a dagger in his side. The pain with the crash of adrenaline leaves him dizzy, and his nerves are on edge. His energy plummets, hands going limp. But he can't stop. Not yet. There are still urgent matters to attend to.

Scraping together what little energy he has left, Ethan tries to twist around in his seat, but he hisses in pain instead. The car swerves, Andrea gasping, eyes wide. "What's wrong?"

Star shifts, her fingers touching his cheek. He grits his teeth, shaking his head. He tries to turn again, but it's no use. His ribs won't permit it. He grimaces, looking up into Star's fear-filled eyes. He sucks in a breath. "My side."

She touches it, her low voice soft. "You're hurt."

The steering wheel's leather creaks from the strength of Andrea's grip. "You're hurt? And you didn't say anything?"

His teeth are grinding. "It's fine."

Star shifts further off him, and he misses her keenly. The seatbelt constricts her movements, but she presses her palm against his bruised, throbbing side. A hum vibrates through the space, pins and needles prickling their way across his skin beneath her palm. She huffs a breath, sweat glistening across her forehead, her hand spasming. She gives him a tight smile. "That should do it."

It feels better already. He strokes her hair back, unsticking the parts that cling to her perspiration. "You didn't need to do that."

"But I did." Concern flashes in her eyes. "A rib like that could have punctured a lung. Please be careful, Ethan."

"But look at you. It took something from you to do it."

She's matte again, her hair limp. She takes his stroking fingers in hers, her small smile wavering. "I'll be okay. But you're mortal. Don't hesitate next time."

He nods, eyes still searching her face. "Are you sure you're fine?"

"I'll be okay. I'm just tired." Her fingers tremble lightly from where they rest against his. "It was a lot of magic today."

Having no choice but to believe her, Ethan nods, bringing her fingers to his lips. He shifts again, easily twisting around to peer out the back window. He can barely see Alec's legs. His unmoving, bloodied legs. "Andy, pull off at the next stop."

Andrea startles, blinking rapidly from whatever mind space she'd sunken into. "Why?"

"We need to check on Alec." He straightens, pointing. "There. Pull off."

"But what about the fish guy?"

He swallows, his hand clenching, but he keeps his tone even to hide his fear. "It'll be fine. I doubt he could be chasing us on foot without being seen, even if he is using magic. Just pull over."

His sister obeys, exiting the freeway with all the grace and fluidity of a tween going on her first joyride. She practically slams on the brakes, Ethan throwing his free hand out when they lurch forward violently. Andrea releases a shuddering breath, shifting into park with an unsteady hand. Only when she shuts off the engine does Ethan dare to unbuckle the seatbelt.

He turns away from Star. "Stay in the car, okay?"

Her hand snatches his and forces him to stop, his car door halfway open. Her voice is a whisper. "I want to go with you."

He doesn't like it. Alec might've saved them, but he doesn't trust the man as far as he can throw him. "Are you sure?"

She nods with grim determination. "Yes."

Andrea holds up a still trembling hand. "Can I stay in the car?"

In the car, out of the car. Doesn't really matter in the end. Everywhere is unsafe. Ethan throws the door all the way open. "Okay."

Ethan's shoes crunch the gravel. Star takes his offered hand and lands lightly next to him. They peer over the edge of the truck bed, and Ethan hisses through his teeth at the gruesome sight. "Fuck, man. Are you alive?"

Alec lays in a pool of his own blood, hand pressed tightly against his midsection. The black leather of his outfit makes it hard to discern his injuries, but Ethan does not doubt their severity. Caked blood mars his face. Slowly, Alec blinks open his bruised eyes. His voice is hushed. "Yeah. Alive."

Star reaches into the truck bed, fingers nearly grazing him, but stops when Alec gives a painful headshake and says, "No. If you keep doing that, it will be like sending up a beacon of your location." He waves them off. "I'm fine. Just leave me back here. The sun is helping the magic heal me."

Star's fingers linger barely an inch above Alec. "You saved us. Thank you, Alec." She offers a small smile, her face softening. "I think you've proven yourself trustworthy. Would you still like to come with us?"

Alec swallows and manages a tight, jolting nod that hurts Ethan to watch. "I would be honored."

After how close the Lophian got, it's a relief to have him on their side, even if a part of Ethan loathes the idea. At least their motives align for now, which is better than nothing. Ethan's gaze travels up and down the length of the priest again. "Do you need water? We can stop at a gas station and grab some."

"No. It's better not to linger." Alec's eyes close again. "I just need time."

Ethan's fingers gently close around Star's, drawing her beside him and back to the truck. He opens the backseat door for her, holding it while she climbs in. This would've been the smarter place to go before, but he wasn't exactly thinking straight at the time. Besides, the backseat really is just for decoration in this truck model. It's a choice of being smooshed in the front or smooshed in the back. At least back here Star can lay down with her head in his lap if she wants.

He clears his throat, trying to get Andrea's attention. She doesn't move, staring wide-eyed straight ahead. He tries again. "Andy?"

She blinks, turning slowly toward him.

He wets his lips, suddenly realizing how shaken his sister is. "Do you want me to drive?"

The words startle her out of her shock. She shakes her head furiously, hands slapping against the steering wheel. "No ...I can drive."

He raises a brow. "You sure?"

"Yes." She reaches for the key and turns the engine back to life. "I need to. I'd go crazy otherwise."

"Makes sense." He gestures toward Star in the backseat. "Alright if I sit back here?"

Andrea's head moves in an odd, sloppy movement that could be called a nod. "Yep. Sure. You got it."

Ethan hesitates. "You sure—"

"For God's sake, Ethaniel, I'm fine! Now get in the fucking truck so we can go."

"Alright." He slams the front passenger door shut before climbing in the back with Star. He's barely secured his seatbelt before Andrea peels onto the road.

They ride in absolute silence. Star leans back in Ethan's arms, and he's content to hold her, breathe her in, reassure himself that she's still here. Whole. Alive. And physically okay.

Intermittently, Ethan turns back to knock on the back window, and Alec's bloodied hand will lift and knock back before lowering out of sight.

Andrea chews nearly all her nails to bleeding. She turns on the radio to fill the emptiness.

The sight of the Parkfield cabin does little to lift their spirits. Ethan looks around, seeing phantoms of happy memories. But now, no border collies run about. Just a quiet, empty house in the darkening twilight.

The oak tree is massive in the distance. Lush. Full. Such a juxtaposition compared to what he's feeling.

Andrea puts the car in park, and her arm flops weakly back down. The silence stretches in a trauma-filled spell that is only broken by Alec's movements in the back. He shifts from the truck bed, groaning and flopping over the edge. It's enough to get them moving. Ethan reaches around to unclasp his seatbelt, while Andrea's door creaks open before she jumps down.

He hears her muffled voice from outside the truck. "Christ. You okay?"

Ethan opens the door when Alec replies, "It looks worse than it is. The magic finished healing me on the way here."

"A shower might be a good idea. You're a bit, you know, bloodied everywhere."

"Yeah...maybe that. Later. I need to think first."

Ethan exits the car, holding out his hand for Star. She grasps it delicately, hopping down. She's muted again, dulled. He squeezes her hand gently. "Let's get inside."

She shakes her head, eyes trained on the tree longingly. "Not yet. I want to be alone with the oak."

His heart clenches, but her words back in San Francisco are the only thing that has his hand loosening around hers. She said she needs it, that she hurts without it, and seeing her in her current state, he has no choice but to agree. "Okay."

Her fingers slip from his, and he has the manic impulse to snatch them back. His whole body feels cold without her heat pressed to him. Just like the hollow feel of the house, he too is an empty shadow of his former self.

Flashes of the earlier fight invade his psyche, and he shoves them violently away.

Andrea steps up to him, glancing in Star's direction "Do you think that's a good idea?"

Ethan's breath shudders. "I don't know. I just...don't know." He gives himself a vicious shake, refocusing and squaring his shoulders. "Help me unload."

The three of them make quick time, Ethan dropping Star's and his bags in the master bedroom. Uncertainty nags him. What if Star doesn't want to sleep with him? Then he'll just have to sleep outside the door. It doesn't matter if the priest almost died trying to save them today, there is no way in hell he's going to allow Alec anywhere near her alone. Over his dead body.

Not that he can do much. He barely helped her the last two times she was in danger. Alec was the one who risked his life to distract the creature long enough for them to get away. An overwhelming sense of ineptness washes over Ethan, his body tightening and heart plummeting. What good is he? He swore to help Star, but what has he really done?

His hands scrub his face, combing his hair back through his fingers, his hair tie falling to the floor. He looks down at it but can't muster the energy to pick it up off the ground. He sighs, dragging himself out of the room, his hair falling in his face. He needs to feed everyone. He needs to make sure they're settled in. Even if his stomach is a knotted mess, he needs to go to the kitchen to see if there is enough food to scrape together dinner.

He nearly stumbles into Andrea and Alec in the living room. They're standing very close, both staring at him intently. He gets the sense that he's interrupted something.

Alec's green eyes dart to Andrea, who is wetting her lips. Ethan's anxiety spikes.

She takes a steadying breath before speaking. "Ethan."

He doesn't like that tone. It's too carefully even.

She continues, "We think that you should go to Star and convince her to finish the priming."

Cold rage flashes through him. His eyes dart to Alec, but some of the violence he feels must show in his face. Alec makes a placating gesture. "Not with me, friend. I doubt her feelings toward me have changed that much."

Andrea interrupts. "You, Ethan. *You* should finish priming her."

Words escape Ethan, the shock is too much.

Alec keeps his tone carefully neutral. "I can tell that it's already initiated. It doesn't take much to see it is you she's chosen to begin this with."

Ethan shakes his head. "Stop. Just stop. You're talking like she even knew what that was before."

"She might not have had the word for it, but it is in her nature to seek it out. You might've noticed the increase in desire, not just with you, but with others around her. Don't forget I was at the club too—"

Ethan snaps harshly, "Yes, I'll never forget that."

Alec has the decency to look embarrassed. "Yes, fair enough. But the patrons around us were drunk off the building magic. The Life magic. It's seeping off her. Every second we delay, the more it builds, and the easier it will be to track." His expression is severe. "The Lophian will not delay. His magic is more powerful than I expected. He must've taken the risk and devoured more than one pearl. It's the only explanation for his near-perfect human body. The magic to make such a transformation is no small task. The cost on his soul was severe. The pain..." Alec shakes his head. "It would've been excruciating."

His green eyes sharpen and meet Ethan's. "The Lophian is too powerful now. It's a miracle I survived its attack. Our only blessing is that it's burning through its magic quickly, but we don't know the full depth of its well. Yes, it is burning quickly, but to what end? My own magic is massive, the pearl I ate a potent one. It is impossible to guess the strength of the creature." He lets out a shuddering breath. "I'm not sure I can win in a fight against it."

"Ethan." He turns to see his sister's pleading eyes. "You almost died twice now. It's coming back, and it's going to keep coming back over and over." Her voice takes a hint of hysteria. "They're going to *eat* her, Ethan. The only way to stop it is if we win—if *humanity* wins. And we already have a head start! Play the game. Win it. Make this all end."

Ethan stares into his sister's large, terrified eyes and feels them chip away at his very soul. His resolution weakens, his body tired. He takes a steadying breath, turning toward Alec again. "And what happens exactly? What is priming? Sex?"

Alec nods. "Essentially. It will be more intense than that. The magic will kick in and merge with your essence. It's Life magic, it will read you to determine how to manifest, as well as figure out which side's Contender you are."

A memory blossoms in Ethan's mind of when Star first landed. That intense, pleasurable, all-consuming energy that filled him and changed her. Gave her form. The first form, before her chosen human one.

Alec's voice draws him back to the present. "Or at least that's what I've read. The magic has a mind of its own, but apparently some Contenders can force it to their will."

Ethan's breath shivers. "And then what happens?"

"We protect her while she processes it. Or gestates it, if you will. Then the magic will birth into this world." Alec gestures to the window. "It's already begun. She went to her astrobleme."

Andrea blinks. "Her what?"

"Astrobleme. Crater. Whatever. She went to the tree, which is feeding off the residual magic in the soil from when she fell. While she primes and gestates, she will seek comfort in it. Or perhaps it aids her in some way? There are many theories on it."

"And then what?"

Alec blinks. "Then we win. The Lophian dies or flees back to the water if it survives the cost of eating of two pearls. Humanity continues to hold dominion over the Earth."

Ethan loses his grip on his temper for a moment, his voice booming in the space. "What about Star!"

Andrea and Alec exchange looks. Her fists clench, lips thinning, and Ethan feels like he'll go mad from the anxiety. Alec speaks calmly in that agitating matter-of-fact way. "The Vessel will have served its purpose."

Ethan feels sick. "And then?"

"And then..." Alec swallows, hesitating. "It will be no more. The remaining blood will be mixed with the earth, and pearls will be formed for the Order. Then, we wait for the next game."

Ethan's ears ring. Andrea's mouth moves, but Ethan can't hear her. He staggers back, feet tripping over themselves. He grabs the armchair nearest to him, bowing over it while he tries to regain control over himself. His breathing is labored, his skin clammy. Andrea's words start to sound, but he cannot decipher them. She touches his shoulder, but he smacks it away, straightening.

Rage boils within him, burning off the shock. "She is not a *Vessel*. She has a name. A body. A life. A goddamn fucking will! And all she wants," his voice cracks, "all she's ever wanted was to live and be happy! She made a fucking tattoo on her skin to remember all the happiness and memories she's made here. She's joyful and kind and doesn't wish to hurt anything, but so protective of the things she loves, and you want me to help you destroy that? Destroy her?"

Andrea's eyes shimmer as he rounds on her. "And you agree?"

His sister wraps her arms around herself, sadness washing over her for a moment before anger flickers. Andrea always struggled with that, feeling sadness when anger is easier to process. "You almost died, Ethan!"

He scoffs. "And?"

"And? AND?!" She stomps her foot loudly. "You're my brother! I love you! It's terrible and sad and unfair for Star that this is what her experience is drawing toward, but what about you? How far will you go to save her? You have a life here, people who love and cherish you here. Who will *mourn* you. Who will never be the same without you." She sniffles, tears filling and escaping her eyes. "I will never be the same without you. You're my brother, but you're more than that. You are my person, Ethan. Don't be a selfish dick, because I will be destroyed without you. Who the fuck will I call every single day? Who will make me breakfast and coffee and love me so unconditionally?" Her voice turns shrill. "You raised me. You accepted me. All of me. Dad found out I was gay and cut me off. You found out I was gay and asked me to not have sex in the living room again, and then made my girlfriend breakfast. So yes. If it's between you and Star, I choose you. I'll always choose you!"

Ethan's eyes burn, his throat tight. "Andy. I'll be fine—"

"No, you won't! I know you, Ethan. I saw you in the parking garage. You'll keep throwing yourself into danger if it means helping Star use her magic to protect herself. But what if she can't help you next time?"

He grasps for words. "Andy, what do you expect me to do? Sit back?"

"Yes! Choose your own safety!" She's screaming now, tears steadily streaming down her face. "Don't just throw yourself away for something you've known for less than a month! Choose life! Choose humanity!" She sucks in breath, her tears threatening to take her voice away. "Choose me. Don't leave me."

He pulls her into a hug, and Andrea dissolves into sobs, clutching him tightly. Her whole frame wracks with it. He presses a kiss to her short hair, his eyes closing. His heart aches, his head pounds. A tear escapes, and he sucks in a shuddering breath. "I love you, Andy." She cries harder in response. He tries to assure her that it will be fine and that he won't leave her, but the words get stuck in his throat, and he swallows them down.

Time stretches until eventually Andrea cries herself out, her shoulders occasionally twitching with hiccups. Ethan continues to hold her. It's a familiar hold, one they've done countless times before. He takes solace in it.

Alec speaks, and Ethan glares at him over Andrea's head. "There are unfortunately only two outcomes to our predicament. Either the Lophian claims her or you prime her. So, you must ask yourself which one would be better."

Ethan's lip curls. Both options suck ass in his opinion, but he's so tired and angry he can't bring himself to speak. He lets his emotions bleed into his face to show his displeasure.

Alec runs his hand over his buzzed hair. "I know. I get it."

Ethan growls low. "You can't begin to understand. You didn't even know she had a mind."

Alec grimaces, shame tinging his cheeks. "True. But I do now, and it makes the game we're forced to play unfathomably cruel. But here we are."

His gaze hardens, his voice lowering. "I heard what the Lophian said. I do not believe it will devour her. Do not think it is a coincidence the creature chose a male human form. I think it's going to try to prime Star for Life magic and trick the magic into conforming to its will. And it will not be kind. It will not take her feelings or dignity into consideration. It will do whatever it needs to achieve its end." Alec turns away, pacing the length of the room. "Just take that into consideration."

Ethan's stomach rolls, and his arms tighten around Andrea. He looks down, unable to bear staring at anything. "I need...I need to think." Andrea twitches, and he elaborates. "You're asking me to willingly participate in killing someone I've grown to care deeply about." His voice sharpens when both Andrea and Alec look like they're about to argue. "No. Fuck you both, she's *alive*. Living and breathing. I need time to consider."

Alec nods with a heavy sigh. "Understandable. I doubt the Lophian is going to show up any second, so I think we have at least a day or two." His fists curl. "But I've underestimated it before. So. You know. Don't take too long."

Ethan is pretty sure if he stays another moment inside this room with Alec, he's going to open his gun locker and shoot the man. He gives Andrea one last squeeze and avoids her eyes when he pulls back. The sadness and pain in them will break him.

The sun is well set at this point, darkness bathing the meadow. Well, near darkness. A light luminosity comes from Star's crater, lighting the tree in an eerie underglow of pale pink.

The crickets chirp so loudly, it's near deafening. Ethan stands on his porch at an utter loss of what to do. His head hurts. His heart hurts. Fuck, his whole body hurts. His sister is scared. He's scared. And Star...

Star...

Ethan swallows, throat burning.

He's moving before he fully comprehends what he plans to do. The dry grass crunches under his feet as his eyes adjust to the oppressive darkness. The moon is full and heavy above, bathing the meadow in a heavenly glow.

And then there is the crater. Where it all began.

His toes touch the edge. It's nearly full of water now. Or, is it water? His blood no longer taints it, and it looks to be a lightly shimmering liquid. The opalescent sheen is similar to the magic that swarmed him when he first found Star.

He can hear Star's sobs from the inner depths of the oak, the roots so wild that it obscures her.

He carefully takes off his shoes, setting them neatly on the ground next to him. He sets his phone, keys, and everything else in his pockets beside them. Fully clothed, he sinks into the watery substance. It's cool, but pleasantly so, with the same consistency he would expect of normal water. He wades out, the ends of his hair dragging on the surface of the water.

Memories of their last time together here come to him, that terrible night when everything was shattered apart. Their wonderful peace, their growing affection for each other. Even the dogs he finds himself missing. He would've gladly gotten Star as many dogs as she wished. Maybe bought this place off Lisa or convinced her to let him rent it long-term. He could do his work remote. Andrea would've had breakfast with them every day. They would've lived so happily out here, in peace. It would've been wonderful, a life that would've ended the debilitating ennui he suffered for so long.

A life of love. A life of passion.

A beautiful dream. Nothing more.

He loops under a branch, ducking beneath the water to clear a few more. Then, he's in the very center, where the roots bow out as if they are taking shape around a bulb. Star lies draped over them, her whole body wracked with the force of her tears, narrow shoulders trembling. Her wet hair plasters to her, dull against her ashy skin.

He dunks under once more to push his hair back and out of his face. The action brings him close enough to reach out a tentative hand to touch her shoulder. She shivers, turning and collapsing into his hold. His arms wrap so tightly around her, his face against her neck as she does the same. She cries and cries, and he feels tears burn trails down his face, his breath stuttering.

They stay like that, protected by the oak, hidden from the world, and wrapped in their own grief until their tears run dry, the exhaustion setting in. Ethan holds Star up above the water, his head resting against hers. Her hair is dry now and gives off a sweet scent. Something about it makes his mouth water and his heart ache with want, which in turn enflames his grief.

Alec's words haunt him. They don't have much time, the thing he wishes they had above all else.

Time. Just a little bit more time.

Star's voice is a low whisper that echoes oddly in this magical space. "I tried, Ethan. I tried so hard."

He tilts his head slightly, trying to decipher her meaning.

Her arms tighten around him. "I wanted to kill the Lophian. I thought, if I do that, then it will be okay. I could do it. Stop all this. But when I tried," she trembles lightly, "my magic failed. It failed me, Ethan, and I don't understand why. Why would it do that? It seems to be a part of me. The more I look upon it, the more I see it. Yes. Me. Mine. And it's something that I can weave into my fabric of existence, because that's what it is. It is me. But then, when I called upon it..." Her voice is almost gone. "It failed me."

He has no answer, not sure what to say to make it better.

Her voice is small, more of a breath than anything else. "What do I do? Tell me what to do, Ethan."

Stay with me. Be with me. Forever. But that's not one of two shitty options the universe is giving them. He swallows painfully, his throat tight. "I can't do that, Star. I can't make this choice for you." He takes a deep breath, then another. And a third for luck. "Whatever you want, Star. I'll do whatever you want. If you want to run, then we'll run. We'll run so fucking far so fast that they'll never find us. And we'll keep running and going." He'll go back inside, get his gun, shoot Alec in the head if he has to, say goodbye to Andrea no matter how much it hurts him to do so, and speed away. He'd do it. He knows he would. The overwhelming sense to go and do just that almost has him moving.

Star begins to cry again. "I wish we could, but we can't." She leans back, looking at him with her beautiful blue eyes, the cosmos swirling in the dark centers. "Astra told me so in dreams. It took me so long to piece them together, but like I told you, the puzzle pieces just started to click together. Remember what Jenny said about Amaterasu?"

He nods and she continues. "She was one of us. A star. She fell in love with her Contender. She figured out that if she bled herself a little at a time, she could keep herself too weak to fully enter the priming. She made her beloved emperor pearls. Many, many pearls." Star's lip trembles. "But the cost. The creature..."

When Star's eyes go far and she falls silent, Ethan speaks up. "A Lophian?"

Star blinks, but she continues to stare off in the distance. "No...the thing Alec calls the Harvester. It was..." She flinches so violently, water sloshes between them. Ethan adjusts quickly to keep her in his arms. Her voice becomes strained. "It was enraged that the game was not being played. He hurt us." She sobs. "He hurt us until the heavens filled with our *screams*. But Amaterasu turned her eyes away from our suffering and continued to bleed herself. The pain of the bleeding was excruciating, but she suffered through it. We do not replenish blood like humans do. Sacred blood. Sacred pearls. She made many to keep her beloved's line strong. Kept his people strong, until she bled her last drop and withered away to nothing. Dust in the wind. The game complete, with no winners."

Star swallows, her eyes meeting Ethan's again. They shine with a haunting that he feels in his bones. "The Harvester was patient. He waited. Waited until the last of the pearls were used by her beloved's descendants. And he struck a mighty death blow. Death magic this world has never seen the likes of. The game rigged. The Land wept its agony. Tainted." She shudders, eyes closing in pain. "His cruel vengeance complete."

When she opens her eyes again, Ethan can see the deep sorrow in them, and he feels it echoing in his soul. "There is no running, Ethan." She strokes a hand lovingly down his face. "I get so few options in my long life. So many that have been robbed from me. But this? *This* is something I get to choose for myself." Her fingertips graze his lips. "I want you to prime me, Ethan."

This time, he closes his eyes, his heart aching. His voice strains. "Do you know what will happen if I do?"

"Yes." The water shifts, and he opens his eyes to see her so close, their bodies flush with each other. "I understand. It will end the game. But there is only one priming." Her lips brush against his. "I choose you, Ethan, willingly and wholeheartedly. My one gift. My blessing. The thing I get for myself."

She kisses him, and it's sweet, soft, filled with such loving trust. His lips move against hers. "I don't think I can." His voice cracks, the words whisper out. "I love you, Star."

She smiles, leaning back. She glows, eyes filling with tears. "I love you too, Ethan. That is why I want this." Her beautiful eyes fill with such a sad sort of joy that he feels his own eyes burn. "You've given me so much in our short time together. Such joyful memories. Please. Give me this one last one. One that will see me to the end."

It hurts. Everything hurts. But he stares in her eyes and knows his answer. He swore he would help her, and if this is what she wants, then this is what he'll give her.

Because he loves her. Because she loves him. For this one night, they can lie and pretend it will be the first of many. "Okay."

Fourteen

This time when Star kisses him, he does not hesitate. He kisses back, pouring all his love and adoration into it. Star's arms tight around his neck until she's flushed against him, her body warming and her hair returning to its luscious state. His hands run over her body, gripping her a touch too hard at times to feel the way his fingers sink into her thighs, her backside, her arms. She doesn't hold back either, immediately sliding her hands under his shirt to smooth over his skin, nails lightly raking across his back.

Gasps and whimpers, breathless huffs. Star sheds him of his clothing, his shirt floating away, his belt sinking, his pants opening and joining the rest. She strokes him, her eyes flashing hungrily. He moans, pulling her back, kissing her so deeply she melts into it, her whole body going malleable, her mouth curling into a smile against his. Her shirt joins his, and he revels in the feel of her breasts overwhelming his hands, his mouth licking and sucking when she arches back. Her nails scrape his scalp, her thighs wrapping around his hips.

A hum vibrates through him, through both of them. The water flashes, growing steadily brighter. Ethan lifts his head, looking around in wonderment, but Star grips his hair, drawing him back to her lips. She pulls him down, and he hesitates, looking at the water around her, but Star just smiles. "It's okay. Come with me."

Ethan licks his lips, eyeing the pearlescent water, searching Star, and then nods. He takes a deep breath, letting her pull him into a kiss, then down into the water they go. They seem to sink and sink, deeper than the pool actually is. Star is kissing him, her soft body delicious against his, her strong legs gripping his hips, her hands releasing his hair in favor of wrapping her arms around his shoulders.

He needs air. It's been too long. He tries to pull back and up, but Star doesn't let go. "It's okay." Her voice echoes oddly in his ears, in his mind, through his body. She pulls back just enough, her swirling blue eyes watching him, her mass of hair floating around. She smiles, bubbles escaping her mouth. "Breathe, Ethan. Just breathe."

Doubts flood his mind, but he doesn't have much of a choice. His body is demanding air, and he chokes, panicking. The liquid enters his lungs...and he exhales. He blinks, meeting Star's glowing eyes. They breathe the water together, Ethan's body warming and humming.

Star kisses him again. "Trust me."

And he does.

They kiss, touch, wind around each other, weightless in the impossibly deep crater, breathing the strange water. Pleasure begins to pulse in him, his body shivering with it. It's like it was before, when Star first crashed into his life, but so much better.

Star goes to slide down his body, open-mouthed kisses raining down, but he stops her, pulling her back up. He strips her of the last of her clothes and sinks deeper into the water, draping her legs over his shoulders. He licks her sex, and her gasps and moans of pleasure ring like bells around him. Her body undulates, back bowing, hands sliding through her hair in a luxurious bend. He shivers, eyes momentarily closing as he enjoys the moment. He could drown in Star, spend days leisurely eating her to her insatiable heart's content.

He free-falls into the enjoyment of pleasuring her. He lets her roll her hips and buck as she wants, gripping his hair until his scalp burns. He moans with her, his hands sliding up her body, unable to get enough, pleasure echoing softly through him. He tilts his head, shivering when she does, moving his hand back to circle his thumb slowly around her entrance.

Her nails rake across his scalp, gripping it in a mindless move that has him gasping, her orgasm colliding into her. She screams a resounding "YES" that could reach the heavens, her back bowing further. Then she spreads her thighs wide, begging "more, more, more" while grinding against his face.

He smiles against her. Such a greedy thing.

He obliges, smoothing his hands over her spread thighs as he licks. Her orgasm keeps building higher and higher, the light around them pulsing with it. She grabs her knees, spreading herself wider, and he tongue-fucks her, his arm looping around a thigh so his thumb can rub her clit. She sobs his name, arching wildly, and he moans against her.

The spongy, muddy ground of the crater hits Ethan's back. He blinks, surprised, looking down at it. Star slips from his hold, and he turns back to her. She smiles brightly, her skin glowing pure white. She kisses him, tongue swiping deep in his mouth, and he grips her tightly, her naked body pressed against his.

She sits up, thighs straddling his hips, her hands on his chest. His eyes flare when she looks at him with giddy excitement. Her voice is a husky whisper that he can feel echo all the way from the tips of his toes to his cock. "You have no idea how long I've waited to do this."

He smiles, her excitement intoxicating. "If I remember correctly, you were rather good at riding..."

Her smile curls in a dark, sensual way that sends Ethan shivering with a spark of anticipation. She slides her hands covetously up his stomach to rest on his pecs, her strength pinning him in place. His teeth sink into his bottom lip as he waits patiently for her next move. She lifts up, head tilting, teasing him, teasing herself before sinking down to take him to the root in two lust-filled drops. His hands convulse on her thighs, pleasure washing over him, his hips rolling.

Star's back bows, and she rocks her hips, nails nicking his chest. "Oh fuck, *yes!*"

It's his only warning.

She rides him with the same joyful abandon she has for all new experiences. Her head tosses back, her hips slamming down on him, her voice filling the space. She chases her pleasure, using him in that way he's fantasized. It nearly breaks Ethan's self-control. He grips her hips tightly, the sounds coming from him like nothing he's ever heard. His toes curl and splay, his heels digging into the muddy ground as he fights his basic instinct to come. It feels too good, Star going too fast, her walls gripping him too tightly. Oh *fuck*, he needs to hold back. He needs to keep control. He needs to wait.

He opens his eyes to meet hers, finding a wicked glint in them that almost tips him over the edge. She licks her lips, moving faster to watch the panic flash over his face. He's going to fail, he just knows it. She wants something from him, something dark and cruel, and it sparks a level of pleasure he's never experienced. A gasped plea escapes his lips, and she falters with a needy gasp. "Please, Star. I'm going to come. Please."

She moans deeply, teeth sinking into her lips, and he's begging now, an almost continuous string pouring from him. The pleasure in him grows and grows, his hips shivering, his back arching. Her eyes flutter, nails raking angry trails as she spasms. She gives a strangled cry, almost losing rhythm, but he thrusts up, not letting her lose the beginning tendrils of her orgasm until it finally hits, his name on her tongue like a prayer.

His control snaps like a thread. He cries out, hips snapping up to meet her as he comes, and comes, and fucking *comes*. His eyes roll back, and he seems to not be stopping, Star still riding him and making the most sinful of sounds. His lungs seize, neck straining, dick pulsing, and right when he thinks he's about to pass out, she collapses on his chest, limp and panting.

The space around them still echoes with the sounds, like there are many of them in a large cavern, all coming to the same mind-blowing peak at slightly different times. Ethan and Star stay wrapped around each other, listening to the echoes until, finally, the last whisper dies away. All that is heard is their resonant breathing.

Ethan idly strokes Star's back as she lays on his chest. Realization dawns on him slowly. He's still hard, probably due to the nature of the priming. Meaning, he can keep going until she's satisfied, and knowing Star, that won't be anytime soon. He's looking at hours of worshiping her perfect body, and that is the only good thing about this situation.

She lifts her arm to study her tattoo, running her fingertips over each and every one of her charms. "You've given me so much joy, Ethan. Thank you." Before he can respond, she lifts up just enough to kiss him slowly, luxuriating in the feel. She murmurs against his lips. "I love you, Ethan."

His heart aches, and he finds himself unable to keep the words to himself. He needs her to know how deep his love runs. If he doesn't, he knows the regret will haunt him for the rest of his days. "I love you, Star." His thumb grazing her jaw. "If..." He swallows thickly. "If I can't have you, I'll have no one else. There will only ever be one of you. One us." He shakes his head. "I'll never marry. I won't find someone else. This is it."

"But, Ethan..." Her eyes flicker with sadness. "I want you to be happy."

"Hey." He gives her a soft smile, one that is only for her. "I thought I'm yours?"

Her eyes flair, her arms tightening. "You are mine."

"Then that settles it." He whispers against her lips, feeling her smile against him. "I love you, Star. Now and forever. Nothing in this universe will change that."

"Ethan. Thank you." She kisses him, and he feels her heart pour into it.

Hours pass, perhaps even days. Ethan completely loses his sense of time as they kiss and kiss, bodies joining over and over, mindless, overwhelming pleasure eating away sense of self, until Star blinks at him with fully blue eyes, no whites visible. A pleasure like he's never felt takes over him, and he cries out, shivering, moving harder, eyes rolling back, Star slapping against him, her nails raking burning trails down his back. When she comes, her voice has an oddly harmonic effect, power pulsing and humming, and he feels like his soul is being sucked from him, his back bowed, his hips snapping powerfully as he empties into her for the final time.

Exhaustion, bone-deep and all-consuming, weighs his body down. He sinks deeper and deeper into the mud, his eyes closing, Star's warm body the only thing anchoring him as his unconsciousness washes him away.

Ethan is in a place he doesn't recognize. A white, echoing space. Vast emptiness with such brightness.

Star.

She stands away from him, her side to him, her lavender hair floating all around. A woman stands before her, long white hair pouring off of her like a river flowing. She holds a glinting star in each hand, and her eyes glow white like the space around them. Jenny's vase flashes before him, and his eyes flare in recognition. Astra.

Star's voice echoes from afar. "Please. Tell me."

Astra's voice harmonizes oddly with itself, distant yet also a whisper in his ear. "Death is the only outcome."

"No." Star's eyes fill with tears. "I want more time."

"There is no running." Flashes of another woman, one who slices her skin, and liquid pearls pour forth like the tears from her eyes. Amaterasu. "There is only death." A flash, a bomb exploding, lives destroyed, the Land weeping in agony. "Death is the only outcome."

Star's arms wrap around herself. "Please. *Please*."

Many voices, echoing everywhere. "There is only death. Death. Death. Death. Yours or his. Death." The room suctions, Ethan's ears popping, and Astra speaks once more. "There is no other outcome."

"No!" Star's eye flash in rage. "No. He is *mine*. I will not allow him to die!" Her teeth bare in a snarl. "Ethan will live. We will live. Together!"

"Yours or his. Let go of the dream..."

Humming echoes in the room. Suddenly, Astra speaks in one voice, and Ethan sees a woman beneath a man as he ruts into her, her eyes glowing iridescent white, her back arched in ecstasy. She cries out, mouth stretched wide as her pleasure peaks. She gasps, her voice barely a whisper. "There is no running. Death is the only outcome." She shivers violently, legs tightening around his hips. "There is only death. Yours, or his. There is no other possibility." Her eyes are clearing, and Ethan sees her dilated pupils with the cosmos swirling within them turning to him. Their eyes connect, and he sucks in a breath as he's swallowed by her stare, as if her soul links with his. Magic hums. She whispers, tears filling her eyes. "Let go of the dream, but never the love."

From afar, Star takes a shuddering, sob-choked breath, but he cannot see her. Her voice cracks. "I understand."

The vision is sucking away from him, and Ethan desperately reaches out into the darkness in vain hope of finding Star within, but it's no use. The dream is disappearing like wisps of smoke between his fingers. Panic fills him, his body beginning to dissolve into the void as well.

As the particles of his form fade away, he makes one last wish, one last vehement plea to the heavens to make it all come to an end. *Please, let her come through this. Please, let her make it out alive. Please. I love her. Please.*

Take me instead. Please. Don't hurt her. Please...please...whatever she needs... take from me... Save her...

A dark, terrifying, guttural laugh echoes, growing, filling the space, and his exposed soul trembles in fear.

Ethan awakens, surfacing from the water with a mighty gasp. The dawn light burns his eyes, his lungs heaving for more and more air. He blinks blurrily, one hand holding Star's limp body to his chest, the other combing back his dripping hair. He's shivering, the water rippling away from him in little tremors. He doesn't let go of Star, tightening his hold so her head rests on his shoulder.

He *hurts*. His bones ache like they're hollow. All over, muscular weakness has him in a vise, and all he can do is hold Star to him while he keeps them both above the surface. They stay like that for what feels like hours.

The oak's roots shift in the dawn. No longer a tight ball, they now branch out, allowing some visuals to leak through. The first sign of movement clenches his heart painfully, body flinching, but it is only Andrea, circling and circling the crater, his shotgun in her tight fist. He catches glimpses of Alec here and there, squatting down to observe the roots better. They leave them be, and Ethan is thankful for it.

He needs a moment to collect his thoughts and strength.

Star's voice is the softest of whispers in his ear. "It wasn't always like this. We used to be free..." Her head tilts toward him. "So long ago. Lifetimes ago. Before this world was even living. Then *he* captured us...somehow...like a mighty net in his body... At first it wasn't so bad. We watched. It was nice. Watching. Always watching." Ethan rests his face against hers, listening to her recollection. "And then the game started...and he plucked us one by one. Tossed to the starved wolves. Torn apart." She flinches. "Drops of pure magic in a magicless world, we changed everything, and it delighted the creature." He feels a burning tear stain his cheek. "A cruel, malicious monster."

Star's arms are floating in the water, and they begin twitching. He takes her hands in his, wrapping both their arms around her middle. Her voice cracks. "We have great magic, but the creature has cursed us. Such a simple curse, one that he managed to weave so deep into our essence that we cannot differentiate it from what we are. We can use our magic as long as it's not to protect ourselves. Cruel. So unbelievably cruel. It's why I can help you, but I can't save myself from the inevitable."

A breeze kicks up, the oak leaves rustling. Star's low voice is heavy with the weight of her confession. "I watched you, Ethan."

Ethan stills, and his heart skips. Slowly, he raises his head from where he rested against her. "You...watched me?"

She attempts to nod. "I waited to jump by you because I wanted to be with you, to connect with you. I wanted it so much that even with no memory, I created a link between our souls with this." Her left arm twitches, and he turns it to reveal their tattoos side by side.

Ethan smooths his thumb over Star's hand, his voice rasping. "Why?"

"You were so sad and lonely, Ethan. I wanted to help you not be so anymore." Her voice trails as her tears slip down her face. "I understand what it is like to be lonely."

Ethan's inhale is harsh, his throat tightening as a pressure builds in his eyes until he squeezes them shut. Star weakly tugs their joined hands to wrap around her body. She's so quiet, the crunching of Andrea's boots circling the crater almost drowns her out. "I don't understand why Astra would talk to me. Why me? Is it because I am the oldest? My magic ancient and strong? But why not the others..." Her fingers twitch against his. "She was always clever. Astra. Watching to solve, not out of enjoyment. Some of us...are specialized. Astra was a prophet. We thought she was prophesizing for the human that took her." Ethan's body goes cold, and his eyes open when Star whispers, "There is no running. Death is the only outcome. Yours, or his. There is no other possibility."

Ethan's mind echoes with the last line, the one Star did not say. *Let go of the dream, but never the love.*

His heart hammers so hard that he's sure Star can feel it against her shoulder. But she continues, unaware. "It would've been a logical reaction to the end of priming due to her magic's nature. And the man did kill the sea creature that came to devour Astra's body..." She shakes her head weakly. "But no. I see now what happened. The curse wouldn't let her prophesize to save herself, so she used the last of her magic to try to save me. Or maybe it's just me that she happened to see. I don't know.

"Perhaps she saw a vision of us trying to run away together and that vile monster watching us from above retaliating with some horrific punishment." She swallows thickly, her voice cracking. "It makes sense. After all, she did send me visions of Amaterasu. A warning of how unreserved the creature is with its cruelty. It worked. We didn't run and now we're at the end."

Ethan's heart clenches, his stomach rolling and acid pressing against the back of his throat.

Her words have a tremor to them. "Ethan...you must live. I can only face this knowing you'll make it through. Maybe that's what Astra saw. An ease for my end." Her breath is strained. "Ethan..."

His voice rasps from his repressed tears. "Yes, Star?"

"My blood..." The shaking is getting worse. "When I landed. It mixed with the earth." She gasps, neck arching back on his shoulder. "Dive to the bottom and find the pearls. Use them."

It takes Ethan a few breaths before he's able to speak. "I don't want to leave you."

"You must." She tries to shift out of his hold but is too weak to get far. "Do it, Ethan. Give them to Alec. He'll know what to do." With a gasp, she manages to move her body to the very limit of his reach. "Go. Leave me, Ethan. Please. I need time."

Against every fiber of his being, he lets go of Star. She floats, body curling into a tight fetal position, her arms wrapped over her head. His chest tightens like a vise, and his eyes burn. He knows he'll see her like this in his nightmares for the rest of his life, but he listens to her final wish. Alec said that they need to protect her while she primes, and Ethan will not fail her.

He gulps a breath before diving under the opalescent water and plunging his fingers into the soft earth below.

It takes Ethan all morning, but he unearths three silvery pearls from the muddy bottom of the crater. They glint a pinkish lavender that is so similar to Star's hair that Ethan nearly drowns trying to keep from screaming from the injustice of it all.

Alec kept sending him back down, again and again, to make sure they hadn't missed any until Ethan was sure he's about to pass out. He breathes heavily from where he collapsed on the crater's shore, chugging from the water bottle Andrea hands him. The ever-blooming wildflowers tickle his neck, and one golden poppy in particular annoys the shit out of him. He swipes it away, but it bobs back to bounce against his lips. He's loath to kill any of Star's flowers, even if he's crushing many of them under his weight. He holds the poppy away so that he can choke down the protein bar Andrea retrieved from the house without accidentally eating a petal. His stomach rolls, cramping something awful when the food hits his sour stomach, but he keeps it down while under Andrea's sharp, motherly glare. It would be annoying if he didn't understand her motives for forcing him to eat. He's shaky, pale. The last of his strength left him when he finished diving for the pearls.

Star isn't responding to them anymore. She's curled up tight floating in the center of the tree. Once in a while, he'll catch a whimper, see the water ripple from her trembling. He tries his best not to think about it. The whole thing makes him sick. His throat is nearly swollen closed from his surging emotions, and he's barely able to breathe. His protein bar threatens to come back up, but he swallows it back down stubbornly. He doesn't need to add puking to his wretched state. Besides, Andrea would probably make him eat another one, and the first was torturous enough.

Another heartrending whimper reaches him from under the tree, and he shuts his eyes tightly to keep the tears from spilling. Star told him what he needed to do. He needs to focus on that and keep her safe. He has to respect her wishes, no matter how wrong it feels to do so.

Alec's breath shivers out of him, drawing Ethan's focus from his grief. The priest hasn't moved from where he sits cross-legged on the dry grass, the pearls in a little bowl Andrea brought over from the cabin. Ethan's sister plants the butt of Ethan's shotgun on the ground, crouching down to look at the little things gleaming lavender in the sun. She glances at Alec. "Well?"

Alec steeples his fingers, shaking his head. Nods. Then shakes. Ethan closes his eyes and chugs some more water, his patience running dry. He's so tired and utterly drained. All he can do is be trapped in this hellish, grief-stricken existence while he waits for Star to die.

Andrea scoffs loudly. "Just say something! Fuck!"

Alec sighs harshly, Ethan looking over at them again. "Okay. Here's the thing. I already ate a pearl."

"Yes. We're all aware. So, eat another. Fish guy did it."

"Yeah, and risked everything for it! Look. We're not meant to house that much power. One pearl? Yeah. Okay. But *two*?" He points at the bowl. "I have no idea how potent that shit is, and I'm not feeling like getting my guts turned inside out because I chose poorly in this game."

Andrea's eyes flare. "That can happen?"

"With more than one, yes. A hundred percent. It's one of the reasons why we don't pop these things like they're free mints. The Lophian must be desperate to risk it."

Andrea asks the question Ethan is too tired to speak. "Aren't *we* that desperate?"

Alec grimaces. "Kind of. Look. We could each take one, but I have no idea what would happen. It's never been done before."

Her brows raise. "Never?"

"No. It's not allowed, or at least, that's what we've been led to believe. Each side has one Contender. That Contender takes the pearl like a ticket-to-enter kind of thing. No one has broken the rule before—or, at any rate, never survived long enough to fess up to it. It's the reason a thousand Lophians aren't crawling out of the sea to hunt us down. The game is meant to be played one on one. So, who knows what would happen if you took it while I'm alive."

"Okay. No offense, but what if you're not alive? Could we take one then?"

Alec frowns thoughtfully. "I guess. No one who hasn't mastered Tantaloria's *Seventy-Five Thousand Rubrics of Magic Wielding* has ever tried taking a pearl before. The magic may very well just rip you apart. Also, no offense, but you're both kind of useless."

Both siblings glare at the priest, and Alec holds up his hands. "I'm just saying. Hand to hand? I've spent my entire life honing my skills, and that's the bare minimum. Knowing how to command the magic to bend to your will is a whole other thing." He shrugs. "Best to keep to guns, if it makes you feel better to have one."

Andrea points her finger in his face. "Listen, asshole. I could outshoot you any time, any day. Don't fucking doubt that. And Ethan isn't half bad either. Teach us the basics, and we'll be able to figure the rest out once you're dead."

It takes him a few tries, but Ethan musters up enough energy to force the words from his throat. "I'm not taking one."

Andrea blinks at him. "Why?"

"Besides the being torn apart thing?" He lifts a shoulder. "It feels wrong. It's Star's blood, and everything I've heard about this monster-god thing makes me believe it's some sort of cruel, fucked-up trick to cause her kind pain. So, no thank you." He swallows. "She's already suffering enough."

"Fine. Well. How about this. We'll each keep a pearl in case shit goes down. Like if Alec dies and we're about to get wrecked. I'd rather die fighting than running, and maybe Ethan will grow a pair and swallow it when the fish steps over our carcasses."

Alec sighs. "Fair enough."

She arches a brow at Ethan. "Sound good?"

He nods weakly, trying not to think too hard about it. She has a point. When all else fails, he will risk everything to keep the Lophian from getting to Star before she's done doing whatever it is she's doing in that water. Alec holds the bowl out, and Andrea pockets her pearl. Ethan tries to lift his hand for his, but it's too difficult. Andrea scoffs angrily, snatches the pearl, and pushes it into his wet jeans pocket.

Alec sighs again. "Okay. First and only magic lesson. How do you move your arm?"

Andrea blinks. "That's not a lesson."

"Yes, it is. It's the most important one. How do you move your arm?"

She waggles her arm. "I don't know. I just do."

"Exactly. Same goes for magic." Alex points at her. "You just do. Inherently, completely, *unflinchingly* command it like it is a part of your body. You want to walk? You walk. You want to breathe? You take a breath. You want to blast something away from you? You blast it as hard as you fucking can. There is no other way to command it, or it will turn on you." He shakes his head. "And try not to think too hard about all the fucked-up ways it could do that. It'll give the magic ideas. You take that pearl, and you feel it in your very soul that you command it and nothing else."

Andrea eyes the last pearl in the bowl. "Is it really that simple?"

"Yes. Everything else is knowing what it can do and understanding the strength and limitations. So, for now, focus on chasing away any doubts you may have about the magic while I continue to sit here and weigh the risk of being ripped apart from the inside out."

Ethan and Alec silently sit together on the crater's shore for hours. Ethan stares at the arching branches of the oak above him, unable to free himself from his thoughtless, unseeing grief that weighs heavily upon his soul. Alec doesn't help. The priest is a buzzing annoyance at his side who occasionally mutters while contemplating Star's pearl. Ethan skin twitches with the agitation. What he wouldn't give to shove the priest farther away from him and, coincidentally, away from Star's immobile body floating in the roots. It might be petty of him, but he can't shed his general disdain for the man.

It is what it is.

Ethan's hand lifts to rub the uncomfortable weight on his chest.

Andrea suddenly appears in his vision, glaring down at him. "Is this what you're doing with your day? Lying around moping?"

Ethan swallows painfully, his voice gravelly. "Mostly." He can't ease this tightness in his chest. It's shifting to his shoulders.

Andrea sneers. "Pathetic."

The word mildly stings, but he's not paying too much attention. He keeps rubbing his chest, trying to shake this ache.

"She needs you."

His eyes focus again. He's not even sure when they unfocused. Andrea charges on. "She is vulnerable. She is—"

His heart thuds painfully, uneven. "Andy."

"—dying and you can't get off the ground to help protect her."

He swallows again, his ears roaring, his chest tightening. "Andy."

"Get the fuck up, Ethan! Shower, eat, get a gun and—"

He sucks in a painful breath. "I can't breathe."

Pain erupts in a wave of agonizing pins and needles all over his chest, prickling their way along his neck toward his face. Ethan claws at himself, eyes shutting tightly, fighting to draw in air. Chaos roars in his ears, his heart hammering, his chest *burning*.

Someone grabs his shoulder, fighting him to roll him onto his back. But he can't. He stays curled on his side, clawing and gasping until he can't even do that, his lungs like lead weights in his chest. His eyes snap open, spots in his vision. Something wrenches him onto his back, a hand slamming onto his sternum.

Magic roars through him, sizzling his insides to what feels like a crisp. Ethan takes a mighty gasp of air, and it sears him, but he does it again and again. Copper floods his mouth, and he realizes he's bitten his tongue. He turns his head to spit out the mouthful of blood, still gulping down air as much as he can, each second getting easier and easier.

He blinks, the spots in his vision bleeding away to sparkles and, finally, to clearness. Andrea is ashen, her hazel eyes too wide, hands clasped to her chest. Tears stream down her face, and Ethan tries to comfort her, but the pain in his limbs is intense. Alec hovers over him, his hand on Ethan's chest pinning him down.

Ethan swallows, his tongue healing with a humming rush. His voice is nearly gone, but he forces out a "thanks."

Alec nods, his dark brows furrowed. "You okay?"

Ethan shakes his pounding head. The pain is bleeding away, and he tries to concentrate, but his arms still won't move. The burning, the prickling. Slowly, it sidles down to his left arm, and he manages to rotate it to stare at the tattoo there. He whips his head toward the tree. The water is vibrating. He chokes, gasping, and manages to point.

Alec notices, leaping to his feet.

Star is glowing, but it is not her usual coloring. It's a chaotic clash of light and dark, as if thunder is roiling under her skin. She thrashes, sloshing water, her mouth stretched in a silent scream. Ethan forces his body to roll over, fighting the overwhelming weight of his limbs. His fingers dig into the ground, pulling him forward. The single-minded obsessive thought thundering in his head screams at him to get to her. To help her. To save her.

Andrea grabs his shoulder. "Don't."

He gasps. "I have to help her."

"No. We don't know what's happening. She's magical, Ethan. She might hurt you."

He shakes his head. "No. She'd never."

His body lurches forward, but Andrea holds him back, her arms linked tightly around his chest. Alec steps up to the crater's edge, the furrow in his brow deepening, his jaw slack. Ethan watches the priest, waiting for some insight, the flashing chaos of Star's silent agony blinding in his peripheral vision.

Alec shakes his head, stepping back. "That's—what—" He shoots Ethan a glare. "What did you do?"

Ethan's eyes flare. "Me?"

"Yeah." Alec points toward Star. "That is not normal. She shouldn't be doing that. It's supposed to be some sort of, I don't know, cocooning. Not," he waves his hands, "whatever the hell that is."

Ethan looks toward Star, cold fear washing over him. Did he do this to her? He can't imagine how. Star led their coupling.

Alec's harsh words cut through his introspection. "Did you prime her?"

Ethan blinks at Alec. "Yeah."

"Fucked her?"

Ethan's face contorts in poorly contained rage. "Jesus Christ!"

"Did you fuck her?"

Ethan is on his feet so quickly that Alec startles. After a day of being barely able to move, he's suddenly back to strength. Not completely, but the adrenaline and cortisol help make up the difference. "Yes! We had sex. Happy?"

"No!" Alec points again. "That is wrong!"

They're chest to chest now. Ethan's anger and hurt are looking for an outlet, and unleashing on Alec feels good enough for him. More than good enough. He's been itching to punch the idiot in the face for a second time, since the first was so satisfactory. "It's not like you gave me an instruction manual. Star wanted to be primed. I did whatever she wanted and yes, that included sex. So fuck off!"

"Hey!" Andrea wedges herself between them, shoving. She might be shoving a brick wall for all the good it does against Alec, but she makes Ethan stumble back a few steps. "Stop it! We're scared and stressed and might die from an overpowered fish, but fighting each other is not the answer. It's not going to help Star." She glares at Ethan viciously. "You want to help her?"

His sister's words from earlier hit him hard. His fists ball, and he forces all the exhaustion down, letting the adrenaline take its course. "Yes."

She glares at Alec. "And you want to win?"

Alec scoffs, "Naturally!"

"Then think, assholes! What the hell is happening?"

Alec sighs roughly, his livid gaze turning back to Star. The priest paces the length of the crater, squatting down and examining her. It takes everything Ethan has not to tackle the man to the ground and pummel him, even more to stop himself from diving in the pool of strange liquid. In defense of Andrea's caution, the water *is* starting to crackle with the same mysterious energy as Star's body.

It hurts him to wait on the sidelines. He wasted so much time in a grief-filled haze. The sun is setting, and he did nothing but stare at the sky while Star was alone. Suffering.

He rubs his chest, eyes burning. Andrea rests a hand on him, leaning into his side in an act of comfort. He wets his lips and shakes off the sadness.

If they survive, he will mourn Star for years to come. But for now, he needs to focus.

Alec makes his full circle. He seems calmer as well, like the walk helped focus him. "Okay. So, you went in and had sex."

Ethan pushes down his defensiveness. "Yes."

"Many times?"

He grits his teeth. "As many as she wanted."

"Like more than twice?"

"Christ! Yes! Many times." Ethan forces a calming breath, his anger roaring up.

Alec chews a lip, eyes narrowing. "And conventional sex?"

Ethan snaps. "Yes!" Andrea shoots him a scolding glare, and he tries to even out his breathing. "What does that have to do with it?"

"Because the texts all say that the magic is birthed into the world. That it gestates within the Vessel. So, my line of thinking is that vaginal sex is required. Sorry for the invasive questions." He runs his hand over his buzzed head. "Just trying to look at all angles."

Ethan goes cold, a thought occurring. He barely hears Andrea's two cents. "Okay, but isn't birth painful? Maybe this is just a part of it that no one cared to write about?"

Alec replies before Ethan can bring himself to speak. "I feel like the magical storm that is currently going on would be painstakingly noted with great flowery language. Trust me. Some of these texts are graphically detailed."

Ethan swallows, his mouth dry. "Do any of them say anything about sterility?"

Alec looks confused, but Andrea's eyes widen. The priest speaks while Andrea touches her lips. "No? Not sure if anyone really knew if they were sterile back then." He catches Andrea's reaction, and his gaze narrows on Ethan. "Why?"

Stomach plummeting, Ethan forces the words out. "I'm sterile."

Alec's brows furrow. "How do you know?"

"I had a vasectomy years ago."

The silence stretches.

"You fucking asshole!"

Alec lunges at Ethan. Andrea tries to stop him, but Ethan throws her out of the way just as Alec takes him to the ground. The wind knocks out of Ethan's lungs, and for the second time today, he fights to gasp in air. Alec grabs his collar, one hand lifting to punch. Andrea throws herself on Alec, wrapping her arms around his raised fist and screaming at him to stop. Alec trembles, eyes full of rage. "You've doomed us all!"

Ethan feels those words deep down in his soul. He wishes Alec would punch him. It would make this moment so much easier to bear with some physical pain to focus on. Andrea is yelling, eyes blazing. "You don't know that! You said it yourself that no one back then would've known if they were infertile. This could have nothing to do with it. The birthing magic is metaphorical, remember?"

Alec whips around to snap back. "Yeah, but none of them surgically sterilized themselves either! Now look at her!" He points at Star's chaotic light display. "Fuck! Just fucking fuck FUCK! We're going to die because I didn't do it myself!" He shoves himself up, Andrea falling back to crouch protectively next to Ethan. He stomps away with a last roared, "FUCK!"

Andrea doesn't take her eyes off Alec while she speaks to Ethan. "You okay?"

"No." He forces himself to sit up. "I fucked it up."

Andrea's hand tightens. "You don't know that."

"No, Andrea. He's right."

Ethan watches Alec's manic pacing, his jaw tensing. He leans toward his sister, his words so quiet only she can hear. "Go get the guns."

Andrea hesitates for only a moment. She takes his pistol out of the holster on her belt and presses it in Ethan's hand. She gets up swiftly and recovers his shotgun. She slings it over her shoulders before racing back to the house.

Ethan stands slowly, keeping his hands relaxed at his side. He angles his body so that his leg blocks Alec's view of the gun in his hand. His dark eyes focus on the pacing priest as the man circles and circles, kicking rocks and screaming.

Ethan counts the seconds, his breaths, as his mind sharpens, exhaustion easing away.

Finally, Alec makes his way back, a glint of something in his eyes. "Okay, I have an idea."

Ethan waits silently for him to continue.

"Maybe we can just do a do-over. I'll go in—"

"No."

Alec blinks. "But—"

Ethan keeps his body relaxed, keeps the gun hidden. "Star said there is only one priming."

Alec throws his hand toward Star. "Yes, but what if it was just partial? Maybe that's what we're seeing. I can go and finish it."

"I said..." Ethan steps back, hand lifting to train the gun on Alec's forehead. "No."

Fifteen

The only noise Ethan hears over the sloshing water in Star's crater is the pounding of his own heart. He stares down Alec, gun trained on the man's head. All he needs to do is pull the trigger and Star will be safe. Safe from this man and his crazed Order. Safe from being forced to prime against her will with someone else. Safe from whatever the hell the Harvester is.

He can do it. He can pull the trigger and be done with it.

Do it and save her. Do it and keep her safe. Something whispers in his ear, a cold, terrible voice that echoes with endless cruelty, *Do it.*

He's heard that voice before. It laughed at Ethan's desperate pleas to save the woman he loves. His hand trembles, his chest tightens, and he gasps for air. His mind is clouded, his vision tunneling around Alec.

A plan blooms before his eyes. He kills Alec, saving Star from this immediate threat, and then they can run away together and just keep running and running and running. *Run.*

Hurt bleeds into Alec's voice, snapping Ethan out of the dark, tunneled space he's sunken into. "Really? After everything I've done for you?" Alec's demeanor hardens, shoulders squaring. "I saved your life. Twice. I fought for you. I fought for your sister. And this is how I'm repaid?" His eyes narrow. "The Order is right. Outsiders cannot be trusted."

Ethan's throat is tight, his teeth clenched. He can shoot Alec, but the Lophian is still out there and coming closer. The memory of Ethan hurt and hopeless when facing the creature pushes past the panic building within him. It focuses him, helps him breathe through the dark mind space.

Andrea is right. Their best chance at survival is to work together.

Ethan swallows past the lump in his throat, blinking hard to clear his tunneling vision. His voice is calmer than he expects. "You did save us. It's why I haven't pulled the trigger." It's a struggle, but he manages to force his chest to take its first full intake of breath since Andrea handed him his gun. "Alec. Star said there is only one priming. That's it. Not multiple. She wanted only me and no one else. Even though I appreciate what you've done, I won't let you hurt her. Do you understand?" His eyes narrow. "I will not let you *rape* her, Alec."

Alec grows ashen, and he takes a step back, his hands becoming fists. His green eyes fill with shame before he drops his gaze, his voice raw with emotion. "You're right. Fuck. I'm sorry. It's just..." The way he taps his forehead, like he's trying to shake a voice from his head, sends a wave of coldness down Ethan's arms. Perhaps they both had that cruel voice whispering in their ears. "The stress got to me, but I'm cool now." He waves at Ethan. "You can lower the gun."

But Ethan doesn't, his eyes stay trained on Alec. What if Alec is lying and Ethan is making a mistake by not killing the man?

As Alec's eyes dart from the gun to Ethan, a flicker of uncertainty and distrust sharpens his gaze. He's still, too still, like a snake preparing to strike, and Ethan's finger curls around the trigger. *Do it.*

The crunching grass from behind him snaps Ethan out of his dark thoughts with a gasp. Cold sweat blooms down his spine, and he shudders in the summer heat. His free hand scrapes the escaped tendrils of hair from his bun out of his face. That must be Andrea returning from the house, and each approaching sound eases the tension in Ethan's shoulders. Andrea will help Ethan sort this out.

Unless...she's in on it.

At the absurdity of the thought, Ethan sucks in a hissing breath through his teeth, whipping his arm down and taking his finger off the trigger. "Sorry. I just..." He gestures at his forehead in hopes of conveying the unsaid jumble of feelings inside him and re-engages the safety. "Got carried away."

Alec nods stiffly, his eyes drifting over Ethan's shoulder. He stands still, eyes widening, and a creeping sensation crawls up the back of Ethan's neck, his heartrate spiking. Ethan hesitates for one infinite second, the uncertainty of Alec's motives niggling at him, before he turns around to see what caught the man's attention, his gaze sweeping the vista.

Andrea smiles brightly about halfway to them from the house, Ethan's spare shotgun secured in her hand. It's an older, less interesting version of the Mossberg Andrea had claimed. She holds up a bag of shells for him to see.

Then, Ethan's gaze drifts past her to the corner of the house, where a pale, dark-haired man stands. Sharp teeth glint in a feral snarl.

Ethan's heart plummets, time slowing. A scream echoes in his mind, his heart pounding, his vision blurring as pure panic drowns his sanity. Not his sister. Please, God, not his sister. He'd begged the universe to take anything but Star. He never thought it'd claim something else in her stead.

His exhale rushes out of him, his eyes burning. No. Fuck, *no*. He can't lose Andrea. His pistol whips up, and he takes aim. His bellow echoes through the valley. "ANDREA! DOWN!" Then, he fires rapidly. Andrea hits the dirt, the tall, brown grass obscuring her.

The Lophian raises his large hand. The bullets freeze midair, and Ethan gasps for breath.

Andrea reappears and starts running to him.

The bullets vault toward her, controlled by the Lophian's magic. Ethan roars, unsure if he's screamed a word or just made a primal noise of fear and pain. His limbs are anchored, eyes burning, gun empty. Please, God. Save her.

A sudden explosion rocks Ethan, and Andrea is knocked off her feet, the force throwing her to the ground again. Ethan sucks in a breath, turning to see Alec's hand raised next to his face. The man takes a steadying breath, sweat blooming across his forehead. Whatever Alec did, he made the bullets combust and ended this deadly ping-pong game. It cost him greatly though; his scarred hand trembles before going limp at his side. His shoulders roll in, eyes dulling for a moment, and Ethan prepares to catch him if he falls.

Movement across the field draws Ethan's attention again, and he focuses on the threat before them. The creature is slowly advancing across the field with no sign of fatigue. Andrea drags herself up and takes off, her long legs

moving her swiftly toward them. The Lophian throws his hand out and
Ethan screams, but instead of his sister exploding, his truck ignites in a ball
of chaotic flame that threatens to take out the house.

There is no running today.

Andrea nearly collides into Ethan, their free hands seeking each other
out in assurance.

Ethan can't tear his gaze away from the approaching Lophian. "Are you
hurt?" he shouts to Andrea, at the same time she asks him, "Did it get you?"

Their clasped hands tremble. Ethan pulls her close. "Run, Andy. Get
out while you can."

She shakes her head, her voice cracking. "No. I'm staying so you don't
fucking die."

His throat is tight, and he fights to swallow. "It might not make a
difference."

Andrea growls, "Then we die together." She throws down her bag of
ammo, snapping open the shotgun and loading it with steady hands. "Let's
do this, Alec."

Alec steps up unsteadily beside Ethan. He turns the pearl between his
scarred fingers, the sheen of purple and pink clenching Ethan's heart. Maybe
it's the light tricking him, but the opalescence is stronger than before, and
Ethan catches a hint of the unique sweetness of Star's hair.

His teeth clench, the pressure behind his eyes building. *Sacred blood.*
Sacred pearls. The pearl gleams like the determination in Star's eyes before it
disappears into Alec's mouth. The priest swallows.

His green eyes go wild, body doubling over with a scream of agony so
sharp that Ethan's ears buzz out, his hands clamping to them. Alec's knee
hits the ground, his hands scratching bleeding trails into his skull. His body
hums, power pulsing like it's trying to rip free, but he roars, forcing it back
down over and over with each painful thud of Ethan's heartbeat.

Andrea isn't distracted by Alec like Ethan is. She has her ammo lined up
how she wants and preps the second shotgun. She thrusts the readied weapon
toward Ethan, and he switches his pistol for it. He shoulders it, taking aim at
the Lophian. The creature is unhurried, its face a blank mask, black eyes so cold
that Ethan feels frost in his heart just from meeting the gaze. He cocks his gun,
ready. Andrea does the same, sinking to one knee. They don't dare fire, not yet.

With one last pain-filled pulse that ruffles Ethan's hair, Alec straightens. A glowing aura of magic shimmers about him, little crackles of electricity traveling down his body. His eyes glow white, his head turning. His gaze locks with Ethan's.

"If I fail, take the pearl." His voice echoes oddly. "Death is the only outcome. Yours, or his. There is no running."

Let go of the dream, but never the love.

Ethan's world spins, and he takes a stumbling step back. The echo in Alec's voice. It was Astra's, Ethan is sure of it. His lips part to ask the ghost of the fallen star something, anything that can help, but Alec's irises return to their normal green, his pupils blown wide. The man straightens, turning toward his adversary. Alec reaches into his pocket, pulling out his small metal rod, and spins his spear into existence.

The tip drags along the ground as Alec walks, the earth lightly rumbling. The Lophian hums, magic crackling and clashing in the air. Two Contenders, like the vase depicted. The roar of the ocean, so far away, sounds loudly in the space, and the Lophian raises its clawed hand. A mirror of Alec's staff appears in his grasp, spinning before arcing down.

They collide, the grass flattening from the force. Ethan throws his arm up to shield his eyes from the debris. Magic whirls all around, and a metallic tang fills his mouth. The darkening sky flashes with the force of each strike, crackles of power threatening to set the dry grass aflame.

Ethan forces his gaze away to turn back toward Star's oak. It tosses in a nonexistent wind, the water no longer opalescent. It's a deep, inky black with bolts of white lightning crackling along the surface. A shiver trembles down his spine at the sight, and the hairs on the back of his neck and along his arms raise.

Something screams at him, his mind spinning to make sense of it all. Through all the chaos, he focuses on the one thing that he now knows with absolute certainty. There is still more he can do, and it's not standing here with a gun. He grabs Andrea's shoulder, fingers digging into the bone. "I need to help Star."

Andrea flinches under his grip, wrenching her shoulder free. She blinks, looking back briefly before training her gaze upon the apocalyptic battle before her. "This is helping Star."

Ethan shakes his head wildly. "No, it's not. Listen, Andy. Something weird is going on."

"No shit."

"No, *weirder*. Do you remember Star telling you about Astra?"

Andrea's brows furrow. "The Vessel on the vase?"

"Yes! She's been speaking to Star." Those white eyes meeting his flash in his vision. "But I don't think she's just talking to Star. She's also been speaking to me. I just fucking know it." His eyes dart up the tree to look to the darkening sky, the moon beginning to rise even though the sun is not fully set. "Astra said, 'Let go of the dream, but never the love.' Star thought it was a message for her, but what if it's not? What if it's for me?"

"Wait, what? What dream?"

He grips the back of his neck. "I don't know. The dream of us being together? Of surviving? Of running away? I don't know, but what I do know is the 'never the love' part." His eyes harden. "I can't do much, but that I can do."

He dumps his guns on the ground next to Andrea. She splutters, "Where are you going?"

Ethan is moving quickly, running to the oak tree. "To help her."

Andrea's high-pitched, panic-laced shriek lances a jolt of guilt through him. "No, Ethan! Come back!"

But it's too late to apologize. Hopefully, one day Andrea will find some way to forgive him for not choosing her after her heartfelt pleas, but he will never forgive himself if he doesn't try to save Star. Star wants him to live, Andrea wants him to live, but Ethan can't stay on the sidelines any longer. Not when Astra has given him hope that there might be a chance, even a small one, that he could save Star. Even if it means he'll die for her chance to live free. *I'm coming, Star. Hold on.*

His boot hits the edge of the crater, the soft dirt folding under his weight, the wildflowers that are in continuous bloom arching their necks to him. He jumps, his eyes trained on the strange fluid beneath the tree and the crackling electricity.

The world splinters away as he crashes into Star's pool. The electricity thunders, pain sizzling up his body. He goes into shock, seizing, convulsing. He breaks through the surface and gasps for air against the pain. It nearly has him clawing back up the side, but he grinds his teeth, eyes opening, and roars through the agony. He turns toward the center of the pool. The light within the roots blinds him, but he squints against it. Step by agonizing step, he forces his body forward. He says one word repeatedly, a word that his pounding heart pulses through his veins. "STAR!"

The burning in his left arm guides him as is the tattooed compass is real, growing more painful the closer to the center he gets. But he's blocked. He pants, his vision flashing when a strong bolt of electricity nearly robs him of his will. The roots have formed a tight ball around the core of the pool. His arm throbs, pointing to it. To Star.

He pushes his hands against the wood. "STAR!" But no answer. He pulls on the roots, his fingers turning white, his shoulders straining. His teeth crack, and he hisses, "Star! Please, please, fuck!" But it's no use. The wood doesn't budge. His eyes burn, his vision blurring as helplessness sweeps over him.

He's going to die in the pool yelling at a tree like a fucking idiot. He squeezes his eyes shut, and tears spill forth, leaving a hot acid trail down his face. He wipes furiously and pauses when his hands burn. He blinks his eyes open and gazes down at his fingers. His tears. They...glow.

The tang of magic hums. Ethan doesn't fully understand what's happening or why, but his fists clench. His hardened gaze flicks to the roots before him. He wipes his face with both hands, his fingers gleaming with lavender and pink. He digs them into a seam within the roots.

"Open...OPEN!" He heaves against the wood as he tries to rip it apart, tears burning his eyes and face. "Fuck you, OPEN!" Raw determination has him roaring, his vision flashing white. "GIVE HER TO ME!"

The wood shifts. Ethan's body screams, but inch by inch, he forces the roots to split until a small sliver parts. Unable to get any more of it to move, he thrusts his left arm into the gap, water sloshing as he swings it widely back and forth, the prickling along his tattoo his only guide.

Ethan's fingers graze something soft and warm. He gasps, shoving himself harder against the ball of roots. His foot slips on the spongy ground, and he nearly loses track of Star when he goes under. His heart is spluttering, his chest tight as if something is sitting on it. His free hand fists his shirt, his other still wedged into the crack he made. Spots form in his vision.

Cruel, cold words slither in his ear. *You're dying, Ethan.*

It's the same uncanny voice that tempted him to shoot Alec. Ethan trembles, and the familiar heartless laugh that taunted his pleas during the priming sounds again, reverberating within his skull like a bell being struck. *You're still as useless as always, but there's time to change that. Get out now and you can be the hero...all you must do...is kill the Contenders...go...before it's too late...*

Ethan's head lolls, his hair floating around him as he sinks deeper. Water fills his mouth and lungs, and they seize. It's not like before during the priming. He can't breathe it. He's drowning. His heart is failing. He's going to die if he doesn't leave. His arm begins to slip out of the roots, his body going limp as the pain eases away with a prickling chill.

Within the roots, something twitches against his slack hand. It wraps around his finger gently. A bloom of warmth spreads within him, his sputtering heart hammering with the familiar vibration of magic that's somehow inside him. It's responding to the touch against his fingers. A hand.

His eyes snap open, gripping the hand within his. Star. She's in there and he must save her. Ethan's foot grinds into the spongy mud, and he shoves off it. His head breaks free of the water, his mouth wide as he chokes and gasps, clearing his lungs of the strange water. He sucks in air, eyes blazing. He digs his feet into the mud and thrusts his left arm further to grip Star's wrist firmly. He's made it this far and he's not going to stop now.

He throws his body back with all his strength until he draws her arm out through the gap. He cries, gasping, tears pouring forth to drench his beard. They drip in the water, cool sweet lavender blooming like ink among the chaotic black.

A terrifying scream of unnatural rage echoes in his mind, but he shoves it away, shoves it back, focusing on his one task: saving the woman he loves. He tears at the roots, his right hand slicing open, but it doesn't stop him. His blood drips out, further diluting the water, until there is no black left around him. Finally, the hole is wide enough for Star's body, and he wrenches on her arm with all his might.

Star spills free and collides into his chest. He wraps himself around her dark, marbled, naked body, drawing her tight to him, his eyes squeezing shut. He chokes out a single word. "Star."

Her chest inflates, and she gasps. Her hands tremble against this face. She sobs. "Ethan...Ethan, no." Panic pitches her deep voice high. "Run. Get out of the water. You'll die."

He shakes his head furiously. "I'm not leaving you."

She tries to shove him, but she's too weak. She chokes on air, her body twisting. "I can't control it. I'll kill you. Ethan. This form will burst apart, and I will erupt into magic. You will *die*! I can't—I can't—" She sobs harder. "I can't kill you."

He shakes his head. "Then we'll die together."

Star screams. "Ethan!"

"Star." He strokes her hair back, tilting her head so he can look into her neon-blue eyes. He's getting weaker, that weight on his chest worse. He whispers when he means to yell. "I love you."

He kisses her. Star's tears stream down her face, mingling with his. She kisses him back, her arms tight around his neck, her fingers snarling in his hair to ruin what's left of his bun. They kiss and kiss. Spots in his vision build and threaten to take him, but he can't lose consciousness. Not yet. She needs him.

Star breaks away first, her head throwing back. Her chest pumps against his, her body trembling. Cracks form along her flesh, but Ethan holds her hard, pressing the splintering skin back together by force. Star sobs, whimpering, "Not Ethan. Please. Don't take him too."

He buries his face in her neck, breathes in her scent. If this idiotic plan doesn't work, at least they'll be together. He whispers his love against her throat, his arms tightening, his tears soaking into her skin.

Vibrating, rumbling magic trembles the water, ripples forming and the tree swaying. Star roars, her eyes glowing a blue so dark, it's nearly black. She lowers her head to press against his neck. He kisses her hair, nuzzling. "Together."

Power blasts, the world trembling. Ethan's eyes close.

Star convulses, seizes, her flesh cracking more and more, her sacred blood dripping to mingle with the lavender water. She heaves in breath, her voice changing, deeper, beautiful, like the darkness of night with the cosmos lighting the world. "You will not take him." Her fingers turn to claws and she shrieks, "HE IS MINE."

Ethan's soul shivers, and the world around him explodes. The water surges like a wave, the black oil descending upon them. Darkness wraps around him, trying to pour into his mouth, his eyes, his ears, but a pulse shivers the liquid. The silvery lavender from his tears slides up him, coating him, coating Star. It shimmers like the stars, cool and lovely.

Star lifts her head from Ethan's neck, her eyes no longer that darkness but the white glow. She screams, the noise so sharp it threatens to burst his eardrums, like it did when she killed the first fish monster, but the silvery water protects him, keeps him whole and untouched. The blackness bursts apart like oil being skimmed from the ocean. Droplets hover all around, Ethan's hair floating with Star's, their strands wrapping together. Then, fire erupts.

The dark oils sizzle with an ungodly scream, acidic smoke curling up and absorbing into the oak. The leaves above shiver as tiny flowers bloom and acorns form, then wither to be absorbed and cycled again. The blooms along the crater edge drip down into the water, the muddy earth coating in aquatic grass.

The cracks along Star's body seal up one by one until she is whole again in Ethan's arms, her pale skin shimmering like the first time she created her body.

Star's lashes flutter, and the blaze wisps away, the suspended water tumbling back down in a gentle rain.

Star goes limp in his hold, and Ethan panics before he feels her steadily breathing in his arms. Alive.

He presses his forehead against hers and weeps, one of his arms around her shoulders keeping her above water and the other softly stroking her to reassure himself she is still whole. The water shifts, and Star's hand surfaces to cup his face, her eyes sleepily opening. Her thumb collects a tear, her brows furrowing. "Ethan...are we dead?"

He laughs, his smile so wide it hurts, and shakes his head. "No, beautiful. We're alive."

"But...how?"

He gently catches her hand in his so that he can kiss her strong pulse, his heart dancing with his surging elation. "You said it was easier to use your magic when it came to saving me. I figured what better way to save yourself than by putting myself in danger."

Her breath hitches, her voice firm in reprimand. "Ethan. You could've died if I hadn't overcome the curse."

He smiles wider, his eyes dancing. "Did it work? Did you break the curse?"

Her lips pinch, her annoyed face so cute that he laughs again. She softens marginally, her finger extending from where he holds her hand to brush his lips. "I did break it for only myself. I don't think the others above are affected. My memories are back too." She pauses when he kisses her tracing fingers, her blue eyes locked on the movement. "When I created my connection with you, I think I accidentally embedded a drop of my magic in you as well. Maybe when I landed, or when I made my tattoo from yours. Perhaps that's why it tingles. I think you woke it when you were trying to save me. It's what saved you in the end."

He brushes his nose against hers. "You could never hurt me, Star."

She mumbles angrily, but her hands leave his to wrap around him. "Never do that again, Ethan. Your sweet smile can only work so many times to gain my forgiveness."

He huffs, their lips touching. "I doubt that."

He kisses her so softly, so sweetly, that he forgets everything around them. There is just the two of them, Star's arms around him, her chest against his. The sun is gone, and the flashing lights of the battle that still rages isn't enough to pull Ethan away from having this moment with Star. Finally, they can live. Together.

In his long, endless life, the creature has been called many things. The Reaper. The Harvester. The Shepherd. The Hunger. The Devourer.

But never has he been called a Failure.

Rage roils down his massive form, his gelatinous body rippling with hot fury. He screams his unholy call, his claws gripping the edge of the universe until the reality creaks from the pressure of his power.

He knew that the *thing*, the one they call "Star," was going to be a nuisance in his Game. It's why he waited so long to drop her. She is as old as he, maybe older, and that thought alone makes his head thrash. How *dare* she defy his power.

A gurgling growl ripples down his long form, the little specks of living light peppering his flesh not daring to wink. He turns his massive head to gaze upon the little creatures that he swallowed all those millennia ago. The resulting vibration of fear from their tiny forms is the only pleasure he feels beneath his rage.

His horrible eyes land on the hole left behind from when he ripped that wretched Star from his body. Then, his gaze slides to the littlest light beside it. The one with a tinge of red.

His long tentacles curl, eyes narrowing with malicious glee. He *will* make Star pay for her insolence. The sky will sing with her siblings' screams. One by one, he will hurt them until the Star begs for forgiveness.

And he knows exactly which sibling to start with.

Sixteen

Star rips away from Ethan's kiss with a sharp gasp, her eyes peeled wide as she stares up through the roots and branches of her oak. Her body trembles, tears welling in her eyes. Her body wracks, and she whispers, "Sidra."

Ethan looks up, searching frantically. "What? What is it?"

Star swallows thickly, her eyes squeezing shut before she looks away sharply. Despair twists her features, and her eyes are full of pain when she finally looks upon him. "I am free, but they are not. The creature is hurting them. I can hear their screams."

Ethan's breath hisses in. "The Harvester?"

"We call him the Devourer, for that is what he does. He devours. A creature so cruel and hateful, a blight upon our existence. And he's furious that we've defied his Game."

She cups Ethan's face, and her hand trembles. "Ethan..." But the words get caught in her throat, her large eyes shimmering with welling tears. He strokes her bare back, and it calms her enough to continue. "I've watched you for longer than you know. I was up there, so fascinated, so enthralled by life in this world. Always. Like an addiction. I think it's how the creature was able to swallow us all those centuries ago. I looked down at this world when I should've looked up. It's my fault." Her voice cracks. "I reacted too late to stop it."

His face softens, heart aching with sympathy. "Star—"

"And then there was you."

His breath catches. "Me?"

Tears cling to her lashes like glittering stars. "I've watched you for so long. Admired your strength, your deep love for the women in your life. Always unwavering love, even when some did not deserve it. Such love." She presses their foreheads together, her fingers tight in his hair. Her breath tickles his lips as she whispers, "I think that's when I started to fall in love with you. I dreamed of a life down here, a life with you. Life as a human woman who you loved and cared for." Her breath hiccups, her voice nearly too low to hear. "I wanted to be loved by you so badly. And it's why I was chosen."

His eyes flare, but he does not dare speak. Star huffs a few breaths, flinching violently at whatever it is that he cannot hear. Finally, she continues. "The Devourer could not resist sending me, the oldest, the strongest, down to die in the ocean, a place I feared most for the kind of horrible, cruel magic it would force me to birth. But there is more than that. I'd die knowing that you were on this land so heartbroken and in need of someone to be loved by, and I'd be trapped in the sea." Her shoulders wrack. "I would've died in my worst nightmare, and I could not stand it. So many years and *years* of my siblings horrifically killed while being so powerless. It was too much."

Ethan's teeth grind as Star's voice rasps with anger. "I fought the creature when he reached for me." Her hands shake, her shoulders becoming rigid. "It made him angrier, but I held onto his hateful body with all of my strength, strength I'd been slowly storing for that moment, for when the world turned enough so that I'd land by you...and I jumped."

Star falls silent. The distant sounds of Alec and the Lophian's fight mingle with their breaths. Ethan's mouth is open, his eyes wide. Star whispers, "Do you hate me for being so selfish?"

His mouth snaps shut and he swallows, his eyes burning. "Star. I could never hate you."

Her shoulders sag, knees buckling, and he catches her before she sinks below the surface. She sobs so hard that she struggles to breathe. They hold each other tightly, Ethan too scared to think about what is happening or what could happen. Astra's prophecy tries to whisper to him, but he shoves it away. It's not fair. They survived the priming. They broke Star's curse. They're both *alive*. This should be the part where the two of them ride off into the sunset. Hell, he could find an actual horse to make it real poetic. Anger burns in him, and he tightens his hold on her, nearly missing it when Star begins to speak again.

"I'm scared, Ethan. I know what I must do, but I...I don't know if I'm brave enough to do it." She grips his shoulders painfully, her voice full of panicked desperation. "Tell me. Tell me to stay with you and run. Please, Ethan. Tell me to run away with you and abandon it all, and I will." She gasps, her tears mingling with his. "I love you, Ethan. I just want to be with you."

His heart aches, screaming at him to tell her to do just that. To stay with him, to run with him. They could live happily ever after. Be free. Together.

Like Amaterasu, they'll never look up again.

"Star." Fuck, he hates this. Every single horrific moment of this moment. "I want to. God, I want to, but I can't." Bile rises, but he swallows it back to say, "I don't think we could live like that knowing all that we've abandoned. I love you, Star. I will always love you, no matter what. Nothing will ever change that. I'm yours." He kisses her neck, whispering against her skin. "Always yours."

A little sob escapes her, but she wipes it away. She pulls back to look at him, her eyes blazing. She grips his forearm, her skin flickering with darkness. "Help me out of the crater." Her low voice rasps with a snarl. "It's time to finish this."

Ethan takes a shuddering breath and nods.

The water ripples smoothly around them, Ethan's arm firmly wrapped around her middle as he guides them to the crater's edge. He drags her up and over the lip, but they nearly topple back down from the blast on the other side of the oak. Ethan chances a look to see Alec and the Lophian locked together. The Lophian kicks Alec's ankle out, and the priest hits the ground hard, but before the Lophian can land a blow, a gunshot cracks through the valley. The Lophian stumbles back, and Alec has time to regain his footing.

Andrea kneels on the opposite side of the crater, Ethan's Mossberg still against her shoulder. Relief sweeps him. Whatever is about to happen with Star, he's glad his sister has at least a whole massive tree buffering her from it.

Ethan heaves, pulling them to their feet. It takes Star a moment to regain use of her legs, but when she does, the grass flattens around them like a wind is blowing it down. Star's eyes turn to him, and he's caught in the deep neon blue. She pulls him forward, her kiss like pure electricity. Her lips mumble against his. "I love you more than the stars in the sky, Ethan. Never forget that." She strokes his face reverently. "I'll keep you safe. I promise. Now get down."

He nods, and she guides him to the bed of wildflowers to lay between her legs. Magic tingles down his body, the world taking a pearlescent sheen for a moment. His gaze locks with Star's, and she searches his face, memorizing it before straightening, the whites of her eyes giving way to blue. She tilts her head back, looking up at the dark night sky. Her voice echoes loudly, magic humming all around. "*You.*"

She claps her hands together before opening her arms wide, a hiss of vibration popping Ethan's ears. The sky splits like a seam, Star tearing it asunder with her magic to reveal what was hidden to him all along. A second sky, more vibrant and beautiful than he ever imagined.

But then the second sky shifts, and Ethan's mind goes numb. Something stretches, its massive form oozing across the cosmos. He tries to make sense of the shape, but his mind struggles with it, his sanity rejecting it over and over, his stomach turning. It's like he's seeing the night sky through a moon jelly, and he follows the vague outline while his eyes struggle to focus. Long clawed hands grip the sky, keeping its body hovering above, its immense, terrible form housing the brightest glinting of stars of the second sky. Its tentacled face turns, and three eyes open to peer down at them.

Cold terror fills Ethan, like he's trapped in a nightmare he can't wake up from, his very bones trembling. Those eyes. It's like looking into empty, black pits of malice. Eyes that would watch prey torn limb from limb just to witness its pain and torment before leaving its mutilated body alive to suffer.

Star's voice soothes over him, strong, full of rage and power. Her skin ripples with magic, hair floating all around as she looks up and screams, "You hunted us. Devoured us. Trapped us. A hellish punishment for the sin of merely existing. But really..." She points a finger at the creature, and its eyes narrow. "*You* were resentful. Fearful of our joined power, and we were too kind to see it while we had the chance." Her skin flickers, and a deep marbling takes over. "Not anymore. I failed my siblings then, but I will not fail them now."

A hiss, one that nearly makes Ethan lose control of his bodily functions, slithers through his mind. "This tantrum of yours bores me. And you know what will happen when I'm bored."

This time Ethan hears the screams. The stars flicker, the high-pitched cries grating upon his mind as his tears build. It's so awful, so horrible, that he begins to beg for it to stop.

The tentacles on the creature's face curl and stretch. "Fall to your knees before the Contenders, little droplet, and maybe I'll spare them further discomforts. You know I can do far worse than this little prodding."

Ethan sucks in a harsh breath, hot and cold flashing over his body until he sweats. The screaming, oh God, the *screaming*. What could be worse than what it's currently doing to them?

"No." Star's fists clench. "I am not yours to sacrifice. *We* are not toys for your sick pleasure!" Her bright skin shimmers with the glorious glow of a nebula, a beauty like nothing Ethan has seen before. Star, his sweet Star, is a goddess of light and vengeance, her wrath and power awe-inspiring.

Star splays her fingers, arms out, lavender hair whipping in the wind. "Astra has a message for you, disgusting one." Power pulses. Her mortal form burns away, flesh turning to dust and blowing in the wind. She stands above Ethan in the glowing form she landed in, shining with the nebula's beauty. "Your mistake was thinking you could tame us."

Before Ethan can blink, Star blasts away from him, the force leaving his ears ringing. The ground bursts apart to form two craters where her feet stood moments before. The magic that she placed over Ethan shivers but holds. His arms raise to shield himself from spraying dirt, but he forces them down when he hears Star's bellowed roar tremble the world. "LET THEM GO!"

She arcs into the sky like a shooting star in reverse, a shimmering trail marking her rapid ascent. Each second is a painful thud of his heart, his lungs frozen, eyes wide. She's so small, the monster so large. Panic overtakes Ethan and he prays, prays so fucking hard, frozen on the ground, his mouth dry.

He can hear the impact as she strikes the creature's face, a small speck between its three eyes. The thing rears back with a mind-rending shriek. Ethan raises his hands to cover his ears, teeth gritting. Cracks form and splinter, and the creature thrashes and writhes as Star's power forces its way deeper and deeper inside.

The creature shudders, its repulsive body arching, tensing. The splintering slows to a snail's pace. One by one, the fissures stop expanding, until there is just one long crack inching its way closer and closer to one of the glowing stars along the edge of its grotesque form.

Ethan's heart thunders, his breath seizing. He whispers, "Come on, come *on*," as he watches the crack move inch by agonizing inch closer to the little star. It glows bright, flickering flashes of red frantically like it, too, is begging for Star to reach it.

Star's tendril pauses, the glowing cracks dulling. The creature is pulled in tight, fighting to crush Star. *His* Star. Ethan chokes, his throat swollen. "Star!"

The light flashes once, twice...then surges. The light tendril spears through the jellylike flesh toward the little red star.

He hears the melodic *ching* of connection.

The red orb blasts apart, and the creature's eldritch scream tears through the heavens again. One after another, cracks form, stretching from star to star, like electricity burning its way through wood. All the glowing orbs tremble, getting brighter and brighter until the night sky flashes day, searing Ethan's retinas. He throws his arms across his face to filter the light enough to keep watching. The creature's hideous body blasts apart, scattering across the cosmos in fragments until it is nothing but dust in the fabric of existence. The Earth trembles. The Devourer is no more.

The magic protecting Ethan blows away like dust. His arms are still covering his face, his eyes wide and unblinking as he struggles to comprehend the aftermath of what happened.

Star's gone. She's really gone. Grief. Overwhelming, soul-crushing grief hits him like a horse kick to the chest. Tears burn down his face, and he sucks in a shocked breath. He cries silently, chest heaving with the strength of it. The moment stretches. Minutes, hours...he's unsure as he weeps. Not until someone touches him does he suck in a harsh breath, arms flinching down to blink blurrily up at his smiling sister. Tears are streaming down her face, making her eyes glisten in the dark twilight. Her usually strong voice is barely above a whisper. "Look up."

He does, and his breath catches.

The stars are dancing. They twine and leap, spinning around each other. The joyful celebration is almost too much for him to bear. He chokes on a sob, the strength of it wracking his body, but he forces his eyes to stay open, to watch the merriment. It's beautiful, the jubilation warming his cracked and withered soul.

Free.

They're all finally free.

Star did it. Astra's prophecy achieved. Their suffering ended.

Andrea stretches out next to him in one of Star's craters, hugging him tightly and laugh-crying, pointing out her favorite revelers. He allows himself to melt into the comfort of her hold, his trembling hand gripping the arm across his chest tightly. He nods in agreement, but he can barely see through the unending tears.

Alec limps his way over to them, drenched in blood. Deep wounds are carved out of his flesh, and his shoulder dislocated. He looks up at the sky with a small smile before looking down at them both. Andrea pats the soft ground next to her, and he eases himself down with an agonized groan that even Ethan feels. Andrea wraps her other arm around Alec's shoulders, tugging him against her with minimal accommodation for his injuries. The priest hisses a pained breath but is too exhausted to put up a fight. He leans his weight against her, mindful of his shoulder.

The three of them watch the dance together.

Ethan forces out the question. "The Lophian?"

Alec clears his throat, his voice thick with emotion. "Fled. No Vessel, no reason to fight. Probably halfway to the ocean by how fast it was moving." He nudges Andrea. "Probably thought you were going to snipe him down."

Andrea huffs. "And did I exaggerate my marksmanship?"

"No, you did not. Thank fuck."

"You're welcome, from your—what did you say? Essentially useless compadres? Deadweights? Meat shields?"

"I don't recall saying all that, but yes. You more than proved your worth. Otherwise, I'd be a very dead priest." He pauses. "Or man, at this point."

Andrea shifts to look at Alec better. "What's this? Not going back to the Order?"

"No point, is there? No more Harvester. No more Game of Fallen Stars. Guess I'll find something else to do." Alec's head thuds against Andrea's shoulder. "Know of anyone hiring?"

"Hm. Dunno. Can you ride a horse as well as you can fight?"

"Eh. Sure. How hard can it be?"

Ethan tunes them out, watching the stars dance in the night sky. It's an odd mix of grief and joy. He wonders if one of them could be his Star, and if she's happy.

He hopes she survived and that she's happy dancing with her siblings.

He smiles through his tears. Just for her. Because he knows it would bring her great happiness to see it, to know that she is the root of it. That he's still hers. Forever.

Seventeen

"Okay I'm heading out."

Ethan tilts his head back far enough to see Andrea bustle out of his cabin through the screen door. Her boots thud noisily on the porch's dry wood as she comes over to offer him a fresh beer. He takes the cold bottle, condensation absent in the dry evening. He rocks on the rocking chair, taking a slow sip. "In a rush to get back to your roommate?"

She scoffs. "If I wanted to live with the living embodiment of obsessive-compulsive disorder, I'd go back to staying with my mother. The man takes neat freak to a whole new level." She leans a hip against the porch railing. "Don't get me wrong, at first it was awesome. Like having a free maid even more thorough than you were. But then it got weird when I caught Alec scrubbing the baseboards with a toothbrush." She examines her freshly painted pink nails. "I think the Order and priesthood deeply damaged him. Chris is about to lose her ever-loving mind if he puts a coaster under her drink one more time." She pauses, her hazel eyes scanning Ethan critically. "How are you holding up?"

Depressed as all hell. Can't sleep. Barely eating. Cried in the shower. Twice. Apparently, one shower cry wasn't good enough today. According to his therapist, water is an emotion regulator. Ethan calls bullshit on that one, though it is easier to drown out the sound under the spray.

He takes a swig. "Peachy."

"Mm-hm."

His thumbnail picks at the logo of his beer, peeling the paper back. "Therapy is helping."

"Yeah?"

Aside from his doubt about water helping him self-regulate, crying only twice is a vast improvement from the first week after the...incident. He flicks some of the picked-off paper from his fingernails. "It's tricky talking about it to Margaret without sounding like a complete lunatic, but we're figuring it out. And you'll be pleased to know that I left the house to go get the medication the psychiatrist prescribed me."

"Oh!" Andrea's eyes flare, standing a little straighter. "That is good. Ethan, I'm so—" Her lips tighten with unspoken emotion. For years, Andrea advocated for him to take medication when his mother wouldn't hear of it. This small act from Ethan means so much to his sister. She ducks and scuffs her boot on the porch. "I'm proud of you. Really."

"Yeah. Not going to lie, taking care of myself is the worst." He gives her a half grin. "Much easier to take care of you."

"Hm. Poor you. Your mess of a sister is no longer messy. Woebegone."

"Yeah. And I heard back from work."

"Yeah? And?"

"They approved remote work. I told Lisa I'll sign the long-term lease for this place at the end of the week." He peels the slightly damp paper from the glass, making a little pile on the arm of his chair. "I think focusing on getting this place set up with a home office will be a good project for me. It'll give me something productive to do. And Lisa said I can make whatever improvements I want as long as the place doesn't get fucked up."

Andrea's lips turn into a small frown. "That's great and everything, but are you sure you wouldn't rather move somewhere else? Maybe somewhere without so many, you know..." She grimaces. "Memories?"

His gaze drifts to the darkening silhouette of Star's oak. Margaret asked him the same thing this morning. He shakes his head. "No. I'd rather stay here." His mouth softens into a small smile. "She loved it here. Who knows? Might even get a dog."

"You hate dogs."

"I'm ambivalent toward them. Besides, it would be nice to have some company."

Andrea's eyes narrow, her nails drumming on the wood railing. "Okay. Fine. You're not wrong there, I guess. But maybe a cat? I feel like you'd really flourish as a cat guy."

"Maybe." Star loved dogs. Would she have loved cats as well? Probably. Star loved just about everything. He takes a sip. "I'll think about it."

"Hm." His sister's lips purse, and he knows the question that is coming. It comes every other day, in various forms of probing and hints. "So, it's been three weeks..."

He nods. "So it has."

"Which makes next week four weeks..."

"That is how weeks work, yes."

She glares. "Fine. Are you going to talk to your mom?"

He clicks his tongue, pausing. "It's...well...kind of."

Andrea's silence is near violent.

He sighs, rubbing his forehead. "I don't know, Andy. I'm still not sure what I'd even say to her, or if I want to talk to her again." His eyes tighten. "I'm much happier without her in my life, and that's fucking depressing but it's true. So, no. I'm not in a rush to talk to her again."

Andrea nods, eyes shining in empathy. "Yeah. I think that's best, though I'll miss the Christmas with Josette show. No one can get drunker and messier than that woman and her sisters."

He huffs a small laugh. "Sorry to deprive you of your favorite holiday special."

"Eh. I'll get over it."

Andrea extends her hand to him, and he meets her halfway with his own. Her fingers squeeze his, and it fills him with warmth.

He smiles, soft and genuine. "I love you, Andy. I'm glad you're my sister."

Andrea beams. "Aw, Ethaniel." She kicks his shoe. "Did your therapist tell you to say that?"

"As a matter of fact, yes she did."

"I knew I liked her for a reason."

The atmosphere is getting a little too heavy for Ethan's tastes. Time for her to go. He nods toward the ATV. "Go back to your house-priest. I'm fine. Really." Then he can get to his favorite activity of the day.

"Yeah, yeah, yeah." Andrea's boots are heavy on the porch steps. "For the record, I love you too, and I'm glad you're my brother-father."

"Can you not call me that? It's weird, and misleading for strangers." He nods his goodbye. "Drive safe."

She throws a leg over the seat. "Always. Try to sleep, okay? I left you some edibles on the kitchen table to help."

He forces a small smile. "Thanks. Night, Andy."

"Night, Ethaniel."

He watches his sister drive off, the light from the living room the only shining thing left in the vicinity. The rocking chair creaks softly over and over, mixing with the crickets. It's familiar. Almost comforting if he wasn't choking on grief.

He tilts his head back and looks up at the night sky to watch the stars dance. It's his favorite time of day and one of the few constants that help him feel joy, especially during that first week. He'll stay on the porch for hours, all night at times, watching their revelry. It's been three weeks, and they're still going strong.

Apparently, the night sky ripping apart to reveal a cosmic horror chilling up there and then exploded didn't sit well with the general populace. The chaos that followed was near catastrophic. Ethan, happily living his best hermit life, only got updates through Andrea, his living, breathing filter. Being in San Francisco during the panic is not something he'd ever want to experience firsthand. There were riots and looting and religious groups going insane. Some people even went into bunkers, others screaming that this was the end of days.

He did make one exception, and that was when the various governments of the world decided to investigate the tear in the sky. They sent a couple of probes up there to get a closer look at the dancing stars. Ethan obsessively scanned through every single article and coverage on it, hoping something would show *his* star dancing. But he's not that lucky. It's like they're in a different reality. Everything that goes up to try to capture it misses it, like passing through an illusion. That's when the conspiracy theorists really got their foothold in the populace. Ethan unplugged his Wi-Fi after that. He didn't need to know more.

It's a relief to him that the magical stars exist up there, dancing. Living free. Untouchable. It's safer for them that way.

But the tear is getting smaller, like the universe is carefully knitting itself back together stitch by stitch. Andrea showed him the measurements that several leading theorists are posting wildly about on social media. What that means, he's not sure, but the tight ball in his chest constricts until it hurts to breathe.

The small hope, the one he doesn't permit himself to linger on, that maybe Star will return, aches with each passing day that the tear gets smaller. Looking at the tightening edges now has a pressure building in him until he feels it in his eyes. His lips press tight together while he holds his breath, like that will keep the wave of grief at bay.

He gasps, chest heaving, eyes closing for a moment. He focuses on his breath and lets the painful thoughts of Star filter through him. Margaret said it wasn't good to ignore his grief, but fuck, acknowledging it hurt like a bitch. His lip trembles with his breath, and he peels his eyes open again. He looks away from the night sky, collecting himself.

He takes another swig to find his beer empty. He sighs. Of course it is. Maybe he should go take one of the edibles Andrea brought him, but that would require getting up. The inconvenience of it all slumps his shoulders, and he leans to the side to set the bottle down on the floor beside him. His fingers trail on the glass, hypnotized by the glinting light dancing along the curve.

His brows furrow, fingers pausing. The brightness reflecting in the dark glass is growing.

He looks up.

Soft as a whisper, a glowing orb the size of the cabin touches down next to Star's oak. His breath catches, eyes widening. The Earth gently trembles, the leaves shaking. Ethan is moving before he realizes it, stumbling down the steps, running faster and faster, hope soaring, heart in his throat.

The glow is taking shape, his eyes burning against it, but he forces them to remain open, to squint against the blinding light, to blink through the welling tears. A bright form is walking toward him, then running. He collides with it, sweeping it up into his arms as Star's human body encompasses her unearthly form. He kisses her, his lips going numb against her power before she kisses him back with her returned lips, her blue eyes shining with tears, her smile glowing as brightly as her essence.

She's here. She's actually here. Alive. Unharmed. *Real.* He always hoped, but never dared to dream. He tries to speak, but he can't seem to stop kissing her, breathing her in.

He gasps against her mouth. "Thank God. I couldn't—I wanted—" He can't continue because the jumble of feelings is too much for him to put into words.

She smiles, stroking his jaw with both hands to slide down his neck, her fingers resting on his pulse to feel it thudding painfully fast. "I know, Ethan. Now kiss me. I've missed you terribly."

He obeys enthusiastically, and she shivers in his arms. He lets his mind go, his body taking control, and Star meets him with an equally starved fervor. Her hands comb through his hair, yanking his bun out to tangle in the length. They kiss and kiss, Ethan's hands greedy upon her naked body. She rips his shirt, nails raking across his skin, and he groans into the kiss, sweeping her up and then down on the ground, the dry grass crunching beneath them.

Her hand slides into his pants, and he murmurs, "Should we go inside?"

She shakes her head. Her soft, low voice, something he's missed since the day it disappeared from his life. "Can't wait."

He nods back, speaking between kisses, hips shivering against her strokes. "What about them? Up there?"

"Don't worry about it." The mischievous smile has his heart skipping a beat. "We like to watch."

"Oh *fuck*." He kisses her deeply, letting her strip him of his clothes. "I love you."

"Good." She bites his lips and purrs. "Now show me."

He moans into their kiss, his naked body wonderfully pressed against hers. She's still hot from her celestial form, and the heat burns him in a delicious sting. Her hand wraps around his cock and presses it against her wet core, her legs spread wide and toes sinking into the earth like roots. She tosses her head back with a delighted gasp, his hips rolling and the head of his cock rubbing against her clit. He buries his face into her neck and groans, shivering with a pent-up want that is dying to rip free. He's so desperate for her. Their first lovemaking was too full of sadness, but now...

Star turns to press her lips against his ear, her puffed breaths tickling him. "Ethan, I need you." Her fingers press against the head of his cock, her hips tilting, and he slips inside her clenching, wet heat. They moan together, Star's back arching to press her beautiful body into his. "Yes, Ethan, *yes!*"

He nips her neck, and her pleasured gasp has him biting. He slips his arm under her hips to angle them, stroking inside her slow and steady, inching deeper and deeper, searching until Star's arms snap around him. "Ethan, *there.*"

"Fuck, Star." He snaps his hips, her nails digging into his back and then raking along it, leaving behind stinging red trails. He shivers, arching into the sensation.

She's trembling, her skin glowing, and it's so fucking beautiful that he has to release her neck to lift up to watch. Her shimmering eyes meet his, and pleasure ripples down his spine in tingling waves of awareness, coaxing his cock harder and his thrusts shorter. Star gasps, grabbing her own thighs and holding them wide for him. A welcome for Ethan to do whatever he wants to her willing body. He almost loses pace, pleasure throbbing at the sight. "I love it when you do that."

She smiles through her continual soft noises of pleasure. "Please, Ethan. I need you."

He gasps. "Tell me if I'm too rough."

Stars laughs, eyes sparkling. "Oh, Ethan. *Harder.*"

"*Fuck.* You're so perfect." He falls upon her, his hips snapping, his knees tearing into the grass as he fucks her. He snakes his other hand in her hair, finally wrapping it around his wrist and gripping it at the base to hold her in place. She's chanting his name with each bottom-out he slams into her, her body shivering, her mouth wide as she pleads for more. His cock is pulsing, the pleasure of being able to freely love her a buzz in his skull that nearly tips him into a too-early orgasm.

He lets go of her hair, and she frowns in disappointment. He smiles wickedly. Her breath catches and she twitches, her heat clenching around him. Goddamn it, she does make it hard to focus. He pulls his other arm out from under her, then finally, he grabs those fucking perfect thighs and swings them over his shoulders.

Her eyes flare when he leans forward, folding her in half. His lips brush hers. "Hold on, beautiful."

He fucks her and she *loves* it, her joyous cries filling the night sky. He can't stop, he can't slow, his sanity slipping away. Star, his Star, is here and she loves him and her body is so wet and willing for whatever the hell he wants. He moves faster, harder, because it makes her squeal, because it makes her clench and pulse, her toes flex, her thighs tremble. The slapping of his hips and the lewd wet sounds nearly have him coming. Her nails rake the earth by her head, her hands twisting in the grass, her hips quivering with the building pleasure.

Her glowing skin begins to flicker, pulse, her eyes flashing a lighter blue. And then she throws her head back and comes, screaming his name to the heavens, her call echoing in the hills, and he smiles brightly, pleasure pulsing through him as she comes and comes. Magic pulses with it, her sex sucking him in greedily, and the air shimmers with a blast. The earth under them erupts in crisp green grass, wildflowers blooming wildly into the night. Star arches, trembling, throbbing, glistening with sweat, and it's too much.

Ethan's spine rounds as he pounds into her, coming hard and fast. His vision flashes, his mouth wide as he swears his soul rips from his body from the force of his pleasure. Star rocks hungrily against him, moaning at the feel of him coming deep inside her. It's too much and Ethan collapses on top of her, releasing her legs.

They pant heavily, their bodies slick with sweat. It's that post-good-fucking feeling that Ethan's been craving with Star but was denied by the priming. Her fingers stroke his hair lazily, combing through his loose curls. He smiles and his face aches, unused to showing such happiness after weeks of grief.

Star's breathless voice sends a little pleasure down his body. He made her that way. He made her come so hard that magic burst from her, her skin now a glow-free human tone, like she needed to get that last burst of magic free to settle back into her body. It's so wonderful and beautiful that he nearly misses what she says. "I've missed you so much, Ethan. It was terrible."

He lifts himself up to gaze down at her face. She smiles softly, stroking his mouth, and he kisses each of the fingertips she presses against his lips. Finally, he asks, "Where were you? Why did it take so long?"

"I was home, with my kind. We were so happy to be free again, to be able to move however we want. But I was hurt. The creature almost crushed me, and they helped me heal."

She pulls him back down for another soft kiss. "Ethan. Thank you."

"Hm." He drags his teeth along her bottom lip, feeling the shiver course through her. "For what?"

"You saved us. You saved me. And because of that, we're all free."

His brows furrow. "You mean when I jumped into the crater?"

"It's more than that." Her fingertips trail over his brow, smoothing the creases until he relaxes. "It was the priming. You, Ethan. So wonderful and selfless. You wielded the priming's magic, forced it to birth what you wanted. And what you wanted more than anything was to save me. So pure and single-minded was your desire that not even the Devourer could tempt you away from your selfless wants. You are truly amazing. We are in awe of you."

Her eyes trail over his shoulder, and she beams up at the night sky. "Oh, Ethan. You should've heard the heated debates we had about what you did and how it all worked to break the curse. So long have we had to be careful about what we said. Just whisper or glint covertly. But now, we can speak freely. Speculate. Dream. Argue." Her eyes mist. "It's amazing."

He strokes her face. "Star."

She looks back at him. "Yes, Ethan?"

The pain in his heart almost robs him of his voice. "Are you going back?"

She wets her lips, her eyes shining with worry and face pinching. "Do you want that?"

His breathing shivers, his hands stroking her face reverently. "Star." His lips graze hers, and he feels her small gasp against them. His voice is barely a hushed whisper, tingling desire crackling between them like a living thing. "Don't go back. Stay with me. Please. Be mine like I am yours."

She giggles, and he kisses her. And kisses her. She tries to answer but he can't stop. Finally, she purrs against his lips. "Yes, Ethan. Always."

Epilogue

Sidra gazes at the world from her perch in the cosmos. Her glowing form flickers, red flashing with a spark of green. The others dance, still celebrating their newfound freedom. They call to her, trying to draw her back into their jubilation, but Sidra can't find the joy needed for such merrymaking.

Sidra's ever-watchful gaze travels to the priest, this "Alec." A green-eyed wolf among sheep... And now Star is down there as one of those defenseless sheep.

Sidra's light stutters, the fear dimming her astral form. Her dearest friend, her mentor, her companion, is trapped in that suffocating flesh sack, her light out of reach. And that light is dim, difficult for Sidra to even see from her perch. Star is drained from the battle with the creature and from jumping once again to be with her mortal lover. Star needs time to heal, to generate, and Earth is not the place for such things. Star should be up here with them where they can protect her, where they can wrap her in their warm light.

Sidra shrinks, her light trembling. It was glorious being free with Star up here again, and Sidra was whole once more nestled against her dear friend. Star, who was there when Sidra was birthed to this existence in a flash of cosmic magic. Star, so ancient and strong, wrapped Sidra in her light while Sidra quivered with the shock of creation. Star, who gently eased Sidra into existence as a solo light in their great cosmos. And then, Star turned her gaze down to the world...and the creature arrived.

Sidra dims so dark that she is more deep red than glowing light.

She turns her gaze up into the vastness of deep space. Few creatures would dare bother them, but that didn't stop the Devourer from taking advantage of their peaceful existence. Sidra's red light quivers, drawing the attention of her siblings. But Sidra doesn't want their comfort.

She looks down upon the human world, at the sister she misses with a deep, horrible ache. She hopes Star will return, but Sidra knows she won't. Star is blissfully happy with her human lover. Sidra watches as Star basks in the wanton, earthly pleasures of a body, glowing not with her light but with a love Sidra is unfamiliar with. A different kind of ache tightens and twists within her. What would it be like...to experience such a thing...

Sidra leans forward, touching the edge of her perch. The seam Star ripped between the two realities is knitting together. It's why Star jumped when she did, fearful of missing an easy descent to be with her human beloved.

Sidra's gaze trails to that lingering priest, the traitor to his Order, the current threat to her friend. Star is too trusting of such a human. His kind, his horrific Order's willingness to play the Game, cannot be trusted, no matter how...*alluring* such a deceitful human's body might be. No, he will betray her friend. Sidra is sure of it.

Star needs Sidra, as much as Sidra desperately needs Star. It makes her choice easier, like this is her only option.

Sidra leans and slips from her perch to fall through the rip, plummeting to the human world.

Thank you for reading! Did you enjoy? Please add your review because nothing helps an author more and encourages readers to take a chance on a book than a review.

And don't miss more from S.E. Berkeley coming soon. Be sure to visit seberkeleyauthor.com

Until then, discover A HAPPY BEGINNING, by City Owl Author, B.A. Richards. Turn the page for a sneak peek!

You can also sign up for the City Owl Press newsletter to receive notice of all book releases!

Sneak Peek A Happy Beginning

BY B.A. RICHARDS

"Are you one of the grooms?"

Alard Fairchild looked up from his phone, the world coming back into focus around him. Men and women swarmed about the hotel's lobby, a buzzing presence of optimism and nerves energizing the space. Multiple accents and languages reverberated off the mahogany wall panels, a noisy overture overwhelming his senses.

The woman in front of him came closer, pushing her ebony bangs from her ocher-colored eyes. "Do you speak English?" she asked, bending forward toward his face. Alard smelled the rose oil drifting from her skin, luring him closer to her lips.

His brain caught up a moment later, and he abruptly sat back, shaking his head to clear it. "No...yes." The confusion on her face made him laugh at his own awkwardness. "Sorry, I mean, yes, I speak English, and no, I'm not part of the wedding."

"Oh." A flash of disappointment in her eyes. "I had hoped you were my fiancé."

"You don't know your own fiancé?"

"It's an arranged marriage." She sat on the plush bench next to Alard, draping a garment bag over her lap. "My parents made the match through our church. I'm supposed to meet him today for the first time." She sighed and plastered on a smile and faced him. "Hi, I'm Shelia."

"Alard." He held out his hand, and she shook it, trying not to let the bag slip off her lap. He looked back at the lobby, focusing on the men in the crowd. "Maybe I can help? Does he look like me?"

"All my mother told me was that he had dark hair and hazel eyes. You have both of those."

It wasn't a lot to work with, but Alard pushed himself up. He scanned the crowd, examining all the dark-haired young men wandering about. It didn't take long before he found another man pacing with a picture in his hand. "Why don't you see if that's him?"

He helped her stand, holding the garment bag as Shelia straightened her dress. "Do I look good?" She bit her lower lip as she snuck a glance over Alard's shoulder.

"You look every inch a princess."

Shelia blushed, then shifted onto her toes to kiss Alard's cheek. "If that is so, you're a prince for saving me. Thank you." She took the garment bag and made her way across the room. Alard watched as they connected and hugged.

A minute later, Alard's phone buzzed from his pocket. He quickly pulled it out and asked, "Hello?" while his free hand covered his other ear to block out the conversations.

"Sorry, Al. I'm almost there. You won't believe the traffic out here." His law partner, James Wilson, shouted above the background noise.

"I think I can." Alard reached for his briefcase. "Listen, James, the lobby is insane. I'll meet you at the corner of Canal and Chartres and we can talk over a drink."

"Sounds like a plan."

Alard wove through the condensing mass of humanity toward the Canal Street exit. Ahead of him, two men entered the lobby through the hotel's spinning glass door. The taller one wore a well-tailored suit with an alluring blue tie. A black lanyard with a name tag hung around his neck, and he carried a leather briefcase. The second man was dressed in khakis with an untucked dress shirt and sunglasses perched on top of his head. They were talking to each other, not noticing as Alard popped out from between two brides and right into their path.

The men avoided colliding with Alard by mere inches, the only casualty being Alard's phone knocked to the floor.

"It's okay," Alard said automatically, leaning down to grab his phone. James continued complaining about the afternoon traffic from the tiny speaker.

As he picked up the phone, his knuckles brushed up against the fingers of one of the men—the one with the sunglasses. For the barest of seconds, Alard held his breath, feeling warm as his vision brightened.

"I'm okay," he continued, flustered. "You okay?" Alard asked the other men.

"Yeah, I'm good. Sorry about that." Sunglasses spoke, and Alard felt his dark brown eyes roam over his body.

Alard straightened and returned the appreciative glance. The man's coloring reminded Alard of a bow of dark walnuts waiting to be devoured. His soft, plump lips lifted into a smirk, as if asking, *do you like what you see?*

Alard attempted not to blush. "No, it's fine, really. The lobby is crowded."

"Al, are you even listening?" James's whine from the phone broke the moment, and Alard put it back to his ear. "Yeah, sorry. I'll be there in a minute."

Sunglasses's friend cleared his throat, looking at his watch. "Raz, we don't have much time before dinner."

Alard nodded to both men. "I should go anyway. Again, sorry." He moved toward the rotating door, taking one quick look back at the good-looking man. His eyes shifted, and he allowed himself to see the magic flowing through the room. A warm white glow emanated from where the couples gathered. Alas, where Sunglasses stood, the magic swirled away, not touching him.

Of course, Alard thought as he blinked his eyes back to normal and exited the hotel. *He's just human.*

The haze of cigarette smoke outside, right past the door, had Alard coughing while he turned to walk to the end of the block. At the streetcar station in the middle of the road, James jumped out the back door. He straightened his Hawaiian shirt and adjusted the strap of his laptop case on his shoulder. His blond hair was a mess that he tried to fix with his fingers as he crossed the street. "You'd think it was Mardi Gras with the amount of people on the street today. Did I miss something on the..." he stopped, looking around at people entering the hotel just behind Alard. "What's with all the wedding dresses?"

Alard chuckled as he slung his arm over his confused colleague's shoulder. "Mass wedding at the conference center tomorrow, from what I've been able to make out." He led James down the side street behind the hotel.

"Think I can pick someone up on the way home?" James asked.

"Not unless you plan to marry them in the morning."

James shook his head. "Nope, no way. Me and marriages don't work. Ask my ex-wife."

"Don't need to. I was there when she burned the effigy in your courtyard."

"That's right." As they entered the next block, James turned them down Bourbon Street. "You got a place in mind for that drink?"

"Of course."

James groaned, raking his fingers through his hair again. "Al, we live in New Orleans—the city known for its music and nightlife. There is more than one fucking jazz bar in the city."

"I'm aware, but Fritzel's is the *best* fucking jazz bar in the city."

"Says you."

Alard laughed. "Plus, I was thinking about visiting the second floor."

The doors to Fritzel's sat wide open, waiting for night to fall and the crowds to appear. The stone walls of the English jazz bar were hidden behind a plethora of pictures, signs, and memorabilia. No lights hung over-head. The ambiance provided by an odd assortment of table lamps on shelves and an unused fireplace. Doorways and mirrors were framed with string lights, giving the bar a softer glow in its unique atmosphere.

Alard walked to the bartender, placing a fifty on the table. The woman smiled, tilting her head towards the back door in the second room. "Welcome back, handsome. Heading upstairs?"

"Of course, but do me a favor, Constance? Give James a double so he'll stop complaining."

"I'm not complaining!" James flopped onto a bar stool, his head falling back. "I'm just saying we can go to other places now and then."

"You're always complaining. I think you would die if you didn't have anything to complain about." Alard nodded when Constance dropped the half-filled whiskey glass in front of James. "You don't have to come up, you know."

"*You're* the one who wanted to talk." James rolled his eyes, sipping his whiskey.

"Catherine hasn't shown up yet," Constance told James. James gave her an appreciative nod, and she walked away to serve a new group of customers.

"Now what was so important that you needed to talk?" James was scrutinizing Alard's posture. James was a master at reading body language, which made him excel at cross-examining witnesses on the rare instance when divorce cases went to trial. Other times, like now, it made Alard self-conscious.

"It's something that would be better talked about upstairs." Alard snuck a look at his friend.

James narrowed his eyes, then sighed. "Fine, Mr. Drama Queen, but you owe me another drink." He stood up and walked to the back door.

Alard got up and followed. "I already bought you a drink!"

"Yeah, but you're making me go upstairs. That's a two-drink minimum request."

"Who's the drama queen now?" Alard laughed as they arrived at the closed door. He knocked three times. The door opened and a large gentleman stood in the doorway. He was tall, skin as dark as midnight, and his eyes were silver. His gaze flickered between the two, glaring at James a moment before resting back on Alard. "Yes?"

"The vampire sent us," Alard whispered, not wanting the passphrase to be overheard by the band ten feet away.

The gatekeeper stared at Alard a moment longer, then stepped back and let them through. Alard led James up a flight of stairs. The left side of the staircase was covered in mismatched windows woven together into a wall. The view out the windows was of a central, currently empty courtyard surrounded by four walls of glass and railings. Twinkle lights lit the way up the stairs, and at the landing was a bureau filled with knickknacks behind the display doors. To the right was a set of French doors with pink light casting through them. To the left was a balcony open to the courtyard. A cat bed, bowl of water, and an empty paper plate with the remains of food sat on the landing by the railing.

A mangy tawny cat crawled out from under the bureau and stretched as they reached the top stair. Alard crouched down and rubbed behind her ears. "Hello, pretty girl. Are you behaving yourself?"

The cat purred, pressing her head up into Alard's hand before walking towards James. James bent down and ran a hand along the cat's spine. "Hey, Misty girl."

Misty left the men and walked back to her cat bed, sat down, and started to clean herself. Alard stood back up, moved past James, and opened the French doors.

The room beyond the doors was dim, the main light emanating from red light bulbs in the ceiling fan, circulating the scent of rose and licorice. The two-room establishment contained a mini kitchenette and lounge in the back, a sitting room in the front, and a wall with a pass-through and doorway between them.

A crushed velvet couch and matching chair sat in front of the sitting room fireplace with a round glass table between them. A miniature planetarium rested on top of a pile of leather-bound books. The Lepus constellation shone on the wall above the fireplace, a red dot among the white stars highlighting Hind's Crimson Star.

"Hello!" A cheerful voice called through the kitchen pass-through separating the two rooms. Fairy lights framed the window-like opening, a whiter light shining beyond in the mini kitchen. Two absinthe fountains sat on a ledge beside the fridge—one red, the other green—ready for the evening's guests.

In front of the fountains stood a woman in her sixties wearing a tan peasant blouse and black leather pants. Rainbow suspenders and military boots completed the outfit. Her pixie length hair was bright pink, spiked up in front and tilted to look like a faux hawk. When she saw Alard, her eyes widened. "Prince Alard! I wasn't expecting you today."

Alard waved his head, blushing. "You don't have to use my title, Monique."

"Yes, don't embarrass the princeling," James mocked from where he had sunk into the couch. "Everyone knows he hates that."

"I don't hate it. I'm just not a prince when I'm here." Alard walked into the second room and gave the older woman a hug. The kitchenette and lounge were brighter with an orange bulb over the wooden picnic bench of a table. A chandelier lit the kitchenette, adding to the charm of what served as a bar.

"First, you're a prince no matter where you are, Alard." Monique stepped back and touched his cheek. "Even if you've resorted to associating with humans like that one."

"Aw, I love you too, Moans." James raised his whiskey glass in salute.

"And second?" Alard asked.

"I might live here, but I'm still one of your subjects," Monique said. "It would be rude not to address you properly when you enter the room."

Laughing, Alard slid onto a barstool at the pass-through window. "I'm going to miss you both," he stated.

"They gave you a date?" Monique put a glass in front of him, the green absinthe adding an earthy scent to the rose and licorice in the air.

Alard nodded, picking up the glass, whirling the liquor around in it. "One human week."

"I'm sorry." Monique placed her hand on Alard's free one, squeezing gently. "I know being here means a lot to you."

"They couldn't have waited until we at least finished the Morrison case?" James groaned.

"Oh yeah, that would have gone over well," Alard said. "Mom, Dad, yeah, can we put off the wedding until after I finish this human divorce case? The kingdoms have been divided for over a thousand years. What's two more weeks?"

James lifted his head. "You think they'd go for it?"

Alard shot a glare at his best friend. "Seriously?"

"Ignore him." Monique leaned on the windowsill. "Are you ready for this?"

"Not in the least." Alard sipped his drink, savoring the taste of wormwood and fennel. "I understand why Meyda and I have to do this, but neither of us really wants to."

"I can understand her not wanting to marry you," James stated.

Monique gave James a look. "How much has he had to drink?" she asked.

"Not enough." James held up the empty glass. "Al owes me one more."

Monique walked around and handed James a bottle that had three fingers of whiskey left. "Knock yourself out." She turned and sat on the other barstool beside Alard. "Meyda doesn't want to marry you?"

"She doesn't want to marry anyone," Alard said. "We've been best friends since we were kids. She's never once been interested in anyone romantically or sexually, and that's fine. She's happy with her books and her pets."

"But?"

"When we marry...I know I can honor her choices, but our parents, hell, the entire kingdom, will expect an heir. We've talked about adoption, since you know, it worked for me becoming the heir. But her parents...everything is just so complicated." Alard rested his forehead in his hands, taking a deep breath. "And that's not even considering that I very much enjoy being intimate, but if I do so with someone not my wife, I dishonor my marriage to her."

"But you two do love each other, right?"

Alard drank the rest of his absinthe. "Like friends. Siblings."

Monique reached over to squeeze Alard's knee. "There have been generations of royalty that have never had the luxury in choosing who they married. Give it a few years, and once you've settled into your rule, the two of you can work to modernize the ideas in the court to compensate for both your preferences."

Alard ran his hand through his hair, sighing. "I don't know if the fairy realm will take well to human definitions of sexuality."

"You'll be their king. Also, I think you should have more faith in your subjects."

"Probably."

Shadows outside the French doors made Monique stand up. She caressed Alard's cheek before leaning in to kiss the top of his head. "You have spent too much time among the humans, Alard. It's given you much, but I think you may have forgotten a part of yourself in the process."

Alard leaned into the affection. "I needed to know who the human I could have been was."

"And he is a good person." Monique made her way back behind her absinthe bar, readying herself for customers. "But you're more than human, my lord. Don't forget that."

The shadows formed into a group of three women through the glass panes. One tried the French doors, but it didn't budge. She knocked, trying to peer in.

"Pet the damn cat!" James slurred from where he was slumped on the couch.

Alard reached over to take the empty bottle from James. "I think you've had enough."

"Never." James looked up at Alard with bloodshot eyes and a lazy grin. "You got a week left, buddy. There's no such thing as too much. Time to live it up and make some bad choices."

"Right, like that will ever end well."

Don't stop now. Keep reading with your copy of A HAPPY BEGINNING, by City Owl Author, B.A. Richards.

Don't miss more from S.E. Berkeley coming soon, and find out more at seberkeleyauthor.com

Until then, discover A HAPPY BEGINNING, by City Owl Author, B.A. Richards

Step into the heart of New Orleans, where legends of vampires, witches, spells, and curses are as alive as the city itself. But what if there's a nugget of truth to the stories?

Alard Fairchild isn't your average man—he's a fairy prince from the Kingdoms of Earth and Sky, hiding in plain sight as a poverty lawyer in the French Quarter. All he wants is a normal, human life. That is, until he meets Razi Miller, a hot tourist with a wild side who's looking for a little adventure—and ends up entangled in something far more dangerous than he ever expected.

After one unforgettable night together, Raz wakes up to find himself magically bonded to Alard by an ancient marriage tattoo. Neither of them knows how it happened or why, but one thing's for sure: the consequences are far-reaching—and deadly.

As Raz is dragged into a hidden world of legendary creatures and mystical portals between realms, he faces a terrifying new reality: Alard is already betrothed to Meyda, the ruthless Princess of Fire and Ice. Their accidental marriage could ignite a brutal war between the kingdoms, and Raz is now a pawn in a deadly political game.

With danger closing in, Alard and Raz must work together to undo the chaos they've unwittingly unleashed. But the more time they spend together, the more they realize the one thing neither of them can control... is love.

Packed with sizzling romance, high-stakes adventure, dark magic, and dragons! A Happy Beginning will keep you hooked until the very last page.

Please sign up for the City Owl Press newsletter for chances to win special subscriber-only contests and giveaways as well as receiving information on upcoming releases and special excerpts.

All reviews are **welcome** and **appreciated**. Please consider leaving one on your favorite social media and book buying sites.

Escape Your World. Get Lost in Ours! City Owl Press at www.cityowlpress.com.

Acknowledgments

I'd like to begin by thanking you, dear reader, for taking the time to pick up my book. Your support means the world to me.

Now onto the hard part. So many people to thank and only so much space to do it! I'd like to begin by thanking the team at City Owl Press, Tina Moss and Yelena Casale, for acquiring my angsty little book. Thank you for taking a chance on me! And thank you to my wonderful editor, Jessica Shearer, for weathering the shit storm that was life during the edit process. We made it! High fives all around!

I'm so grateful for my husband and my two babies. Without his support, I wouldn't have had the time or editorial skills to make this dream a reality. Without my babies, I wouldn't have had the inspiration to chase this once unattainable dream. You three are my world and greatest loves.

I'd like to thank my parents for this bottomless well of confidence that formed from their unwavering belief that I was amazing at everything I attempted. It served me well when facing the endless rejection that is life in publishing. I'd also like to thank them for the genetic predisposition for anxiety to balance out the confidence so I turned out semi-normal. Appreciate you both! I'd like to thank my Aunt Barb, who is no longer with us, but would've bought every book in the store and passed it out to all her thousands of friends. Her laughter is the root of my humor and I miss her endlessly. And then there is my sister, Jacquelyn, who taught me how to be a badass bitch. Her strength and endurance inspires me to be greater than I am. I am thankful to have her in my life.

Being an author might be a solitary occupation, but I'd be nowhere without my group chats so I must thank them all by their names: the 2025 Small Press Debuts for being my cheerleaders, the Bi Panic (at the disco) for being my tea serving guides, and the SECRET BOOK CLUB for being my safe space. Then there are the individuals who I would be utterly lost without. Berna for being my first author friend and best critique partner. Sarah for being my first reader and fan. Aspen for being my boss bitch friend who *gets it*. And so many, many, more. Thank you all.

About the Author

S.E. Berkeley resides in southern California with her loving partner, feral children, and psychic cat. When she's not endlessly fetching snacks for small children, she enjoys hiking through her beloved state's wilderness and daydreaming of her next heart-pounding romantasy.

seberkeleyauthor.com

X x.com/SEBerkeley

instagram.com/seberkeleyauthor

tiktok.com/@seberkeleyauthor

bsky.app/profile/seberkeley.bsky.social

threads.com/@seberkeleyauthor

About the Publisher

City Owl Press is a cutting edge indie publishing company, bringing the world of romance and speculative fiction to discerning readers.

Escape Your World. Get Lost in Ours!

www.cityowlpress.com

 facebook.com/CityOwlPress

 x.com/cityowlpress

 instagram.com/cityowlbooks

 pinterest.com/cityowlpress

 tiktok.com/@cityowlpress